Blood
Is
Not
Enough

Blood Is Not Enough

17 Stories of Vampirism

Edited by
Ellen Datlow

WILLIAM MORROW AND COMPANY, INC.
NEW YORK

APR 17 1989

Library of Congress Cataloging-in-Publication Data

Blood is not enough / edited by Ellen Datlow.
    p.   cm.
  ISBN 0-688-08526-1
  1. Vampires—Literary collections.   I. Datlow, Ellen.
PN6071.V3B5 1989
808.8'0375—dc19

88-29064
CIP

Printed in the United States of America

First Edition

1 2 3 4 5 6 7 8 9 10

BOOK DESIGNED BY MANUELA PAUL

For my parents

Acknowledgments

I would like to thank the following people for help in putting together this book: Astrid Anderson Bear, Michael Swanwick, Ginjer Buchanan, Ed Bryant, Brian McCann, Pat Lobrutto, Brian Thomsen, Tom Disch, Bruce McAllister, Shelley Frier, Merrilee Heifetz, Jim Frenkel, David Hartwell.

I'd also like to thank Greg Cox for letting me pick his brain over egg creams. And for giving me an early draft of his upcoming book from Borgo Press, *The Transylvanian Library: A Consumer's Guide to Vampire Fiction*. It was invaluable for background on the subject.

Contents

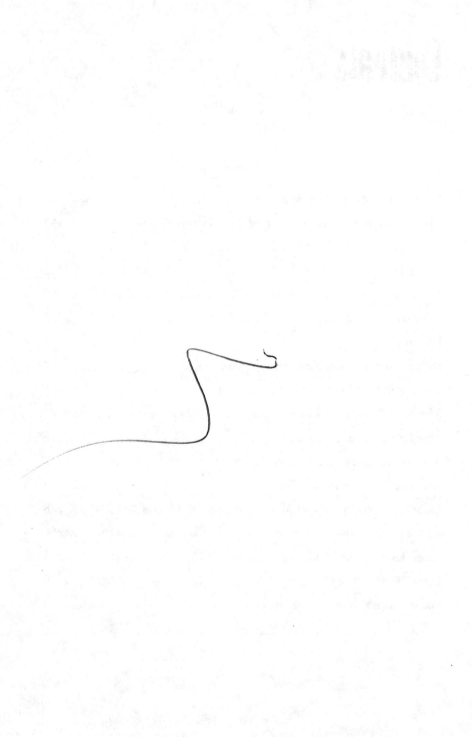

Introduction

As an adolescent I was fascinated by the Dracula movies with the exotic Bela Lugosi and the sexy Christopher Lee, and later in college was repulsed by the original *Nosferatu the Vampire*—not a very sexy creature as far as I was concerned. But my first experience of the overt sex appeal of vampires came about by accident. I ran out to see Frank Langella on Broadway in *Dracula* because the set was designed by Edward Gorey, whose work I adore and collect. Wow! Langella was one sexy vampire. I forgot all about Gorey's sets by the end of the second act when Dracula carries Lucy unconscious to bed and leans over her neck. Curtain.

The play prompted me finally to read Bram Stoker's *Dracula*. Ordinarily, I am not a fan of gothic style but I was stunned by the story's power. This despite being jaded by overexposure to the mythic creatures in books, movies, and television. I can imagine the shock of Victorian readers at the book's blatant sexuality. The biting of the neck, the passivity of the victim (traditionally young and female and attractive), the loss of will, can all be taken as a cautionary metaphor for the power of unbound lust. Stoker's *Dracula* has set the standard against which every vampire novel or story written since is measured.

There has been a distinct evolution in vampire literature over the years. Many of the early stories and novels seemed to start from scratch—the characters knowing nothing about vampirism or the existence of vampires. As a result much of the action was taken up in identifying the cause of those strange little red marks on the throats of victims who mysteriously became listless and began to sleepwalk. These days, there is a self-awareness in vampire literature. Although some of the literature still insists that the characters remain adamantly ignorant of the vampire in their midst, I doubt today's reader finds this kind of material very believable. This new sophistication on the part of the reader's expectations has quite a positive effect on the literature. It forces writers to find new ways to interest and surprise and scare.

I know that the vampires I've always found most interesting are not just your ordinary bloodsuckers. One of my favorites is Miriam Blaylock, the tragic immortal of Whitley Strieber's *The Hunger,* who carries the remains of her human lovers with her over the centuries, doomed to a loneliness impossible to fully comprehend. Another fascinating protagonist is Suzy McKee Charnas's Dr. Edward Weyland of *The Vampire Tapestry,* who while trying to blend in with humans and undergoing forced psychotherapy, eventually becomes so co-opted by our race that he has difficulty seeing us as "prey," a perception necessary for a vampire to retain in order to survive. Then there is Michael McDowell's vampire in his story "Halley's Passing," who while retaining the brutal violence characteristic of vampires, has completely forgotten, and obviously outgrown, the original reason for his actions—the need for blood. What these vampires have in common is that they all have an inner life apart from their blood-taking. They are either plagued by ethics (or at least doubts) concerning their condition, or their condition has changed in ways that overwhelm and threaten their existence. Originally a supernatural creature which survived like an animal on instinct, without much thought and surely no self-reflection, the vampire has evolved into a being with some human characteristics, and an individuality the reader can relate to.

Now we can have ethical versus unethical vampires like those in George R. R. Martin's novel *Fevre Dream* or vampires as heroes as in Chelsea Quinn Yarbro's *The Saint-Germain Chronicles.* Books are written from the vampire's point of view (Anne Rice's trilogy); vampires are psychoanalyzed (the *Unicorn Tapestry* novella by Charnas); and writers delve into the actual ramifications of vampirism. As a result, the writers have a much larger canvas to work with and are able to produce in-depth portraits of vampires in more varied circumstances. Since I've always been interested in the unusual, the quirky, the perverse in all my reading, this kind of odd vampire led to my interest in the wider range of vampiric behavior and the broader concept of vampirism. In traditional vampire fiction, blood is the essence. When I talk about vampirism I mean the draining of energy, the sucking of the will, the life force itself. Or as William Burroughs writes in *The Adding Machine: Selected Essays:*

They always take more than they leave by the basic nature of the vampiric process of inconspicuous but inexorable consumption. The vampire converts quality, live blood, vitality, youth, talent into quantity food and time, for himself. He perpetuates the most basic betrayal of the spirit, reducing all human dreams to his shit.

There have been quite a few anthologies on vampires, inevitably containing the occasional story of vampirism as well. Recently, *Vampires,* edited by Alan Ryan, does a nice job of putting the vampire story into an historical perspective. *Vamps,* edited by Martin H. Greenberg and Charles G. Waugh, collects stories exclusively about female vampires. These anthologies and others before them deal mostly with the taking of blood. But vampirism can go beyond black capes and teeth marks on the neck. In *Blood Is Not Enough* there are manipulative telepaths, life-sucking aliens, modern incubi, the resurrected dead. "Lazarus," by Leonid Andreyev, is the oldest story in the book, first published in the early 1900's, and only three others—"Try a Dull Knife" (1969), "The Girl With the Hungry Eyes" (1949), and Gahan Wilson's "The Sea Was Wet as Wet Can Be" (1967)—were published more than ten years ago. Many of the stories are original to this book, commissioned to explore this theme. Some came to me through my position as Fiction Editor of *Omni,* and a couple were recommended by colleagues in the field.

Some of the characters in these stories don't even realize they're vampires ("Return of the Dust Vampires," "Time-Lapse," "Lazarus," and "Dirty Work"). Others try to deny what they are, like the vampire in "The Silver Collar." Blood is shed often enough, but blood is not enough. The raison d'être of most of these vampires is the draining of energy, life, will. Somehow both the erotic and the horrific show through them. And it seems that vampirism becomes one of the main themes of our culture in this century.

Ellen Datlow

Roger seem to mind the good-natured jesting, since he was soon joining in the laughter with his peculiar *haw-haw-haw*.

Nina loved it all. Both gentlemen showered attention on her, and although Charles never failed to show the primacy of his affection for me, it was understood by all that Nina Hawkins was one of those young women who invariably becomes the center of male gallantry and attention in any gathering. Nor were the social strata of Charleston blind to the combined charm of our foursome. For two months of that now-distant summer, no party was complete, no excursion adequately planned, and no occasion considered a success unless we four were invited and had chosen to attend. Our happy dominance of the youthful social scene was so pronounced that Cousins Celia and Loraine wheedled their parents into leaving two weeks early for their annual August sojourn in Maine.

I am not sure when Nina and I came up with the idea of the duel. Perhaps it was during one of the long, hot nights when the other "slept over"—creeping into the other's bed, whispering and giggling, stifling our laughter when the rustling of starched uniforms betrayed the presence of our colored maids moving through the darkened halls. In any case, the idea was the natural outgrowth of the romantic pretensions of the time. The picture of Charles and Roger actually dueling over some abstract point of honor relating to *us* thrilled both of us in a physical way that I recognize now as a simple form of sexual titillation.

It would have been harmless except for the Ability. We had been so successful in our manipulation of male behavior—a manipulation that was both expected and encouraged in those days—that neither of us had yet suspected that there was anything beyond the ordinary in the way we could translate our whims into other people's actions. The field of parapsychology did not exist then; or rather, it existed only in the rappings and knockings of parlor-game séances. At any rate, we amused ourselves for several weeks with whispered fantasies, and then one of us—or perhaps both of us—used the Ability to translate the fantasy into reality.

In a sense, it was our first Feeding.

I do not remember the purported cause of the quarrel, perhaps some deliberate misinterpretation of one of Charles's jokes. I cannot recall who Charles and Roger arranged to have serve as seconds on that illegal outing.

Carrion Comfort

DAN SIMMONS

What attracts me to this story (and intrigues me) is the southern gentility of these human monsters as they reminisce over the parts they played in the death of innocents. Most people have the ability to manipulate others by psychological gamesmanship—but what if you could do it by sheer force of will? Simmons has since expanded the novelette into a novel, as yet unpublished.

Nina was going to take credit for the death of the Beatle, John. I thought that was in very bad taste. She had her scrapbook laid out on my mahogany coffee table, newspaper clippings neatly arranged in chronological order, the bald statements of death recording all of her Feedings. Nina Drayton's smile was radiant, but her pale-blue eyes showed no hint of warmth.

"We should wait for Willi," I said.

"Of course, Melanie. You're right, as always. How silly of me. I know the rules." Nina stood and began walking around the room, idly touching the furnishings or exclaiming softly over a ceramic statuette or piece of needlepoint. This part of the house had once been the conservatory, but now I used it as my sewing room. Green plants still caught the morning light. The light made it a warm, cozy place in the daytime, but now that winter had come the room was too chilly to use at night. Nor did I like the sense of darkness closing in against all those panes of glass.

"I love this house," said Nina.

She turned and smiled at me. "I can't tell you how much I look forward to coming back to Charleston. We should hold all of our reunions here."

I knew how much Nina loathed this city and this house.

"Willi would be hurt," I said. "You know how he likes to show off his place in Beverly Hills—and his new girlfriends."

"And boyfriends," Nina said, laughing. Of all the changes and darkenings in Nina, her laugh has been least affected. It was still the husky but childish laugh that I had first heard so long ago. It had drawn me to her then—one lonely, adolescent girl responding to the warmth of another as a moth to a flame. Now it served only to chill me and put me even more on guard. Enough moths had been drawn to Nina's flame over the many decades.

"I'll send for tea," I said.

Mr. Thorne brought the tea in my best Wedgwood china. Nina and I sat in the slowly moving squares of sunlight and spoke softly of nothing important: mutually ignorant comments on the economy, references to books that the other had not gotten around to reading, and sympathetic murmurs about the low class of persons one meets while flying these days. Someone peering in from the garden might have thought he was seeing an aging but attractive niece visiting her favorite aunt. (I drew the line at suggesting that anyone would mistake us for mother and daughter.) People usually consider me a well-dressed if not stylish person. Heaven knows I have paid enough to have the wool skirts and silk blouses mailed from Scotland and France. But next to Nina I've always felt dowdy.

This day she wore an elegant, light-blue dress that must have cost several thousand dollars. The color made her complexion seem even more perfect than usual and brought out the blue of her eyes. Her hair had gone as gray as mine, but somehow she managed to get away with wearing it long and tied back with a single barrette. It looked youthful and chic on Nina and made me feel that my short artificial curls were glowing with a blue rinse.

Few would suspect that I was four years younger than Nina. Time had been kind to her. And she had Fed more often.

She set down her cup and saucer and moved aimlessly around the room again. It was not like Nina to show such signs of nervousness. She stopped in front of the glass display case. Her gaze passed over the Hummels and the pewter pieces and then stopped in surprise.

"Good heavens, Melanie. A pistol! What an odd place to put an old pistol."

"It's an heirloom," I said. "A Colt Peacemaker from right after the War Between the States. Quite expensive. And you're right, it *is* a silly place to keep it. But it's the only case I have in the house with a lock on it and Mrs. Hodges often brings her grandchildren when she visits—"

"You mean it's *loaded*?"

"No, of course not," I lied. "But children should not play with such things . . ." I trailed off lamely. Nina nodded but did not bother to conceal the condescension in her smile. She went to look out the south window into the garden.

Damn her. It said volumes about Nina that she did not recognize that pistol.

On the day he was killed, Charles Edgar Larchmont had been my beau for precisely five months and two days. There had been no formal announcement, but we were to be married. Those five months had been a microcosm of the era itself—naive, flirtatious, formal to the point of preciosity, and romantic. Most of all, romantic. Romantic in the worst sense of the word: dedicated to saccharine or insipid ideals that only an adolescent—or an adolescent society—would strive to maintain. We were children playing with loaded weapons.

Nina, she was Nina Hawkins then, had her own beau—a tall, awkward, but well-meaning Englishman named Roger Harrison. Mr. Harrison had met Nina in London a year earlier, during the first stages of the Hawkinses' Grand Tour. Declaring himself smitten—another absurdity of those times—the tall Englishman had followed her from one European capital to another until, after being firmly reprimanded by Nina's father (an unimaginative little milliner who was constantly on the defensive about his doubtful social status), Harrison returned to London to "settle his affairs." Some months later he showed up in New York just as Nina was being packed off to her aunt's home in Charleston in order to terminate yet another flirtation. Still undaunted, the clumsy Englishman followed her south, ever mindful of the protocols and restrictions of the day.

We were a gay group. The day after I met Nina at Cousin Celia's June ball, the four of us were taking a hired boat up the Cooper River for a picnic on Daniel Island. Roger Harrison, serious and solemn on every topic, was a perfect foil for Charles's irreverent sense of humor. Nor did

I do remember the hurt and confused expression on Roger Harrison's face during those few days. It was a caricature of ponderous dullness, the confusion of a man who finds himself in a situation not of his making and from which he cannot escape. I remember Charles and his mercurial swings of mood—the bouts of humor, periods of black anger, and the tears and kisses the night before the duel.

I remember with great clarity the beauty of that morning. Mists were floating up from the river and diffusing the rays of the rising sun as we rode out to the dueling field. I remember Nina reaching over and squeezing my hand with an impetuous excitement that was communicated through my body like an electric shock.

Much of the rest of that morning is missing. Perhaps in the intensity of that first, subconscious Feeding, I literally lost consciousness as I was engulfed in the waves of fear, excitement, pride—of *maleness*—emanating from our two beaus as they faced death on that lovely morning. I remember experiencing the shock of realizing, *this is really happening,* as I shared the tread of high boots through the grass. Someone was calling off the paces. I dimly recall the weight of the pistol in my hand—Charles's hand, I think; I will never know for sure—and a second of cold clarity before an explosion broke the connection, and the acrid smell of gunpowder brought me back to myself.

It was Charles who died. I have never been able to forget the incredible quantities of blood that poured from the small, round hole in his breast. His white shirt was crimson by the time I reached him. There had been no blood in our fantasies. Nor had there been the sight of Charles with his head lolling, mouth dribbling saliva onto his bloodied chest while his eyes rolled back to show the whites like two eggs embedded in his skull.

Roger Harrison was sobbing as Charles breathed his final, shuddering gasps on that field of innocence.

I remember nothing at all about the confused hours that followed. The next morning I opened my cloth bag to find Charles's pistol lying with my things. Why would I have kept that revolver? If I had wished to take something from my fallen lover as a sign of remembrance, why that alien piece of metal? Why pry from his dead fingers the symbol of our thoughtless sin?

It said volumes about Nina that she did not recognize that pistol.

*   *   *

"Willi's here," announced Nina's amanuensis, the loathsome Miss Barrett Kramer. Kramer's appearance was as unisex as her name: short-cropped, black hair, powerful shoulders, and a blank, aggressive gaze that I associated with lesbians and criminals. She looked to be in her mid-thirties.

"Thank you, Barrett dear," said Nina.

Both of us went out to greet Willi, but Mr. Thorne had already let him in, and we met in the hallway.

"Melanie! You look marvelous! You grow younger each time I see you. Nina!" The change in Willi's voice was evident. Men continued to be overpowered by their first sight of Nina after an absence. There were hugs and kisses. Willi himself looked more dissolute than ever. His alpaca sport coat was exquisitely tailored, his turtleneck sweater successfully concealed the eroded lines of his wattled neck, but when he swept off his jaunty sports-car cap the long strands of white hair he had brushed forward to hide his encroaching baldness were knocked into disarray. Willi's face was flushed with excitement, but there was also the telltale capillary redness about the nose and cheeks that spoke of too much liquor, too many drugs.

"Ladies, I think you've met my associates, Tom Luhar and Jenson Reynolds?" The two men added to the crowd in my narrow hall. Mr. Luhar was thin and blond, smiling with perfectly capped teeth. Mr. Reynolds was a gigantic Negro, hulking forward with a sullen, bruised look on his coarse face. I was sure that neither Nina nor I had encountered these specific cat's-paws of Willi's before. It did not matter.

"Why don't we go into the parlor?" I suggested. It was an awkward procession ending with the three of us seated on the heavily upholstered chairs surrounding the Georgian tea table that had been my grandmother's. "More tea, please, Mr. Thorne." Miss Kramer took that as her cue to leave, but Willi's two pawns stood uncertainly by the door, shifting from foot to foot and glancing at the crystal on display as if their mere proximity could break something. I would not have been surprised if that had proved to be the case.

"Jense!" Willi snapped his fingers. The Negro hesitated and then brought forward an expensive leather attaché case. Willi set it on the tea table and clicked the catches open with his short, broad fingers. "Why don't you two see Mrs. Fuller's man about getting something to drink?"

When they were gone Willi shook his head and smiled apologetically at Nina. "Sorry about that, Love."

Nina put her hand on Willi's sleeve. She leaned forward with an air of expectancy. "Melanie wouldn't let me begin the Game without you. Wasn't that *awful* of me to want to start without you, Willi dear?"

Willi frowned. After fifty years he still bridled at being called Willi. In Los Angeles he was Big Bill Borden. When he returned to his native Germany—which was not often because of the dangers involved—he was once again Wilhelm von Borchert, lord of dark manor, forest, and hunt. But Nina had called him Willi when they had first met in 1931 in Vienna, and Willi he had remained.

"You begin, Willi dear," said Nina. "You go first."

I could remember the time when we would have spent the first few days of our reunion in conversation and catching up with one another's lives. Now there was not even time for small talk.

Willi showed his teeth and removed news clippings, notebooks, and a stack of cassettes from his briefcase. No sooner had he covered the small table with his material than Mr. Thorne arrived with the tea and Nina's scrapbook from the sewing room. Willi brusquely cleared a small space.

At first glance one might see certain similarities between Willi Borchert and Mr. Thorne. One would be mistaken. Both men tended to the florid, but Willi's complexion was the result of excess and emotion; Mr. Thorne had known neither of these for many years. Willi's balding was a patchy, self-consciously concealed thing—a weasel with mange; Mr. Thorne's bare head was smooth and unwrinkled. One could not imagine Mr. Thorne ever having *had* hair. Both men had gray eyes—what a novelist would call cold, gray eyes—but Mr. Thorne's eyes were cold with indifference, cold with a clarity coming from an absolute absence of troublesome emotion or thought. Willi's eyes were the cold of a blustery North Sea winter and were often clouded with shifting curtains of the emotions that controlled him—pride, hatred, love of pain, the pleasures of destruction.

Willi never referred to his use of the Ability as *Feedings*—I was evidently the only one who thought in those terms—but Willi sometimes talked of The Hunt. Perhaps it was the dark forests of his homeland that he thought of as he stalked his human quarry through the sterile streets

21

of Los Angeles. Did Willi dream of the forest, I wondered. Did he look back to green wool hunting jackets, the applause of retainers, the gouts of blood from the dying boar? Or did Willi remember the slam of jack-boots on cobblestones and the pounding of his lieutenants' fists on doors? Perhaps Willi still associated his Hunt with the dark European night of the ovens that he had helped to oversee.

I called it Feeding. Willi called it The Hunt. I had never heard Nina call it anything.

"Where is your VCR?" Willi asked. "I have put them all on tape."

"Oh, Willi," said Nina in an exasperated tone. "You know Melanie. She's *so* old-fashioned. You know she wouldn't have a video player."

"I don't even have a television," I said. Nina laughed.

"Goddamn it," muttered Willi. "It doesn't matter. I have other records here." He snapped rubber bands from around the small, black notebooks. "It just would have been better on tape. The Los Angeles stations gave much coverage to the Hollywood Strangler, and I edited in the . . . Ach! Never mind."

He tossed the videocassettes into his briefcase and slammed the lid shut.

"Twenty-three," he said. "Twenty-three since we met twelve months ago. It doesn't seem that long, does it?"

"Show us," said Nina. She was leaning forward, and her blue eyes seemed very bright. "I've been wondering since I saw the Strangler interviewed on *Sixty Minutes*. He *was* yours, Willi? He seemed so—"

"*Ja, ja,* he was mine. A nobody. A timid little man. He was the gardener of a neighbor of mine. I left him alive so that the police could question him, erase any doubts. He will hang himself in his cell next month after the press loses interest. But this is more interesting. Look at this." Willi slid across several glossy black-and-white photographs. The NBC executive had murdered the five members of his family and drowned a visiting soap-opera actress in his pool. He had then stabbed himself repeatedly and written 50 SHARE in blood on the wall of the bathhouse.

"Reliving old glories, Willi?" asked Nina. "DEATH TO THE PIGS and all that?"

"No, goddamn it. I think it should receive points for irony. The girl had been scheduled to drown on the program. It was already in the script outline."

22

"Was he hard to Use?" It was my question. I was curious despite myself.

Willi lifted one eyebrow. "Not really. He was an alcoholic and heavily into cocaine. There was not much left. And he hated his family. Most people do."

"Most people in California, perhaps," said Nina primly. It was an odd comment from Nina. Years ago her father had committed suicide by throwing himself in front of a trolley car.

"Where did you make contact?" I asked.

"A party. The usual place. He bought the coke from a director who had ruined one of my—"

"Did you have to repeat the contact?"

Willi frowned at me. He kept his anger under control, but his face grew redder. "*Ja, ja*. I saw him twice more. Once I just watched from my car as he played tennis."

"Points for irony," said Nina. "But you lose points for repeated contact. If he were as empty as you say, you should have been able to Use him after only one touch. What else do you have?"

He had his usual assortment. Pathetic skid-row murders. Two domestic slayings. A highway collision that turned into a fatal shooting. "I was in the crowd," said Willi. "I made contact. He had a gun in the glove compartment."

"Two points," said Nina.

Willi had saved a good one for last. A once-famous child star had suffered a bizarre accident. He had left his Bel Air apartment while it filled with gas and then returned to light a match. Two others had died in the ensuing fire.

"You get credit only for him," said Nina.

"*Ja, ja.*"

"Are you absolutely sure about this one? It *could* have been an accident."

"Don't be ridiculous," snapped Willi. He turned toward me. "*This* one was very hard to Use. Very strong. I blocked his memory of turning on the gas. Had to hold it away for two hours. Then forced him into the room. He struggled not to strike the match."

"You should have had him use his lighter," said Nina.

"He didn't smoke," growled Willi. "He gave it up last year."

23

"Yes," smiled Nina. "I seem to remember him saying that to Johnny Carson." I could not tell whether Nina was jesting.

The three of us went through the ritual of assigning points. Nina did most of the talking. Willi went from being sullen to expansive to sullen again. At one point he reached over and patted my knee as he laughingly asked for my support. I said nothing. Finally he gave up, crossed the parlor to the liquor cabinet, and poured himself a tall glass of bourbon from father's decanter. The evening light was sending its final, horizontal rays through the stained-glass panels of the bay windows, and it cast a red hue on Willi as he stood next to the oak cupboard. His eyes were small, red embers in a bloody mask.

"Forty-one," said Nina at last.

She looked up brightly and showed the calculator as if it verified some objective fact. "I count forty-one points. What do you have, Melanie?"

"*Ja,*" interrupted Willi. "That is fine. Now let us see your claims, Nina." His voice was flat and empty. Even Willi had lost some interest in the Game.

Before Nina could begin, Mr. Thorne entered and motioned that dinner was served. We adjourned to the dining room—Willi pouring himself another glass of bourbon and Nina fluttering her hands in mock frustration at the interruption of the Game. Once seated at the long, mahogany table, I worked at being a hostess. From decades of tradition, talk of the Game was banned from the dinner table. Over soup we discussed Willi's new movie and the purchase of another store for Nina's line of boutiques. It seemed that Nina's monthly column in *Vogue* was to be discontinued but that a newspaper syndicate was interested in picking it up.

Both of my guests exclaimed over the perfection of the baked ham, but I thought that Mr. Thorne had made the gravy a trifle too sweet. Darkness had filled the windows before we finished our chocolate mousse. The refracted light from the chandelier made Nina's hair dance with highlights while I feared that mine glowed more bluely than ever.

Suddenly there was a sound from the kitchen. The huge Negro's face appeared at the swinging door. His shoulder was hunched against white hands and his expression was that of a querulous child.

". . . the hell you think we are sittin' here like goddamned—" The white hands pulled him out of sight.

"Excuse me, ladies." Willi dabbed linen at his lips and stood up. He still moved gracefully for all of his years.

Nina poked at her chocolate. There was one sharp, barked command from the kitchen and the sound of a slap. It was the slap of a man's hand—hard and flat as a small-caliber-rifle shot. I looked up and Mr. Thorne was at my elbow, clearing away the dessert dishes.

"Coffee, please, Mr. Thorne. For all of us." He nodded and his smile was gentle.

Franz Anton Mesmer had known of it even if he had not understood it. I suspect that Mesmer must have had some small touch of the Ability. Modern pseudosciences have studied it and renamed it, removed most of its power, confused its uses and origins, but it remains the shadow of what Mesmer discovered. They have no idea of what it is like to Feed.

I despair at the rise of modern violence. I truly give in to despair at times, that deep, futureless pit of despair that poet Gerard Manley Hopkins called carrion comfort. I watch the American slaughterhouse, the casual attacks on popes, presidents, and uncounted others, and I wonder whether there are many more out there with the Ability or whether butchery has simply become the modern way of life.

All humans feed on violence, on the small exercises of power over another. Bur few have tasted—as we have—the ultimate power. And without the Ability, few know the unequaled pleasure of taking a human life. Without the Ability, even those who do feed on life cannot savor the flow of emotions in stalker and victim, the total exhilaration of the attacker who has moved beyond all rules and punishments, the strange, almost sexual submission of the victim in that final second of truth when all options are canceled, all futures denied, all possibilities erased in an exercise of absolute power over another.

I despair at modern violence. I despair at the impersonal nature of it and the casual quality that has made it accessible to so many. I had a television set until I sold it at the height of the Vietnam War. Those sanitized snippets of death—made distant by the camera's lens—meant nothing to me. But I believe it meant something to these cattle that surround me. When the war and the nightly televised body counts ended, they demanded more, *more,* and the movie screens and streets of this sweet and dying nation have provided it in mediocre, mob abundance. It is an addiction I know well.

They miss the point. Merely observed, violent death is a sad and sullied tapestry of confusion. But to those of us who have Fed, death can be a *sacrament*.

"My turn! My turn!" Nina's voice still resembled that of the visiting belle who had just filled her dance card at Cousin Celia's June ball.

We had returned to the parlor. Willi had finished his coffee and requested a brandy from Mr. Thorne. I was embarrassed for Willi. To have one's closest associates show any hint of unplanned behavior was certainly a sign of weakening Ability. Nina did not appear to have noticed.

"I have them all in order," said Nina. She opened the scrapbook on the now-empty tea table. Willi went through them carefully, sometimes asking a question, more often grunting assent. I murmured occasional agreement although I had heard of none of them. Except for the Beatle, of course. Nina saved that for near the end.

"Good God, Nina, that was you?" Willi seemed near anger. Nina's Feedings had always run to Park Avenue suicides and matrimonial disagreements ending in shots fired from expensive, small-caliber ladies' guns. This type of thing was more in Willi's crude style. Perhaps he felt that his territory was being invaded. "I mean . . . you were risking a lot, weren't you? It's so . . . damn it . . . so *public*."

Nina laughed and set down the calculator. "Willi *dear*, that's what the Game is *about*, is it not?"

Willi strode to the liquor cabinet and refilled his brandy snifter. The wind tossed bare branches against the leaded glass of the bay window. I do not like winter. Even in the South it takes its toll on the spirit.

"Didn't this guy . . . what's his name . . . buy the gun in Hawaii or someplace?" asked Willi from across the room. "That sounds like his initiative to me. I mean, if he was *already* stalking the fellow—"

"Willie dear." Nina's voice had gone as cold as the wind that raked the branches. "No one said he was *stable*. How many of yours are stable, Willi? But I made it *happen*, darling. I chose the place and the time. Don't you see the irony of the *place*, Willi? After that little prank on the director of that witchcraft movie a few years ago? It was straight from the script—"

"I don't know," said Willi. He sat heavily on the divan, spilling brandy on his expensive sport coat. He did not notice. The lamplight reflected from his balding skull. The mottles of age were more visible at night, and his neck, where it disappeared into his turtleneck, was all ropes and tendons. "I don't know." He looked up at me and smiled suddenly, as if we shared a conspiracy. "It could be like that writer fellow, eh, Melanie? It could be like that."

Nina looked down at the hands in her lap. They were clenched and the well-manicured fingers were white at the tips.

The Mind Vampires. That's what the writer was going to call his book.

I sometimes wonder if he really would have written anything. What was his name? Something Russian.

Willi and I received telegrams from Nina: COME QUICKLY YOU ARE NEEDED. That was enough. I was on the next morning's flight to New York. The plane was a noisy, propeller-driven Constellation, and I spent much of the flight assuring the overly solicitous stewardess that I needed nothing, that, indeed, I felt fine. She obviously had decided that I was someone's grandmother, who was flying for the first time.

Willi managed to arrive twenty minute before me. Nina was distraught and as close to hysteria as I had ever seen her. She had been at a party in lower Manhattan two days before—she was not so distraught that she forgot to tell us what important names had been there—when she found herself sharing a corner, a fondue pot, and confidences with a young writer. Or rather, the writer was sharing confidences. Nina described him as a scruffy sort with a wispy little beard, thick glasses, a corduroy sport coat worn over an old plaid shirt—one of the type invariably sprinkled around successful parties of that era, according to Nina. She knew enough not to call him a beatnik, for that term had just become passé, but no one had yet heard the term *hippie,* and it wouldn't have applied to him anyway. He was a writer of the sort that barely ekes out a living, these days at least, by selling blood and doing novelizations of television series. Alexander something.

His idea for a book—he told Nina that he had been working on it for some time—was that many of the murders then being committed were actually the result of a small group of psychic killers, he called them *mind vampires,* who used others to carry out their grisly deeds.

He said that a paperback publisher had already shown interest in his

27

outline and would offer him a contract tomorrow if he would change the title to *The Zombie Factor* and put in more sex.

"So what?" Willi had said to Nina in disgust. "You have me fly across the continent for this? I might buy the idea myself."

That turned out to be the excuse we used to interrogate this Alexander somebody during an impromptu party given by Nina the next evening. I did not attend. The party was not overly successful according to Nina but it gave Willi the chance to have a long chat with the young would-be novelist. In the writer's almost pitiable eagerness to do business with Bill Borden, producer of *Paris Memories, Three on a Swing,* and at least two other completely forgettable Technicolor features touring the drive-ins that summer, he revealed that the book consisted of a well-worn outline and a dozen pages of notes.

He was sure, however, that he could do a treatment for Mr. Borden in five weeks, perhaps even as fast as three weeks if he were flown out to Hollywood to get the proper creative stimulation.

Later that evening we discussed the possibility of Willi simply buying an option on the treatment, but Willi was short on cash at the time and Nina was insistent. In the end the young writer opened his femoral artery with a Gillette blade and ran screaming into a narrow Greenwich Village side street to die. I don't believe that anyone ever bothered to sort through the clutter and debris of his remaining notes.

"It could be like that writer, *ja,* Melanie?" Willi patted my knee. I nodded. "He was mine," continued Willi, "and Nina tried to take credit. Remember?"

Again I nodded. Actually he had been neither Nina's nor Willi's. I had avoided the party so that I could make contact later without the young man noticing he was being followed. I did so easily. I remember sitting in an overheated little delicatessen across the street from the apartment building. It was over so quickly that there was almost no sense of Feeding. Then I was aware once again of the sputtering radiators and the smell of salami as people rushed to the door to see what the screaming was about. I remember finishing my tea slowly so that I did not have to leave before the ambulance was gone.

"Nonsense," said Nina. She busied herself with her little calculator. "How many points?" She looked at me. I looked at Willi.

"Six," he said with a shrug. Nina made a small show of totaling the numbers.

"Thirty-eight," she said and sighed theatrically. "You win again, Willi. Or rather, you beat *me* again. We must hear from Melanie. You've been so quiet, dear. You must have some surprise for us."

"Yes," said Willi, "it is your turn to win. It has been several years."

"None," I said. I had expected an explosion of questions, but the silence was broken only by the ticking of the clock on the mantelpiece. Nina was looking away from me, at something hidden by the shadows in the corner.

"None?" echoed Willi.

"There was . . . one," I said at last. "But it was by accident. I came across them robbing an old man behind . . . but it was completely by accident."

Willi was agitated. He stood up, walked to the window, turned an old straight-back chair around and straddled it, arms folded. "What does this mean?"

"You're quitting the Game?" Nina asked as she turned to look at me. I let the question serve as the answer.

"Why?" snapped Willi. In his excitement it came out with a hard *v*.

If I had been raised in an era when young ladies were allowed to shrug, I would have done so. As it was, I contented myself with running my fingers along an imaginary seam on my skirt. Willi had asked the question, but I stared straight into Nina's eyes when I finally answered, "I'm tired. It's been too long. I guess I'm getting old."

"You'll get a lot *older* if you do not Hunt," said Willi. His body, his voice, the red mask of his face, everything signaled great anger just kept in check. "My God, Melanie, you *already* look older! You look terrible. This is *why* we hunt, woman. Look at yourself in the mirror! Do you want to die an old woman just because you're tired of using *them*?" Willi stood and turned his back.

"Nonsense!" Nina's voice was strong, confident, in command once more. "Melanie's *tired*, Willi. Be nice. We all have times like that. I remember how *you* were after the war. Like a whipped puppy. You wouldn't even go outside your miserable little flat in Baden. Even after we helped you get to New Jersey you just sulked around feeling sorry for yourself. Melanie *made up* the Game to help you feel better. So quiet! *Never* tell a lady who feels tired and depressed that she looks terrible. Honestly, Willi, you're such a *Schwachsinniger* sometimes. And a crashing boor to boot."

I had anticipated many reactions to my announcement, but this was the one I feared most. It meant that Nina had also tired of the game. It meant that she was ready to move to another level of play.

It had to mean that.

"Thank you, Nina darling," I said. "I knew you would understand."

She reached across and touched my knee reassuringly. Even through my wool skirt, I could feel the cold of her fingers.

My guests would not stay the night. I implored. I remonstrated. I pointed out that their rooms were ready, that Mr. Thorne had already turned down the quilts.

"Next time," said Willi. "Next time, Melanie, my little love. We'll make a weekend of it as we used to. A week!" Willi was in a much better mood since he had been paid his thousand-dollar prize by each of us. He had sulked, but I had insisted. It soothed his ego when Mr. Thorne brought in a check already made out to WILLIAM D. BORDEN.

Again I asked him to stay, but he protested that he had a midnight flight to Chicago. He had to see a prizewinning author about a screenplay. Then he was hugging me good-bye, his companions were in the hall behind me and I had a brief moment of terror.

But they left. The blond young man showed his white smile, and the Negro bobbed his head in what I took as a farewell. Then we were alone.

Nina and I were alone.

Not quite alone. Miss Kramer was standing next to Nina at the end of the hall. Mr. Thorne was out of sight behind the swinging door to the kitchen. I left him there.

Miss Kramer took three steps forward. I felt my breath stop for an instant. Mr. Thorne put his hand on the swinging door. Then the husky little brunette opened the door to the hall closet, removed Nina's coat, and stepped back to help her into it.

"Are you sure you won't stay?"

"No, thank you, darling. I've promised Barrett that we would drive to Hilton Head tonight."

"But it's late—"

"We have reservations. Thank you anyway, Melanie. I *will* be in touch."

"Yes."

"I mean it, dear. We must talk. I understand *exactly* how you feel, but you have to remember that the Game is still important to Willi. We'll have to find a way to end it without hurting his feelings. Perhaps we could visit him next spring in Karinhall or whatever he calls that gloomy old Bavarian place of his. A trip to the Continent would do wonders for you, dear."

"Yes."

"I *will* be in touch. After this deal with the new store is settled. We need to spend some time together, Melanie . . . just the two of us . . . like old times." Her lips kissed the air next to my cheek. She held my forearms tightly. "Good-bye, darling."

"Good-bye, Nina."

I carried the brandy glass to the kitchen. Mr. Thorne took it in silence.

"Make sure the house is secure," I said. He nodded and went to check the locks and alarm system. It was only nine forty-five, but I was very tired. *Age,* I thought. I went up the wide staircase, perhaps the finest feature of the house, and dressed for bed. It had begun to storm, and the sound of the cold raindrops on the window carried a sad rhythm to it.

Mr. Thorne looked in as I was brushing my hair and wishing it were longer. I turned to him. He reached into the pocket of his dark vest. When his hand emerged a slim blade flicked out. I nodded. He palmed the blade shut and closed the door behind him. I listened to his footsteps recede down the stairs to the chair in the front hall, where he would spend the night.

I believe I dreamed of vampires that night. Or perhaps I was thinking about them just prior to falling asleep, and a fragment had stayed with me until morning. Of all mankind's self-inflicted terrors, of all its pathetic little monsters, only the myth of the vampire had any vestige of dignity. Like the humans it feeds on, the vampire must respond to its own dark compulsions. But unlike its petty human prey, the vampire carries out its sordid means to the only possible ends that could justify such actions— the goal of literal immortality. There is a nobility there. And a sadness.

Before sleeping I thought of that summer long ago in Vienna. I saw

31

Willi young again—blond, flushed with youth, and filled with pride at escorting two such independent American ladies.

I remembered Willi's high, stiff collars and the short dresses that Nina helped to bring into style that summer. I remembered the friendly sounds of crowded *Biergartens* and the shadowy dance of leaves in front of gas lamps.

I remembered the footsteps on wet cobblestones, the shouts, the distant whistles, and the silences.

Willi was right; I had aged. The past year had taken a greater toll than the preceding decade. But I had not Fed. Despite the hunger, despite the aging reflection in the mirror, *I had not Fed.*

I fell asleep trying to think of that writer's last name. I fell asleep hungry.

Morning. Bright sunlight through bare branches. It was one of those crystalline, warming winter days that make living in the South so much less depressing than merely surviving a Yankee winter. I had Mr. Thorne open the window a crack when he brought in my breakfast tray. As I sipped my coffee I could hear children playing in the courtyard. Once Mr. Thorne would have brought the morning paper with the tray, but I had long since learned that to read about the follies and scandals of the world was to desecrate the morning. I was growing less and less interested in the affairs of men. I had done without a newspaper, telephone, or television for twelve years and had suffered no ill effects unless one were to count a growing self-contentment as an ill thing. I smiled as I remembered Willi's disappointment at not being able to play his video cassettes. He was such a child.

"It is Saturday, is it not, Mr. Thorne?" At his nod I gestured for the tray to be taken away. "We will go out today," I said. "A walk. Perhaps a trip to the fort. Then dinner at Henry's and home. I have arrangements to make."

Mr. Thorne hesitated and half-stumbled as he was leaving the room. I paused in the act of belting my robe. It was not like Mr. Thorne to commit an ungraceful movement. I realized that he too was getting old. He straightened the tray and dishes, nodded his head, and left for the kitchen.

I would not let thoughts of aging disturb me on such a beautiful morning. I felt charged with a new energy and resolve. The reunion the night before had not gone well but neither had it gone as badly as it might have. I had been honest with Nina and Willi about my intention of quitting the Game. In the weeks and months to come, they—or at least Nina—would begin to brood over the ramifications of that, but by the time they chose to react, separately or together, I would be long gone. Already I had new (and old) identities waiting for me in Florida, Michigan, London, southern France, and even in New Delhi. Michigan was out for the time being. I had grown unused to the harsh climate. New Delhi was no longer the hospitable place for foreigners it had been when I resided there briefly before the war.

Nina had been right about one thing—a return to Europe would be good for me. Already I longed for the rich light and cordial *savoir vivre* of the villagers near my old summer house outside of Toulon.

The air outside was bracing. I wore a simple print dress and my spring coat. The trace of arthritis in my right leg had bothered me coming down the stairs, but I used my father's old walking stick as a cane. A young Negro servant had cut it for father the summer we moved from Greenville to Charleston. I smiled as we emerged into the warm air of the courtyard.

Mrs. Hodges came out of her doorway into the light. It was her grandchildren and their friends who were playing around the dry fountain. For two centuries the courtyard had been shared by the three brick buildings. Only my home had not been parceled into expensive town houses or fancy apartments.

"Good morning, Miz Fuller."

"Good morning, Mrs. Hodges. A beautiful day, isn't it?"

"It is that. Are you off shopping?"

"Just for a walk, Mrs. Hodges. I'm surprised that Mr. Hodges isn't out today. He always seems to be working in the yard on Saturdays."

Mrs. Hodges frowned as one of the little girls ran between us. Her friend came squealing after her, sweater flying. "Oh, George is at the marina already."

"In the daytime?" I had often been amused by Mr. Hodges's departure for work in the evening, his security-guard uniform neatly pressed, gray hair jutting out from under his cap, black lunch pail gripped firmly under his arm.

Mr. Hodges was as leathery and bowlegged as an aged cowboy. He was one of those men who were always on the verge of retiring but who probably realized that to be suddenly inactive would be a form of death sentence.

"Oh, yes. One of those colored men on the day shift down at the storage building quit, and they asked George to fill in. I told him that he was too old to work four nights a week and then go back on the weekend, but you know George. He'll never retire."

"Well, give him my best," I said.

The girls running around the fountain made me nervous.

Mrs. Hodges followed me to the wrought-iron gate. "Will you be going away for the holidays, Miz Fuller?"

"Probably, Mrs. Hodges. Most probably." Then Mr. Thorne and I were out on the sidewalk and strolling toward the Battery. A few cars drove slowly down the narrow streets, some tourists stared at the houses of our Old Section, but the day was serene and quiet.

I saw the masts of the yachts and sailboats before we came in sight of the water as we emerged onto Broad Street.

"Please acquire tickets for us, Mr. Thorne," I said. "I believe I would like to see the fort."

As is typical of most people who live in close proximity to a popular tourist attraction, I had not taken notice of it for many years. It was an act of sentimentality to visit the fort now. An act brought on by my increasing acceptance of the fact that I would have to leave these parts forever. It is one thing to plan a move; it is something altogether different to be faced with the imperative reality of it.

There were few tourists. The ferry moved away from the marina and into the placid waters of the harbor. The combination of warm sunlight and the steady throb of the diesel caused me to doze briefly. I awoke as we were putting in at the dark hulk of the island fort.

For a while I moved with the tour group, enjoying the catacomb silences of the lower levels and the mindless singsong of the young woman from the Park Service. But as we came back to the museum, with its dusty dioramas and tawdry little trays of slides, I climbed the stairs back to the outer walls. I motioned for Mr. Thorne to stay at the top of the stairs and moved out onto the ramparts.

Only one other couple—a young pair with a cheap camera and a baby in an uncomfortable-looking papoose carrier—were in sight along the wall.

It was a pleasant moment. A midday storm was approaching from the west and it set a dark backdrop to the still-sunlit church spires, brick towers, and bare branches of the city.

Even from two miles away I could see the movement of people strolling along the Battery walkway. The wind was blowing in ahead of the dark clouds and tossing whitecaps against the rocking ferry and wooden dock. The air smelled of river and winter and rain by nightfall.

It was not hard to imagine that day long ago. The shells had dropped onto the fort until the upper layers were little more than protective piles of rubble. People had cheered from the rooftops behind the Battery. The bright colors of dresses and silk parasols must have been maddening to the Yankee gunners. Finally one had fired a shot above the crowded rooftops. The ensuing confusion must have been amusing from this vantage point.

A movement down below caught my attention. Something dark was sliding through the gray water—something dark and shark silent. I was jolted out of thoughts of the past as I recognized it as a Polaris submarine, old but obviously still operational, slipping through the dark water without a sound. Waves curled and rippled over the porpoise-smooth hull, sliding to either side in a white wake. There were several men on the tower. They were muffled in heavy coats, their hats pulled low. An improbably large pair of binoculars hung from the neck of one man, whom I assumed to be the captain. He pointed at something beyond Sullivan's Island. I stared. The periphery of my vision began to fade as I made contact. Sounds and sensations came to me as from a distance.

Tension. The pleasure of salt spray, breeze from the north, northwest. Anxiety of the sealed orders below. Awareness of the sandy shallows just coming into sight on the port side.

I was startled as someone came up behind me. The dots flickering at the edge of my vision fled as I turned.

Mr. Thorne was there. At my elbow. Unbidden. I had opened my mouth to command him back to the top of the stairs when I saw the cause of his approach. The youth who had been taking pictures of his pale wife was now walking toward me. Mr. Thorne moved to intercept him.

"Hey, excuse me, ma'am. Would you or your husband mind taking our picture?"

I nodded and Mr. Thorne took the proffered camera. It looked minuscule in his long-fingered hands. Two snaps and the couple were satisfied that their presence there was documented for posterity. The young man grinned idiotically and bobbed his head. Their baby began to cry as the cold wind blew in.

I looked back to the submarine, but already it had passed on, its gray tower a thin stripe connecting the sea and sky.

We were almost back to town, the ferry was swinging in toward the ship, when a stranger told me of Willi's death.

"It's awful, isn't it?" The garrulous old woman had followed me out onto the exposed section of deck. Even though the wind had grown chilly and I had moved twice to escape her mindless chatter, the woman had obviously chosen me as her conversational target for the final stages of the tour. Neither my reticence nor Mr. Thorne's glowering presence had discouraged her. "It must have been terrible," she continued. "In the dark and all."

"What was that?" A dark premonition prompted my question.

"Why, the airplane crash. Haven't you heard about it? It must have been awful, falling into the swamp and all. I told my daugher this morning—"

"What airplane crash? When?" The old woman cringed a bit at the sharpness of my tone, but the vacuous smile stayed on her face.

"Why last night. This morning I told my daughter—"

"Where? What aircraft are you talking about?" Mr. Thorne came closer as he heard the tone of my voice.

"The one last night," she quavered. "The one from Charleston. The paper in the lounge told all about it. Isn't it terrible? Eighty-five people. I told my daughter—"

I left her standing there by the railing. There was a crumpled newspaper near the snack bar, and under the four-word headline were the sparse details of Willi's death. Flight 417, bound for Chicago, had left Charleston International Airport at twelve-eighteen A.M. Twenty minutes later the aircraft had exploded in midair not far from the city of Columbia. Fragments of fuselage and parts of bodies had fallen into Congaree Swamp, where fishermen had found them. There had been no survivors. The FAA and FBI were investigating.

There was a loud rushing in my ears, and I had to sit down or faint. My hands were clammy against the green-vinyl upholstery. People moved past me on their way to the exits.

Willi was dead. Murdered. Nina had killed him. For a few dizzy seconds I considered the possibility of a conspiracy—an elaborate ploy by Nina and Willi to confuse me into thinking that only one threat remained. But no. There would be no reason. If Nina had included Willi in her plans, there would be no need for such absurd machinations.

Willi was dead. His remains were spread over a smelly, obscure marshland. I could imagine his last moments. He would have been leaning back in first-class comfort, a drink in his hand, perhaps whispering to one of his loutish companions.

Then the explosion. Screams. Sudden darkness. A brutal tilting and the final fall to oblivion. I shuddered and gripped the metal arm of the chair.

How had Nina done it? Almost certainly not one of Willi's entourage. It was not beyond Nina's powers to Use Willi's own cat's-paws, especially in light of his failing Ability, but there would have been no reason to do so. She could have Used anyone on that flight. It *would* have been difficult. The elaborate step of preparing the bomb. The supreme effort of blocking all memory of it, and the almost unbelievable feat of Using someone even as we sat together drinking coffee and brandy.

But Nina could have done it. Yes, she *could* have. And the timing. The timing could mean only one thing.

The last of the tourists had filed out of the cabin. I felt the slight bump that meant we had tied up to the dock. Mr. Thorne stood by the door.

Nina's timing meant that she was attempting to deal with both of us at once. She obviously had planned it long before the reunion and my timorous announcement of withdrawal. How amused Nina must have been. No wonder she had reacted so generously! Yet, she had made one great mistake. By dealing with Willi first, Nina had banked everything on my not hearing the news before she could turn on me. She knew that I had no access to daily news and only rarely left the house anymore. Still, it was unlike Nina to leave anything to chance. Was it possible that she thought I had lost the Ability completely and that Willi was the greater threat?

I shook my head as we emerged from the cabin into the gray afternoon light. The wind sliced at me through my thin coat. The view of the gangplank was blurry, and I realized that tears had filled my eyes. For Willi? He had been a pompous, weak old fool. For Nina's betrayal? Perhaps it was only the cold wind.

The streets of the Old Section were almost empty of pedestrians. Bare branches clicked together in front of the windows of fine homes. Mr. Thorne stayed by my side. The cold air sent needles of arthritic pain up my right leg to my hip. I leaned more heavily upon father's walking stick.

What would her next move be? I stopped. A fragment of newspaper, caught by the wind, wrapped itself around my ankle and then blew on.

How would she come at me? Not from a distance. She was somewhere in town. I knew that. While it is possible to Use someone from a great distance, it would involve great rapport, an almost intimate knowledge of that person. And if contact were lost, it would be difficult if not impossible to reestablish at a distance. None of us had known why this was so. It did not matter now. But the thought of Nina still here, nearby, made my heart begin to race.

Not from a distance. I would see my assailant. If I knew Nina at all, I knew that. Certainly Willi's death had been the least personal Feeding imaginable, but that had been a mere technical operation. Nina obviously had decided to settle old scores with *me,* and Willi had become an obstacle to her, a minor but measurable threat that had to be eliminated before she could proceed. I could easily imagine that in Nina's own mind her choice of death for Willi would be interpreted as an act of compassion, almost a sign of affection. Not so with me. I felt that Nina would want me to know, however briefly, that she was behind the attack. In a sense, her own vanity would be my warning. Or so I hoped.

I was tempted to leave immediately. I could have Mr. Thorne get the Audi out of storage, and we could be beyond Nina's influence in an hour—away to a new life within a few more hours. There were important items in the house, of course, but the funds that I had stored elsewhere would replace most of them. It would be almost welcome to leave everything behind with the discarded identity that had accumulated them.

No. I could not leave. Not yet.

From across the street the house looked dark and malevolent. Had *I* closed those blinds on the second floor? There was a shadowy movement in the courtyard, and I saw Mrs. Hodges's granddaughter and a friend scamper from one doorway to another. I stood irresolutely on the curb and tapped father's stick against the black-barked tree. It was foolish to dither so—I knew it was—but it had been a long time since I had been forced to make a decision under stress.

"Mr. Thorne, please check the house. Look in each room. Return quickly."

A cold wind came up as I watched Mr. Thorne's black coat blend into the gloom of the courtyard. I felt terribly exposed standing there alone. I found myself glancing up and down the street, looking for Miss Kramer's dark hair, but the only sign of movement was a young woman pushing a perambulator far down the street.

The blinds on the second floor shot up, and Mr. Thorne's face stared out whitely for a minute. Then he turned away, and I remained staring at the dark rectangle of window. A shout from the courtyard startled me, but it was only the little girl—what was her name?—calling to her friend. Kathleen, that was it. The two sat on the edge of the fountain and opened a box of animal crackers. I stared intently at them and then relaxed. I even managed to smile a little at the extent of my paranoia. For a second I considered using Mr. Thorne directly, but the thought of being helpless on the street dissuaded me. When one is in complete contact, the senses still function but are a distant thing at best.

Hurry. The thought was sent almost without volition. Two bearded men were walking down the sidewalk on my side of the street. I crossed to stand in front of my own gate. The men were laughing and gesturing at each other. One looked over at me. *Hurry.*

Mr. Thorne came out of the house, locked the door behind him, and crossed the courtyard toward me. One of the girls said something to him and held out the box of crackers, but he ignored her. Across the street the two men continued walking. Mr. Thorne handed me the large front-door key. I dropped it in my coat pocket and looked sharply at him. He nodded. His placid smile unconsciously mocked my consternation.

"You're sure?" I asked. Again the nod. "You checked all of the rooms?" Nod. "The alarms?" Nod. "You looked in the basement?" Nod. "No sign of disturbance?" Mr. Thorne shook his head.

My hand went to the metal of the gate, but I hesitated. Anxiety filled my throat like bile. I was a silly old woman, tired and aching from the chill, but I could not bring myself to open that gate.

"Come." I crossed the street and walked briskly away from the house. "We will have dinner at Henry's and return later." Only I was not walking toward the old restaurant. I was heading away from the house in what I knew was a blind, directionless panic. It was not until we reached the waterfront and were walking along the Battery wall that I began to calm down.

No one else was in sight. A few cars moved along the street, but to approach us someone would have to cross a wide, empty space. The gray clouds were quite low and blended with the choppy, white-crested waves in the bay.

The open air and fading evening light served to revive me, and I began to think more clearly. Whatever Nina's plans had been, they certainly had been thrown into disarray by my day-long absence. I doubted that Nina would stay if there were the slightest risk to herself. No, she would be returning to New York by plane even as I stood shivering on the Battery walk. In the morning I would receive a telegram, I could see it. MELANIE ISN'T IT TERRIBLE ABOUT WILLI? TERRIBLY SAD. CAN YOU TRAVEL WITH ME TO THE FUNERAL? LOVE, NINA.

I began to realize that my reluctance to leave immediately had come from a desire to return to the warmth and comfort of my home. I simply had been afraid to shuck off this old cocoon. I could do so now. I would wait in a safe place while Mr. Thorne returned to the house to pick up the one thing I could not leave behind. Then he would get the car out of storage, and by the time Nina's telegram arrived I would be far away. It would be *Nina* who would be starting at shadows in the months and years to come. I smiled and began to frame the necessary commands.

"Melanie."

My head snapped around. Mr. Thorne had not spoken in twenty-eight years. He spoke now.

"Melanie." His face was distorted in a rictus that showed his back teeth. The knife was in his right hand. The blade flicked out as I stared. I looked into his empty, gray eyes, and I knew.

"Melanie."

The long blade came around in a powerful arc. I could do nothing to stop it. It cut through the fabric of my coat sleeve and continued into my side. But in the act of turning, my purse had swung with me. The knife tore through the leather, ripped through the jumbled contents, pierced my coat, and drew blood above my lowest left rib. The purse had saved my life.

I raised father's heavy walking stick and struck Mr. Thorne squarely in his left eye. He reeled but did not make a sound. Again he swept the air with the knife, but I had taken two steps back and his vision was clouded. I took a two-handed grip on the cane and swung sideways again, bringing the stick around in an awkward chop. Incredibly, it again found the eye socket. I took three more steps back.

Blood streamed down the left side of Mr. Thorne's face, and the damaged eye protruded onto his cheek. The rictal grin remained. His head came up, he raised his left hand slowly, plucked out the eye with a soft snapping of a gray cord, and thew it into the water of the bay. He came toward me. I turned and ran.

I *tried* to run. The ache in my right leg slowed me to a walk after twenty paces. Fifteen more hurried steps and my lungs were out of air, my heart threatening to burst. I could feel a wetness seeping down my left side and there was a tingling—like an ice cube held against the skin—where the knife blade had touched me. One glance back showed me that Mr. Thorne was striding toward me faster than I was moving. Normally he could have overtaken me in four strides. But it is hard to make someone run when you are Using him. Especially when that person's body is reacting to shock and trauma. I glanced back again, almost slipping on the slick pavement. Mr. Thorne was grinning widely. Blood poured from the empty socket and stained his teeth. No one else was in sight.

Down the stairs, clutching at the rail so as not to fall. Down the twisting walk and up the asphalt path to the street. Pole lamps flickered and went on as I passed. Behind me Mr. Thorne took the steps in two jumps. As I hurried up the path, I thanked God that I had worn low-heel shoes for the boat ride. What would an observer think seeing this bizarre, slow-motion chase between two old people? There were no observers.

I turned onto a side street. Closed shops, empty warehouses. Going left would take me to Broad Street, but to the right, half a block away, a lone figure had emerged from a dark storefront. I moved that way, no longer able to run, close to fainting. The arthritic cramps in my leg hurt more than I could ever have imagined and threatened to collapse me on the sidewalk. Mr. Thorne was twenty paces behind me and quickly closing the distance.

The man I was approaching was a tall, thin Negro wearing a brown nylon jacket. He was carrying a box of what looked like framed sepia photographs.

He glanced at me as I approached and then looked over my shoulder at the apparition ten steps behind.

"Hey!" The man had time to shout the single syllable and then I reached out with my mind and *shoved*. He twitched like a poorly handled marionette. His jaw dropped, and his eyes glazed over, and he lurched past me just as Mr. Thorne reached for the back of my coat.

The box flew into the air, and glass shattered on the brick sidewalk. Long, brown fingers reached for a white throat. Mr. Thorne backhanded him away, but the Negro clung tenaciously, and the two swung around like awkward dance partners. I reached the opening to an alley and leaned my face against the cold brick to revive myself. The effort of concentration while Using this stranger did not afford me the luxury of resting even for a second.

I watched the clumsy stumblings of the two tall men for a while and resisted an absurd impulse to laugh.

Mr. Thorne plunged the knife into the other's stomach, withdrew it, plunged it in again. The Negro's fingernails were clawing at Mr. Thorne's good eye now. Strong teeth were snapping in search of the blade for a third time, but the heart was still beating and he was still usable. The man jumped, scissoring his legs around Mr. Thorne's middle while his jaws closed on the muscular throat. Fingernails raked bloody streaks across white skin. The two went down in a tumble.

Kill him. Fingers groped for an eye, but Mr. Thorne reached up with his left hand and snapped the thin wrist. Limp fingers continued to flail. With a tremendous exertion, Mr. Thorne lodged his forearm against the other's chest and lifted him bodily as a reclining father tosses a child above him. Teeth tore away a piece of flesh, but there was no vital damage. Mr. Thorne brought the knife between them, up, left, then right. He severed half the Negro's throat with the second swing, and blood fountained over both of them. The smaller man's legs spasmed twice, Mr. Thorne threw him to one side, and I turned and walked quickly down the alley.

Out into the light again, the fading evening light, and I realized that I had run myself into a dead end. Backs of warehouses and the windowless, metal side of the Battery Marina pushed right up against the waters of the bay. A street wound away to the left, but it was dark, deserted, and far too long to try.

I looked back in time to see the black silhouette enter the alley behind me.

I tried to make contact, but there was nothing there. Nothing. Mr. Thorne might as well have been a hole in the air. I would worry later how Nina had done this thing.

The side door to the marina was locked. The main door was almost a hundred yards away and would also be locked. Mr. Thorne emerged from the alley and swung his head left and right in search of me. In the dim light his heavily streaked face looked almost black. He began lurching toward me.

I raised father's walking stick, broke the lower pane of the window, and reached in through the jagged shards. If there was a bottom or top bolt I was dead. There was a simple doorknob lock and crossbolt. My fingers slipped on the cold metal, but the bolt slid back as Mr. Thorne stepped up on the walk behind me. Then I was inside and throwing the bolt.

It was very dark. Cold seeped up from the concrete floor and there was a sound of many small boats rising and falling at their moorings. Fifty yards away light spilled out of the office windows. I had hoped there would be an alarm system, but the building was too old and the marina too cheap to have one. I walked toward the light as Mr. Thorne's forearm shattered the remaining glass in the door behind me. The arm withdrew. A great kick broke off the top hinge and splintered wood around the bolt. I glanced at the office, but only the sound of a radio talk show came out of the impossibly distant door. Another kick.

I turned to my right and stepped to the bow of a bobbing inboard cruiser. Five steps and I was in the small, covered space that passed for a forward cabin. I closed the flimsy access panel behind me and peered out through the Plexiglas.

Mr. Thorne's third kick sent the door flying inward, dangling from long strips of splintered wood. His dark form filled the doorway. Light from a distant streetlight glinted off the blade in his right hand.

Please. Please hear the noise. But there was no movement from the office, only the metallic voices from the radio. Mr. Thorne took four paces, paused, and stepped down onto the first boat in line. It was an open outboard, and he was back up on the concrete in six seconds. The second boat had a small cabin. There was a ripping sound as Mr. Thorne kicked open the tiny hatch door, and then he was back up on the walkway. My boat was the eighth in line. I wondered why he couldn't just hear the wild hammering of my heart.

I shifted position and looked through the starboard port. The murky Plexiglas threw the light into streaks and patterns. I caught a brief glimpse of white hair through the window, and the radio was switched to another station. Loud music echoed in the long room. I slid back to the other porthole. Mr. Thorne was stepping off the fourth boat.

I closed my eyes, forced my ragged breathing to slow, and tried to remember countless evenings watching a bowlegged old figure shuffle down the street. Mr. Thorne finished his inspection of the fifth boat, a longer cabin cruiser with several dark recesses, and pulled himself back onto the walkway.

Forget the coffee in the thermos. Forget the crossword puzzle. Go look!

The sixth boat was a small outboard. Mr. Thorne glanced at it but did not step onto it. The seventh was a low sailboat, mast folded down, canvas stretched across the cockpit. Mr. Thorne's knife slashed through the thick material. Blood-streaked hands pulled back the canvas like a shroud being torn away. He jumped back to the walkway.

Forget the coffee. Go look! Now!

Mr. Thorne stepped onto the bow of my boat. I felt it rock to his weight. There was nowhere to hide, only a tiny storage locker under the seat, much too small to squeeze into. I untied the canvas strips that held the seat cushion to the bench. The sound of my ragged breathing seemed to echo in the little space. I curled into a fetal position behind the cushion as Mr. Thorne's leg moved past the starboard port. *Now.* Suddenly his face filled the Plexiglas strip not a foot from my head. His impossibly wide grimace grew even wider. *Now.* He stepped into the cockpit.

Now. Now. Now.

Mr. Thorne crouched at the cabin door. I tried to brace the tiny louvered door with my legs, but my right leg would not obey. Mr. Thorne fist slammed through the thin wooden strips and grabbed my ankle.

"Hey there!"

It was Mr. Hodges's shaky voice. His flashlight bobbed in our direction.

Mr. Thorne shoved against the door. My left leg folded painfully. Mr. Thorne's left hand firmly held my ankle through the shattered slats while the hand with the knife blade came through the opening hatch.

"Hey—" My mind shoved. Very hard. The old man stopped. He dropped the flashlight and unstrapped the buckle over the grip of his revolver.

Mr. Thorne slashed the knife back and forth. The cushion was almost knocked out of my hands as shreds of foam filled the cabin. The blade caught the tip of my little finger as the knife swung back again.

Do it. Now. Do it. Mr. Hodges gripped the revolver in both hands and fired. The shot went wide in the dark as the sound echoed off concrete and water. *Closer, you fool. Move!* Mr. Thorne shoved again and his body squeezed into the open hatch. He released my ankle to free his left arm, but almost instantly his hand was back in the cabin, grasping for me. I reached up and turned on the overhead light. Darkness stared at me from his empty eye socket. Light through the broken shutters spilled yellow strips across his ruined face. I slid to the left, but Mr. Thorne's hand, which had my coat, was pulling me off the bench. He was on his knees, freeing his right hand for the knife thrust.

Now! Mr. Hodges's second shot caught Mr. Thorne in the right hip. He grunted as the impact shoved him backward into a sitting position. My coat ripped, and buttons rattled on the deck.

The knife slashed the bulkhead near my ear before it pulled away.

Mr. Hodges stepped shakily onto the bow, almost fell, and inched his way around the starboard side. I pushed the hatch against Mr. Thorne's arm, but he continued to grip my coat and drag me toward him. I fell to my knees. The blade swung back, ripped through foam, and slashed at my coat. What was left of the cushion flew out of my hands. I had Mr. Hodges stop four feet away and brace the gun on the roof of the cabin.

Mr. Thorne pulled the blade back and poised it like a matador's sword. I could sense the silent scream of triumph that poured out over the stained teeth like a noxious vapor. The light of Nina's madness burned behind the single, staring eye.

Mr. Hodges fired. The bullet severed Mr. Thorne's spine and continued on into the port scupper. Mr. Thorne arched backward, splayed out his arms, and flopped onto the deck like a great fish that had just been landed. The knife fell to the floor of the cabin, while stiff, white fingers continued to slap nervelessly against the deck. I had Mr. Hodges step forward, brace the muzzle against Mr. Thorne's temple just above the remaining eye, and fire again. The sound was muted and hollow.

There was a first-aid kit in the office bathroom. I had the old man stand by the door while I bandaged my little finger and took three aspirin.

My coat was ruined, and blood had stained my print dress. I had never cared very much for the dress—I thought it made me look dowdy—but the coat had been a favorite of mine. My hair was a mess. Small, moist bits of gray matter flecked it. I splashed water on my face and brushed my hair as best I could. Incredibly, my tattered purse had stayed with me although many of the contents had spilled out. I transferred keys, billfold, reading glasses, and Kleenex to my large coat pocket and dropped the purse behind the toilet. I no longer had father's walking stick, but I could not remember where I had dropped it.

Gingerly I removed the heavy revolver from Mr. Hodges's grip. The old man's arm remained extended, fingers curled around air. After fumbling for a few seconds I managed to click open the cylinder. Two cartridges remained unfired. The old fool had been walking around with all six chambers loaded! *Always leave an empty chamber under the hammer.* That is what Charles had taught me that gay and distant summer so long ago when such weapons were merely excuses for trips to the island for target practice punctuated by the shrill shrieks of our nervous laughter as Nina and I allowed ourselves to be held, arms supported, bodies shrinking back into the firm support of our so-serious tutors' arms. *One must always count the cartridges,* lectured Charles, as I half-swooned against him, smelling the sweet, masculine shaving soap and tobacco smell rising from him on that warm, bright day.

Mr. Hodges stirred slightly as my attention wandered. His mouth gaped, and his dentures hung loosely. I glanced at the worn leather belt, but there were no extra bullets there, and I had no idea where he kept any. I probed, but there was little left in the old man's jumble of thoughts except for a swirling tape-loop replay of the muzzle being laid against Mr. Thorne's temple, the explosion, the—

"Come," I said. I adjusted the glasses on Mr. Hodges's vacant face, returned the revolver to the holster, and let him lead me out of the building.

It was very dark out. We had gone six blocks before the old man's violent shivering reminded me that I had forgotten to have him put on his coat. I tightened my mental vise, and he stopped shaking.

The house looked just as it had . . . my God . . . only forty-five minutes earlier. There were no lights. I let us into the courtyard and searched my overstuffed coat pocket for the key. My coat hung loose and the cold night air nipped at me. From behind lighted windows across the courtyard came the laughter of little girls, and I hurried so that Kathleen would not see her grandfather entering my house.

Mr. Hodges went in first, with the revolver extended. I had him switch on the light before I entered.

The parlor was empty, undisturbed. The light from the chandelier in the dining room reflected off polished surfaces. I sat down for a minute on the Williamsburg reproduction chair in the hall to let my heart rate return to normal. I did not have Mr. Hodges lower the hammer on the still-raised pistol. His arm began to shake from the strain of holding it. Finally, I rose and we moved down the hall toward the conservatory.

Miss Kramer exploded out of the swinging door from the kitchen with the heavy iron poker already coming down in an arc. The gun fired harmlessly into the polished floor as the old man's arm snapped from the impact. The gun fell from limp fingers as Miss Kramer raised the poker for a second blow.

I turned and ran back down the hallway. Behind me I heard the crushed-melon sound of the poker contacting Mr. Hodges's skull. Rather than run into the courtyard I went up the stairway. A mistake. Miss Kramer bounded up the stairs and reached the bedroom door only a few seconds after me. I caught one glimpse of her widened, maddened eyes and of the upraised poker before I slammed and locked the heavy door. The latch clicked just as the brunette on the other side began to throw herself against the wood. The thick oak did not budge. Then I heard the concussion of metal against the door and frame. Again.

Cursing my stupidity, I turned to the familiar room, but there was nothing there to help me. There was not as much as a closet to hide in, only the antique wardrobe. I moved quickly to the window and threw up the sash. My screams would attract attention but not before that monstrosity had gained access. She was prying at the edges of the door now. I looked out, saw the shadows in the window across the way, and did what I had to do.

Two minutes later I was barely conscious of the wood giving away around the latch. I heard the distant grating of the poker as it pried at the recalcitrant metal plate. The door swung inward.

Miss Kramer was covered with sweat. Her mouth hung slack, and drool slid from her chin. Her eyes were not human. Neither she nor I heard the soft tread of sneakers on the stairs behind her.

Keep moving. Lift it. Pull it back—all the way back. Use both hands. Aim it.

Something warned Miss Kramer. Warned Nina, I should say; there was no more Miss Kramer. The brunette turned to see little Kathleen standing on the top stair, her grandfather's heavy weapon aimed and cocked. The other girl was in the courtyard shouting for her friend.

This time Nina knew she had to deal with the threat. Miss Kramer hefted the poker and turned into the hall just as the pistol fired. The recoil tumbled Kathleen backward down the stairs as a red corsage blossomed above Miss Kramer's left breast. She spun but grasped the railing with her left hand and lurched down the stairs after the child. I released the ten-year-old just as the poker fell, rose, fell again. I moved to the head of the stairway. I had to see.

Miss Kramer looked up from her grim work. Only the whites of her eyes were visible in her spattered face. Her masculine shirt was soaked with her own blood, but still she moved, functioned. She picked up the gun in her left hand. Her mouth opened wider, and a sound emerged like steam leaking from an old radiator.

"Melanie . . ." I closed my eyes as the thing started up the stairs for me.

Kathleen's friend came in through the open door, her small legs pumping. She took the stairs in six jumps and wrapped her thin, white arms around Miss Kramer's neck in a tight embrace.

The two went over backward, across Kathleen, all the way down the wide stairs to the polished wood below.

The girl appeared to be little more than bruised. I went down and moved her to one side. A blue stain was spreading along one cheekbone, and there were cuts on her arms and forehead. Her blue eyes blinked uncomprehendingly.

Miss Kramer's neck was broken. I picked up the pistol on the way to her and kicked the poker to one side. Her head was at an impossible angle, but she was still alive. Her body was paralyzed, urine already stained the wood, but her eyes still blinked and her teeth clicked together obscenely. I had to hurry. There were adult voices calling from the Hodgeses' town house. The door to the courtyard was wide open. I turned to the girl. "Get up." She blinked once and rose painfully to her feet.

I shut the door and lifted a tan raincoat from the coatrack.

It took only a minute to transfer the contents of my pockets to the raincoat and to discard my ruined spring coat. Voices were calling in the courtyard now.

I kneeled down next to Miss Kramer and seized her face in my hands, exerting pressure to keep the jaws still. Her eyes had rolled upward again, but I shook her head until the irises were visible. I leaned forward until our cheeks were touching. My whisper was louder than a shout.

"I'm coming for you, Nina."

I dropped her head onto the wood and walked quickly to the conservatory, my sewing room. I did not have time to get the key from upstairs; so I raised a Windsor side chair and smashed the glass of the cabinet. My coat pocket was barely large enough.

The girl remained standing in the hall. I handed her Mr. Hodges's pistol. Her left arm hung at a strange angle and I wondered if she had broken something after all. There was a knock at the door, and someone tried the knob.

"This way," I whispered, and led the girl into the dining room.

We stepped across Miss Kramer on the way, walked through the dark kitchen as the pounding grew louder, and then were out, into the alley, into the night.

There were three hotels in this part of the Old Section. One was a modern, expensive motor hotel some ten blocks away, comfortable but commercial. I rejected it immediately. The second was a small, homey lodging house only a block from my home. It was a pleasant but nonexclusive little place, exactly the type I would choose when visiting another town. I rejected it also. The third was two and a half blocks farther, an old Broad Street mansion done over into a small hotel, expensive antiques in every room, absurdly overpriced. I hurried there. The girl moved quickly at my side. The pistol was still in her hand, but I had her remove her sweater and carry it over the weapon. My leg ached, and I frequently leaned on the girl as we hurried down the street.

The manager of the Mansard House recognized me. His eyebrows went up a fraction of an inch as he noticed my disheveled appearance. The girl stood ten feet away in the foyer, half-hidden in the shadows.

"I'm looking for a friend of mine," I said brightly. "A Mrs. Drayton."

The manager started to speak, paused, frowned without being aware of it, and tried again. "I'm sorry. No one under that name is registered here."

"Perhaps she registered under her maiden name," I said. "Nina Hawkins. She's an older woman but very attractive. A few years younger than I. Long, gray hair. Her friend may have registered for her . . . an attractive, young, dark-haired lady named Barrett Kramer—"

"No, I'm sorry," said the manager in a strangely flat tone. "No one under that name has registered. Would you like to leave a message in case your party arrives later?"

"No," I said. "No message."

I brought the girl into the lobby, and we turned down a corridor leading to the restrooms and side stairs. "Excuse me, please," I said to a passing porter. "Perhaps you can help me."

"Yes, ma'am." He stopped, annoyed, and brushed back his long hair. It would be tricky. If I was not to lose the girl, I would have to act quickly.

"I'm looking for a friend," I said. "She's an older lady but quite attractive. Blue eyes. Long, gray hair. She travels with a young woman who has dark, curly hair."

"No, ma'am. No one like that is registered here."

I reached out and grabbed hold of his forearm tightly. I released the girl and focused on the boy. "Are you sure?"

"Mrs. Harrison," he said. His eyes looked past me. "Room 207. North front."

I smiled. *Mrs. Harrison.* Good God, what a fool Nina was. Suddenly the girl let out a small whimper and slumped against the wall. I made a quick decision. I like to think that it was compassion, but I sometimes remember that her left arm was useless.

"What's your name?" I asked the child, gently stroking her bangs. Her eyes moved left and right in confusion. "Your name!"

"Alicia." It was only a whisper.

"All right, Alicia. I want you to go home now. Hurry, but don't run."

"My *arm* hurts," she said. Her lips began to quiver. I touched her forehead again and *pushed*.

"You're going home," I said. "Your arm does not hurt. You won't remember anything. This is like a dream that you will forget. Go home. Hurry, but do not run." I took the pistol from her but left it wrapped in the sweater. "Bye-bye, Alicia."

She blinked and crossed the lobby to the doors. I handed the gun to the bellhop. "Put it under your vest," I said.

"Who is it?" Nina's voice was light.

"Albert, ma'am. The porter. Your car's out front, and I'll take your bags down."

There was the sound of a lock clicking and the door opened the width of a still-secured chain. Albert blinked in the glare, smiled shyly, and brushed his hair back. I pressed against the wall.

"Very well." She undid the chain and moved back. She had already turned and was latching her suitcase when I stepped into the room.

"Hello, Nina," I said softly. Her back straightened, but even that move was graceful. I could see the imprint on the bedspread where she had been lying. She turned slowly. She was wearing a pink dress I had never seen before.

"Hello, Melanie." She smiled. Her eyes were the softest, purest blue I had ever seen. I had the porter take Mr. Hodges's gun out and aim it. His arm was steady. He pulled back the hammer and held it with his thumb. Nina folded her hands in front of her. Her eyes never left mine.

"Why?" I asked.

Nina shrugged ever so slightly. For a second I thought she was going to laugh. I could not have borne it if she had laughed—that husky, childlike laugh that had touched me so many times. Instead she closed her eyes. Her smile remained.

"Why Mrs. Harrison?" I asked.

"Why, darling, I felt I owed him *something*. I mean, poor Roger. Did I ever tell you how he died? No, of course I didn't. And you never asked." Her eyes opened. I glanced at the porter, but his aim was steady. It only remained for him to exert a little more pressure on the trigger.

"He *drowned*, darling," said Nina. "Poor Roger threw himself from that steamship—what was its name?—the one that was taking him back to England. So strange. And he had just written me a letter promising marriage. Isn't that a *terribly* sad story, Melanie? Why do you think he did a thing like that? I guess we'll never know, will we?"

"I guess we never will," I said. I silently ordered the porter to pull the trigger.

Nothing.

I looked quickly to my right. The young man's head was turning toward me. *I had not made him do that.* The stiffly extended arm began to swing in my direction. The pistol moved smoothy like the tip of a weather vane swinging in the wind.

No! I strained until the cords in my neck stood out. The turning slowed but did not stop until the muzzle was pointing at my face. Nina laughed now. The sound was very loud in the little room.

"Good-bye, Melanie *dear*," Nina said, and laughed again. She laughed and nodded at the porter. I stared into the black hole as the hammer fell. On an empty chamber. And another. And another.

"Good-bye, Nina," I said as I pulled Charles's long pistol from the raincoat pocket. The explosion jarred my wrist and filled the room with blue smoke. A small hole, smaller than a dime but as perfectly round, appeared in the precise center of Nina's forehead. For the briefest second she remained standing as if nothing had happened. Then she fell backward, recoiled from the high bed, and dropped face forward onto the floor.

I turned to the porter and replaced his useless weapon with the ancient but well-maintained revolver. For the first time I noticed that the boy was not much younger than Charles had been. His hair was almost exactly the same color. I leaned forward and kissed him lightly on the lips.

"Albert," I whispered, "there are four cartridges left. One must always count the cartridges, mustn't one? Go to the lobby. Kill the manager. Shoot one other person, the nearest. Put the barrel in your mouth and pull the trigger. If it misfires, pull it again. Keep the gun concealed until you are in the lobby."

We emerged into general confusion in the hallway.

"Call for an ambulance!" I cried. "There's been an accident. Someone call for an ambulance!" Several people rushed to comply. I swooned and leaned against a white-haired gentleman. People milled around, some peering into the room and exclaiming. Suddenly there was the sound of three gunshots from the lobby. In the renewed confusion I slipped down the back stairs, out the fire door, into the night.

Time has passed. I am very happy here. I live in southern France now, between Cannes and Toulon, but not, I am happy to say, too near St. Tropez.

I rarely go out. Henri and Claude do my shopping in the village. I never go to the beach. Occasionally I go to the townhouse in Paris or to my pensione in Italy, south of Pescara, on the Adriatic. But even those trips have become less and less frequent.

There is an abandoned abbey in the hills, and I often go there to sit and think among the stones and wild flowers. I think about isolation and abstinence and how each is so cruelly dependent upon the other.

I feel younger these days. I tell myself that this is because of the climate and my freedom and not as a result of that final Feeding. But sometimes I dream about the familiar streets of Charleston and the people there. They are dreams of hunger.

On some days I rise to the sound of singing as girls from the village cycle by our place on their way to the dairy. On those days the sun is marvelously warm as it shines on the small white flowers growing between the tumbled stones of the abbey, and I am content simply to be there and to share the sunlight and silence with them.

But on other days—cold, dark days when the clouds move in from the north—I remember the shark-silent shape of a submarine moving through the dark waters of the bay, and I wonder whether my self-imposed abstinence will be for nothing. I wonder whether those I dream of in my isolation will indulge in their own gigantic, final Feeding.

It is warm today. I am happy. But I am also alone. And I am very, very hungry.

I suspect that the vampire myth is as persistent, resilient, and satisfying as it is because there is a bit of the vampire in each of us. Much has been written about the blood symbolism in vampire tales, much about the latent erotic imagery, but little is said about the simple attraction of *control*. If you believe as I do that any exercise of power over another person is an incipient act of violence, then the vampire represents the ultimate violence—an extension of power over others to the grave and beyond.

"Carrion Comfort" has its genesis in a variety of places. There is a marvelous scene in the otherwise laughable 1931 *Dracula* where Bela Lugosi has a contest of wills with the aging Van Helsing. The old man staggers forward a few paces under the vampire's influence and then pulls back painfully, slowly, struggling against invisible bonds. "You have a strong vill, Van Helsing," smiles Lugosi. But we know who will win the contest in the end.

And of course any story or novel about extrasensory powers of control must recognize Frank M. Robinson's *The Power* (1956) as a seminal influence.

In the end, however, it was the simple image of these three old people meeting in pleasant reunion, sunlight moving across their aged skin and young eyes, that proved the prime mover for "Carrion Comfort." As many of us suspect, the road to success is littered with the brittle bones of our victims. After a while we do not notice.

We are what we devour.

Dan Simmons

The Sea Was Wet as Wet Could Be

GAHAN WILSON

Lewis Carroll's Alice in Wonderland *and* Through the Looking Glass *are among my favorite works of fantasy. The books, in addition to being charming and entertaining, are deft commentaries on the economic, social, and political conditions of the times. And beneath some of the cute rhymes lurks genuine horror. So it is with "The Walrus and the Carpenter." Gahan Wilson's "The Sea Was Wet as Wet Could Be" is the story that prompted me to begin* Blood Is Not Enough.

I felt we made an embarrassing contrast to the open serenity of the scene around us. The pure blue of the sky was unmarked by a single cloud or bird, and nothing stirred on the vast stretch of beach except ourselves. The sea, sparkling under the freshness of the early morning sun, looked invitingly clean. I wanted to wade into it and wash myself, but I was afraid I would contaminate it.

We are a contamination here, I thought. We're like a group of sticky bugs crawling in an ugly little crowd over polished marble. If I were God and looked down and saw us, lugging our baskets and our silly, bright blankets, I would step on us and squash us with my foot.

We should have been lovers or monks in such a place, but we were only a crowd of bored and boring drunks. You were always drunk when you were with Carl. Good old, mean old Carl was the greatest little drink pourer in the world. He used drinks like other types of sadists used whips. He kept beating you with them until you dropped or sobbed or went mad, and he enjoyed every step of the process.

We'd been drinking all night, and when the morning came, somebody, I think it was Mandie, got the great idea that we should all go out on a picnic. Naturally, we thought it was an inspiration, we were nothing if not real sports, and so we'd packed some goodies, not forgetting the liquor, and we'd piled into the car, and there we were, weaving across the beach, looking for a place to spread our tacky banquet.

We located a broad, low rock, decided it would serve for our table, and loaded it with the latest in plastic chinaware, a haphazard collection of food and a quantity of bottles.

Someone had packed a tin of Spam among the other offerings and, when I saw it, I was suddenly overwhelmed with an absurd feeling of nostalgia. It reminded me of the war and of myself soldierboying up through Italy. It also reminded me of how long ago the whole thing had been and how little I'd done of what I'd dreamed I'd do back then.

I opened the Spam and sat down to be alone with it and my memories, but it wasn't to be for long. The kind of people who run with people like Carl don't like to be alone, ever, especially with their memories, and they can't imagine anyone else might, at least now and then, have a taste for it.

My rescuer was Irene. Irene was particularly sensitive about seeing people alone because being alone had several times nearly produced fatal results for her. Being alone and taking pills to end the being alone.

"What's wrong, Phil?" she asked.

"Nothing's wrong," I said, holding up a forkful of the pink Spam in the sunlight. "It tastes just like it always did. They haven't lost their touch."

She sat down on the sand beside me, very carefully, so as to avoid spilling the least drop of what must have been her millionth Scotch.

"Phil," she said, "I'm worried about Mandie. I really am. She looks so unhappy!"

I glanced over at Mandie. She had her head thrown back and she was laughing uproariously at some joke Carl had just made. Carl was smiling at her with his teeth glistening and his eyes deep down dead as ever.

"Why should Mandie be happy?" I asked. "What, in God's name, has she got to be happy about?"

"Oh, Phil," said Irene. "You pretend to be such an awful cynic. She's *alive*, isn't she?"

56

I looked at her and wondered what such a statement meant, coming from someone who'd tried to do herself in as earnestly and as frequently as Irene. I decided that I did not know and that I would probably never know. I also decided I didn't want anymore of the Spam. I turned to throw it away, doing my bit to litter up the beach, and then I saw them.

They were far away, barely bigger than two dots, but you could tell there was something odd about them even then.

"We've got company," I said.

Irene peered in the direction of my point.

"Look, everybody," she cried, "we've got company!"

Everybody looked, just as she had asked them to.

"What the hell is this?" asked Carl. "Don't they know this is my private property?" And then he laughed.

Carl had fantasies about owning things and having power. Now and then he got drunk enough to have little flashes of believing he was king of the world.

"You tell 'em, Carl!" said Horace.

Horace had sparkling quips like that for almost every occasion. He was tall and bald and he had a huge Adam's apple and, like myself, he worked for Carl. I would have felt sorrier for Horace than I did if I hadn't had a sneaky suspicion that he was really happier when groveling. He lifted one scrawny fist and shook it in the direction of the distant pair.

"You guys better beat it," he shouted. "This is private property!"

"Will you shut up and stop being such an ass?" Mandie asked him. "It's not polite to yell at strangers, dear, and this may damn well be *their* beach for all you know."

Mandie happens to be Horace's wife. Horace's children treat him about the same way. He busied himself with zipping up his windbreaker, because it was getting cold and because he had received an order to be quiet.

I watched the two approaching figures. The one was tall and bulky, and he moved with a peculiar, swaying gait. The other was short and hunched into himself, and he walked in a fretful, zigzag line beside his towering companion.

"They're heading straight for us," I said.

The combination of the cool wind that had come up and the approach of the two strangers had put a damper on our little group. We sat quietly

57

and watched them coming closer. The nearer they got, the odder they looked.

"For heaven's sake!" said Irene. "The little one's wearing a square hat!"

"I think it's made of paper," said Mandie, squinting, "folded newspaper."

"Will you look at the mustache on the big bastard?" asked Carl. "I don't think I've ever seen a bigger bush in my life."

"They remind me of something," I said.

The others turned to look at me.

The Walrus and the Carpenter . . .

"They remind me of the Walrus and the Carpenter," I said.

"The who?" asked Mandie.

"Don't tell me you never heard of the Walrus and the Carpenter?" asked Carl.

"Never once," said Mandie.

"Disgusting," said Carl. "You're an uncultured bitch. The Walrus and the Carpenter are probably two of the most famous characters in literature. They're in a poem by Lewis Carroll in one of the *Alice* books."

"In *Through the Looking Glass*," I said, and then I recited their introduction:

> "The Walrus and the Carpenter
>   Were walking close at hand
> They wept like anything to see
>   Such quantities of sand . . ."

Mandie shrugged. "Well, you'll just have to excuse my ignorance and concentrate on my charm," she said.

"I don't know how to break this to you all," said Irene, "but the little one *does* have a handkerchief."

We stared at them. The little one did indeed have a handkerchief, a huge handkerchief, and he was using it to dab at his eyes.

"Is the little one supposed to be the Carpenter?" asked Mandie.

"Yes," I said.

"Then it's all right," she said, "because he's the one that's carrying the saw."

"He is, so help me, God," said Carl. "And, to make the whole thing perfect, he's even wearing an apron."

"So the Carpenter in the poem has to wear an apron, right?" asked Mandie.

"Carroll doesn't say whether he does or not," I said, "but the illustrations by Tenniel show him wearing one. They also show him with the same square jaw and the same big nose this guy's got."

"They're goddamn doubles," said Carl. "The only thing wrong is that the Walrus isn't a walrus, he just looks like one."

"You watch," said Mandie. "Any minute now he's going to sprout fur all over and grow long fangs."

Then, for the first time, the approaching pair noticed us. It seemed to give them quite a start. They stood and gaped at us and the little one furtively stuffed his handkerchief out of sight.

"We can't be as surprising as all that!" whispered Irene.

The big one began moving forward, then, in a hesitant, tentative kind of shuffle. The little one edged ahead, too, but he was careful to keep the bulk of his companion between himself and us.

"First contact with the aliens," said Mandie, and Irene and Horace giggled nervously. I didn't respond. I had come to the decision that I was going to quit working for Carl, that I didn't like any of these people about me, except, maybe, Irene, and that these two strangers gave me the honest creeps.

Then the big one smiled, and everything was changed.

I've worked in the entertainment field, in advertising and in public relations. This means I have come in contact with some of the prime charm boys and girls in our proud land. I have become, therefore, not only a connoisseur of smiles, I am a being equipped with numerous automatic safeguards against them. When a talcumed smoothie comes at me with his brilliant ivories exposed, it only shows he's got something he can bite me with, that's all.

But the smile of the Walrus was something else.

The smile of the Walrus did what a smile hasn't done for me in years—it melted my heart. I use the corn-ball phrase very much on purpose.

When I saw his smile, I knew I could trust him; I felt in my marrow that he was gentle and sweet and had nothing but the best intentions. His resemblance to the Walrus in the poem ceased being vaguely chilling and became warmly comical. I loved him as I had loved the teddy bear of my childhood.

"Oh, I *say*," he said, and his voice was an embarrassed boom, "I *do* hope we're not intruding!"

"I daresay we are," squeaked the Carpenter, peeping out from behind his companion.

"The, uhm, fact is," boomed the Walrus, "we didn't even notice you until just back then, you see."

"We were talking, is what," said the Carpenter.

> They wept like anything to see
> Such quantities of sand . . .

"About sand?" I asked.

The Walrus looked at me with a startled air.

"We *were*, actually, now you come to mention it."

He lifted one huge foot and shook it so that a little trickle of sand spilled out of his shoe.

"The stuff's impossible," he said. "Gets in your clothes, tracks up the carpet."

"Ought to be swept away, it ought," said the Carpenter.

> 'If seven maids with seven mops
> Swept it for half a year,
> Do you suppose,' the Walrus said,
> 'That they could get it clear?'

"It's too much!" said Carl.

"Yes, indeed," said the Walrus, eying the sand around him with vague disapproval, "altogether too much."

Then he turned to us again and we all basked in that smile.

"Permit me to introduce my companion and myself," he said.

"You'll have to excuse George," said the Carpenter, "as he's a bit of a stuffed shirt, don't you know?"

60

"Be that as it may," said the Walrus, patting the Carpenter on the flat top of his paper hat, "this is Edward Farr, and I am George Tweedy, both at your service. We are, uhm, both a trifle drunk, I'm afraid."

"We are, indeed. We are that."

"As we have just come from a really delightful party, to which we shall soon return."

"Once we've found the fuel, that is," said Farr, waving his saw in the air. By now he had found the courage to come out and face us directly.

"Which brings me to the question," said Tweedy. "Have you seen any *driftwood* lying about the premises? We've been looking high and low and we can't seem to find *any* of the blasted stuff."

"Thought there'd be piles of it," said Farr, "but all there is is sand, don't you see?"

"I would have sworn you were looking for oysters," said Carl.

Again, Tweedy appeared startled.

> 'O Oysters, come and walk with us!'
> The Walrus did beseech . . .

"Oysters?" he asked. "Oh, no, we've *got* the oysters. All we lack is the means to cook 'em."

" 'Course we could always use a few more," said Farr, looking at his companion.

"I suppose we *could,* at that," said Tweedy thoughtfully.

"I'm afraid we can't help you fellows with the driftwood problem," said Carl, "but you're more than welcome to a drink."

There was something unfamiliar about the tone of Carl's voice that made my ears perk up. I turned to look at him, and then had difficulty covering up my astonishment.

It was his eyes. For once, for the first time, they were really friendly.

I'm not saying Carl had fishy eyes, blank eyes—not at all. On the surface, that is. On the surface, with his eyes, with his face, with the handling of his entire body, Carl was a master of animation and expression. From sympathetic, heart-felt warmth, all the way to icy rage, and on every stop in-between, Carl was completely convincing.

But only on the surface. Once you got to know Carl, and it took a while, you realized that none of it was really happening. That was because

Carl had died, or been killed, long ago. Possibly in childhood. Possibly he had been born dead. So, under the actor's warmth and rage, the eyes were always the eyes of a corpse.

But now it was different. The friendliness here was genuine, I was sure of it. The smile of Tweedy, of the Walrus, had performed a miracle. Carl had risen from his tomb. I was in honest awe.

"*Delighted,* old chap!" said Tweedy.

They accepted their drinks with obvious pleasure, and we completed the introductions as they sat down to join us. I detected a strong smell of fish when Tweedy sat down beside me but, oddly, I didn't find it offensive in the least. I was glad he'd chosen me to sit by. He turned and smiled at me, and my heart melted a little more.

It soon turned out that the drinking we'd done before had only scratched the surface. Tweedy and Farr were magnificent boozers, and their gusto encouraged us all to follow suit.

We drank absurd toasts and were delighted to discover that Tweedy was an incredible raconteur. His specialty was outrageous fantasy: wild tales involving incongruous objects, events, and characters. His invention was endless.

> 'The time has come,' the Walrus said,
>   'To talk of many things:
> Of shoes—and ships—and sealing-wax—
>   Of cabbages—and kings—
> And why the sea is boiling hot—
>   And whether pigs have wings.'

We laughed and drank, and drank and laughed, and I began to wonder why in hell I'd spent my life being such a gloomy, moody son of a bitch, been such a distrustful and suspicious bastard, when the whole secret of everything, the whole core secret, was simply to enjoy it, to take it as it came.

I looked around and grinned, and I didn't care if it was a foolish grin. Everybody looked all right, everybody looked swell, everybody looked better than I'd ever seen them look before.

Irene looked happy, honestly and truly happy. She, too, had found the secret. No more pills for Irene, I thought. Now that she knows the secret, now that she's met Tweedy who's given her the secret, she'll have no more need of those goddamn pills.

And I couldn't believe Horace and Mandie. They had their arms around each other, and their bodies were pressed close together, and they rocked as one being when they laughed at Tweedy's wonderful stories. No more nagging for Mandie, I thought, and no more cringing for Horace, now they've learned the secret.

And then I looked at Carl, laughing and relaxed and absolutely free of care, absolutely unchilled, finally, at last, after years of—

And then I looked at Carl again.

And then I looked down at my drink, and then I looked at my knees, and then I looked out at the sea, sparkling, clean, remote and impersonal.

And then I realized it had grown cold, quite cold, and that there wasn't a bird or a cloud in the sky.

> The sea was wet as wet could be,
>   The sands were dry as dry.
> You could not see a cloud, because
>   No cloud was in the sky:
> No birds were flying overhead—
>   There were no birds to fly.

That part of the poem was, after all, a perfect description of a lifeless earth. It sounded beautiful at first, it sounded benign. But then you read it again and you realized that Carroll was describing barrenness and desolation.

Suddenly Carl's voice broke through and I heard him say:

"Hey, that's a hell of an idea, Tweedy! By God, we'd love to! Wouldn't we, gang?"

The others broke out in an affirmative chorus and they all started scrambling to their feet around me. I looked up at them, like someone who's been awakened from sleep in a strange place, and they grinned down at me like loons.

"Come on, Phil!" cried Irene.

Her eyes were bright and shining, but it wasn't with happiness. I could see that now.

> 'It seems a shame,' the Walrus said,
> 'To play them such a trick . . .'

I blinked my eyes and stared at them, one after the other.

"Old Phil's had a little too much to drink!" cried Mandie, laughing. "Come on, old Phil! Come on and join the party!"

"What party?" I asked.

I couldn't seem to get located. Everything seemed disorientated and grotesque.

"For Christ's sake, Phil," said Carl, "Tweedy and Farr, here, have invited us to join their party. There's no more drinks left, and they've got plenty!"

I set my plastic cup down carefully on the sand. If they would just shut up for a moment, I thought, I might be able to get the fuzz out of my head.

"Come *along,* sir!" boomed Tweedy jovially. "It's only a pleasant walk!"

> 'O oysters come and walk with us,'
> The walrus did beseech.
> 'A pleasant walk, a pleasant talk,
> Along the briny beach . . .'

He was smiling at me, but the smile didn't work anymore.

"You cannot do with more than four," I told him.

"*Uhm?* What's that?"

> '. . . we cannot do with more than four,
> And give a hand to each.'

"I said, 'You cannot do with more than four.' "

"He's right, you know," said Farr, the Carpenter.

"Well, uhm, then," said the Walrus, "if you feel you really *can't* come, old chap . . ."

"What, in Christ's name, are you all talking about?" asked Mandie.

"He's hung up on that goddamn poem," said Carl. "Lewis Carroll's got the yellow bastard scared."

"Don't be such a party pooper, Phil!" said Mandie.

64

"To hell with him," said Carl. And he started off, and all the others followed him. Except Irene.

"Are you sure you really don't want to come, Phil?" she asked.

She looked frail and thin against the sunlight. I realized there really wasn't much of her, and that what there was had taken a terrible beating.

"No," I said. "I don't. Are you sure you want to go?"

"Of course I do, Phil."

I thought of the pills.

"I suppose you do," I said. "I suppose there's really no stopping you."

"No, Phil, there isn't."

And then she stooped and kissed me. Kissed me very gently, and I could feel the dry, chapped surface of her lips and the faint warmth of her breath.

I stood.

"I wish you'd stay," I said.

"I can't," she said.

And then she turned and ran after the others.

I watched them growing smaller and smaller on the beach, following the Walrus and the Carpenter. I watched them come to where the beach curved around the bluff, and watched them disappear behind the bluff.

I looked up at the sky. Pure blue. Impersonal.

"What do you think of this?" I asked it.

Nothing. It hadn't even noticed.

> 'Now, if you're ready, oysters dear,
>   We can begin to feed.'
> 'But not on us!' the oysters cried,
>   Turning a little blue,
> 'After such kindness, that would be
>   A dismal thing to do!'

A dismal thing to do.

I began to run up the beach, toward the bluff. I stumbled now and then because I had had too much to drink. Far too much to drink. I heard small shells crack under my shoes, and the sand made whipping noises.

I fell, heavily, and lay there gasping on the beach. My heart pounded in my chest. I was too old for this sort of footwork. I hadn't had any real exercise in years. I smoked too much and I drank too much. I did all the wrong things. I didn't do any of the right things.

I pushed myself up a little and then I let myself down again. My heart was pounding hard enough to frighten me. I could feel it in my chest, frantically pumping, squeezing blood in and spurting blood out.

Like an oyster pulsing in the sea.

'Shall we be trotting home again?'

My heart was like an oyster.

I got up, fell up, and began to run again, weaving widely, my mouth open and the air burning my throat. I was coated with sweat, streaming with it, and it felt icy in the cold wind.

'Shall we be trotting home again?'

I rounded the bluff and then I stopped and stood swaying, and then I dropped to my knees.

The pure blue of the sky was unmarked by a single bird or cloud, and nothing stirred on the whole vast stretch of the beach.

But answer came there none—
And this was scarcely odd, because . . .

Nothing stirred, but they were there. Irene and Mandie and Carl and Horace were there, and four others, too. Just around the bluff.

'We cannot do with more than four . . .

But the Walrus and the Carpenter had taken two trips.

I began to crawl toward them on my knees. My heart, my oyster heart, was pounding too hard to allow me to stand.

The other four had had a picnic, too, very like our own. They, too, had plastic cups and plates, and they, too, had brought bottles. They had sat and waited for the return of the Walrus and the Carpenter.

Irene was right in front of me. Her eyes were open and stared at, but did not see, the sky. The pure blue uncluttered sky. There were a few grains of sand in her left eye. Her face was almost clear of blood. There were only a few flecks of it on her lower chin. The spray from the huge wound in her chest seemed to have traveled mainly downward and to the right. I stretched out my arm and touched her hand.

"Irene," I said.

> But answer came there none—
> And this was scarcely odd, because
> They'd eaten every one.

I looked up at the others. Like Irene, they were, all of them, dead. The Walrus and the Carpenter had eaten the oysters and left the shells.

The Carpenter never found any firewood, and so they'd eaten them raw. You can eat oysters raw if you want to.

I said her name once more, just for the record, and then I stood and turned from them and walked to the bluff. I rounded the bluff and the beach stretched before me, vast, smooth, empty, and remote.

Even as I ran upon it, away from them, it was remote.

I distrusted the *Alice* books from the start. My grown-ups tried to pretend they were children's books and that I should and would enjoy them, so they officially shuffled them in with the *Oz* and *Pooh* collection, but I knew better; I knew they were dangerous and I opened them only rarely and gingerly.

Of course Tenniel's Jabberwock leapt out at me from the start (as it has, I am sure, at many another innocent child), but there were many other horrors: the simultaneously fading and grinning cat; the impeccably cruel Duchess with her "little boy"; something about Bill the Lizard floating helplessly over the chimney; the crazed creatures at the Tea Party—the worst part of it was the thing that pervaded all those images and all the other images in the books (which I knew weren't

about any "Wonderland" at all, but about the very world I
was trying to grow up in, only seen from some terrifyingly
sophisticated point of view); the weird convincingness of
Carroll's horrible message that *nothing, nothing* soever,
made any sense at all!

If it hadn't been for brave, stolid Alice (bless her stout,
young, British heart), herself a child, I don't think I could
have survived those goddamn books.

But there is no Alice in this story.

Gahan Wilson

The Silver Collar

GARRY KILWORTH

"The Silver Collar" is a departure for Garry, who usually writes contemporary or futuristic science fiction. It is the most traditional of the stories in this volume, a gothic fantasy in which the vampire main character is never on stage. It shows the folly of those who believe love can conquer all.

The remote Scottish island came into view just as the sun was setting. Outside the natural harbor, the sea was kicking a little in its traces and tossing its white manes in the dying light. My small outboard motor struggled against the ebbing tide, sometimes whining as it raced in the air as a particularly low trough left it without water to push against the blades of its propeller. By the time I reached the jetty, the moon was up and casting its chill light upon the shore and purple-heather hills beyond. There was a smothered atmosphere to this lonely place of rock and thin soil, as if the coarse grass and hardy plants had descended as a complete layer to wrap the ruggedness in a faded cover, hiding the nakedness from mean, inquisitive eyes.

As the agents had promised, he was waiting on the quay, his tall, emaciated figure stark against the gentle upward slope of the hinterland: a splinter of granite from the rock on which he made his home.

"I've brought the provisions," I called, as he took the line and secured it.

"Good. Will you come up to the croft? There's a peat fire going—it's warm, and I have some scotch. Nothing like a dram before an open fire, with the smell of burning peat filling the room."

"I could just make it out with the tide," I said. "Perhaps I should go now." It was not that I was reluctant to accept the invitation from this eremite, this strange recluse—on the contrary, he interested me—but I had to be sure to get back to the mainland that night, since I was to crew a fishing vessel the next day.

"You have time for a dram," his voice drifted away on the cold wind that had sprung up within minutes, like a breath from the mouth of the icy north. I had to admit to myself that a whisky, by the fire, would set me on my toes for the return trip, and his tone had a faintly insistent quality about it which made the offer difficult to refuse.

"Just a minute then—and thanks. You lead the way."

I followed his lean, lithe figure up through the heather, which scratched at my ankles through my seasocks. The path was obviously not well used and I imagined he spent his time in and around his croft, for even in the moonlight I could discern no other tracks incising the soft shape of the hill.

We reached his dwelling and he opened the wooden door, allowing me to enter first. Then, seating me in front of the fire, he poured me a generous whisky before sitting down himself. I listened to the wind, locked outside the timber and turf croft, and waited for him to speak.

He said, "John, is't it? They told me on the radio."

"Yes—and you're Samual."

"Sam. You must call me Sam."

I told him I would and there was a period of silence while we regarded each other. Peat is not a consistent fuel, and tends to spurt and spit colorful plumes of flame as the gases escape, having been held prisoner from the seasons for God knows how long. Nevertheless, I was able to study my host in the brief periods of illumination that the fire afforded. He could have been any age, but I knew he was my senior by a great many years. The same thoughts must have been passing through his own head, for he remarked, "John, how old are you? I would guess at twenty."

"Nearer thirty, Sam. I was twenty-six last birthday." He nodded, saying that those who live a solitary life, away from others, have great difficulty in assessing the ages of people they do meet. Recent events slipped from his memory quite quickly, while the past seemed so close.

He leaned forward, into the hissing fire, as if drawing a breath from the ancient atmospheres it released into the room. Behind him, the earthen walls of the croft, held together by rough timbers and unhewn stones, seemed to move closer to his shoulder, as if ready to support his words with confirmation. I sensed a story coming. I recognized the pose from being in the company of sailors on long voyages and hoped he would finish before I had to leave.

"You're a good-looking boy," he said. "So was I, once upon a time." He paused to stir the flames and a blue-green cough from the peat illuminated his face. The skin was taut over the high cheekbones and there was a wanness to it, no doubt brought about by the inclement weather of the isles—the lack of sunshine and the constant misty rain that comes in as white veils from the north. Yes, he had been handsome—still was. I was surprised by his youthful features and suspected that he was not as old as he implied.

"A long time ago," he began, "when we had horse-drawn vehicles and things were different, in more ways than one . . ."

A sharp whistling note—the wind squeezing through two tightly packed logs in the croft—distracted me. Horse-drawn vehicles? What was this? A second-hand tale, surely? Yet he continued in the first person.

". . . gas lighting in the streets. A different set of values. A different set of beliefs. We were more pagan then. Still had our roots buried in dark thoughts. Machines have changed all that. Those sort of pagan, mystical ideas can't share a world with machines. Unnatural beings can only exist close to the natural world and nature's been displaced.

Yes, a different world—different things to fear. I was afraid as a young man—the reasons may seem trivial to you, now, in your time. I was afraid of, well, getting into something I couldn't get out of. Woman trouble, for instance—especially one not of my class. You understand?

I got involved once. Must have been about your age, or maybe a bit younger since I'd only just finished my apprenticeship and was a journeyman at the time. Silversmith. You knew that? No, of course you didn't. A silversmith, and a good one too. My master trusted me with one of his three shops, which puffed my pride a bit, I don't mind telling you. Anyway, it happened that I was working late one evening, when I heard the basement doorbell jangle.

I had just finished lighting the gas lamps in the workshop at the back, so I hurried to the counter where a customer was waiting. She had left the door open and the sounds from the street were distracting, the basement of course being on a level with the cobbled road. Coaches were rumbling by and the noise of street urchins and flower sellers was fighting for attention with the foghorns from the river. As politely as I could, I went behind the customer and closed the door. Then I turned to her and said, 'Yes madam? Can I be of service?'

She was wearing one of those large satin cloaks that only ladies of quality could afford and she threw back the hood to reveal one of the most beautiful faces I have ever seen in my life. There was a purity to her complexion that went deeper than her flawless skin, much deeper. And her eyes—how can I describe her eyes?—they were like black mirrors and you felt you could see the reflection of your own soul in them. Her hair was dark—coiled on her head—and it contrasted sharply with that complexion, pale as a winter moon, and soft, soft as the velvet I used for polishing the silver.

'Yes,' she replied. 'You may be of service. You are the silversmith, are you not?'

'The journeyman, madam. I'm in charge of this shop.'

She seemed a little agitated, her fingers playing nervously with her reticule.

'I . . .' she faltered, then continued. 'I have a rather unusual request. Are you able to keep a secret, silversmith?'

'My work is confidential, if the customer wishes it so. Is it some special design you require? Something to surprise a loved one with? I have some very fine filigree work here.' I removed a tray from beneath the counter. 'There's something for both the lady and the gentleman. A cigar case, perhaps? This one has a crest wrought into the case in fine silver wire—an eagle, as you can see. It has been fashioned especially for a particular customer, but I can do something similar if you require . . .'

I stopped talking because she was shaking her head and seemed to be getting impatient with me.

'Nothing like that. Something very personal. I want you to make me a collar—a silver collar. Is that possible?'

'All things are possible.' I smiled. 'Given the time of course. A torc of some kind?'

'No, you misunderstand me.' A small frown marred the ivory forehead and she glanced anxiously towards the shop door. 'Perhaps I made a mistake . . . ?

Worried, in case I lost her custom, I assured her that whatever was her request I should do my utmost to fulfill it. At the same time I told her that I could be trusted to keep the nature of the work to myself.

'No one shall know about this but the craftsman and the customer—you and I.'

She smiled at me then: a bewitching, spellbinding smile, and my heart melted within me. I would have done anything for her at that moment—I would have robbed my master—and I think she knew it.

'I'm sorry,' she said. 'I should have realized I could trust you. You have a kind face. A gentle face. One should learn to trust in faces.

'I want you—I want you to make me a collar which will cover my whole neck, especially the throat. I have a picture here, of some savages in Africa. The women have metal bands around their necks which envelop them from shoulder to chin. I want you to encase me in a similar fashion, except with one single piece of silver, do you understand? And I want it to fit tightly, so that not even your . . .' She took my hand in her own small gloved fingers. 'So that not even your little finger will be able to find its way beneath.'

I was, of course, extremely perturbed at such a request. I tried to explain to her that she would have to take the collar off quite frequently, or the skin beneath would become diseased. Her neck would certainly become very ugly.

'In any case, it will chafe and become quite sore. There will be constant irritation . . .'

She dropped my hand and said, no, I still misunderstood. The collar was to be worn permanently. She had no desire to remove it, once I had fashioned it around her neck. There was to be no locking device or anything of that sort. She wanted me to seal the metal.

'But?' I began, but she interrupted me in a firm voice.

'Silversmith, I have stated my request, my requirements. Will you carry out my wishes, or do I find another craftsman? I should be loath to do so, for I feel we have reached a level of understanding which might be difficult elsewhere. I'm going to be frank with you. This device, well—its purpose is protective. My husband-to-be is not—not like other men, but I love him just the same. I don't wish to embarrass you with talk that's not proper between strangers, and personal to my situation, but the collar is necessary to ensure my marriage is happy—a limited happiness.

Limited to a lifetime. I'm sure you *must* understand now. If you want me to leave your shop, I shall do so, but I am appealing to you because you are young and must know the pain of love—unfulfilled love. You are a handsome man and I don't doubt you have a young lady whom you adore. If she were suffering under some terrible affliction, a disease which you might contract from her, I'm sure it would make no difference to your feelings. You would strive to find a way in which you could live together, yet remain uncontaminated yourself. Am I right?'

I managed to breathe the word 'Yes,' but at the time I was filled with visions of horror. Visions of this beautiful young woman being wooed by some foul creature of the night—a supernatural beast that had no right to be treading on the same earth, let alone touching that sacred skin, kissing—my mind reeled—kissing those soft, moist lips with his monstrous mouth. How could she? Even the thought of it made me shudder in revulsion.

'Ah,' she smiled, knowingly. 'You want to save me from him. You think he is ugly and that I've been hypnotized, somehow, into believing otherwise? You're quite wrong. He's handsome in a way that you'd surely understand—and sensitive, kind, gentle—those things a woman finds important. He's also very cultured. His blood . . .'

I winced and took a step backward, but she was lost in some kind of reverie as she listed his attributes and I'm sure was unaware of my presence for some time.

'. . . his blood is unimpeachable, reaching back through a royal lineage to the most notable of European families. I love him, yet I do not want to become one of his kind, for that would destroy my love . . .'

'And—he loves you of course,' I said, daringly.

For a moment those bright eyes clouded over, but she replied, 'In his way. It's not important that we both feel the same *kind* of love. We want to be together, to share our lives. I prefer him to any man I have ever met and I *will not* be deterred by an obstacle that's neither his fault, nor mine. A barrier that's been placed in our way by the injustice of nature. He can't help the way he is—and I want to go to him. That's all there is to it.'

For a long time neither of us said anything. My throat felt too dry and constricted for words, and deep inside me I could feel something struggling, like a small creature fighting the folds of a net. The situation was beyond my comprehension: that is, I did not wish to allow it to enter my full understanding or I would have run screaming from the shop and made myself look foolish to my neighbors.

'Will you do it, silversmith?'

'But,' I said, 'a collar covers only the throat . . .' I left the rest unsaid, but I was concerned that she was not protecting herself fully: the other parts of her anatomy—the wrists, the thighs.

She became very angry. 'He isn't an *animal*. He's a gentleman. I'm merely guarding against—against moments of high passion. It's not just a matter of survival with him. The act is sensual and spiritual, as well as—as well as—what you're suggesting,' there was a note of loathing in her tone, 'is tantamount to rape.'

She was so incensed that I did not dare say that her lover must have satisfied his need *somewhere*, and therefore had compromised the manners and morals of a gentleman many times.

'Will you help me?' The eyes were pleading now. I tried to look out of the small, half-moon window, at the yellow-lighted streets, at the feet moving by on the pavement above, in an attempt to distract myself, but they were magnetic, those eyes, and they drew me back in less than a moment. I felt helpless—a trapped bird—in their unremitting gaze of anguish, and of course, I submitted.

I agreed. I just heard myself saying, 'Yes,' and led her into the back of the shop where I began the work. It was not a difficult task to actually fashion the collar, though the sealing of it was somewhat painful to her and had to be carried out in stages, which took us well into the night hours. I must have, subconsciously perhaps, continued to glance through the workshop door at the window, for she said once, very quietly, 'He will not come here.'

Such a beautiful throat she had too. Very long, and elegant. It seemed a sacrilege to encase such beauty in metal, though I made the collar as attractive as I made any silver ornament which might adorn a pretty woman. On the outside of the metal I engraved centripetal designs and at her request, some representational forms: Christ on the cross, immediately over her jugular vein, but also Zeus and Europa, and Zeus and Leda, with the Greek god in his bestial forms of the bull and the swan. I think she had been seduced by the thought that she was marrying some kind of deity.

When I had finished, she paid me and left. I watched her walk out, into the early morning mists, with a heavy guilt in my heart. What could I have done? I was just a common craftsman and had no right interfering in the lives of others. Perhaps I should have tried harder to dissuade her, but I doubt she would have listened to my impertinence for more than a few moments. Besides, I had, during those few short hours, fallen in love with her—utterly—and when she realized she had made a mistake, she would have to come back to me again, to have the collar removed.

I wanted desperately to see her again, though I knew that any chance of romance was impossible, hopeless. She was not of my class—or rather, I was not of hers, and her beauty was more than I could ever aspire to, though I knew myself to be a good-looking young man. Some had called *me* beautiful—it was that kind of handsomeness that I had been blessed with, rather than the rugged sort.

But despite my physical advantages, I had nothing which would attract a lady of quality from her own kind. The most I could ever hope for—the very most—was perhaps to serve her in some way.

Three weeks later she was back, looking somewhat distraught.

'I want it to come off,' she said. 'It must be removed.'

My fingers trembled as I worked at cutting her free—a much simpler task than the previous one.

'You've left him,' I said. 'Won't he follow?'

'No, you're quite wrong.' There was a haunted look to her eyes which chilled me to the bone. 'It's not that. I was too mistrustful. I love him too much to withhold from him the very thing he desires. I must give myself to him—wholly and completely. I need him, you see. And he needs me— yet like this I cannot give him the kind of love he has to have. I've been selfish. Very selfish. I must go to him . . .'

'Are you mad?' I cried, forgetting my position. 'You'll become like him—you'll become—'

'How *dare* you! How dare you preach to *me?* Just do your work, silversmith. Remove the collar!'

I was weak of course, as most of us are when confronted by a superior being. I cut the collar loose and put it aside. She rubbed her neck and complained loudly that flakes of skin were coming away in her hands.

'It's ugly,' she said. 'Scrawny. He'll never want me like this.'

'No—thank God!' I cried, gathering my courage.

At that moment she looked me full in the eyes and a strange expression came over her face.

'You're in love with me, aren't you? That's why you're so concerned, silversmith. Oh dear, I am so dreadfully sorry. I thought you were just being meddlesome. It was genuine concern for my welfare and I didn't recognize it at first. Dear man,' she touched my cheek. 'Don't look so sad. It cannot be, you know. You should find some nice girl and try to forget, because you'll never see me again after tonight. And don't worry about me. I know what I'm doing.'

With that, she gathered up her skirts and was gone again, down toward the river. The sun was just coming up, since she had arrived not long before the dawn, and I thought: At least she will have a few hours more of natural life.

After that I tried to follow her advice and put her out of my mind. I did my work, something I had always enjoyed, and rarely left the shop. I felt that if I could get over a few months without a change in my normal pattern of existence, I should be safe. There were nightmares of course, to be gone through after sunsets, but those I was able to cope with. I have always managed to keep my dreams at a respectable distance and not let them interfere with my normal activities.

Then, one day, as I was working on a pendant—a butterfly requested by a banker for his wife—a small boy brought me a message. Though it was unsigned, I knew it was from her and my hands trembled as I read the words.

They simply said, 'Come. I need you.'

Underneath this request was scrawled an address, which I knew to be located down by one of the wharves, south of the river.

She *needed* me—and I knew exactly what for. I touched my throat. I wanted her too, but for different reasons. I did not have the courage that she had—the kind of sacrificial courage that's produced by an overwhelming love. But I was not without strength. If there was a chance, just a chance, that I could meet with her and come away unscathed, then I was prepared to accept the risk.

But I didn't see how that was possible. Her kind, as she had become, possessed a physical strength which would make any escape fraught with difficulty.

I had no illusions about her being in love with me—or even fond of me.

77

She wanted to use me for her own purposes, which were as far away from love as earth is from the stars. I remembered seeing deep gouges in the silver collar, the time she had come to have it removed. They were like the claw marks of some beast, incised into the trunk of a tree. No wonder she had asked to have it sealed. Whoever, *what*ever, had made those marks would have had the strength to tear away any hinges or lock. The frenzy to get at what lay beneath the silver must have been appalling to witness—*experience*—yet she had gone back to him, without the collar's protection.

I wanted her. I dreamed about having her, warm and close to me. That she had become something other than the beautiful woman who had entered my shop was no deterrent. I knew she would be just as lovely in her new form and I desired her above all things. For nights I lay awake, running different schemes over in my mind, trying to find a path which would allow us to make love together, just once, and yet let me walk away safely afterward. Even as I schemed, I saw her beauty laid before me, willingly, and my body and soul ached for her presence.

One chance. I had this one chance of loving a woman a dozen places above my station: a woman whose refined ways and manner of speech had captivated me from the moment I met her. A woman whose dignity, elegance, and gracefulness were without parallel. Whose form surpassed that of the finest silverwork figurine I had ever known.

I had to find a way.

Finally, I came up with a plan which seemed to suit my purposes, and taking my courage in both hands I wrote her a note which said, 'I'm waiting for you. *You* must come to *me*.' I found an urchin to carry it for me and told him to put it through the letter box of the address she had given me.

That afternoon I visited the church and a purveyor of medical instruments.

That evening I spent wandering the streets, alternately praising myself for dreaming up such a clever plan and cursing myself for my foolhardiness in carrying it through. As I strolled through the backstreets, stepping around the gin-soaked drunks and tipping my hat to the factory girls as they hurried home from a sixteen-hour day in some garment manufacturer's sweatshop, or a hosiery, I realized that for once I had allowed my emotions to overrule my intellect. I'm not saying I was an intelligent young man—not above the average—but I was wise enough to know that there was great danger in what I proposed to do, yet the force of my feelings was more powerful than fear. I could not deny them their expression. The heart has no reason, but its drive is stronger than sense dictates.

The barges on the river ploughed slowly against the current as I leaned on the wrought-iron balustrade overlooking the water. I could see the gas lamps reflected on the dark surface and thought about the shadow world that lived alongside our own, where nothing was rigid, set, but could be warped and twisted, like those lights in the water when the ripples from the barges passed through them. Would it take me and twist me into something, not ugly, but insubstantial? Into something that has the appearance of the real thing, but which is evanescent in the daylight and can only make its appearance at night, when vacuous shapes and phantasms take on a semblance of life and mock it with their unreal forms?

When the smell of the mud below me began to waft upward, as the tide retreated and the river diminished, I made my way homeward. There was a sharpness to the air which cut into my confidence and I was glad to be leaving it behind for the warmth and security of my rooms. Security? I laughed at myself, having voluntarily exposed my vulnerability.

She came.

There was a scratching at the casement windowpane in the early hours of the morning and I opened it and let her in. She had not changed. If anything, she was more beautiful than ever, with a paler color to her cheeks and a fuller red to her lips.

No words were exchanged between us. I lay on the bed naked and she joined me after removing her garments. She stroked my hair and the nape of my neck as I sank into her soft young body. I cannot describe the ecstasy. It was—*unearthly*. She allowed me—encouraged me—and the happiness of those moments was worth all the risks of entering Hell for a taste of Heaven.

Of course, the moment came when she lowered her head to the base of my throat. I felt the black coils of her hair against my cheek: smelled their sweet fragrance. I could sense the pulse in my neck, throbbing with blood. Her body was warm against mine—deliciously warm. I wanted her to stay there forever. There was just a hint of pain in my throat—a

79

needleprick, no more, and then a feeling of drifting, floating on warm water, as if I had suddenly been transported to tropic seas and lay in the shallows of some sunbleached island's beaches. I felt no fear—only, *bliss.*

Then, suddenly, she snorted, springing to her feet like no athlete I have ever seen. Her eyes were blazing and she spat and hissed into my face.

'What have you done?' she shrieked.

Then the fear came, rushing to my heart. I cowered at the bedhead, pulling my legs up to my chest in an effort to get as far away from her as possible.

Again she cried, 'What have you done?'

'Holy water,' I said. 'I've injected holy water into my veins.'

She let out another wail which made my ears sing. Her hands reached for me and I saw those long nails, like talons, ready to slash at an artery, but the fear was gone from me. I just wanted her back in bed with me. I no longer cared for the consequences.

'Please?' I said, reaching for her. 'Help me? I want you to help me.'

She withdrew from me then and sprang to the window. It was getting close to dawn: The first rays of the sun were sliding over the horizon.

'You fool,' she said, and then she was gone, out into the murk. I jumped up and looked for her through the window, but all I could see was the mist on the river, curling its way around the rotten stumps of an old jetty.

"Once I had recovered my common sense and was out of her influence, I remember thinking to myself that I would have to make a collar—a silver collar . . ."

The fire spat in the grate and I jerked upright. I had no idea how long Sam had been talking but the peat was almost all ashes.

"The tide," I said, alarmed. "I must leave."

"I haven't finished," he complained, but I was already on my feet. I opened the door and began to walk quickly down the narrow path we had made through the heather, to where my boat lay, but even as I approached it, I could see that it was lying on its side in the slick, glinting mud.

Angry, I looked back at the croft on the hillside. He must have known. He must have known. I was about to march back and take Sam to task, when I suddenly saw the croft in a new perspective. It was like most dwellings of its kind—timber framed, with sods of earth filling the cracks, and stones holding down the turf on the roof. But it was a peculiar shape—more of a mound than the normal four walls and a roof—and was without windows.

My mind suddenly ran wild with frightening images of wood, earth, and rocks. The wooden coffin goes inside the earth and the headstone weights it down. A mound—a burial mound. *He hadn't been able to stay away from her. The same trap that had caught her . . .*

I turned back to the boat and tried dragging it across the moonlit mud, toward the distant water, but it was too heavy. I could only inch it along, and rapidly became tired. The muscles in my arms and legs screamed at me. All the time I labored, one side of my mind kept telling me not to be so foolish, while the other was equally insistent regarding the need to get away. I could hear myself repeating the words. *"He couldn't stay away from her. He couldn't stay away."*

I had covered about six yards when I heard a voice at my shoulder—a soft, dry voice, full of concern.

"Here, John, let me help you . . ."

Sam did help me that day, more than I wished him to. I don't hate him for that, especially now that so many years have passed. Since then I have obtained this job, of night ferryman on the loch, helping young ladies like the one I have in the skiff with me now—a runaway, off to join her lover.

"Don't worry," I try to reassure her, after telling her my story, "we sailors are fond of our tales. Come and join me by the tiller. I'll show you how to manage the boat. Do I frighten you? I don't mean to. I only want to help you . . ."

Writers are so often asked where they get their ideas from and nine times out of ten I can't reply because I don't know myself. However, in this case I know exactly where it came from—my daughter's dream. A couple of nights before her wedding, Chantelle had a nightmare. She told me at breakfast the following morning that she dreamed she had discovered that Mark (her fiancé) was a vampire and that she had to wear a silver collar on their wedding night. So the main ingredient of the story was handed to me on a platter, the credit going to prenuptial nerves.

This is my first story involving the vampire myth. I'm not so much interested in the idea of the creatures themselves as I am in why we need them. Why do we invent blood-sucking monsters to feed our fascination? The idea that blood is a sacred substance, with properties of determining nobility or peasantry, racial superiority or inferiority, criminality or decency, goes back a long way and is still with us in various forms. Blue blood, *bad* blood, red-blooded youths. A whole mythological web has been woven out of this ordinary red, viscous fluid, that is important to us, but no more so than our kidneys. Anybody fancy writing a kidney-eating monster story? Ah, you laugh?

I think we need vampires, not because they drain our lifeblood, but because they change us into someone else and give us the gift of immortality. To live forever—now *there's* the rub.

Garry Kilworth

Try a Dull Knife

HARLAN ELLISON

In my late teens I became an avid Ellison reader. I remember reading "Try a Dull Knife" in 1969 and the chill it gave me. It was one of the stories that helped formulate the concept behind this book. So here it appears, happily, in Blood Is Not Enough.

It was *pachanga* night at The Cave. Three spick bands all going at once, each with a fat momma shaking her meat and screaming ¡*Vaya!* The sound was something visible, an assault in silver lamé and screamhorn. Sound hung dense as smog-cloud, redolent as skunk-scent from a thousand roaches of the best shit, no stems or seeds. Darkness shot through with the quicksilver flashes of mouths open to show gold bridgework and dirty words. Eddie Burma staggered in, leaned against a wall and felt the sickness as thick as cotton wool in his throat.

The deep scar-burn of pain was bleeding slowly down his right side. The blood had started coagulating, his shirt stuck to his flesh, but he dug it: it wasn't pumping any more. But he was in trouble, that was the righteous truth. Nobody can get cut the way Eddie Burma'd been cut and not be in deep trouble.

And somewhere back out there, in the night, they were moving toward him, coming for him. He had to get through to—who? Somebody. Somebody who could help him; because only now, after fifteen years of what had been happening to him, did Eddie Burma finally know what it was he had been through, what had been done to him . . . what was *being* done to him . . . what they would certainly do to him.

He stumbled down the short flight of steps into The Cave and was

83

instantly lost in the smoke and smell and twisting shadows. Ethnic smoke, Puerto Rican smells, lush shadows from another land. He dug it; even with his strength ebbing, he dug it.

That was Eddie Burma's problem. He was an empath. He felt. Deep inside himself, on a level most people never even know exists, he felt for the world. Involvement was what motivated him. Even here, in this slum nightclub where intensity of enjoyment substituted for the shallow glamour and gaucherie of the uptown *boîtes,* here where no one knew him and therefore could not harm him, he felt the pulse of the world's life surging through him. And the blood started pumping again.

He pressed his way back through the crowd, looking for a phone booth, looking for a toilet, looking for an empty booth where he could hide, looking for the person or persons unknown who could save him from the dark night of the soul slipping toward him inexorably.

He caromed off a waiter, Pancho Villa moustache, dirty white apron, tray of draft beers. "Hey, where's the *gabinetto?*" he slurred the request. His words were slipping in their own blood.

The Puerto Rican waiter stared at him. Uncomprehending. "*¿Perdón?*"

"The toilet, the *pissoir,* the can, the head, the crapper. I'm bleeding to death, where's the potty?"

"Ohhh!" Meaning dawned on the waiter. "*¡Excusado . . . atavío!*" He pointed. Eddie Burma patted him on the arm and slumped past, almost falling into a booth where a man and two women were groping one another darkly.

He found the door to the toilet and pushed it open. A reject from a Cuban Superman film was slicking back his long, oiled hair in an elaborate pompadour before the foggy mirror. He gave Eddie Burma a passing glance and went back to the topography of his coiffure. Burma moved past him in the tiny room and slipped into the first stall.

Once inside, he bolted the door, and sat down heavily on the lidless toilet. He pulled his shirt up out of his pants, and unbuttoned it. It stuck to his skin. He pulled, gently, and it came away with the sound of mud squished underfoot. The knife wound ran from just below the right nipple to the middle of his waist. It was deep. He was in trouble.

He stood up, hanging the shirt on the hook behind the door, and pulled hanks of toilet paper from the gray, crackly roll. He dipped the paper in a wad, into the toilet bowl, and swabbed at the wound. Oh, God, *really* deep.

Then nausea washed over him, and he sat down again. Strange thoughts came to him, and he let them work him over:

This morning, when I stepped out the front door, there were yellow roses growing on the bushes. It surprised me; I'd neglected to cut them back last fall, and I was certain the gnarled, blighted knobs at the ends of the branches—still there, silently dead in reproach of my negligence—would stunt any further beauty. But when I stepped out to pick up the newspaper, there they were. Full and light yellow, barely a canary yellow. Breathing moistly, softly. It made me smile, and I went down the steps to the first landing, to get the paper. The parking lot had filled with leaves from the Eucalyptus again, but somehow, particularly this *morning, it gave the private little area surrounding and below my secluded house in the hills a more lived-in, festive look. For the second time, for no sensible reason, I found myself smiling. It was going to be a good day, and I had the feeling that all the problems I'd taken on—all the social cases I took unto myself—Alice and Burt and Linda down the hill—all the emotional cripples who came to me for succor—would shape up, and we'd all be smiling by end of day. And if not today, then certainly by Monday. Friday, the latest.*

I picked up the paper and snapped the rubber band off it. I dropped the rubber band into the big metal trash basket at the foot of the stairs, and started climbing back up to the house, smelling the orange blossoms and the fine, chill morning air. I opened the paper as I climbed, and with all the suddenness of a freeway collision, the morning calm vanished from around me. I was stopped in mid-step, one leg raised for the next riser, and my eyes felt suddenly grainy, as though I hadn't had enough sleep the night before. But I had.

The headline read: EDWARD BURMA FOUND MURDERED.

But . . . I was Eddie Burma.

He came back from memories of yellow roses and twisted metal on freeways to find himself slumped against the side of the toilet stall, his head pressed to the wooden wall, his arms hanging down, the blood running into his pants top. His head throbbed, and the pain in his side was beating, hammering, pounding with a regularity that made him shiver with fear. He could not sit there, and wait.

Wait to die, or wait for them to find him.

He knew they would find him. He knew it.

The phone. He could call . . .

He didn't know whom he could call. But there had to be someone. Someone out there who would understand, who would come quickly and save him. Someone who wouldn't take what was left of him, the way the others would.

They didn't need knives.

How strange that *that* one, the little blonde with the Raggedy Ann shoebutton eyes, had not known that. Or perhaps she had. But perhaps also the frenzy of the moment had overcome her, and she could not simply feed leisurely as the others did. She had cut him. Had done what they all did, but directly, without subtlety.

Her blade had been sharp. The others used much more devious weapons, subtler weapons. He wanted to say to her, "Try a dull knife." But she was too needing, too eager. She would not have heard him.

He struggled to his feet, and put on his shirt. It hurt to do it. The shirt was stained the color of teak with his blood. He could barely stand now.

Pulling foot after foot, he left the toilet, and wandered out into The Cave. The sound of "Mamacita Lisa" beat at him like gloved hands on a plate glass window. He leaned against the wall, and saw only shapes moving moving moving in the darkness. Were they out there? No, not yet; they would never look here first. He wasn't known here. And his essence was weaker now, weaker as he died, so no one in the crowd would come to him with a quivering need. No one would feel it possible to drink from this weak man, lying up against a wall.

He saw a pay phone, near the entrance to the kitchen, and he struggled toward it. A girl with long dark hair and haunted eyes stared at him as he passed, started to say something, then he summoned up strength to hurry past her before she could tell him she was pregnant and didn't know who the father was, or she was in pain from emphysema and didn't have doctor money, or she missed her mother who was still in San Juan. He could handle no more pains, could absorb no more anguish, could let no others drink from him. He didn't have that much left for his own survival.

My fingertips (he thought, moving) *are covered with the scars of people I've touched. The flesh remembers those touches. Sometimes I feel as though I am wearing heavy woolen gloves, so thick are the memories of all those touches. It seems to insulate me, to separate me from mankind. Not mankind from me, God knows, for they get through without pause or difficulty—but me, from mankind. I very often refrain from washing my hands for days and days, just to preserve whatever layers of touches might be washed away by the soap.*

Faces and voices and smells of people I've known have passed away, but still my hands carry the memories on them. Layer after layer of the laying-on of hands. Is that altogether sane? I don't know. I'll have to think about it for a very long time, when I have the time.

If I ever have the time.

He reached the pay phone; after a very long time he was able to bring a coin up out of his pocket. It was a quarter. All he needed was a dime. He could not go back down there, he might not make it back again. He used the quarter, and dialed the number of a man he could trust, a man who could help him. He remembered the man now, knew the man was his only salvation.

He remembered seeing him in Georgia, at a revival meeting, a rural stump religion circus of screaming and Hallelujahs that sounded like !H!A!L!L!E!L!U!J!A!H! with dark black faces or red necks all straining toward the seat of God on the platform. He remembered the man in his white shirtsleeves, exhorting the crowd, and he heard again the man's spirit message.

"Get right with the Lord, before *he* gets right with *you*! Suffer your silent sins no longer! Take out your truth, carry it in your hands, give it to me, all the ugliness and cesspool filth of your souls! I'll wash you clean in the blood of the lamb, in the blood of the Lord, in the blood of the truth of the word! There's no other way, there's no great day coming without purging yourself, without cleansing your spirit! I can handle all the pain you've got boiling around down in the black lightless pit of your souls! Hear me, dear God hear me . . . I am your mouth, your tongue, your throat, the horn that will proclaim your deliverance to the Heavens above! Evil and good and worry and sorrow, all of it is mine, I can carry it, I can handle it, I can lift it from out of your mind and your soul and your body! The place is here, the place is me, give me your woe! Christ knew it, God knows it, *I* know it, and now *you* have to know it! Mortar and trowel and brick and cement make the wall of your need! Let me tear down that wall, let me hear all of it, let me into your mind and let me take your burdens! I'm the strength, I'm the watering place . . . come drink from my strength!"

And the people had rushed to him. All over him, like ants feeding on a dead beast. And then the memory dissolved. The image of the tent revival meeting dissolved into images of wild animals tearing at meat, of hordes of carrion birds descending on fallen meat, of small fish leaping with sharp teeth at helpless meat, of hands and more hands, and teeth that sank into meat.

The number was busy.

It was busy again.

He had been dialing the same number for nearly an hour, and the number was always busy. Dancers with sweating faces had wanted to use the phone, but Eddie Burma had snarled at them that it was a matter of life and death that he reach the number he was calling, and the dancers had gone back to their partners with curses for him. But the line was still busy. Then he looked at the number on the pay phone, and knew he had been dialing himself all that time. That the line would always *always* be busy, and his furious hatred of the man on the other end who would not answer was hatred for the man who was calling. He was calling himself, and in that instant he remembered who the man had been at the revival meeting. He remembered leaping up out of the audience and taking the platform to beg all the stricken suffering ones to end their pain by drinking of his essence. He remembered, and the fear was greater than he could believe. He fled back to the toilet, to wait for them to find him.

Eddie Burma, hiding in the refuse room of a sightless dark spot in the netherworld of a universe that had singled him out for reality. Eddie Burma was an individual. He had substance. He had corporeality. In a world of walking shadows, of zombie breath and staring eyes like the cold dead flesh of the moon, Eddie Burma was a real person. He had been born with the ability to belong to his times; with the electricity of nature that some called charisma and others called warmth. He felt deeply; he moved through the world and touched; and was touched.

His was a doomed existence, because he was not only an extrovert and gregarious, but he was truly clever, vastly inventive, suffused with humor, and endowed with the power to listen. For these reasons he had passed through the stages of exhibitionism and praise-seeking to a state where his reality was assured. Was very much his own. When he came into a room, people knew it. He had a face. Not an image, or a substitute life that he could slip on when dealing with people, but a genuine reality.

He was Eddie Burma, only Eddie Burma, and could not be confused with anyone else. He went his way, and he was identified as Eddie Burma in the eyes of anyone who ever met him. He was one of those memorable people. The kind other people who have no lives of their own talk about. He cropped up in conversations: "Do you know what Eddie said . . . ?" or "Guess what happened to Eddie?" And there was never any confusion as to who was the subject under discussion.

Eddie Burma was a figure no larger than life, for life itself was large enough, in a world where most of those he met had no individuality, no personality, no reality, no existence of their own.

But the price he paid was the price of doom. For those who had nothing came to him and, like creatures of darkness, amorally fed off him. They drank from him. They were the succubi, draining his psychic energies. And Eddie Burma always had more to give. Seemingly a bottomless well, the bottom had been reached. Finally. All the people whose woes he handled, all the losers whose lives he tried to organize, all the preying crawlers who slinked in through the ashes of their non-existence to sup at his board, to slake the thirsts of their emptiness . . . all of them had taken their toll.

Now Eddie Burma stumbled through the last moments of his reality, with the wellsprings of himself almost totally drained. Waiting for them, for all his social cases, all his problem children, to come and finish him off.

I live in a hungry world, Eddie Burma now realized.

"Hey, man! C'mon outta th'crapper!" The booming voice and the pounding on the stall door came as one.

Eddie trembled to his feet and unbolted the door, expecting it to be one of them. But it was only a dancer from The Cave, wanting to rid himself of cheap wine and cheap beer. Eddie stumbled out of the stall, almost falling into the man's arms. When the beefy Puerto Rican saw the blood, saw the dead pale look of flesh and eyes, his manner softened.

"Hey . . . you okay, man?"

Eddie smiled at him, thanked him softly, and left the toilet. The nightclub was still high, still screaming, and Eddie suddenly knew he could not let *them* find this good place, where all this good people were plugged into life and living. Because for *them* it would be a godsend, and they would drain The Cave as they had drained him.

He found a rear exit, and emerged into the moonless city night, as alien as a cavern five miles down or the weird curvature of another dimension. This alley, this city, this night, could as easily have been Transylvania or the dark side of the moon or the bottom of the thrashing sea. He stumbled down the alley, thinking . . .

They have no lives of their own. Oh, this poisoned world I now see so clearly. They have only the shadowy images of other lives, and not even real other lives—the lives of movie stars, fictional heroes, cultural clichés. So they borrow from me, and never intend to pay back. They borrow, at the highest rate of interest. My life. They lap at me, and break off pieces of me. I'm the mushroom that Alice found with the words EAT ME in blood-red on my id. They're succubi, draining at me, draining my soul. Sometimes I feel I should go to some mystical well and get poured full of personality again. I'm tired. So tired.

There are people walking around this city who are running on Eddie Burma's drained energies, Eddie Burma's life-force. They're putt-putting around with smiles just like mine, with thoughts I've second-handed like old clothes passed on to poor relatives, with hand-movements and expressions and little cute sayings that were mine, Scotch-taped over their own. I'm a jigsaw puzzle and they keep stealing little pieces. Now I make no scene at all, I'm incomplete, I'm unable to keep the picture coherent, they've taken so much already.

They had come to his party, all of the ones he knew. The ones he called his friends, and the ones who were merely acquaintances, and the ones who were using him as their wizard, as their guru, their psychiatrist, their wailing wall, their father confessor, their repository of personal ills and woes and inadequacies. Alice, who was afraid of men and found in Eddie Burma a last vestige of belief that males were not all beasts. Burt, the box-boy from the supermarket, who stuttered when he spoke, and felt rejected even before the rejection. Linda, from down the hill, who had seen in Eddie Burma an intellectual, one to whom she could relate all her theories of the universe. Sid, who was a failure, at fifty-three. Nancy, whose husband cheated on her. John, who wanted to be a lawyer, but would never make it because he thought too much about his clubfoot. And all the others. And the new ones they always seemed to bring with them. There were always so many new ones he never knew. Particularly the pretty little blonde with the Raggedy Ann shoebutton eyes, who stared at him hungrily.

And from the first, earlier that night, he had known something was wrong. There were too many of them at the party. More than he could handle . . . and all listening to him tell a story of something that had happened to him when he had driven to New Orleans in 1960 with Tony in the Corvette and they'd both gotten pleurisy because the top hadn't been bolted down properly and they'd passed through a snowstorm in Illinois.

All of them hung to his words, like drying wash on a line, like festoons of ivy. They sucked at each word and every expression like hungry things pulling at the marrow in beef bones. They laughed, and they watched, and their eyes glittered . . .

Eddie Burma had slowly felt the strength ebbing from him. He grew weary even as he spoke. It had happened before, at other parties, other gatherings, when he had held the attention of the group, and gone home later, feeling drained. He had never known what it was.

But tonight the strength did not come back. They kept watching him, seemed to be *feeding* at him, and it went on and on, till finally he'd said he had to go to sleep, and they should go home. But they had pleaded for one more anecdote, one more joke told with perfect dialect and elaborate gesticulation. Eddie Burma had begun to cry, quietly. His eyes were red-rimmed, and his body felt as though the bones and musculature had been removed, leaving only a soft rubbery coating that might at any moment cave in on itself.

He had tried to get up; to go and lie down; but they'd gotten more insistent, had demanded, had ordered, had grown nasty. And then the blonde had come at him, and cut him, and the others were only a step behind. Somehow . . . in the thrashing tangle that had followed, with his friends and acquaintances now tearing at one another to get at him, he had escaped. He had fled, he did not know how, the pain of his knifed side crawling inside him. He had made it into the trees of the little glen where his house was hidden, and through the forest, over the watershed, down to the highway, where he had hailed a cab. Then into the city . . .

See me! See me, please! Just don't always come and take. Don't bathe in my reality and then go away feeling clean. Stay and let some of the dirt of you rub off on me. I feel like an invisible man, like a drinking trough, like a sideboard dripping with sweetmeats . . . Oh God, is this a play, and myself unwillingly the star? How the hell do I get off stage? When do they ring down the curtain? Is there, please God, a man with a hook . . . ?

91

I make my rounds, like a faith healer. Each day I spend a little time with each one of them. With Alice and with Burt and with Linda down the hill; and they take from me. They don't leave anything in exchange, though. It's not barter, it's theft. And the worst part of it is I always needed that, I always let them rob me. What sick need was it that gave them entrance to my soul? Even the pack rat leaves some worthless object when it steals a worthless object. I'd take anything from them: the smallest anecdote, the most used-up thought, the most stagnant concept, the puniest pun, the most obnoxious personal revelation . . . anything! But all they do is sit there and stare at me, their mouths open, their ears hearing me so completely they empty my words of color and scent . . . I feel as though they're crawling into me. *I can't stand any more . . . really I can't.*

The mouth of the alley was blocked.

Shadows moved there.

Burt, the box-boy. Nancy and Alice and Linda. Sid, the failure. John, who walked with a rolling motion. And the doctor, the jukebox repairman, the pizza cook, the used-car salesman, the swinging couple who swapped partners, the discothèque dancer . . . all of them.

They came for him.

And for the first time he noticed their teeth.

The moment before they reached him stretched out as silent and timeless as the decay that ate at his world. He had no time for self-pity. It was not merely that Eddie Burma had been cannibalized every day of the year, every hour of the day, every minute of every hour of every day of every year. The awareness dawned unhappily—in that moment of timeless time—that he had *let* them do it to him. That he was no better than they, only different. They were the feeders—and he was the food. But no nobility could be attached to one or the other. He *needed* to have people worship and admire him. He *needed* the love and attention of the masses, the worship of monkeys. And for Eddie Burma that was a kind of beginning to death. It was the death of his unself-consciousness; the slaughter of his innocence. From that moment forward, he had been aware of the clever things he said and did, on a cellular level below consciousness. He was aware. Aware, aware, aware!

And awareness brought them to him, where they fed. It led to self-consciousness, petty pretensions, ostentation. And that was a thing devoid of substance, of reality. And if there was anything on which his acolytes could not nourish, it was a posturing, phony, *empty* human being.

They would drain him.

The moment came to a timeless climax, and they carried him down under their weight, and began to feed.

When it was over, they left him in the alley. They went to look elsewhere.

With the vessel drained, the vampires moved to other pulsing arteries.

Though I have worked assiduously at living my life by Pasteur's dictum, "Chance favors the prepared mind," and consider it ludicrous and horrifying that the guy in the White House (as I sit writing this in May of 1988) is so loopy that he consults astrologers—a craziness we associate with utter derangement cases like Hitler, who maintained a staff stargazer—I nonetheless amuse myself with the harmless conceit that each of us possesses different kinds of "luck."

(Because I truly believe there is no such thing as "luck," but cannot deny both synchronicity and serendipity in the insensate universe, this is my childlike way of taking into account sheer randomness of circumstance that redounds to our benefit. And I'm not for a second truly serious about it.)

There are people who are "lucky" in love and people who are "lucky" in business and people who are "lucky" when they survive accidents. The kinds of "luck" that I possess are far less significant measured against the totality of my life. They are: parking-space luck; restaurant luck; bad-companion luck.

My friends (and ex-Executive Assistants) Linda Steele and Sarah Wood used to rage at my parking-space luck. It wouldn't matter if the destination was in the heaviest-traffic section of Westwood or Downtown L.A. As I neared the building in which I needed to transact my business, a parking place would open . . . usually smack in front of the entrance. There could be entire armadas of parked cars at my place of arrival . . . and someone would drive away just as we neared

the most convenient spot. Linda and Sarah would revile me
with splenic fervor, going so far as to bet me a buck it
wouldn't happen *this* time.

I made a few dollars off that one.

Then there's restaurant luck. Trust me on this, I am
systemically incapable of picking a bad eatery. Joints that look
as though they've been selected for this year's Cockroach Party
Conclave from the outside, invariably become secret dining
treasures, to be whispered about only among my closest friends
lest the word leak out and *they* invade the place, making it
impossible for me to get a seat when I'm hungry. (We all
know who *they* are: the uptown folks in Gucci loafers, with
their rebuilt noses and friends who are big in debentures and
real estate. You know the ones. They always need to push two
tables together so they can scream at each other more
conveniently.) I can be driving down an Interstate in a part of
the country I've never visited before, and my head will come
up and my nose (unrebuilt) will begin to twitch like a setter
on point, and I'll say to my passengers, "If we take the next
exit, turn right and go off in *that* direction, we'll find a
sensational rib joint." They look at me with proper disbelief.
So I do it, and we find a five-stool counter joint run by an
ancient black man whose arcane abilities with baby-backs is
strictly imperial. Never fails. Ask Silverberg. Ask Len Wein.
Trust me on this.

But the most efficacious luck I command is the luck that
keeps me away from deadbeats. Time-wasters, arrivistes, bums
and mooches. The mooks of the world.

Now, I suppose, dealing with this pragmatically, it is only
what Hemingway called "a built-in, shock-proof shit
detector." The flawless functioning of the onboard computer
that has been programmed with decades of experience and
insight and body-language and tonal inflection and the
behavior of sociopaths. Sherlock Holmes employed this
methodology to scope a visitor to 221B Baker Street within
moments of his/her arrival: deductive logic. That's what this
"luck" must be, I'm certain of it.

94

Whatever the rationale, it works for me. I'm not about to say I've never been flummoxed—there was this lady I once married for 45 days, but that's another novel, for another time—yet the wool has been pulled very rarely. I can spot a twisto with the first sentence uttered. Lames and leaners and hustlers don't do very well with me. I seem to be creep-proof.

And so, almost all of the vast amount of trouble I've gotten myself into, has been no one's fault but my own. I cannot plead that I was "led astray by the wickedness of others." I am, in the Amerind sense of the phrase, absolutely responsible for my life and all the actions that have gone to construct that life. No accessory after the fact, I am precisely who I made me.

Yet in 1963–65, I "went Hollywood" for a while. Not so seriously that you might confuse me with William Holden's corpse floating in Gloria Swanson's swimming pool, but off-direction enough that I spent more time than I had to fritter away, in the company of people who drifted on the tide like diatoms. Some actors, some blue-sky entrepreneurs, some starlets, some taproots-in-Hell users and manipulators. I knew they were wrong the moment I opened the packages, but I'm no different from you: we all go to the zoo to watch the peculiar animals from faraway lands. Temporary fascination is not self-abuse, as long as one retains a sense of perspective; tip-toeing through the minefield satisfies our need for diversion and danger, as long as one doesn't lease a burrow and start buying furniture for permanent residency. As sheepish apologia, I offer the only explanation that ever seems acceptable for the peculiar things we do: it seemed like a good idea at the time.

And so, cute as a bug, I waded hip-deep in a social scene that bore as much relation to Living a Proper Life as Narnia bears to Ashtabula, Ohio. Which is to say, not a whole lot.

I was living in an actual treehouse at that time. A small, charming structure up a steep private road that ended in a parking lot below the house, a flat space surrounded by eucalyptus trees that totally hid the house from casual sight. It cost one hundred and thirty-five bucks a month, and had a small kitchen, a smaller bathroom, a decent-sized living room with a wood-burning fireplace, high beamed ceilings and paneled walls, and a "captain's cabin" bedroom that was, in truth, only a triangular-shaped walled-off section with old-fashioned bay windows all around. I loved that little place on Bushrod Lane.

To that eyrie, 1962–66, came an unending stream of odd types and casual liaisons. The house lay in the bosom of Beverly Glen, at that time a rich enclave of artistic and (what used to be called) bohemian intellects. Lee Marvin and Clint Eastwood, Robert Duvall and Harry Dean Stanton, Robert Blake and Lenny Bruce . . . I knew them all, and a few of them became friends. The parties were intimate, because the house was so small; the fun was constant because it was poor folks fun, pizza and alla that smart chat, unimpaired by dope or booze because I don't do neither, and had no room for it in my environs.

In that venue, I stood off the son of the Detroit Mafia boss and two of his pistoleros with a Remington XP-100 pistol-rifle that fires enormous .221 Fireball cartridges, while I was ridiculously attired only in a bath towel around my waist. In that venue, I met and made friends with the dog Ahbhu, who still lives as Blood in "A Boy and His Dog." In that venue, I managed so fully to fulfill all my adolescent sex-fantasies that I was able to proceed with my life having flensed myself of the dopey dream-hungers that pursue men into middle-age.

And in that venue I wrote "Paingod" and "'Repent, Harlequin!' Said the Ticktockman" and "Lonelyache" and "Soldier" and "Punky and the Yale Men" and "Pretty Maggie Moneyeyes" and "I Have No Mouth, and I Must Scream" and a great many other stories. It was in that venue that I conceived and began editing DANGEROUS VISIONS.

I partied, and I dissipated, and I screwed like a mad thing, but I always worked. Which is why I can look back on that time with pleasure and a smile. But were it not for having *done the writing*—the thing that has always saved me from becoming a bum—the years of my having "gone Hollywood" would reside in memory draped with a sense of loss, a coating of wasted time, a terror at how easily we can all be led astray.

"Try a Dull Knife" came out of that period.

It was the story that marked the end of my sojourn among the bad companions. What had been going on, had been going on for several years; and during that time I went from one bunch of gargoyles to another, with them mooching and leaning, wasting my nights and borrowing my money (of which there was damned little, despite my working steadily in TV, writing *Outer Limits* and *Burke's Law* and *Route 66* and dozens of other shows). I was constantly having to put people up in the tiny treehouse because they were being hunted by even deadlier types. When Bobby Blake needed a place to hide out so his producer couldn't find him, to force him to do retakes on a segment of *The Richard Boone Show* that Bobby had starred in, he went to ground in my living room. We shot a lot of pool in those days. A mountain lion leaped off the jungly hill that loomed over the treehouse and damned near ripped off my arm, right in the middle of a late night party.

And then, like drawing a deep breath, I sat down and wrote "Try a Dull Knife," and it was all over.

For me, the work has always been therapy. Writing and taking showers provides the spark of insight that informs my awareness of what the hell I'm doing in the Real World.

And the oddest part about "Try a Dull Knife" is that I had written the first two paragraphs sometime in 1963, had written those lines without any idea how they would proceed into a story, and had shoved the yellow second-sheet with those words on it into a drawer, and never went near it, never even remembered it, till 1965. Two years after the opening had been written, I was writing another story entirely. It started with the words "Somewhere back out there, in the night, they were moving toward him, coming for him." And as I wrote along, the story taking shape slowly, as slowly as was taking shape the realization that I was surrounded by, and being used by, a glittery species of emotional vampires . . . I realized that I had started the story in the wrong place. I'd begun the yarn at least one beat too late.

And I stopped writing, and without knowing why, I started rooting through that drawer full of odd pieces of snippets for stories that might never be written, that trash-bin of words and ideas that had foundered on the shoals of my lack of craft or insight. I found that yellow second-sheet, and I read what I had written, and I added the word "and" at the beginning of my current project, and . . . the pieces fit exactly.

The onboard computer was just beginning to learn what it needed to know, back in 1963. But the connection had been made, in 1965, and *I* learned a lesson I've never forgotten:

I trust my talent. Implicitly.

I may be a dolt, subject to all the idiocies and false beliefs and false starts to which we are all heir, but the talent knows what the hell it's doing. The talent protects itself. It knows it has to exist in this precarious liaison with a dolt, and it makes damned sure the envelope containing the message doesn't get postmarked to the Dead Letter Office.

"Try a Dull Knife" didn't get finished till 1968, but the writing of the first pages exploded the scene through which I was sloughing. It freed me, and within a week or so I was out in the open again, moving away from the blasted, creepy world in which I had spent my uneasy days and nights, locked in useless embrace with the vampires who abound in unknowing, innocent society.

"Try a Dull Knife" is a story about bloodsuckers. It is also a story about "luck."

Harlan Ellison

Varicose Worms

SCOTT BAKER

The worms in this story drain the energy of their host and are the perfect representatives of their master. The story is also about magic, shamanism, and poetic justice. And it's a truly disgusting story, so don't try it before a meal.

Eminescu Eliade's great good luck had been his last name, that and the fact that not only had he been a cultured cosmopolitan and intelligent man when he'd arrived in Paris (named Eminescu after his country's greatest nineteenth-century poet by parents who'd seen to it that he had a thorough classical education, he'd almost completed his studies as a veterinarian when he'd been forced to flee Romania as the result of an indiscretion with a rather highly placed local official's daughter) but that he'd arrived in Paris hungry, practically penniless and desperate. So desperate that when he'd seen a copy of Mircea Eliade's *Le Chamanisme et les techniques archaïques de l'extase* in a bookstore window on the rue St. Jacques, where it had been accompanied by a notice explaining that Professor Eliade had returned to Paris for a limited time to give a series of lectures at the Musée de l'Homme under the auspices of the Bollingen Foundation, he'd gone to the post office and spent what were almost the last of his few coins for two phone tokens. He called the museum with the first and somehow, despite his halting French and the implausibility of his story, convinced the woman who answered the phone to give him the phone number of the apartment in Montmartre where the professor was staying, then used the other token to call the professor himself and pretend to a family relationship that had as far as he knew no basis in fact.

His meeting with the professor a few days later resulted in nothing but an excellent hot meal and the chance to discuss his namesake's poetry in Romanian with a fellow exile, but the fact that he'd found a copy of the other's book on shamanism in a library and had read it carefully in preparation for the interview changed his life.

Because when, some weeks later, he found himself panhandling in back of the Marché St. Germain with all his clothes worn in thick layers to keep him warm and the rest of his few possessions in two plastic bags he kept tied to his waist with some twine he'd found, or sleeping huddled over the ventilation grating at the corner of the boulevard St. Germain and the rue de l'Ancienne Comédie where the hot dry air from the métro station underneath kept him warm, or under the Pont Neuf (the oldest bridge in Paris despite its name) on nights when it was raining and he couldn't get past the police who sometimes made sure no one got into the Odéon métro station without a ticket—in the weeks and months he spent standing with his fellow *clochards* sheltered from the wind against the urine-stained stone of the Église St. Sulpice, yelling and singing things at the passersby, or in alleyways passing the cheap red wine in the yellow-tinged green bottles with the fat stars standing out in bas-relief on their necks back and forth—he slowly came to realize that certain of his companions were not at all what they seemed, were in fact shamans—urban shamans—every bit as powerful, as fearsome and as wild as the long-dead Tungu shamans whose Siberian descendents still remembered them with such awe. Remembered them only, because long ago all the truly powerful shamans had left the frozen north with its starvation and poverty for the cities where they could put their abilities to better use, leaving only those whose powers were comparatively feeble or totally faked to carry on their visible tradition and be studied by scholars such as Professor Eliade.

And from his first realization of what he'd found and what it meant, it hadn't taken him all that long to put the knowledge to use and become what he'd been now for more than fifteen years: an internationally known French psychiatrist with a lucrative private practice in which the two younger psychiatrists with whom he shared his offices on avenue Victor Hugo were not his partners but his salaried employees. The diplomas hanging framed on his wall were all genuine despite the fact that the name on them—Julien de Saint-Hilaire—was false and that the universities in Paris and Geneva and Los Angeles that had issued them would have been appalled to learn just what he'd actually done to earn them. He had a twenty-two-room apartment in a private hotel overlooking the Parc Monceau that even the other tenants now thought had been in his family since the early sixteen hundreds, maids who were each and every one of them country girls from small villages in the provinces as maids were traditionally supposed to be, and a very beautiful blond-haired American wife, Liz, in her early twenties, who'd been a model for Cacharel before he'd married her and convinced her to give up her career.

He took two, and sometimes three, month-long business trips every year, leaving the routine care of his patients during his absences to Jean-Luc and Michel, both of whom were talented minor shamans though neither of them was as yet aware of just what it was that they did when they dealt with patients.

Last fall, for example, he'd left them with the practice while he attended a psychiatric congress in San Francisco where he and his fellow psychiatrists—or at least that sizable minority among them who were, like himself, practicing shamans—had gotten together in a very carefully locked and guarded auditorium, there to put on their shamanizing costumes so they could steal people's souls and introduce malefic objects into their bodies, thus assuring themselves and their less aware colleagues of an adequate supply of patients for the coming year. He'd learned quite a bit about the proper use of quartz crystals from two young aboriginal shamans attending their first international congress, but had done as poorly as usual in the competitions: The very gifts that made him so good at recovering souls no matter how well his colleagues hid them made it difficult for him to recognize those hiding places where they in turn would be unable to discover the souls *he* hid. But he'd had a good time drinking Ripple and Thunderbird and Boone's Farm Apple Wine from stained paper bags on street corners and in Golden Gate Park, where he and most of the other psychiatrists attending the congress had slept when the weather permitted, and by the time he'd returned to Paris Liz had lost all the weight she'd put on since the trip before.

But it was almost the end of March now, time to start readying himself for his next month-long separation from her and from his comfortable life as Julien de Saint-Hilaire. He had to retrieve the lost, strayed, and stolen souls of those he intended to cure, and damage or find new hiding places for the souls of those patients he intended to retain for further treatment.

101

And besides, Liz was starting to get fat again. It was a vicious circle: They both loved to eat but she couldn't keep up with him without putting on weight, and the fatter she got the more insecure she felt about her appearance, so the more she ate to comfort herself. She was already back to the stage where she was sneaking out to eat napoleons and lemon tarts and exotic ice creams and sherbets in three or four different tea salons every afternoon, doing it all so surreptitiously that if he didn't know beforehand where she was planning to go, it could take him a whole afternoon of searching to catch up with her; in another month or so she'd be getting worried enough to start looking to other men for reassurance again.

And that was something he couldn't, and wouldn't, allow. He had very precise plans for his heir, a boy whose soul was even now undergoing its third year of prenatal preparation in one of the invisible eagle's nests high up on the Eiffel Tower where since the turn of the century the most powerful French politicians and generals had received the training and charisma and made the contacts necessary to ready them for their subsequent roles. And after all the years he'd spent readying Liz to bear his son he wasn't going to let her negate his efforts with another man's seed. She had her pastries, her wines, cognacs, and sleeping pills, her clothing and her restaurants, her money and her social position, and she'd have to stay content with them for at least the next four years, until his son was born.

On the way to his office he stopped off at his second apartment. It was a one-room windowless garret on the rue de Condé that had obviously been somebody's attic at one time. It now boasted a tiny brick fireplace and chimney that he'd fitted with an elaborate and deadly labyrinth which enabled him to enter and leave as a bird without permitting entrance by any other shamans. He picked up some of the pills he kept for Liz. His supply was almost exhausted: He'd have to write the old Indian in Arizona (John Henry Two Feathers Thomas Thompson, whose father had toured with Buffalo Bill's Wild West Show before starting his own medicine show with a white barker for a front) again and get some more.

He put on his two caps—for something as trivial as what he was about to do he didn't really need the power the rest of his costume would have provided him with—and became a pigeon with orange eyes and naked pink legs. He negotiated the chimney maze, making sure the spirits who guarded it recognized him in the form he'd adopted, to emerge on the roof and fly back to his apartment overlooking the Parc Monceau. He and Liz had been up very late making love the night before, with only a brief pause at two in the morning for the cold buffet he'd had his catering service prepare them, and she was still asleep, even snoring slightly in the way she did when she'd had too much to drink or had taken too many sleeping pills the night before, all of which made things easier for him. As did the fact that he'd left the cage with the two mynah birds in it covered when he'd left the apartment. Liz had bought the birds at the Sunday bird market on the Île de la Cité while he'd been away on his last trip and the birds had never learned to tolerate his presence in any of the forms he took. But though they were alert enough to detect the fact that he wasn't what he seemed to be as either a bird or a man, they were too stupid to realize that despite their dark cage the night was over. So he didn't have to worry about the birds making enough noise to awaken Liz.

He slipped in through the window he'd left open in the master bedroom, plucked Liz's sleeping soul from her body and bruised it with his beak in a way he knew from experience would do her no lasting harm but which would give her migraines for the next few weeks. Then he returned her still-sleeping soul to her body and flew back to his garret, where he took off his caps and locked them away in the sky-blue steel steamer trunk he kept them in. He sprayed his hair with a kerosene-smelling children's delousing spray, to take care of the head-lice that made their home in the inner cap, then used a dry shampoo to get rid of both the spray and the smell from the cap itself. He finally locked the door behind him, making sure when he did so that the spirits guarding the apartment would continue to deny entry to anyone but himself, then went back down the five flights of stairs as Julien de Saint-Hilaire, checked with the concierge a moment, and caught a taxi to his office.

He checked with Jean-Luc and Michel when he arrived, but found that except for a matter concerning a long-time patient who was now more than a year behind on his bills and who showed no signs of being ready to pay (which wasn't their responsibility, anyway), they had everything more or less under control. Too much under control, even: Jean-Luc especially was doing those patients he worked with more good than Eminescu wanted them done, but there was no way to get the younger psychiatrist to stop curing them without explaining to him the true nature of his profession and just what it was he was really doing to get the results he was getting, and that was something Eminescu was not yet ready to let him know; perhaps in another twenty or twenty-five years, when he himself would have to begin thinking about conserving his force.

He sat down behind his desk, pretended to busy himself with one patient's case history while he thought about what to do to that patient who was refusing to pay and waited for Liz to phone him.

The call came perhaps half an hour later. She said she'd just awakened and all she could think about was how soon he was going to be going away, and did he know yet exactly when he was going to have to leave for Japan? He told her he'd received confirmation on his flights, and that he'd be leaving in another six days, on a Monday, very early in the morning. She told him that she had an awful headache, it had started as soon as she'd awakened and realized he was going to be leaving, and she asked him to bring her something for the pain, since it was obviously his fault she had the headache because he was going away and she always felt sick and tired and alone and unhappy whenever he left her for more than a few days. He said he'd bring her some of the painkillers he'd given her the last time, the ones that didn't leave her too groggy, and she said, fine, but try to make them a little stronger this time, Julien, even if they do make me a bit groggy. He said he would, but that if she was really feeling that bad perhaps it would be better if he came home early, he could cancel all his afternoon appointments. She said, no, that wouldn't be necessary, but if he'd meet her for lunch he could give her the pills then, she'd pick out the restaurant and make the reservations, come by to pick him up when it was time. About one o'clock?

He said that one o'clock would be perfect. When she arrived he gave her the first two of the old Indian's pills, and on the way to the restaurant soothed her headache. For that he didn't even need his caps, he had enough power left over from just having worn them earlier.

It was an excellent restaurant near the Comédie Française, on rue Richelieu, and he was enormously hungry—flying demanded a great deal of energy; the iron with which his bones had been reinforced and tied together after his initiatory dismemberment was heavy and hard to lift when he was a bird, for all that the iron-wrapped bones gave him the vitality and endurance of a much younger man when in human form—and both he and Liz enjoyed their meal. Afterward he dropped her off outside

Notre Dame (where she had to meet some friends of her aunt's whom she'd been unable to get out of promising to show around), then went back to his apartment on the rue de Condé and put on his entire costume: the raccoon-skin cap with the snap-on tail that John Henry had given him and which he kept hidden under the over-large shapeless felt hat, the greasy false beard and hair (though in one sense they weren't really false at all, since they and the skin to which they were still attached had both been at one time his: more of the old Indian's work), the multiple layers of thermal underwear he wore under the faded work blues that were in turn covered by the old brown leather military trench coat with the missing buttons and half the left sleeve gone, the three pink plastic shopping bags from Monoprix filled with what looked like rags, but weren't, and the two pairs of crusted blue socks he wore under his seven-league work shoes (the ones he had specially made for him in Austria to look as though they were coming apart), so he could trace the pills' progress through Liz's system, and help them along when and if necessary.

It was raining by the time he'd completed his preparations and had begun beating his tambourine and hopping up and down, but he didn't feel like doing anything major about the weather even though he'd planned to go home as a pigeon again. So by the time he arrived back at the apartment he was very wet. But that gave him an excuse to remain perched there on the bedroom windowsill, ignoring the nasty looks the mynah birds were giving him while he ruffled his feathers and looked indignant.

Liz had already gotten rid of her aunt's friends, as he'd been sure she would; she was on the phone again, trying to find someone to go tea-salon hopping with her for the rest of the afternoon. She was having trouble: Very few of her woman friends could keep up with her pastry and sweets consumption and still look the way that Liz demanded the people she was seen with look, while Eminescu had for several years now made a practice of discouraging any and all of her male friends, even the homosexuals, who showed any tendency to spend too much, or even too attentive, time with her.

Not, of course, that he'd ever done so in any way that either Liz or her admirers could have ever realized had anything to do with her husband. The men in question just always had something go horribly wrong when they were with her—sudden, near fatal attacks of choking or vomiting;

running into old wives or girlfriends they'd abandoned pregnant; being mistaken for notorious Armenian terrorists or Cypriot neo-nazi bombers by the CRS and so ending up clubbed unconscious and jailed incommunicado; other things of the same sort—with the result that Liz never had any *fun* with them, and began avoiding even those few hyper-persistent or genuinely lovestruck victims who kept trying to see her anyway.

Which reminded him: It was time for her to get her headache back. As a former veterinary student he was quite familiar with Pavlovian conditioning—had, in fact, been writing his thesis on the ways it had been used to train the attack dogs used by the government in quelling the then-recent Polish workers' insurrection when he'd been forced to flee Romania—and his spiritual experience in later years had proven to him how useful a correct application of its basic principles could be to a shaman like himself. Thus, whenever Liz did something he approved of he rewarded her for it, whenever she did something he disapproved of he punished her, but always in ways that would seem to her to be in some way the direct result of her behavior, and not of any interference or judgment on his part. And that, finally, was the rationale for the use of the pills he gave her whenever he went away: Not only did they keep her properly subdued in his absence and insure that she'd have taken off her excess weight by the time he returned and restored her to normal, but they made her so miserable that when he did return she equated his presence—the secondary stimulus—with the primary stimulus of her renewed health and vitality in the same way she'd learned to equate his absence with her misery.

It was all very rational and scientific, a fact on which he prided himself. Too many of his colleagues were little better than witch-doctors.

"You're my whole happiness," Liz had told him once. "My only reason for staying alive." And that, to be sure, was how he wanted things.

It had taken her five phone calls but she'd finally found someone: Marie-Claude had agreed to accompany her, and they were going to meet at the tea room they liked on the Île St. Louis where the ice cream was so good. And the sun was coming out again. He flew there to wait for them.

From his perch in the tree across the street from the tea salon he could see them easily enough as they entered together, though when they sat down away from the window he had to cock his head just right to watch them through the walls. They both ordered ice cream—Bertillon chocolate, coffee, and chestnut for Liz, the same for Marie-Claude but with coconut in place of the coffee—and while they were waiting for the waitress to bring it convinced each other that it would be all right to have some sherbets with their coffee afterward.

Eminescu waited until Liz's first few swallows of chocolate were reaching her stomach to cock his head at the angle that let him see what was going on inside her.

Her stomach acids and digestive enzymes had already dissolved the pills and liberated the encysted bladder worms, and these in turn were reacting to the acids and enzymes by evaginating—turning themselves inside out, as though they'd been one-finger gloves with the fingers pushed in, but with the fingers now popping out again. Once the young tapeworms (as he'd learned to call them at UCLA, and it was a better name for them than the French *vers solitaires,* because these worms at least were far from solitary) had their scolexes, head-sections, free they could use the suckers and hooks on them to attach themselves to the walls of Liz's intestines, there to begin growing by pushing out new anterior segments—though he'd be back to deal with them before any of the worms was more than five or so meters long, and thus before any of the worms had reached its full sexual maturity.

Three specimens each of three kinds of tapeworm—*Taenia solium, Taenia saginata,* and *Diphyllobothrium latum,* the pork, beef, and fish tapeworms, respectively—he allowed to hook and sucker themselves to Liz's intestinal walls, though not without first ensuring that the individuals he favored would all be fairly slow-growing, as well as unlikely to excrete excessive amounts of those toxic waste products peculiar to their respective species. The myriad other worms whose encysted forms the pills had contained he killed, reaching out from his perch in the tree to pluck them from her intestinal walls with his beak, pinch off and kill their voracious little souls. It was all very well controlled, all very scientific, with nothing left to chance.

He watched her the rest of the afternoon, at that and three other tea salons, to make sure the nine worms he'd selected for her would do her no more damage than he'd planned for them to do, and that none of the other worms the pills had contained had escaped his attention and survived.

When at last he returned to the apartment on the rue de Condé he was weak with hunger. He took a quick shower and ate a choucroute at a nearby brasserie before going back to his office to make sure nothing unexpected had come up in his absence.

And every day until the time came for him to leave, he checked Liz two or three times, to make sure the worms now growing so rapidly inside her would do no lasting harm. He valued Liz a great deal, enjoyed her youth and spontaneity fully as much as he valued the son she was going to bear him, and he had no desire to be unnecessarily cruel to her.

On the morning he'd chosen to leave he went to his second apartment and checked on her one last time as she showered—thinner already and beautiful for all the fatigue on her face and in her posture—then returned to the windowless room and resumed his human form. He was hungry, but for the next month he was Eminescu Eliade again, and there was no way he could use Julien de Saint-Hilaire's money to pay for as much as a merguez-and-fries sandwich from one of the window-front Tunisian restaurants on the rue St. André des Arts without destroying much of his costume's power.

The rat he was to follow was waiting for him as arranged at the bottom of the stairs, behind the trash cans. He put it in one of his plastic bags, where it promptly made a nest for itself out of the rags that weren't really rags. Then he went out to beg the money for the three things he'd need to get started: the bottles of wine he'd have to share with his fellow shamans as long as he remained aboveground, the first-class métro ticket he'd need to enter the labyrinths coexistent with the Parisian métro system, and the *terrine de foie de volailles au poivre vert* from Coesnon's which the rat demanded he feed it each time it guided him through the city's subway labyrinths.

There were a lot of clochards he didn't recognize behind the Marché and on the streets nearby, even a blond-haired threesome—two bearded young men and a girl with her hair in braids—who looked more like hitch-hiking German or Scandinavian students temporarily short of money than like real clochards, for all that they seemed to know most of the others and be on good terms with them. What it added up to was an unwelcome reminder that he'd been spending too much time either abroad or as Julien de Saint-Hilaire, and not nearly enough staying in touch with his city and its spirit world—and that was an error that could well prove fatal to him unless he took steps to correct it. He'd have to stay in Paris that October after all, and miss the Australian congress that had

had him so excited ever since he'd begun to learn the kinds of things one could do with quartz crystals.

It took him five days to get the money he needed: He was out of practice at begging and every few hours, of course, he had to put most of what he'd earned toward the wine he shared with the others. And Coesnon's had tripled their prices during the last year alone. But by the fifth evening he had what he needed, so he walked down the rue de l'Ancienne Comédie to the rue Dauphine, where he bought the four-hundred-and-fifty-franc terrine despite the staff's and other customers' horrified disapproval when he squeezed himself and his bulging sacks into the narrow charcuterie, knocking a platter of blood sausage with apples to the floor in the process, then spent another four hours listening to the mutterings and arguments of the future shamans awaiting birth in the hundreds of tiers of invisible pigeons' nests that completely covered the green bronze statue of Henri IV astride his horse, there on its pedestal atop the little fenced-off step pyramid on the Pont Neuf. But there was nothing useful to be heard—Tabarin and his pompous master Mondor arguing as usual in the nest they shared, Napoleon pleading to be rescued from the tiny statuette of himself that the overly zealous Bonapartist who'd been commissioned to cast Henri's statue had hidden in the king's right arm, thus inadvertently imprisoning his hero's spirit there until such time as someone should destroy the statuette or rescue him—and so after listening a while he proceeded on diagonally across the Île de la Cité to Chatelet where he entered the métro system.

He bought himself a first-class ticket and pretended to drop it as he went to insert it in the machine so he could release the rat. It scurried away from him through the thick crowds and he had to run after it as soon as the machine disgorged his enigmatically stamped ticket, plastic bags, rags and leather overcoat flapping as he ran. Four or five times he lost sight of the rat—once because some fifteen- or sixteen-year-olds thought it would be fun to trip him and see how long they could keep him from getting back to his feet before somebody stopped them—but each time he found the rat again and at last it led him in through one of the urinals to the first of the labyrinth's inner turnings. There he fed it the first half of the terrine and the stamped métro ticket.

The corridors were less crowded when he emerged from the urinal, the light dimmer and pinker, and with each subsequent turning away from the public corridors into the secret ways which led through the land of the

dead there were more and more of the German shepherds whose powerful
bodies housed the souls of those few dead who'd been granted leave of the
Undercity for a day and a night in return for guarding Paris itself, fewer
and fewer people, and those few only the dying and mentally ill, the
North African blacks who worked as maintenance men and cleaners in the
métro system, and shamans like himself—plus once a politician whose
name he couldn't recall but to whom he'd made the proper ritual
obeisances anyway.

When he regained his feet and wiped the filth from his forehead he
found the corridor around him had changed yet again. The murky and
polluted bottom waters of the Seine flowed sluggishly past and around
him without touching him, and his guide now wore the baggy bright-red
shorts with the two big gold buttons on the front that told him he'd
finally escaped the outer world entirely and entered the land of the dead.

He fed the rat the rest of the terrine and began retracing the route he
knew should take him back to the place where he'd hidden the soul of the
first of those patients whom he intended to have make a miraculous
recovery upon his return, a retired general suffering from the delusion that
he was a young and bearded bouquiniste making his living selling
subversive literature and antique pornographic postcards from a bookstall
by the Seine.

But Hell had changed, changed radically and inexplicably in the year
he'd spent away from it, and it took him almost seven weeks before he was
able to escape it again by a route that led up and out through the sewer
system. Because someone, somehow, had found his patients' souls where
he'd buried them in the river mud and filth, had dug them up and left in
their place small, vicious but somehow indistinct, creatures that had
attacked him and tried to devour his soul. He'd been strong enough to
fight them off, though they'd vanished before the mud cloud they'd
stirred up had settled and he'd had a chance to get a closer look at them.
But though he'd found his patients' souls and recovered them from their
new hiding places without overmuch trouble, none of his usual contacts
among the dead had been willing or able to tell him who his enemy was,
or what the things that had attacked him had been.

He'd planned to stay Eminescu Eliade for a while after his return to the
surface so he could try to locate his enemy where he knew the man had to
be hiding, among the clochards who had not yet achieved professional

recognition in a second identity (because while professional ethics allowed stealing other psychiatrists' patients' souls, even encouraged it as tending to keep everyone alert and doing their best, leaving creatures such as the things that had attacked him to devour a fellow psychiatrist's soul was specifically forbidden by the Ordre des médecins)—but when he took the form of a pigeon and returned to the apartment he shared with Liz to see how she was doing and make sure the tapeworms in her intestines hadn't done her any real harm in the extra weeks, ready to perhaps even kill one or two of them if they were getting a little too long, he saw that something further had gone wrong, horribly wrong.

Liz was in the kitchen in her striped robe, spooning chestnut purée from a one-kilo can frantically into her mouth as though she were starving, and his first impression was that he'd never before seen her looking so disgustingly fat and sloppy. But then he realized that though her belly was distended and she looked as though she'd neither slept nor washed in a few days she was if anything skinnier than she'd been when he'd seen her last. Much skinnier. And that the swollen puffiness that so disfigured her face came from the fact that she was crying, and that her legs—her legs that had always been so long and smooth and beautiful, so tawny despite her naturally ash-blond hair that she'd always refused to wear any sort of tinted or patterned stockings, even when her refusal had cost her work—her legs were streaked with long, twitching fat blue veins. Varicose veins, as though she were a fat and flaccid woman in her sixties.

He cocked his pigeon's head to the right and looked in through her abdominal walls to see what was happening within her intestines, in through the skin and muscles of her legs to understand what was going on there.

Only to find that the tapeworms had reached sexual maturity despite all the careful checking he'd done on them before his departure, and that not only had their intertwined ten-meter bodies almost completely choked her swollen and distended intestines, but that their hermaphroditic anterior segments had already begun producing eggs. And those eggs—instead of having been excreted as they should have been, to hatch only when and if stimulated by the distinctive digestive juices of the pigs, cows, or fish whose particular constellation of acids and enzymes alone could provide their species of worm with its necessary stimuli—those eggs were hatching almost immediately, while they were

111

still within Liz's digestive tract, and the minute spherical embryos were anchoring themselves to the intestinal walls with the six long hooks they each sported, then boring through the walls to enter her bloodstream, through which they then let themselves be carried down into her legs. There, in the smaller vessels in her calves and thighs, they were anchoring themselves and beginning to grow, not encysting as normal tapeworm embryos would have done, but instead developing into myriads of long, filament-thin worms that were slowly climbing their way from their anchor points up through her circulatory system toward her heart as they lengthened.

His enemy, whoever his enemy was, had planned the whole farce with his patients' stolen but easily recoverable souls and the things that had been lying in wait for him in their place just to keep him occupied while *he* played around with the worms in Liz, modified them for his own purposes. He must have had her under observation long enough to have known about the fear of all other doctors but himself that Eminescu had long ago conditioned into her, known that he'd have a free hand with her until Eminescu got back. And if Eminescu'd stayed trapped in the secret ways even a few days longer she might well have lost her feet, perhaps even her legs, to gangrene and so been ruined as the potential mother of his son. A week or two beyond that and she could have been dead.

She was constantly moving her legs, twitching them as she gorged herself on the purée, kneading her calves and thighs. Keeping the circulation going as best she could despite the filament worms waving like strands of hungry kelp in her veins, the worms that had so far only impeded, and not yet blocked, the flow of blood through her legs.

It was all very scientific and precise, masterfully devised. Whoever'd done it could have easily killed her, done so with far less effort and imagination than he'd expended on producing her present condition. The whole thing was a challenge, could only be a challenge, traditional in intent for all that the way it had been done was new to him. And what the challenge said was, I want your practice and your position and everything else you have, and I can take it away from you, I've already proved that anything you can do I can do better, and I'm going to go ahead and do it unless you can stop me before I kill you. The challenge was undoubtedly on file with the Ordre des médecins, though there'd be no way for Eminescu to get a look at the records and learn who his challenger was: The relevant laws were older than France or Rome, and were zealously enforced.

But what he could do was take care of Liz and keep her from being damaged any further while he tried to learn more about his opponent. He reached out with his beak, twisted the souls of the filament worms in Liz's legs dead. They were much tougher than he'd anticipated, surprisingly hard to kill, but when at last they were all dead he pulled them carefully free of the blood vessels in which they'd anchored themselves, pulled them out through Liz's muscles and skin without doing her any further damage, then patched the damaged veins and arteries with tissues he yanked from the legs of a group of Catholic schoolgirls who happened to be passing in the street. They were young: They'd recover soon enough. The stagnant and polluted blood, slimy with the worms' waste products, began to flow freely through her system again.

He watched Liz closely for a while to make sure the waste products weren't concentrated or toxic enough to be dangerous to her in the time it would take her liver or other organs to filter them from her blood. When he was sure that any harm they might do her would be trivial enough to be ignored he reached out to take and squeeze the souls of the tapeworms knotted together and clogging her intestines, snatched himself back just in time to save himself when he recognized them: the creatures that had attacked him in the land of the dead. But fearsome though they were on the spiritual plane—and now that he had a chance to examine them better he saw that their souls were not those of tapeworms but of some sort of lampreys, those long eel-like parasitic vertebrates whose round sucking mouths contain circular rows of rasping teeth with which they bore their way in through the scales of the fish they've attached themselves to, so as to suck out the fish's insides and eventually kill it in the process—physically they were still only tapeworms despite their modified reproductive systems. And that meant that he could destroy them by physical—medical—means. Quinacrine hydrochloride and aspidium oleoresin should be more than sufficient, if there hadn't been something better developed recently that he wasn't aware of yet. But to make use of any kind of medicine he'd have to resume his identity as Julien de Saint-Hilaire, if only long enough to return home, soothe Liz and prescribe for her, then make sure she was following the treatment he suggested and that it was working for her.

But before he did that he had to try to learn a little more about his challenger, so he returned to his apartment on the rue de Condé and resumed his human form. His efforts in the Undercity and just now as a bird had totally depleted his body's reserves of fat and energy; he was gaunt and trembling, so that those passersby he approached after making his way down the back stairs to the street who weren't frightened away by his diseased look were unusually generous. After he'd made the phone call that confirmed that, yes, an official challenge had been registered against Julien de Saint-Hilaire, he was able to buy not only the wine he needed to approach his fellow clochards but some food from the soup kitchen behind the Marché as well.

He slept that night in the métro, curled up on the benches with three other clochards, one of whom was a woman, though as much a shaman as himself or the other two. The woman had a bottle of cheap rosé; they passed it back and forth while they talked, and he listened to them while saying as little himself as possible, trying to find out if they knew anything about his enemy without revealing what he was doing, but either they knew nothing about his opponent or they were siding with him against Eminescu and keeping their knowledge hidden. Which was quite possible: He'd seen it happen that way a few times before, with older shamans who were particularly arrogant and disliked, though he'd never imagined it could happen to him.

The next day he spent sitting on a bench on the Pont Neuf, panhandling just enough to justify his presence there while he tried to learn something from the spirits in their nests on the statue of Henri IV. He even promised to free Napoleon from the statuette in which the former Emperor was trapped and promised him a place in one of the highest eagle's nests on the Eiffel Tower from which he'd be able to make a triumphant return to politics, if only he'd tell Eminescu his enemy's name or something that would help him find him. But Napoleon had been imprisoned there in the statuette in King Henri's statue's right arm pleading with and ranting at the shamans who refused to so much as acknowledge his existence for too many years and he'd become completely insane: He refused to reply to Eminescu's questions, continued his habitual pleas and promises even after Eminescu had begun hurting him and threatening to silence his voice forever unless he responded rationally.

Eminescu finally left him there, still ranting and pleading: It would have been pointless to waste any more of his forces in carrying out the threats he'd made. He had enough money to pay his entry to the Eiffel Tower, so he flew there as a pigeon, cursing the unaccustomed heaviness of his iron-wrapped bones, then transformed himself back into a clochard in the bushes and went up to the observation deck in the elevator, there found his son and General de Gaulle in their respective nests and asked their advice. De Gaulle—perhaps because the nest in which he was preparing his triumphal return was next to Eminescu's son's nest and the two had come to know each other fairly well—was always polite to Eminescu, wherein the other politicians and military men, able to sense the fact that he wasn't truly French and themselves chauvinistic to the core, refused to even speak to him.

But neither de Gaulle nor his son knew anything useful, and his son seemed weaker and less coherent than the last time Eminescu had spoken to him, as though the forces conspiring against his birth were already beginning to make him fade. Still, at least he was safe from any sort of direct attack: The invisible eagles that guarded his nest allowed no one not of their own kind to approach the tower in anything but human form, and would have detected and killed any mere shaman like Eminescu or his enemy who'd attempted to put on an eagle's form to gain entry.

He returned to the rue de Condé so he could beat his tambourine and sing and dance without danger of interruption, and thus summon the maximum possible power. It was night by the time he felt ready, so he took the form of an owl and returned to the apartment overlooking the Parc Monceau, perched outside the bedroom window, terrifying the mynah birds, and killed the tapeworm embryos that had made their way into Liz's bloodstream again. It was easier this time: He had a lot more strength available to him as an owl, though it was harder to hold the form and he paid for that strength later on, when he regained his humanity.

He examined the worms in Liz's intestines with the owl's sharper eyes to see if there was some way he could destroy them without harming Liz or risking his own safety, saw that even as an owl he didn't have enough concentrated spiritual strength at his disposal to destroy all the worms together. There would have been a way to do it with quartz crystals, replacing those sections of her intestines to which the tapeworms had anchored themselves with smooth crystal so they'd lose their purchase and be eliminated from her body, but he was far from skillful enough yet to carry out the operation without killing her, since loose quartz crystals in her body would be like just so many obsidian knives, and he lacked the experience needed to mold the quartz to her flesh and infuse it with her spirit so as to make it a living part of her.

He could have done it if he'd had a chance to go to that Australian convention he'd planned to attend in the fall. As it was he'd have to try to find another way.

That night he slept under the Pont Neuf on some sheets of cardboard a previous sleeper had left behind him, satisfying the tremendous hunger his efforts as an owl had awakened in him as best he could from the garbage cans behind Coesnon's and some of the other gourmet boutiques on the rue Dauphine.

The next morning he flew to his offices on Avenue Victor Hugo as a pigeon and spent a long time watching Jean-Luc and Michel. It had been months since he'd last been there as anything but Julien de Saint-Hilaire and he wanted to make sure that neither of them had developed the kind of power his challenger so obviously had. They were, after all, the two persons most likely to covet his position and the two most prepared to fill it when he was gone, despite the fact that a challenge from either of them would have been a clear violation of medical ethics and that his challenger had registered his challenge with the Ordre des médecins in thoroughly proper fashion.

He watched them working, soothing souls in pain, coaxing lost or strayed souls back to the bodies they'd left. They were both small, slim and dark, both immensely sincere, and they were both fumbling around blindly in the spirit realm for souls that they could have recovered in instants if they'd known what it was they were really doing. No, their instincts were good, but they were still just what he'd always thought them to be, talented amateurs with no idea of the true nature of their talents, even though those talents seemed to be growing, in Jean-Luc's case in particular.

Since he was there Eminescu used the opportunity to undo some of the good Michel had done a young schizophrenic he had no intention of seeing recover, then returned to the rue de Condé, and from there, as Julien de Saint-Hilaire, to his apartment overlooking the park, stopping only briefly on the way to buy and eat seven hundred and fifty grams of dark chocolates.

Liz was asleep, passed out half dressed on the living room sofa with a partially eaten meal cold on a tray on the table beside her. The kitchen was littered with empty and half-empty cans and bottles.

The servants were all gone and he knew Liz well enough to be sure she'd sent them away, unable to bear the idea of having anyone who knew her see what had happened to her legs, just as she would have been unable to face being examined by another doctor.

She twitched in her sleep, shifting the position of her legs on the sofa, then moved them back the way they'd been. The blue veins in her thighs and calves looked perhaps a little less fat and swollen than they'd seemed when he'd first found out what'd happened to her, but only slightly so: Even though he'd gotten rid of the worms in the veins themselves and replaced a tiny fraction of the damaged vessels it would take a long time for the rest to regain their elasticity. He might even have to replace them altogether.

He'd stopped at a pharmacy run by a minor shaman he knew on the way over to order the various medicines he'd need to deal with the tapeworms as well as a comprehensive selection of those sleeping and pain pills which Liz had a tendency to abuse when he failed to keep her under close enough supervision but which would serve now to keep her more or less anesthetized and incapable of worrying too much for the next few weeks, until his present troubles were over one way or another. And there was at least the consolation of knowing that if he did succeed in discovering his opponent's identity and destroying him, the other's attack on Liz would have served to further reinforce the way Eminescu'd conditioned her to associate his every absence with unhappiness and physical misery, his return with health and pleasure.

He picked up the phone, intending to awaken her with a faked call to the pharmacy so as to make it seem as though he'd just entered, taken one look at her lying there with her legs all swollen and marbled with twitching blue veins and had immediately and accurately diagnosed her condition and so known exactly what he'd have to do without needing to subject her to the indignity of further examinations or tests. It was what she expected of him: Liz had always had a childlike faith in doctors and medicine for all her fear of them. But at the last moment he put the phone down again and went back into the bedroom to take a careful look at the two mynah birds in their cage.

His presence alarmed them: They started hopping nervously back and forth between their perches, making little hushed cries of alarm as if afraid that if they were any louder they'd draw his attention to them. But hushed as their cries were they were still making more noise than he wanted them to, so he closed the heavy door behind him to cut off the sound and keep them from awakening Liz. Without his cap and costume he couldn't examine them to find out if they were just the rather stupid birds they appeared to be or if one or even both of them were spies for his enemy, perhaps that enemy himself in bird-form. (But could two shamans together challenge a third? He had the impression it was forbidden, but that there was perhaps a way for a challenger to make use of a second shaman's aid.) In any case, the mynah birds were living creatures over whom he exercised no control and which had been introduced into his home with neither his knowledge nor his permission at a time when he'd been away, and he couldn't trust them.

He opened the cage door, reached in quickly with both hands and grabbed the birds before they could escape or make more than one startled squeak apiece, then wrung their necks and threw them out the window, aiming the bodies far enough to the right so that Liz wouldn't see them if she just took a casual look out the window. He could retrieve them later and take them back with him to examine more closely at his other apartment before Liz'd had a chance to leave the house and discover them dead.

He left the cage door open and opened the window slightly, to provide an explanation for their absence when Liz noticed they were gone, then covered the cage to keep her from noticing it immediately.

He went back into the living room. Liz had turned over again and was scratching her right calf in her sleep, leaving angry red scratches all up and down it. He played out the scene he'd planned beforehand with the faked call to the pharmacy, reassured her as soon as the sound of his voice awakened her: He was back, he'd known what had happened to her as soon as he took one look at her, it was a side-effect of certain illegal hormones that people had been injecting dairy cows with recently and which had been showing up, for some as yet unexplained reason, in high concentrations only in certain crèmes pâtissières used in such things as napoleons and eclairs, and he knew how to cure her condition, it wasn't even really anything to worry about, she wouldn't need surgery and in a few weeks she'd be completely cured, there wouldn't be any scars or anything else to show for the episode but some unpleasant memories, her legs would be as beautiful as before and she shouldn't worry, she should just trust him.

She'd burst into tears as soon as she'd seen him there, was holding on to him and crying with relief by the time he'd finished telling her not to worry, that everything was going to be all right.

The bell rang: the pharmacy, one of the few in Paris willing to deliver, with the medicines he'd ordered. He paid the delivery man, tipping him extravagantly as always, then went back into the bedroom where Liz'd run to hide herself when she heard the bell and gave her two sleeping pills and a pain pill. Only when she was completely groggy and he'd tucked her into bed did he explain his absence, telling her about the two weeks he'd spent completely isolated in a tiny village in the mountains where the Japanese government was carrying out an experimental mental health program and from which it had been impossible to phone her, though he didn't understand how she could have failed to receive the long, long telegram he'd sent her from Tokyo after he'd tried so many times to get her on the phone without once succeeding.

She started nodding out near the end of the explanation, as he'd intended: She'd never remember exactly what it was that he'd told her but only that he'd explained things, and he could always modify his story later and then tell her that the modified story was exactly the same as the one he'd told her before. Though that was probably just an unnecessary precaution: She always believed even the most implausible stories he told her, just as she seemed to have believed his story about the hormones.

He got her to take the various pills, powders, and liquids he'd obtained to treat the tapeworms with—there'd been a number of new medicines he'd been totally unaware of on the market, yet another reminder of how out of touch he'd been allowing himself to become—then gave her two more sleeping pills to make sure she'd stay unconscious for a while. He waited until she was asleep and snoring raggedly, then left.

He retrieved the two mynah birds from the bushes, put them in a plastic sack and caught a taxi to his other apartment, where he put on his costume to examine them.

But the birds were just mynah birds, as far as he could tell when he took them apart, and when he returned once again to his other apartment as a pigeon and flew in through the bathroom window he'd left open for himself he saw that the medicines he'd used were having no effect whatsoever on the tapeworms—no effect, that is, except to stimulate them to a frantically accelerated production of new eggs.

Once again his enemy had anticipated him, known what his next move would be long before he himself had done so and had arranged to use it against him. He was being laughed at, played for a fool, a clown.

But for all the anger that knowledge awakened in him there was nothing he could do about it yet. He had to stay there beside Liz on the bed for hours, stalking nervously back and forth on his obscenely pink legs as he plucked embryo after embryo from her bloodstream and destroyed them, until he was so hungry and exhausted he could barely keep himself conscious. Then he had no choice but to return to his other apartment— resting every two or three blocks in a tree or on a window ledge—so he could resume his identity as Julien de Saint-Hilaire long enough to pay for a large meal in a restaurant.

He ate an immense meal at an Italian restaurant a few blocks away, followed it with a second, equally large, meal at a bad Chinese restaurant he usually avoided and felt better.

He tried telephoning John Henry Two Feathers Thomas Thompson but was told that the old Indian's number was no longer in service and that there was no new listing for him. Eminescu didn't know if that meant he was dead, or had moved, or had just obtained an unlisted number. But there was no one Eminescu could trust who lived near enough to his former teacher to contact him, and he didn't have the time to fly to America and try to find him himself, either as a bird or by taking a plane as Julien de Saint-Hilaire. So he sent the old Indian a long telegram, and hoped that he'd not only get it, but that he'd have something to say that would help Eminescu.

He bought a sandwich from a sidewalk stand and ate it on the way back to the rue de Condé apartment, then resumed his caps and costume and returned to the Parc Monceau apartment yet one more time as a pigeon to try to deal with the embryos, yet despite the huge meals he'd eaten and the hours he'd spent in his other identity he was still too hungry and too exhausted to keep it up for more than a few hours before the embryos started getting past him despite everything he could do. And the worms in Liz's intestines seemed to be producing their eggs ever faster now, as though the process he'd begun when he gave her the medicines was still accelerating.

Defeated and furious, he returned to his other apartment, passed out as soon as he regained his human form. When he reawakened he barely had enough strength to crawl over to the sink where he'd left the two dismembered mynah birds and strip the meat from their bones and devour it.

There was no way he could hope to save Liz if he continued the way he was going. All he was really doing was destroying himself, using up all the forces which he'd need to protect himself from his opponent when it finally came to a direct attack on him. For a moment he was tempted to just abandon Liz, give up his identity as Julien de Saint-Hilaire and let her die or be taken over by the challenger when he moved into the Julien de Saint-Hilaire role in Eminescu's place. But he'd come too far, was too close to the true power and security he knew his son would provide him with, the assurance that he himself would be born in one of the Eiffel Tower's eagles' nests, to abandon everything now. Besides, Liz still pleased him, though it wasn't just that, just the kind of sentimental weakness that he knew would destroy him if he ever let it get the upper hand. No, what mattered was that Liz was *his,* his to dispose of and no one else's, and his pride was such that he could never allow anyone else to take her away from him. That pride he knew for his strength, as all sentimentality was weakness: Without his pride he was nothing.

He had to save her life, but he couldn't do it as a pigeon, nor even as an owl. Yet they were in the heart of Paris; the only other animal forms he could put on safely—cats, perhaps ducks or other small birds, insects, rats, and mice—would be equally ineffectual. If he tried to put on an eagle's form the invisible eagles atop the Eiffel Tower would detect him and destroy him for his presumption, for all that he had a son they were raising as one of their own; if he put on a wolf's or a dog's form the dead who patrolled the city as German shepherds would bring him down, for only they were allowed to use canine form, and Paris had for centuries been forbidden to wolves. And if he tried to put on a bear's body—a bear's form would be ideal, as far as he knew he was the only shaman in France who knew how to adopt it and there'd be no way his enemy could have been prepared to deal with it, but there was also no way he could shamble

121

the huge, conspicuous body across Paris undetected, nor anyone he could trust to transport it for him, and for all the force that being a bear would give him, the dogs would still be able to bring him down if they attacked as a pack, and he'd be vulnerable as well to humans with guns.

Unless he was willing to give up the complete separation of his two identities which he'd always maintained for his own protection, and took his costume and tambourine with him to the other apartment, and made the transformation there. The problem wasn't just the basically trivial difficulty of explaining his clochard-self's presence to Liz and the domestics (and that, anyway, would be no problem at all with the servants gone and Liz full of pills) but that the more people who knew he was both Eminescu Eliade and Julien de Saint-Hilaire, the less safe he was. Both identities were, of course, registered with the Ordre des médecins and there were a very few of his French psychiatric colleagues who knew him as both, though most knew only that he was both shaman and psychiatrist, but those few who did know were all men to whom he'd chosen to reveal himself because he was satisfied they posed no real threat to him, while at the same time they knew he in turn would never threaten them, thus rendering mutual trust possible. The clochards with whom he spent his time as Eminescu Eliade, of course, knew that he was a shaman, just as he knew which among them were also shamans, but though they knew that he had to have some sort of second identity, none of them, as far as he was aware, knew that that second identity was that of Julien de Saint-Hilaire. Thus none of them could attack him while he was in his psychiatrist's role, far from his caps, costume and drum, and so virtually defenseless.

It was Julien de Saint-Hilaire, and not Eminescu Eliade, who'd been challenged and who was under attack. Yet even so he knew that as long as he kept his unknown enemy from learning that the two were one and the same (and his opponent *couldn't* know that yet, or Eminescu would have already been dead) Eminescu Eliade would remain, if not safe, at least always free to escape to safety and anonymity. All of which would be lost if the other caught him taking his costume and drum to the other apartment.

Lost, unless he could destroy the worms in Liz and get his shamanizing aids back to the rue de Condé before the other realized what Eminescu was doing. Or unless he managed to kill the other before he'd had a chance to make use of the information he'd gained, and before he'd had a chance to reveal it to anyone else.

And Eminescu was tired of having to defend himself, of worrying about his safety, tired and very angry. He wanted to hurt his enemy, not just avoid him or survive his attacks. The other had to have a lot of his power—and that meant a lot of his soul—in the worms: If Eminescu could destroy them he might well cripple his enemy so that he could finish him off later, at his leisure. And too, this was the only way he could save Liz, and his unborn son.

He took his father's skull from the silver hatbox in the trunk, held it out at arm's length with both hands and asked it whether or not he'd succeed in saving Liz without betraying himself to his enemy. There was no reply, the skull became neither lighter nor heavier, but that proved nothing: His father rarely responded and those few times that the skull's weight had seemed to change Eminescu had been unable to rule out the possibility that the brief alteration in its heaviness he'd felt had been no more than the result of unconscious suggestion, like the messages he'd seen Liz seem to receive when she played with her Ouija board.

He put the skull and the rest of his shamanizing equipment back in the trunk and locked it, then went downstairs as Julien de Saint-Hilaire. He ate yet another two meals at nearby restaurants, then found the concierge's husband and got him to help move the heavy steamer trunk downstairs. Back at the other apartment he tipped the taxi driver who'd brought him there substantially extra to help carry the trunk up the rear stairs. When the driver left he dragged it into the apartment and locked it in the unused spare bedroom at the far end of the apartment, where Liz was least likely to be disturbed by the noise he'd make beating his tambourine and chanting, and where she was least likely to realize that a door to which she'd never had the key was now locked against her.

She was still in the bedroom, asleep. He called his catering service and asked them to deliver cold cuts for a party of fifteen in an hour, then went downstairs and bought a side of beef and a half dozen chickens from his butcher. The butcher and his two assistants helped him up the stairs and into the kitchen with the meat. When they were gone he dragged the beef into the spare bedroom, followed it with the chickens.

The caterers managed to deliver the cold cuts without waking Liz. He ate some of them, laid the others out where he'd be able to get at them easily when he made the transformation back to human, though since he wouldn't be flying he at least wouldn't have to waste the kinds of energy it took to get his iron-weighted body airborne. Then he locked all the doors and windows carefully and turned off the phone and doorbell, so as to make sure that nothing disturbed or awakened Liz before he was finished with her.

It was good to put his caps and costume on in the Parc Monceau apartment for the first time, good to beat his tambourine there in the spare room with the late-afternoon sun coming in through the curtains screening the window. Good to put on the bear's form after so many years of forcing himself to stay content with being no more than a pigeon or owl or rat. It had been fifteen—no, seventeen—years since he'd last been a bear, there in that box canyon in Arizona with John Henry Two Feathers Thomas Thompson, and he'd forgotten what joy it was to be huge and shaggy and powerful, forgotten the bear's keen intelligence and cunning, the enormous reserves of strength its anger gave it.

Forgotten too the danger of losing himself in the bear, of letting the seeming inexhaustibility of the forces at his disposal seduce him into going too far beyond his limits, so that when the time came for him to resume his human form he'd lack the energy to animate his body and so die.

Outside a dog began to bark, and then another. He couldn't tell if they were just dogs barking, or some of the dead who'd detected his transformation, but even if they were just dogs they were a reminder that the longer he stayed a bear the more chance there was that his enemy would detect him, realize what he was doing and counterattack.

More dogs, a growing number of them living animals now, howling all around his building and even within it: He recognized the excited voices of the thirteen whippets the film distributor on the first floor kept, the sharp yapping of the old lady on the second floor's gray poodle and the deeper and stupider baying of her middle-aged daughter's obnoxious Irish setter. Lights were beginning to go on in other buildings. Which meant he had to hurry, leave the meat and chickens he'd planned to eat before he began for later, so he could get to Liz and soothe her immediately, before even drugged as she was the noise woke her.

Soothe her and then destroy the worms before the disturbance the dead were making brought his enemy. If he wasn't already here, or coming.

He'd left the door to the room he was using slightly ajar. Now he pushed it open with his snout, squeezed through the narrow doorway and shambled down the long hall toward the master bedroom. He was already hungry, though he still had some margin before he'd be in danger.

Halfway down the hall to the bedroom he knocked a tall glass lamp from a table. It hit the parquet floor and shattered loudly, and for a moment he was sure that the noise would be enough to awaken Liz after all: She metabolized her sleeping pills very rapidly and would already be beginning to get over the effects of the ones he'd given her. But when he reached the bedroom and poked his head in to check on her she was still asleep, though the howling outside and within the building was still getting louder and louder. There had to be fifty or sixty dogs out there by now, perhaps even more.

He shambled the rest of the way into the room, reared up and balanced himself on his hind legs at the foot of the bed, then reached out and plucked Liz's soul from her body, locked it away from all pain and sensation in her head. As though her skull were a mother's womb inside which she lay curled like a haggard but voluptuous foetus, her whole adult body there within her head, filling it and overflowing it slightly, one hand dangling from her right ear, a foot and ankle and short length of calf protruding from her half-open mouth.

He turned her over with his paws and made a quick incision in her belly with his long claws, pulled the flesh apart so he could reach in and flip her intestines free of her abdomen. He ripped them open and seized the worms in his teeth, ripped them free of her intestinal walls and then tore them apart, killing the scolexes and each and every segment before he swallowed them. It was easy, amazingly easy, like the time John Henry Two Feathers Thomas Thompson had taught him to flip trout from a stream with his paws, and though the tapeworms were lampreys as well as worms they couldn't get a grasp on his shaggy body with their sucking mouths, their concentric circles of razor-sharp rasping teeth, so it was only a matter of moments before he'd killed them all and devoured their dead bodies.

All eight of them, where there should have been nine.

He cursed himself for the way he'd let the noise the dogs were making outside the apartment rush him into beginning without examining Liz very, very carefully again first, realized that at no time since he'd returned

125

from the Undercity had he thought to count the worms in her belly, that he'd just assumed that all nine were still there.

But there was no time now to try to solve the problem of the ninth worm's escape or disappearance; he had to try to get Liz's intestines back together and inside her and functioning before she bled to death, and before the hunger growing ever more insistent within him reached the point where it could be fatal.

He licked the insides of her intestines clean with his long tongue, making sure he got each and every egg and embryo and crushed the life out of them between his teeth before he swallowed them. Then he pushed the ripped intestines back into shape with his nose and tongue, licked them until they'd stopped bleeding and begun to heal, licked them a little more and then nosed them back into place in her abdominal cavity, licked the incision in her belly until it closed and healed, continued to lick it until no further trace of its presence remained.

Then he reached into her legs and bloodstream, pulled the embryos and filament worms he found there from her body, killed and devoured them.

And it had been easy, almost too easy. He would have thought the whole thing another diversion, only a means of luring him here in his shaman's self, had it not been for the fact that there was no one else in France who knew he was able to take on the form of a bear. There were very few people left anywhere in Europe who knew how to do so, and those few were all far to the North, in the Scandinavian countries.

Besides, there was still the missing tapeworm to consider.

Liz's soul still filled her head. He very carefully checked her body to make sure it was now free of worms, eggs, embryos, and toxins before he released her soul, let it begin slowly filtering down out of her head into the rest of her body.

The veins in her legs were still blue and fat, undoubtedly painful: The filament worms had damaged all the tiny valves in the vessels that kept the blood from pooling there. But all that was, now that the worms had been removed, was ordinary varicose veins; he should be able to heal them easily enough, and if they proved for some reason more difficult to deal with than he expected them to be he could always steal healthy veins from other people's legs for her. From that patient who was so late paying his bills, if his blood type was right and his circulatory system in good condition.

His hunger had passed the danger point, especially with his human form weakened as it was by his previous efforts, but he forced himself to go over the bedroom and both the attached bathrooms meticulously, looking for the ninth worm. It wasn't there. Perhaps the medicines he'd given Liz had destroyed it; perhaps the first worm's death had been the signal which had stimulated the other worms to their accelerated egg production. In any case, the worm was gone.

Liz was sleeping soundly now, would remain asleep for another five or six hours while her soul reintegrated itself with her body. More than long enough for him to change the bloodstained sheets and blankets and mattress cover.

He fell once on his way back through the corridor to the spare bedroom, got a good look at himself in the hall mirror as he was getting back up. He looked almost dead of starvation, a bit like a weasel or wolverine, but with neither the sleekness nor the grace.

He made it back into the spare bedroom and pushed the door closed behind him, though he had no way to lock it before he regained his human form. He devoured the cold cuts on their platter, ate the chickens and began ripping chunks of meat from the side of beef.

And when he'd cracked open the last bone and licked it clean of the last of the marrow it had contained he triggered his transformation.

He lay there, Eminescu Eliade, too tired to move or do anything else, just letting the strength begin flowing gently back into him from his caps and costume. There'd been enough energy in the food he'd eaten to keep him alive, just barely enough, but it would be a while before he'd be strong enough to pull his tambourine to him, tap out the rhythms on it he could use to summon the strength he'd need to get to his feet and change back into Julien de Saint-Hilaire, then get something more to eat from the kitchen and finally clean up Liz and the bed.

Everything was silent, completely silent, both within the apartment and outside. He had a throbbing pain in his head and he felt dizzy and a little nauseated and very hungry. The floor was too hard for him now that he'd lost the flesh that had formerly cushioned his bones and it hurt him even through his many layers of swaddling clothing. He'd have to find a way to explain to Liz the twenty kilos or more he'd lost so suddenly.

He lay there, half-dozing, letting the strength return to him.

And then he must have passed out, because when he opened his eyes

127

again Liz was kneeling over him, still covered with dry blood but dressed now, her robe wrapped around her. He tried to tell her something, he wasn't sure quite what, but she shook her head and put her fingers to her lips. She was smiling, but it was a strange, tight-lipped smile and he felt confused.

The door opened behind him, letting in a current of cold air. Jean-Luc and Michel came in together, holding hands.

Liz snatched Eminescu's two caps from his head and put them on her own before he'd had a chance to realize what she was doing, and by then it was too late to even try to change himself back into a bear, or into anything else.

She motioned to Jean-Luc and Michel. They bent down to kiss her on both cheeks in greeting while she did the same to them, then took up their positions, Jean-Luc kneeling across from her on the opposite side of Eminescu's body, Michel down by his feet. Jean-Luc helped her strip Eminescu's leather coat from him while Michel took his seven-league shoes and his socks from his feet. Without his caps he had no strength with which to even try to resist them, and with each article and layer of clothing they stripped from him he was weaker still, until at the end he no longer had the strength to so much as lift his head.

When he was naked and shivering in the cold air Liz took off her robe and gave it to Jean-Luc to hold while she dressed herself in Eminescu's many layers of rags. Then together she and Jean-Luc wrapped him in her discarded robe while Michel picked up Eminescu's tambourine and began to beat it.

Naked and weakened as he was, he could sense nothing of the power they were summoning and using. He had never felt it, not even in the end, never detected in any of them the slightest sign of the power that had defeated and destroyed him, and in a way that was almost as bad as the fact of the defeat itself, that he would never know if Liz or one of the other two had been his true enemy, keeping his or her powers hidden from Eminescu in some way he would never now get the chance to understand, or if all three of them together had been only the instrument for some challenger whose identity he would never know.

Liz knelt down beside him again, pulled the beard from his face and put it on her own. She leaned over him then, began nuzzling his cheek and then kissing him on the mouth.

Without ceasing to kiss him she brought her hands up, jammed her fingers into his mouth and pried it wide, held his jaw open despite his feeble efforts to close it while she stuck her tongue in his mouth.

Her tongue explored his mouth, then uncoiled its flat, twelve-meter body and slid slowly down his throat into its new home.

Varicose Worms" started as a title, inspired by the combination of someone I saw walking on the street and a long-standing fascination/revulsion for internal/intestinal parasites. Since I had been immersed in the Ashlu Cycle, in which I had been trying to treat shamanism with total seriousness, for a number of years, I felt like having some fun with the ideas I'd been using and treating them more ironically for a change.

Scott Baker

Lazarus

LEONID ANDREYEV

The oldest story in Blood Is Not Enough, *"Lazarus" was published in the early 1900s. It's about what might have happened after Jesus Christ resurrected Lazarus, three days dead, who up to that point had been a normal man of his times. From this biblical miracle, Andreyev began an incredible story of existential horror, which is more in the eye of the beholder than in poor, undead Lazarus.*

When Lazarus left the grave, where for three days and three nights he had been under the enigmatical sway of death, and returned alive to his dwelling, for a long time no one noticed in him those sinister things which made his name a terror as time went on. Gladdened by the sight of him who had been returned to life, those near to him made much of him, and satisfied their burning desire to serve him, in solicitude for his food and drink and garments. They dressed him gorgeously, and when, like a bridegroom in his bridal clothes, he sat again among them at the table and ate and drank, they wept with tenderness. And they summoned the neighbors to look at him who had risen miraculously from the dead. These came and shared the joy of the hosts. Strangers from far-off towns and hamlets came and adored the miracle in tempestuous words. The house of Mary and Martha was like a beehive.

Whatever was found new in Lazarus' face and gestures was thought to be some trace of a grave illness and of the shocks recently experienced. Evidently the destruction wrought by death on the corpse was only arrested by the miraculous power, but its effects were still apparent; and what death had succeeded in doing with Lazarus' face and body was like an artist's unfinished sketch seen under thin glass. On Lazarus' temples, under his eyes, and in the hollows of his cheeks, lay a deep and cadaverous blueness; cadaverously blue also were his long fingers, and around his finger-nails, grown long in the grave, the blue had become purple and dark. On his lips, swollen in the grave the skin had burst in places, and thin reddish cracks were formed, shining as though covered with transparent mica. And he had grown stout. His body, puffed up in the grave, retained its monstrous size and showed those frightful swellings in which one sensed the presence of the rank liquid of decomposition. But the heavy corpselike odor which penetrated Lazarus' grave-clothes and, it seemed, his very body, soon entirely disappeared, the blue spots of his face and hands grew paler, and the reddish cracks closed up, although they never disappeared altogether. That is how Lazarus looked when he appeared before people, in his second life, but his face looked natural to those who had seen him in the coffin.

In addition to the changes in his appearance, Lazarus' temper seemed to have undergone a transformation, but this had attracted no attention. Before his death Lazarus had always been cheerful and carefree, fond of laughter and a merry joke. It was because of this brightness and cheerfulness, with not a touch of malice and darkness that the Master had grown so fond of him. But now Lazarus had grown grave and taciturn, he never jested, nor responded with laughter to other people's jokes; and the words which he very infrequently uttered were the plainest, most ordinary and necessary words, as deprived of depth and significance as those sounds with which animals express pain and pleasure, thirst and hunger. They were the words that one can say all one's life, and yet they give no indication of what pains and gladdens the depth of the soul.

Thus, with the face of a corpse, which for three days had been under the heavy sway of death, dark and taciturn, already appallingly transformed, but still unrecognized by anyone in his new self, he was sitting at the feast table among friends and relatives, and his gorgeous nuptial garments glittered with yellow-gold and bloody scarlet. Broad waves of jubilation, now soft, now tempestuously sonorous surged around him; warm glances of love were reaching out for his face, still cold with the coldness of the grave; and a friend's warm palm caressed his blue, heavy, hand. Music played—the tympanum and the pipe, the cithara and the harp. It was as though bees hummed, grasshoppers chirped, and birds warbled over the happy house of Mary and Martha.

One of the guests incautiously lifted the veil. By a thoughtless word he broke the serene charm and uncovered the truth in all its naked ugliness. Ere the thought formed itself in his mind, his lips uttered with a smile: "Why do you not tell us what happened yonder?"

All grew silent, startled by the question. It was as if it occurred to them only now that for three days Lazarus had been dead, and they looked at him, anxiously awaiting his answer. But Lazarus kept silence.

"You do not wish to tell us," wondered the man; "is it so terrible yonder?"

And again his thought came after his words. Had it been otherwise, he would not have asked this question, which at that very moment oppressed his heart with its insufferable horror. Uneasiness seized all present, and with a feeling of heavy weariness they awaited Lazarus' words, but he was sternly and coldly silent, and his eyes were lowered, As if for the first time, they noticed the frightful blueness of his face and his repulsive obesity. On the table, as if forgotten by Lazarus, rested his bluish-purple wrist, and to this all eyes turned, as if it were from it that the awaited answer was to come. The musicians were still playing, but now the silence reached them too, and even as water extinguishes scattered embers, so were their merry tunes extinguished in the silence. The pipe grew silent; the voices of the sonorous tympanum and the murmuring harp died away; and as if the strings had burst, the cithara answered with a tremulous, broken note. Silence.

"You do not wish to say?" repeated the guest, unable to check his chattering tongue. But the stillness remained unbroken, and the bluish-purple hand rested motionless. And then he stirred slightly and everyone felt relieved. He lifted up his eyes, and lo! straightway embracing everything in one heavy glance, fraught with weariness and horror, he looked at them—Lazarus who had arisen from the dead.

It was the third day since Lazarus had left the grave. Ever since then many had experienced the pernicious power of his eye, but neither those who were crushed by it forever, nor those who found the strength to resist in it the primordial sources of life, which is as mysterious as death, never could they explain the horror which lay motionless in the depth of his black pupils. Lazarus looked calmly and simply with no desire to conceal anything, but also with no intention to say anything; he looked coldly, as one who is infinitely indifferent to those alive. Many carefree people came close to him without noticing him, and only later did they learn with astonishment and fear who that calm stout man was that walked slowly by, almost touching them with his gorgeous and dazzling garments. The sun did not cease shining when he was looking nor did the fountain hush its murmur, and the sky overhead remained cloudless and blue. But the man under the spell of his enigmatical look heard no more the fountain and saw not the sky overhead. Sometimes he wept bitterly, sometimes he tore his hair and in a frenzy called for help; but more often it came to pass that apathetically and quietly he began to die, and so he languished many years, before everybody's eyes wasted away, colorless, flabby, dull, like a tree silently drying up in a stony soil. And of those who gazed at him, the one who wept madly sometimes felt again the stir of life; the others never.

"So you do not wish to tell us what you have seen yonder?" repeated the man. But now his voice was impassive and dull, and deadly gray weariness showed in Lazarus' eyes. And deadly gray weariness covered like dust all the faces, and with dull amazement the guests stared at each other and did not understand wherefore they had gathered here and sat at the rich table. The talk ceased. They thought it was time to go home, but could not overcome the weariness which glued their muscles, and they kept on sitting there, yet apart, and torn away from each other, like pale fires scattered over a dark field.

But the musicians were paid to play, and again they took their instruments, and again tunes full of studied mirth and studied sorrow began to flow and to rise. They unfolded the customary melody, but the guests harkened in dull amazement. Already they knew not why it is necessary, and why it is well, that people should pluck strings, inflate their cheeks, blow in thin pipes, and produce a bizarre, many-voiced noise.

"What bad music!" said someone.

The musicians took offense and left. Following them, the guests left one after another, for night was already come. And when placid darkness encircled them and they began to breathe with more ease, suddenly

Lazarus' image loomed up before each one in formidable radiance; the blue face of a corpse, grave clothes gorgeous and resplendent, a cold look in the depths of which lay motionless an unknown horror. As though petrified, they were standing far apart, and darkness enveloped them, but in the darkness blazed brighter and brighter the supernatural vision of him who for three days had been under the enigmatical sway of death. For three days had he been dead: Thrice had the sun risen and set, but he had been dead. And now he is again among them, touches them, looks at them, and through the black disks of his pupils, as through darkened glass, stares the unknowable Yonder.

No one was taking care of Lazarus, for no friends, no relatives were left to him, and the great desert, which encircled the holy city, came near the very threshold of his dwelling. And the desert entered his house, and stretched on his couch, like a wife, and extinguished the fires. No one was taking care of Lazarus. One after the other, his sisters—Mary and Martha—forsook him. For a long while Martha was loath to abandon him, for she knew not who would feed him and pity him. She wept and prayed. But one night, when the wind was roaming in the desert and with a hissing sound the cypresses were bending over the roof, she dressed noiselessly, and secretly left the house. Lazarus probably heard the door slam; it banged against the sidepost under the gusts of the desert wind, but he did not rise to go out and look at her that was abandoning him. All the night long the cypresses hissed over his head and plaintively thumped the door, letting in the cold, greedy desert.

Like a leper he was shunned by everyone, and it was proposed to tie a bell to his neck, as is done with lepers, to warn people against sudden meetings. But someone remarked, growing frightfully pale, that it would be too horrible if by night the moaning of Lazarus' bell were suddenly heard under the pillows, and so the project was abandoned.

And since he did not take care of himself, he would probably have starved to death, had not the neighbors brought him food in fear of something that they sensed but vaguely. The food was brought to him by children; they were not afraid of Lazarus, nor did they mock him with naive cruelty, as children are wont to do with the wretched and miserable. They were indifferent to him, and Lazarus answered them with the same coldness; he had no desire to caress the black little curls, and to look into their innocent shining eyes. Given to Time and to the desert, his house was crumbling down, and long since had his famishing goats wandered away to the neighboring pastures. His bridal garments became threadbare. Ever since that happy day when the musicians played, he had worn them unaware of the difference of the new and the worn. The bright colors grew dull and faded; vicious dogs and the sharp thorns of the desert turned the tender fabric into rags.

By day, when the merciless sun slew all things alive, and even scorpions sought shelter under stones and writhed there in a mad desire to sting, he sat motionless under the sun's rays, his blue face and the uncouth, bushy beard lifted up, bathing in the fiery flood.

When people still talked to him, he was once asked, "Poor Lazarus, does it please you to sit thus and to stare at the sun?"

And he had answered: "Yes, it does."

So strong, it seemed, was the cold of his three days' grave, so deep the darkness, that there was no heat on earth to warm Lazarus, nor a splendor that could brighten the darkness of his eyes. That is what came to the mind of those who spoke to Lazarus, and with a sigh they left him.

And when the scarlet, flattened globe would lower, Lazarus would set out for the desert and walk straight toward the sun, as if striving to reach it. He always walked straight toward the sun, and those who tried to follow him and to spy upon what he was doing at night in the desert, retained in their memory the black silhouette of a tall stout man against the red background of an enormous flattened disk. Night pursued them with her horrors, and so they did not learn of Lazarus' doings in the desert, but the vision of the black on red was forever branded on their brains. Just as a beast with a splinter in its eye furiously rubs its muzzle with its paws, so they too foolishly rubbed their eyes, but what Lazarus had given was indelible, and Death alone could efface it.

But there were people who lived far away, who never saw Lazarus and knew of him only by report. With daring curiosity, which is stronger than fear and feeds upon it, with hidden mockery, they would come to Lazarus who was sitting in the sun and enter into conversation with him. By this time Lazarus' appearance had changed for the better and was not so terrible. The first minute they snapped their fingers and thought of how stupid the inhabitants of the holy city were; but when the short talk was over and they started homeward, their looks were such that the inhabitants of the holy city recognized them at once and said: "Look, there is one more fool on whom Lazarus has set his eye"; and they shook their heads regretfully, and lifted up their arms.

There came brave, intrepid warriors, with tinkling weapons; happy youths came with laughter and song; busy tradesmen, jingling their money, ran in for a moment, and haughty priests leaned their crosiers against Lazarus' door, and they were all strangely changed, as they came back. The same terrible shadow swooped down upon their souls and gave a new appearance to the old familiar world.

Those who still had the desire to speak, expressed their feelings thus:

"All things tangible and visible grew hollow, light and transparent, similar to lightsome shadows in the darkness of night;

"For that great darkness, which holds the whole cosmos, was dispersed neither by the sun nor by the moon and the stars, but like an immense black shroud enveloped the earth and like a mother embraced it;

"It penetrated all the bodies, iron and stone, and the particles of the bodies, having lost their ties, grew lonely; and it penetrated into the depth of the particles, and the particles of particles became lonely;

"For that great void, which encircles the cosmos, was not filled by things visible, neither by the sun, nor by the moon and the stars, but reigned unrestrained, penetrating everywhere, severing body from body, particle from particle;

"In the void, hollow trees spread hollow roots threatening a fantastic fall; temples, palaces, and houses loomed up and they were hollow; and in the void men moved about restlessly, but they were light and hollow like shadows;

"For time was no more, and the beginning of all things came near their end: the building was still being built, and builders were still hammering away, and its ruins were already seen and the void in its place; the man was still being born, but already funeral candles were burning at his head, and now they were extinguished, and there was the void in place of the man and of the funeral candles;

"And wrapped by void and darkness the man in despair trembled in the face of the horror of the infinite."

Thus spake the men who had still a desire to speak. But, surely, much more could those have told who wished not to speak, and died in silence.

At that time there lived in Rome a renowned sculptor. In clay, marble, and bronze he wrought bodies of gods and men, and such was their beauty that people called them immortal. But he himself was discontented and asserted that there was something even more beautiful, that he could not embody either in marble or in bronze. "I have not yet gathered the glimmers of the moon, nor have I my fill of sunshine," he was wont to say, "and there is no soul in my marble, no life in my beautiful bronze." And when on moonlight nights he slowly walked along the road, crossing the black shadows of cypresses, his white tunic glittering in the moonshine, those who met him would laugh in a friendly way and say:

"Are you going to gather moonshine, Aurelius? Why then did you not fetch baskets?"

And he would answer, laughing and pointing to his eyes:

"Here are the baskets wherein I gather the sheen of the moon and the glimmer of the sun."

And so it was: The moon glimmered in his eyes and the sun sparkled therein. But he could not translate them into marble, and therein lay the serene tragedy of his life.

He was descended from ancient patrician race, had a good wife and children, and suffered from no want.

When the obscure rumor about Lazarus reached him, he consulted his wife and friends and undertook the far journey to Judea to see him who had miraculously risen from the dead. He was somewhat weary in those days and he hoped that the road would sharpen his blunted senses. What was said of Lazarus did not frighten him: He had pondered much over Death, did not like it, but he disliked also those who confused it with life. "In this life are life and beauty," thought he; "beyond is Death, and enigmatical; and there is no better thing for a man to do than to delight in life and in the beauty of all things living." He had even a vainglorious desire to convince Lazarus of the truth of his own view and restore his soul to life, as his body had been restored. This seemed so much easier because the rumors, shy and strange, did not render the whole truth about Lazarus and but vaguely warned against something frightful.

*   *   *

Lazarus had just risen from the stone in order to follow the sun which was setting in the desert, when a rich Roman, attended by an armed slave, approached him and addressed him in a sonorous voice: "Lazarus!"

And Lazarus beheld a superb face, lit with glory, and arrayed in fine clothes, and precious stones sparkling in the sun. The red light lent to the Roman's face and head the appearance of gleaming bronze: That also Lazarus noticed. He resumed obediently his place and lowered his weary eyes.

"Yes, you are ugly, my poor Lazarus," quietly said the Roman, playing with his golden chain; "you are even horrible, my poor friend; and Death was not lazy that day when you fell so heedlessly into his hands. But you are stout, and, as the great Caesar used to say, fat people are not ill-tempered; to tell the truth, I don't understand why men fear you. Permit me to spend the night in your house; the hour is late, and I have no shelter."

Never had anyone asked Lazarus' hospitality.

"I have no bed," said he.

"I am somewhat of a soldier and I can sleep sitting," the Roman answered. "We shall build a fire."

"I have no fire."

"Then we shall have our talk in the darkness, like two friends. I think you will find a bottle of wine."

"I have no wine."

The Roman laughed.

"Now I see why you are so somber and dislike your second life. No wine! Why, then we shall do without it; there are words that make the head go round better than the Falernian."

By a sign he dismissed the slave, and they remained alone. And again the sculptor started speaking, but it was as if, together with the setting sun, life had left his words; and they grew pale and hollow, as if they staggered on unsteady feet, as if they slipped and fell down, drunk with the heavy lees of weariness and despair. And black chasms grew up between the worlds, like far-off hints of the great void and the great darkness.

"Now I am your guest, and you will not be unkind to me, Lazarus!" said he. "Hospitality is the duty even of those who for three days were dead. Three days, I was told, you rested in the grave. There it must be cold . . . and thence comes your ill habit of going without fire and wine. As to me, I like fire; it grows dark here so rapidly. . . . The lines of your eyebrows and forehead are quite, quite interesting: They are like ruins of strange palaces, buried in ashes, after an earthquake. But why do you wear such ugly and queer garments? I have seen bridegrooms in your country, and they wear such clothes—are they not funny?—and terrible? . . . But are you a bridegroom?"

The sun had already disappeared, a monstrous black shadow came running from the east, it was as if gigantic bare feet began rumbling on the sand, and the wind sent a cold wave along the backbone.

"In the darkness you seem still larger, Lazarus, as if you have grown stouter in these moments. Do you feed on darkness, Lazarus? I would fain have a little fire—at least a little fire. I feel somewhat chilly, your nights are so barbarously cold. Were it not so dark, I should say that you were looking at me, Lazarus. Yes, it seems to me you are looking. . . . Why, you are looking at me, I feel it—but there you are smiling."

Night came, and filled the air with heavy blackness.

"How well it will be, when the sun will rise tomorrow, anew. . . . I am a great sculptor, you know; that is how my friends call me. I create. Yes, that is the word . . . but I need daylight. I give life to the cold marble, I melt sonorous bronze in fire, in bright hot fire. . . . Why did you touch me with your hand?"

"Come," said Lazarus. "You are my guest."

They went to the house. And a long night enveloped the earth.

The slave, seeing that his master did not come, went to seek him, when the sun was already high in the sky. And he beheld his master side by side with Lazarus: In profound silence they were sitting right under the dazzling and scorching rays of the sun and looking upward. The slave began to weep and cried out: "My master, what has befallen you, master?"

The very same day the sculptor left for Rome. On the way Aurelius was pensive and taciturn, staring attentively at everything—the men, the ship, the sea, as if trying to retain something. On the high sea a storm burst upon them, and all through it Aurelius stayed on the deck and eagerly scanned the seas looming near and sinking with a dull boom.

At home his friends were frightened at the change which had taken place in Aurelius, but he calmed them, saying meaningly: "I have found it."

And without changing the dusty clothes he wore on his journey, he fell to work, and the marble obediently resounded under his sonorous hammer. Long and eagerly he worked, admitting no one, until one morning he announced that the work was ready and ordered his friends to be summoned, severe critics and connoisseurs of art. And to meet them he put on bright and gorgeous garments, that glittered with yellow gold—and scarlet byssus.

"Here is my work," said he thoughtfully.

His friends glanced, and a shadow of profound sorrow covered their faces. It was something monstrous, deprived of all the lines and shapes familiar to the eye, but not without a hint at some new, strange image.

On a thin, crooked twig, or rather on an ugly likeness of a twig, rested askew a blind, ugly, shapeless, outspread mass of something utterly and inconceivably distorted, a mad heap of wild and bizarre fragments, all feebly and vainly striving to part from one another. And, as if by chance, beneath one of the wildly-rent salients a butterfly was chiseled with divine skill, all airy loveliness, delicacy, and beauty with transparent wings, which seemed to tremble with an impotent desire to take flight.

"Wherefore this wonderful butterfly, Aurelius?" said somebody falteringly.

But it was necessary to tell the truth, and one of his friends who loved him best said firmly: "This is ugly, my poor friend. It must be destroyed. Give me the hammer."

And with two strokes he broke the monstrous mass into pieces, leaving only the infinitely delicate butterfly untouched.

From that time on Aurelius created nothing. With profound indifference he looked at marble and bronze, and on his former divine works, where everlasting beauty rested. With the purpose of arousing his former fervent passion for work and awakening his deadened soul, his friends took him to see other artists' beautiful works, but he remained indifferent as before, and the smile did not warm up his tightened lips. And only after listening to lengthy talks about beauty, he would retort wearily and indolently: "But all this is a lie."

By day, when the sun was shining, he went into his magnificent, skillfully built garden, and having found a place without a shadow, he exposed his bare head to the glare and heat. Red and white butterflies fluttered around; from the crooked lips of a drunken satyr, water streamed down with a splash into a marble cistern, but he sat motionless and silent, like a pallid reflection of him who, in the far-off distance, at the very gates of the stony desert, sat under the fiery sun.

And now it came to pass that the great, deified Augustus himself summoned Lazarus. The imperial messengers dressed him gorgeously, in solemn nuptial clothes, as if Time had legalized them, and he was to remain until his very death the bridegroom of an unknown bride. It was as if an old, rotting coffin had been gilded and furnished with new, gay tassels. And men, all in trim and bright attire, rode after him, as if in bridal procession indeed, and those foremost trumpeted loudly, bidding people to clear the way for the emperor's messengers. But Lazarus' way was deserted: His native land cursed the hateful name of him who had miraculously risen from the dead, and people scattered at the very news of his appalling approach. The solitary voice of the brass trumpets sounded in the motionless air, and the wilderness alone responded with its languid echo.

Then Lazarus went by sea. And his was the most magnificently arrayed and the most mournful ship that ever mirrored itself in the azure waves of the Mediterranean Sea. Many were the travelers aboard, but like a tomb was the ship, all silence and stillness, and the despairing water sobbed at the steep, proudly curved prow. All alone sat Lazarus exposing his head to the blaze of the sun, silently listening to the murmur and splash of the wavelets, and afar seamen and messengers were sitting, a vague group of weary shadows. Had the thunder burst and the wind attacked the red sails, the ships would probably have perished, for none of those aboard had either the will or the strength to struggle for life. With a supreme effort some mariners would reach the board and eagerly scan the blue, transparent deep, hoping to see a naiad's pink shoulder flash in the hollow of an azure wave, or a drunken gay centaur dash along and in frenzy splash the wave with his hoof. But the sea was like a wilderness, and the deep was dumb and deserted.

With utter indifference Lazarus set his feet on the street of the eternal city, as if all her wealth, all the magnificence of her palaces built by

141

giants, all the resplendence, beauty, and music of her refined life were but the echo of the wind in the desert quicksand. Chariots were dashing, and along the streets were moving crowds of strong, fair, proud builders of the eternal city and haughty participants in her life; a song sounded; fountains and women laughed a pearly laughter; drunken philosophers harangued, and the sober listened to them with a smile; hoofs struck the stone pavements. And surrounded by cheerful noise, a stout, heavy man was moving, a cold spot of silence and despair, and on his way he sowed disgust, anger, and vague, gnawing weariness. Who dares to be sad in Rome? the citizens wondered indignantly, and frowned. In two days the entire city already knew *all* about him who had miraculously risen from the dead, and shunned him shyly.

But some daring people there were, who wanted to test their strength, and Lazarus obeyed their imprudent summons. Kept busy by state affairs, the emperor constantly delayed the reception, and seven days did he who had risen from the dead go about visiting others.

And Lazarus came to a cheerful Epicurean, and the host met him with laughter: "Drink, Lazarus, drink!" he shouted. "Would not Augustus laugh to see you drunk?"

And half-naked drunken women laughed, and rose petals fell on Lazarus' blue hands. But then the Epicurean looked into Lazarus' eyes and his gaiety ended forever. Drunkard remained he for the rest of his life; never did he drink, yet forever was he drunk. But instead of the gay revery which wine brings with it, frightful dreams began to haunt him, the sole food of his stricken spirit. Day and night he lived the poisonous vapors of his nightmares, and Death itself was not more frightful than its raving, monstrous forerunners.

And Lazarus came to a youth and his beloved, who loved each other and were most beautiful in their passions. Proudly and strongly embracing his love, the youth said with serene regret: "Look at us Lazarus, and share our joy. Is there anything stronger than love?"

And Lazarus looked. And for the rest of their life they kept loving each other, but their passion grew gloomy and joyless, like those funeral cypresses whose roots feed on the decay of the graves and whose black summits in a still evening hour seek in vain to reach the sky. Thrown by the unknown forces of life into each other's embraces, they mingled tears with kisses, voluptuous pleasures with pain, and they felt themselves doubly slaves, obedient slaves to life, and patient servants of the silent Nothingness. Ever united, ever severed, they blazed like sparks and like sparks lost themselves in the boundless Dark.

And Lazarus came to a haughty sage, and the sage said to him: "I know all the horrors you can reveal to me. Is there anything you can frighten me with?"

But before long the sage felt that the knowledge of horror was far from being the horror itself, and that the vision of Death was not Death. And he felt that wisdom and folly are equal before the face of Infinity, for Infinity knows them not. And it vanished, the dividing-line between knowledge and ignorance, truth and falsehood, top and bottom, and the shapeless thought hung suspended in the void. Then the sage clutched his gray head and cried out frantically: "I can not think! I can not think!"

Thus under the indifferent glance for him, who miraculously had risen from the dead, perished everything that asserts life, its significance and joys. And it was suggested that it was dangerous to let him see the emperor, that it was better to kill him, and having buried him secretly, to tell the emperor that he had disappeared no one knew whither. Already swords were being whetted and youths devoted to the public welfare prepared for the murder, when Augustus ordered Lazarus to be brought before him next morning, thus destroying the cruel plans.

If there was no way of getting rid of Lazarus, at least it was possible to soften the terrible impression his face produced. With this in view, skillful painters, barbers, and artists were summoned, and all night long they were busy over Lazarus' head. They cropped his beard, curled it, and gave it a tidy, agreeable appearance. By means of paints they concealed the corpselike blueness of his hands and face. Repulsive were the wrinkles of suffering that furrowed his old face, and they were puttied, painted, and smoothed; then, over the smooth background, wrinkles of good-tempered laughter and pleasant carefree mirth were skillfully painted with fine brushes.

Lazarus submitted indifferently to everything that was done to him. Soon he was turned into a becomingly stout, venerable old man, into a quiet and kind grandfather of numerous offspring. It seemed that the smile, with which only a while ago he was spinning funny yarns, was still lingering on his lips and that in the corner of his eye serene tenderness was hiding, the companion of old age. But people did not dare change his nuptial garments, and they could not change his eyes, two dark and frightful glasses through which the unknowable Yonder looked at men.

Lazarus was not moved by the magnificence of the imperial palace. It was as if he saw no difference between the crumbling house, closely pressed by the desert, and the stone palace, solid and fair, and indifferently he passed into it. The hard marble of the floors under his feet grew similar to the quicksand of the desert, and the multitude of richly dressed and haughty men became like void air under his glance. No one looked into his face, as Lazarus passed by, fearing to fall under the appalling influence of his eyes; but when the sound of his heavy footsteps had sufficiently died down, the courtiers raised their heads and with fearful curiosity examined the figure of a stout, tall, slightly bent old man, who was slowly penetrating into the very heart of the imperial palace. Were Death itself passing, it would be faced with no greater fear: For until then the dead alone knew Death, and those alive knew Life only—and there was no bridge between them. But this extraordinary man, although alive, knew Death, and enigmatical, appalling, was his cursed knowledge. "Woe!" people thought; "he will take the life of our great, deified Augustus"; and then sent curses after Lazarus, who meanwhile kept on advancing into the interior of the palace.

Already did the emperor know who Lazarus was, and prepared to meet him. But the monarch was a brave man, and felt his own tremendous, unconquerable power, and in his fatal duel with him who had miraculously risen from the dead he wanted not to invoke human help. And so he met Lazarus face to face.

"Lift not your eyes upon me, Lazarus," he ordered. "I heard your face is like that of Medusa and turns into stone whomsoever you look at. Now, I wish to see you and talk with you, before I turn into stone," he added in a tone of kingly jesting, not devoid of fear.

Coming close to him, he carefully examined Lazarus' face and his strange festal garments. And although he had a keen eye, he was deceived by his appearance.

"So. You do not appear terrible, my venerable old man. But the worse for us, if horror assumes such a respectable and pleasant air. Now let us have a talk."

Augustus sat, and questioning Lazarus with his eye as much as with words, started the conversation: "Why did you not greet me as you entered?"

Lazarus answered indifferently: "I knew not it was necessary."

"Are you a Christian?"

"No."

Augustus approvingly shook his head.

"That is good. I do not like Christians. They shake the tree of life before it is covered with fruit, and disperse its odorous bloom to the winds. But who are you?"

With a visible effort Lazarus answered: "I was dead."

"I had heard that. But who are you now?"

Lazarus was silent, but at last repeated in a tone of weary apathy: "I was dead."

"Listen to me, stranger," said the emperor, distinctly and severely giving utterance to the thought that had come to him at the beginning, "my realm is the realm of Life, my people are of the living, not of the dead. You are here one too many. I know not who you are and what you saw there; but, if you lie, I hate lies, and if you tell the truth, I hate your truth. In my bosom I feel the throb of life; I feel strength in my arm, and my proud thoughts, like eagles, pierce the space. And yonder in the shelter of my rule, under the protection of laws created by me, people live and toil and rejoice. Do you hear the battle cry, the challenge men throw into the face of the future?"

Augustus, as if in prayer, stretched forth his arms and exclaimed solemnly: "Be blessed, O great and divine Life!"

Lazarus was silent, and with growing sternness the emperor went on: "You are not wanted here, miserable remnant, snatched from under Death's teeth, you inspire weariness and disgust with life; like a caterpillar in the fields, you gloat on the rich ear of joy and belch out the drivel of despair and sorrow. Your truth is like a rusty sword in the hands of a nightly murderer, and as a murderer you shall be executed. But before that, let me look into your eyes. Perchance only cowards are afraid of them, but in the brave they awake the thirst for strife and victory; then you shall be rewarded, not executed . . . Now, look at me, Lazarus."

At first it appeared to the deified Augustus that a friend was looking at

145

him, so soft, so tenderly fascinating was Lazarus's glance. It promised not horror, but sweet rest, and the Infinite seemed to him a tender mistress, a compassionate sister, a mother. But stronger and stronger grew its embraces, and already the mouth, greedy of hissing kisses, interfered with the monarch's breathing, and already to the surface of the soft tissues of the body came the iron of the bones and tightened its merciless circle, and unknown fangs, blunt, and cold, touched his heart and sank into it with slow indolence.

"It pains," said the deified Augustus, growing pale. "But look at me, Lazarus, look."

It was as if some heavy gates, ever closed, were slowly moving apart, and through the growing interstice the appalling horror of the Infinite poured in slowly and steadily. Like two shadows entered the shoreless void and the unfathomable darkness; they extinguished the sun, ravished the earth from under the feet, and the roof over the head. No more did the frozen heart ache.

Time stood still and the beginning of each thing grew frightfully near to its end. Augustus' throne, just erected, crumbled down, and the void was already in the place of the throne and of Augustus. Noiselessly did Rome crumble down, and a new city stood on its site and it too was swallowed by the void. Like fantastic giants, cities, states, and countries fell down and vanished in the void darkness, and with uttermost indifference did the insatiable black womb of the Infinite swallow them.

"Halt!" ordered the emperor.

In his voice sounded already a note of indifference, his hands dropped in languor, and in the vain struggle with the onrushing darkness his fiery eyes now blazed up, and now went out.

"My life you have taken from me, Lazarus," said he in a spiritless, feeble voice.

And these words of hopelessness saved him. He remembered his people, whose shield he was destined to be, and keen salutary pain pierced his deadened heart. "They are doomed to death," he thought wearily. "Serene shadows in the darkness of the Infinite," thought he, and horror grew upon him. "Frail vessels with living, seething blood, with a heart that knows sorrow and also great joy," said he in his heart, and tenderness pervaded it.

Thus pondering and oscillating between the poles of Life and Death, he slowly came back to life, to find in its suffering and in its joys a shield against the darkness of the void and the horror of the Infinite.

"No, you have not murdered me, Lazarus," said he firmly, "but I will take your life. Begone."

That evening the deified Augustus partook of his meats and drinks with particular joy. Now and then his lifted hand remained suspended in the air, and a dull glimmer replaced the bright sheen of his fiery eye. It was the cold wave of Horror that surged at his feet. Defeated, but not undone, ever awaiting its hour, that Horror stood at the emperor's bedside, like a black shadow all through his life, it swayed his nights but yielded the days to the sorrows and joys of life.

The following day, the hangman with a hot iron burned out Lazarus' eyes. Then he was sent home. The deified Augustus dared not kill him.

Lazarus returned to the desert, and the wilderness met him with hissing gusts of wind and the heat of the blazing sun. Again he was sitting on a stone, his rough, bushy beard lifted up; and the two black holes in place of his eyes looked at the sky with an expression of dull terror. Afar off the holy city stirred noisily and restlessly, but around him everything was deserted and dumb. No one approached the place where lived he who had miraculously risen from the dead, and long since his neighbors had forsaken their houses. Driven by the hot iron into the depth of his skull, his cursed knowledge hid there in an ambush. As if leaping out from an ambush it plunged its thousand invisible eyes into the man, and no one dared look at Lazarus.

And in the evening, when the sun, reddening and growing wider, would come nearer and nearer the western horizon, the blind Lazarus would slowly follow it. He would stumble against stones and fall, stout and weak as he was; would rise heavily to his feet and walk on again; and on the red screen of the sunset his black body and outspread hands would form a monstrous likeness of a cross.

And it came to pass that once he went out and did not come back. Thus seemingly ended the second life of him who for three days had been under the enigmatical sway of death, and rose miraculously from the dead.

L'Chaim!

HARVEY JACOBS

A short, deft tale that came about as a result of a lunch I had with Harvey. I mentioned the anthology and he was inspired . . . he says it's about yuppies.

Delmore Grobit, who looked like a sponge with his cratered face and yellow suntan, came early to the Tentacle Club. He settled into his favorite chair, a leather throne near the window, found a *National Geographic,* examined photographs of round Polynesian women, and waited for James Guard. He looked up from time to time, observing other members of the club who congregated around the fireplace under the hanging gold symbol of the fraternity, a huge octopus. The same octopus symbol appeared on drinking glasses, match book covers, napkins and on the blazers of more dedicated souls. Delmore Grobit thought the octopus icon pretentious, ugly, and bizarre.

Today was his birthday. The Tentacles would expect him to host a dinner party later in the evening. The tradition bothered Delmore, not because of the expense, which would come back to him in useless gifts, but because the idea of marking the day one came wriggling and screaming into the world made no sense. It was an occasion to forget, not sanctify.

Delmore looked forward to seeing James Guard. He didn't know if James really liked him or if his young friend's affection over the years was feigned. It could be merely gratitude. James had much to be grateful for. Still, he did send thoughtful presents at Christmas and he surely would bring some token tonight. He never forgot his benefactor's birthday.

The Tentacles' reading room seemed claustrophobic, a sure sign of impending spring. It was a winter room without question, ideal sanctuary on nights when the wind was a scream from a toothless mouth. In warmer months that room became oppressive.

As always, James Guard arrived on time and brought his own special energy. He radiated health and optimism. His assurance stopped just short of arrogance. Delmore appreciated his entrances. He saw a lot of himself in the young man.

"Happy birthday, Delmore," James said. "I brought you this small token."

"You shouldn't have, Jim. But thank you." Delmore's arthritic fingers had trouble but he managed to undo the green ribbon. He tore silver paper off a simple white box. Inside, lying on a bed of cotton, was a pair of cufflinks made from ancient Greek coins.

"Do you like them? They're authentic."

"They are very fine, Jim. Splendid."

"The least I could do."

"Ours has been a satisfying association," Delmore said. "I hope you feel the same."

"How else could I feel? You've given me everything. You've allowed me the best kind of life. I owe you more than I could ever think to repay."

"I'll never forget your face when I made you my offer."

"What could you expect? I was at rock bottom, miserable. I fit nowhere. Nobody wanted my paintings. I couldn't hold a job. I couldn't even afford the razor for suicide."

"Don't talk like that."

"Well, what's true is true. You found a loser and turned up a winner. Does that sound immodest?"

"Why be modest?"

"All that faith. All that money. Delmore, I've asked you many times. Why me?"

"Why indeed?"

"How did you find me? I know you said you'd heard about me. But looking back, I know that's impossible. My talent hadn't even begun to show. I was painting like a schoolboy. It had to be something else."

"Questions, questions. You could never just accept your luck."

149

"Do you know what I used to think? That you were my father. That my nun of a mother had one lapse."

"That's terrible."

"Why so terrible? At least it explained you."

"Nothing like that, Jim."

"What, then?"

Zachary, the perennial maître de of the Tentacles Club, shuffled to where they sat. He attempted a smile.

"Yes, Zachary?"

"I want to wish you felicitations, Mr. Grobit. Happy birthday and many, many more."

"Thank you."

"I've taken the liberty of arranging a small dinner party."

"Of course. Take care of the details."

"And the midnight toast?"

"Ah, yes. We must have the midnight toast."

"Certainly. As you know, it is expected . . ."

"I know the rules," Delmore said.

"I will bring the glasses, the Waterford crystal. As for the wine . . ."

"Zachary, we have time. I'm in conversation."

"Excuse me, sir. Forgive me."

"Excused. Forgiven."

Zachary turned slowly and walked toward the fireplace.

"Jim, I want to tell you a story. Many, many long years go, when I was your age, strange as it seems, my life was full of futures. I had begun my business career and I was about to marry a lovely girl of some means."

"I didn't even know you had a wife, Delmore."

"I did. A wife, a daughter, a house. And plans, dreams, goals. Like you, Jim. I bought a bottle of champagne on the day of my wedding. LaTouer '09, the finest wine I could find. I had planned to drink it on my wedding night, sharing the glorious vintage with my bride. But I didn't."

"Why not?"

"I don't know. I decided to save it for an even more special occasion. The birth of a child. Some triumph. I had nothing specific in mind, you see. A future special occasion. Well, there was a child and there were triumphs. But I saved the wine. Each time I decided to save the wine for

150

future celebration. Even when my daughter gave birth to her first son I postponed opening that wine."

"I can understand. That bottle of wine was a guarantee for you, Delmore. As long as it remained unopened there would be a future."

"Exactly. Do you know when I finally opened it? On impulse. On a rainy night in the autumn of the year. I felt thirst. I uncorked the champagne. No special occasion. None were left. My wife was taken by the plague. My daughter and her child were random victims of some war. Do you know what I discovered when I opened the bottle? The wine had turned. It was syrupy and sour. The lovely bubbles were sludge. And I began to laugh. I laughed at the cosmic joke, Jim. I had the last laugh."

"The last laugh?"

"They found me dead in the morning."

"Beg pardon, Delmore?"

"It's rather complicated. A mere technicality. Besides, I had made provision."

"Provision for what?"

"Always questions, Jim. You have such a rapid mind. Provision for an ongoing. Lord knows, it didn't come cheap. They took the better part of my fortune."

"Who did?"

"The Tentacles, of course. They called it my initiation fee."

"I'm afraid I'm lost, Delmore."

"Wine has always interested me. I'm sure it's because of that cursed bottle of champagne. I'm quite an expert on the fruits of the grape, as they say. In fact, most of the Tentacles share that passion, or obsession. It's one of the few blessings of membership here. We spend countless hours talking of years, months, days, splendid crops, ecstatic harvests, orgasmic testings. I know it is an indulgence but I haven't many."

"Delmore, you don't need to apologize to me. If you enjoy a good wine, so be it. What harm done?"

"Which brings us to the toast. On midnight of one's birthday, it is customary that the birthday boy provide a decanter of the finest wine for all the Tentacles to share. Tonight is my night."

"And I am very pleased that you asked me to join you here."

"I thought about my choice, Jim. And don't you know, I found myself thinking of a future special occasion. That is, I had a wine in mind but

I decided to save it. Do we ever change? I realized that I'd already learned my lesson. No more waiting."

"Good. Live for the moment, Delmore."

"It's not only that. I was displaying selfishness. Frankly, Jim, I don't much enjoy this club. But it has become my family. It would be wrong to hold back on the membership. They demand the best one can offer."

"Then give it to them. There's always another bottle of wine. Think positively, Delmore. At this very moment, somewhere, new grapes are maturing. Maybe this will be a vintage year."

"I'm glad you share my feelings. Jim, you've had ten marvelous years."

"Because of you, Delmore. More than I could have expected of a lifetime."

"Yes. And the best thing is, you *know* it. You *appreciate.* So many of the youth are indifferent."

"I do appreciate."

Delmore reached over to embrace James Guard. The young man hugged him. They had never touched like that. Delmore felt a delicious warmth that reminded him of other embraces. He began to weep even as he cut the young man's throat with a quick slash of his silver pocket knife. Blood erupted from the violated neck. Delmore clapped his hands sharply. Zachary came toward them with the decanter but the waiter took forever. Delmore could not abide waste on such a scale.

"Hurry, hurry, for God's sake," Delmore yelled. "It is a minute to midnight. And what we have here is vintage 1955. December of 1955."

"Did you actually find a '55?" said one of the Tentacles. "A December?"

"I did," Delmore said. "I've kept it for a decade."

"This must be a very special occasion," the member said.

Zachary filled the decanter and corked the wound in James Guard's quivering corpse. Glasses were passed to the Tentacles who came to surround Delmore's chair.

"Actually," Delmore said, "it is just another birthday. Not a thousandth or ten thousandth. Just a birthday."

"Cheers," said Zachary, pouring fresh blood. "To Mr. Grobit."

"Drink hearty," Delmore said.

"I have a March, 1962," said another member. "I've kept her practically from birth. She's a social worker. Charming. I was going to save her for a while longer. But why? You've taught me something, Delmore. An occasion is made special if it is specially recognized."

Delmore had another sip. He felt better than he had in ages. The right wine is full of mystery. He could taste elusive ghosts. Tomorrow he would look for another bottle. And he would find it.

Ellen Datlow and I were lunching at a trendy bistro, and we began to speculate on the possibility of a new breed—the Yuppie Vampire. This upscale American vampire would need a whole new life-style (if that is the word) and a new literature to celebrate new standards of taste. To expect such a creature to be satisfied with old, established blood types was obviously wrong. *You eat what you are.* Or, in this case, drink. This insight caused a vessel to throb in Ms. Datlow's tempting neck and she said, "Write it, writer." Hence, *L'Chaim!,* a toast to the nouvelle cuisine of the dark.

Harvey Jacobs

Return of the Dust Vampires

SHARON N. FARBER

Sharon's story is one of several she's written that use her experiences as a medical doctor to great effect. The patient in the story is suffering from a mysterious, wasting disease. Written in 1980, "Return of the Dust Vampires" is a chillingly unintentional harbinger of the AIDS epidemic.

The man and woman ran across the burning sands, their faces surprisingly blank and unconcerned considering that they were being pursued by shambling, dust-colored monsters.

"I can't go on," the blonde cried.

Dr. Insomnia, leaning on the doorjamb, suggested, "Leave her." But the tall man paid no attention. He picked up the woman and stumbled onward, the creatures coming closer . . .

"Turkey," Dr. Todd remarked. "I'd've left her."

Dr. Insomnia looked in the newspaper. " 'Channel 16: *Desert Vampires,* 1955,' " she read. " 'One star'—I'd say they were being charitable."

"The actor there. Room 418."

She peered at the running man framed in long shot heading toward electric towers. "My guinea pig?" She left the call room and went to the nurses' station, skimmed 418's chart, then knocked on his door and entered without waiting. The patient lay in the patchy light from the neighboring research building. Dr. Insomnia woke him gently and introduced herself.

"Dr. Todd is watching one of your films."

"I'd heard interns suffered," he answered softly.

154

"Why should the patients be the only ones? We're going to switch your shots tonight—no more morphine. You'll get intravenous enkephalins for the pain."

"Enkeph . . . Do they work?"

"They're the body's own natural painkiller. But as one of my profs used to say, 'If enkephalins were any good, you could buy them on Delmar Street.' If you have any discomfort, make sure you tell me before we begin treatment tomorrow." She twirled her stethoscope. The man sighed and obligingly pulled himself into a seated position and unlaced his gown.

She compared the strong young figure on the TV to the frail dying man on the bed, thinking that neither could be the true him. The man had wasted away until he was sallow skin delineating bones. Despite his height, a single nurse could lift him. His body was consuming itself, cannibalizing the muscles. His cheeks and temples were hollowed, and even the essential fat in the eye sockets was going, making the dark eyes recede into the skull.

"Breathe, Mr. Dutcher."

"Call me Rich."

Dr. Insomnia removed the earpieces and stared into the shadowed eyes. "Rich Dutcher—wait. 'Time Seekers'?"

The man nodded.

"Well, all right! You were Commander Stone. I had a crush on you that was unbelievable." She smiled with one side of her mouth. "It's taken twenty years, but I've finally got Commander Stone naked and in my clutches."

He said weakly, "Cue up diabolical laughter and fade to cut."

> I enter my office and Jason is in the comfortable chair, light glinting from his wedding band. Hugging him, I don't let go while he empties a bag of take-out food. Tousling his hair while he steals all the water chestnuts and I say, "It's nice of you to visit. It can't be very convenient, since you're dead," and he says, "Did you return my library books?"

Dr. Insomnia poured a cup of departmental coffee, then went to her own cubbyhole where she looked about the stacked journals, offprints, and half-full mugs, expecting to see Chinese food packets. *The dream's after-glow,* she thought. Slowly she drifted into full wakefulness, to alternate this state with one of zombielike exhaustion for sixteen more hours until her daily three or four hours of sleep.

She ripped yesterday from the desk calendar, half smiling as she remembered the luncheon date with Sean. *Only lunchtime affairs for the weary.* The phone rang.

"I'll be right there," she told the project technicians, pouring another mug of coffee. A cartoon on the office wall showed Dr. Insomnia holding an IV bottle and line in one hand, a Foley catheter and bag in the other, labeled respectively "Caffeine In" and "Caffeine Out."

She read the morning paper as the patients were brought in and interfaced, patient and doctor linked by the machine. At eleven Dutcher was wheeled in—a skeleton, swimming inside an expensive robe.

"You understand what we're doing?"

He nodded. "Grasping at straws."

"You're candid."

"I read the informed-consent information, though I didn't really understand most of it. 'Somatic self-image'—you intend to convince me that I'm healthy?" He laughed weakly. "That'll take some convincing."

"The imager reads off a template—in this case, me—and sets up resonant signals in your body. It's related to the placebo effect and to 'faith-healing.' " The technician began applying the patient's monitoring and invasive electrodes. Dr. Insomnia waved with her unwired hand and continued. "I haven't eaten in twenty-four hours. We'll begin by convincing your body that it also is hungry and can handle food. We can't step up your immune response and start fighting those metastases until you're in positive nutritional balance."

He shrugged. "It all sounds like the doubletalk in 'Time Seekers' or those fifties sci-fi flicks—*The Jellyfish from Hell.*"

"Hey, I saw that," the technician said, threading Dutcher's IV line into the imaging machine. He handed Dr. Insomnia her headphones, then stepped toward the patient, holding another pair.

Dr. Insomnia winked. "Close your eyes, lie still—and think of the British Empire."

She watched as Dutcher relaxed under the tranquilizer injection, the tensed muscles that clothed his skeleton gradually losing their harsh definition. The electroencephalograph showed increasing low-voltage slow waves. The pulsing blue light of his heart monitor slowed toward the steady rhythm of Dr. Insomnia's monitor.

The doctor gazed at an article and found the print slightly blurred. She closed the journal. Familiarity made dissection of the sensations difficult. There was the taste of metal, the itch of electrodes, the tingling of fingers and toes, the warm skin flush of blood dissipating heat acquired in passage through the analyzer. Dr. Insomnia felt as if her intellect were fuzzy; her mind seemed poised on the edge of a flood of memories.

She focused on a brief printout of her own EEG—some decreased alpha, increased beta, a hint of theta waves. She was hovering on the border between wakefulness and stage-one sleep.

"Too much feedback?" she asked the tech, her voice deep and isolated under the headphones.

He scanned the gauges, then wrote on a pad, "Everything checks at this end. You've been working all morning. Maybe you're just sleepy."

The blue pulses of the heart monitor synchronized.

Dr. Insomnia tossed the journal onto the floor to join the pile. She turned off the lights, closed her eyes, and concentrated on the patterns made by the random firing of retinal neurons. She imagined a tree, a glacier, a bear skiing down the ice. She thought of less and and then nothing, suddenly shuddered, and leaped back from the edge of sleep.

"Oh shit," she said, as she had nightly for ten years. "I've *got* to get some sleep." Her bed was striped with moonlight through the blinds. She heard the roar of cars on the busy street below, like surf against the beach, the omnipresent rumble becoming briefly silent as traffic moved on the cross street.

She groped for the TV controls. The picture grew out from the center in an expanding presence of light.

An Aztec priest rants on over a supine, writhing woman in a temple which is a redress of a set from *Flash Gordon,* which is in turn a redress from *Green Hell. You can't fool the doctor.* The entire Aztec nation is a half-dozen extras in loincloths.

"No no no," the woman shrieks preparatory to the sacrifice; suddenly conquistadors enter and rescue her. The dying priest is dragged off by acolytes to be mummified—

"Mummified? An Aztec?"

Jump cut to the 1950s present. A small Mexican archaeologist is talking to a tall American one. "Hey, 418!" It is Dutcher, a head taller than anyone else in the movie, his face young but with the important lines already set in. His head is bent in a perpetual tilt to see his fellow actors.

Everything is formula and predictable. The mummified priest walks around disposing of bit players. It's really trying to get at Dutcher's love-interest, who is:

(a) the older archaeologist's daughter, and

(b) the reincarnation of the princess who was rescued before the first commercial.

"Millions for defense. Not one penny for script," Dr. Insomnia mutters. The spooky part is seeing Dutcher frozen in youth and health. Dr. Insomnia's eyelids drift southward as the hero wonders how to electrocute the mummy.

"Throw in a radio while it's bathing," she suggests, and sleeps.

> Mother says, "Eat. There are children starving in Europe." Dinner writhes like a sacrificial victim and melts. I'm running outside into rain, steaming ground like a tropical jungle, snakes in the banana, papaya, pineapple trees. Screeching monkey laughter. Green hell?

"*Aztec Doom* was on last night," she remarked around the hovering technician.

"One of mine?" Rich asked.

"You weren't very good."

"For what they paid, why bother?"

Again the body snapped convulsively as sleep neared. Again the sad grope for the TV controls.

"It's like nothing I've ever seen before," Rich says over the sheet-draped, desiccated corpse. People disappear from the small desert town for another half hour. Then some teen-agers are trapped and barely escape the monster, an actor in a dust-colored mask and bodysuit. Events limp forward. Rich carries the young blonde to the electric towers while the dust vampires pursue, bent on stealing moisture, flesh, life . . .

158

* * *

Dr. Insomnia sat back, feet on her desk, and contemplated her standard morning exhaustion. Her eyes were red as Christopher Lee's in *Satanic Rites of Dracula*. She'd forgotten the last night's dream before she could add it to her journal, but she had vague memories that it had been slow-going, like a Russian novel, or introductory chemistry for humanities majors. A plodding, sinking feeling.

"Quagmired in a marshmallow sea," she said aloud, pleased to have found the proper metaphor. She examined her breakfast doughnut once more, rotating it a full 360 degrees, staring at the multicolored sprinkles in the icing. She tossed it in the trash can, a perfect hook shot. Then she attended a departmental meeting, nodding sagely when necessary, and adopting an interested expression until her facial muscles ached. She felt as Rich must have, filming *Desert Vampires*, enduring take after take of trying to look concerned while other actors stumbled over their lines and speculated endlessly about the corpse.

Rich's handshake was firmer. "I think it's working," he said. "Look, I'm even drinking juice between meals."

She smiled. Never tell the patient he's fooling himself. What had she accomplished with the other five? Some improved appetite, less nausea— marijuana might do the same. At best, they now had better attitudes.

"I saw *Desert Vampires* last night."

"Not too selective."

"Channel 16 from Las Pulgas will run anything. Sometimes I think aliens have determined that TV waves are bad for us—they'll depopulate the earth or turn us into zombies or something. So the aliens buy up UHF stations all over and beam out vacuous nonsense twenty-four hours a day, even though no one's watching."

He looked thoughtful. "I think I was in that one. Fifty-eight. I played second lead to Gerald Mohr."

She hits the jackpot. A rerun of *Time Seekers*.

"It only lasted one season. No one syndicates shows that lasted one season." She lifts one corner of her mouth, her smile self-conscious even when she's alone with the TV. "No one? Channel 16 must take that as a challenge."

Dr. Insomnia loves the show. How can she not? It begins in Time

159

Seekers' top-secret future headquarters. A beehive-hairdoed woman screams. The sun is preparing to go nova. Dr. Meter—she remembers the runt scientist from her youth—whips out his slide rule—(slide rule!)—and announces that they only have 14 hours, 58 minutes and 32.5 seconds left to live.

But as it continues, Dr. Insomnia forgets the camp, early sixties futurism. She falls back into her adolescence, when it was only the reassuring presence of *Time Seekers* every Wednesday that gave her purpose, like a tree pointing out a hidden path in an endless plain or a pyramid standing inflexible against erosion.

The hero, blue-eyed and cleft-chinned, fights off various fiends, eventually arriving at headquarters. Dr. Meter says, "Quick, Rusty. Commander Stone needs you."

Dr. Insomnia holds her breath as the door swings open to the commander's office. The past, especially an adolescent crush, is embarrassing. She always flinches at Herman's Hermits albums or the execrable acting of one of her teen idols. But Stone is a pleasant surprise. Rich is as he should be, face with definite planes and seams in the black and white. Forty-five is kind to him—the lines and shadowed hollows giving character, while the chin is only starting to fall, the stomach to grow, the hair to disappear. His expression is a studied blank, every word and movement minimal but perfectly correct.

"Shit. He can act," she says, quite pleased that she need not be embarrassed.

He sits behind the desk—"Naturally; he's taller than Rusty"—and rattles through the exposition. The hero is almost out the door when Stone's gravelly voice says, offhanded, "Oh, and, Rusty?" Dr. Insomnia says the words along with him. "All time and space depend on you."

The rest of the show is Rusty's heroics through Tudor England and some primitive jungle planet, as he fights thugs and repeatedly rescues a kidnap-prone woman. Insomnia waits for these scattered moments when they cut back to Time Seekers' headquarters. Dr. Meter paces anxiously. Stone sits on the edge of his desk.

"Time is running out."

"I know. We can only hope Rusty succeeds."

And the tag scene: "You did it, Rusty. The Time president wants to thank you."

"He'll have to wait." Sparkle. "I've got a heavy date in Elizabethan England and I don't want to keep the lady waiting." Sprightly music as he winks and leaves. Stone looks furious but, as Dr. Meter shrugs fondly, Stone's expression melts into a rueful grin. Fadeout.

> Fog and drums. A row of conga drummers along the lower border of Hippie Hill in Golden Gate Park. Am I a kid again or—no, I'm me. Hare Krishna chanters. Marijuana smoke overlying eucalyptus scent. Someone playing with soap bubbles; a large one floats over the trees toward Haight Street, unseen behind, the bubble growing and swallowing the park inside it. Standing at the edge of the bubble, translucent, pulsing, rippling with colors like oil on a wet street. A man sits outside the bubble, his back familiar. I must reach him, reach out, reach through the soap wall . . .

"Sorry we're running late. I overslept," she said, marveling at the words.

Rich grinned. "I get to go out in the sun today. I've got some energy to burn." Enthusiasm seemed strange coming from the still cadaverously thin white-haired man.

"Dr. Todd says you're putting away four-course dinners now."

"First course awful, second course dreadful, third . . ."

"In other words, typical hospital food. I'll see if we can have some better meals sent in. Jeeves?" The technician rolled his eyes at the summons and turned on the machinery. White noise welled up in the headphones. Brains grew still in a semblance of sleep . . .

She wheeled Dutcher back to his room. His voice was huskier and slower than Commander Stone's, but it was sounding closer every day. "The best I can say for *Time Seekers* is that it was work. My first steady acting job after I lost the contract with the studio—I was too tall. Didn't make it as a leading man and they couldn't have a character actor dwarfing the romantic lead. Then I did that awful monster stuff and then TV, villains mostly. I've snuffed more people than Baby Face Nelson.

"*Time Seekers* was just an excuse to let them use their back lot and old props. Mongol Horde with Enfield rifles—that sort of stuff. My wife would wake me from a dead sleep and I'd say, 'Time and space depend on you, Rusty.' The hardest part of acting is keeping a straight face."

"Well, you kept one very well," she said. He barely needed help getting from the wheelchair to his bed. Stone had always seemed in control, sitting impassively as the universe about him rocked with chaos. She remembered adolescent nights, lying in the dark inventing a background for the character, fantasies explaining his imperturbability. She laughed aloud. "You know, I don't think I recognize you except when you're in the background, half in shadow and slightly out of focus."

"That's because the star's contract specified that he be the one in focus."

She went to the doorway and stopped. "Another cherished mystery bites the dust. Thanks a lot."

Dr. Insomnia's body did not rest. Like every body, it ceaselessly respired, digested, filtered, metabolized, excreted. And it served as mercenary soldier for six other unwell bodies. One night it looked at short strands of nucleic acids and responded with interferon. Another night a hapten inspired B cells to gear up into plasma cells and churn out immunoglobins. Or a tuberculin test awoke the cell-mediated immunity and marshaled the killer T-cells.

Dr. Insomnia's body went to war while Dr. Insomnia's brain watched *Time Seekers* and then slept. The roar of traffic subsided on the busy street. Solitary trucks rumbled by, shaking the apartment house. The sun rose over the mountains, illuminating the promise of another smog-filled San Yobebe morning. Light slid in between the slats of the venetian blinds. The traffic built back up to surflike regularity.

Dr. Insomnia still slept.

Desert Vampires as it should be, hopeless and terrifying. We're shot down on some desert planet, Time Seeker uniforms ragged and torn, waiting to die of the cruel heat or alien marauders or indigenous monsters. Commander Stone leads us, torn shirt, scraped cheek, mussed hair. He looks delicious. I'm wearing medic clothes; the others are extras; people from work. "Keep walking," Stone orders, threatens, cajoles. "Toward the hills." What's in the hills? More rock and sand and hopelessness. Someone lags behind and disappears with a scream, us too tired to react. Only ashes. They pick us off one by one in the daylight. Jason dies again. Sean stands there with an astonished wide-eyed look and crumbles as sand. He's layers collapsing one by one, while I hide my face in the tatters of Stone's uniform and his gravelly voice says, "Don't worry. I won't let them get you." Screaming: "They've gotten everyone else!" After all my hopes and expectations, I'm only a screamer needing to be rescued and feeling disappointed with myself. But he seems to expect, to like my helplessness. He says gravely, "They can't get me. I'm a regular . . ." In a circle around us, the sand animates, pushing up into the figures of humans and then shambling forward, solidifying, reaching toward us . . .

She awoke with the blankets on the floor, the sheet's indentations across her face, and the twenty-four hour flu in her gut.

The antibody test results came back later that week. "Just plain old influenza virus, last season's variety," Sean, her lunchtime lover, reported in a disappointed voice. "Any flu capable of downing Dr. Insomnia ought to be a brave new strain."

"I should be able to fight something so prosaic."

"Maybe you're tired."

She shook her head. "Maybe I'm not tired enough."

Two of the six patients were dead. Three more merely hung on. Dr. Insomnia fought skirmishes, delayed implacable besiegers who would sooner or later burn, starve, dig them out. Every day, as dessert, they wheeled in Rich Dutcher, looking healthier with each session. Dr. Insomnia looked forward to him as she used to look forward to *Time Seekers,* a joyful cap to a train of miserable events.

"You need more sun," Rich said. "You're pale."

"Thanks, doctor." She coughed and felt a stab of guilt and anxiety. *Mellow out,* she told herself. *It's not like he's immunosuppressed. In fact, right now his reticuloendothelial system is probably a damn sight healthier than yours.* Aloud she said, "Bit of a cold."

They interfaced with the machine. White noise swallowed the remainder of the morning. She blinked, returning to awareness in the warm noon light.

That evening she reviewed Dutcher's chart. Hemoglobin normal. Lymphocyte count high normal. Weight increasing. Radiology noted no new growths, the old ones decreasing to small scars. On the bottom of one page the intern had scribbled, "Query—remission?" The word was sunbursting through clouds.

Rich was awake and cynically watching one of his own movies. "Giant cockroaches," he said. "I had real ones in my apartment while I was making this turkey. They gave me the creeps—my wife had to kill them. But here I am zapping fifty-foot ones with an electric fly swatter."

163

"Are you implying it's unrealistic?"

He snorted, an old man scowling at himself. "Look at me. That's not acting, it's sleepwalking. I'll never be able to live it down. Fifty years after I'm dead they'll be showing this dreck on the late late show."

"Yeah. Like now, you can watch TV and fall in love with Bogart thirty years after he died."

He looked at her sharply, dark eyes in a pool of light. "Do you always get entranced by flickering images?"

She sighed. "It's so much easier to love people who don't exist. Safer too." She shook her head as if waking to the situation. "Revelations at this early hour? I came in to give you some good news."

He listened gravely as she described his progress. "I'm the only one on whom it's really worked?"

"You know what I think it is? Ego. Only someone with a colossal ego could will himself to health. No offense?"

He laughed. "Don't worry. Von Sternberg said actors are cattle, but we're special cattle. We have charisma. We project. We're immortal. Flies in amber."

She hooked a thumb at the TV. "That's more like a dinosaur in a tar pit. Cattle?" She muttered, "Grade A government-inspected beefcake," glancing obliquely at the screen. Rich, stripped to the waist, was climbing another electric tower. The old actor chuckled and left for his therapeutic walk down the hall and back. Dr. Insomnia watched the tiny man scramble about the tower trying to avoid a huge cockroach.

During the commercial she noticed a spiral-bound notebook on the nightstand. She opened it at random.

I'm outside, running in the rain. Trees—banana, pineapple. (Pineapple on trees?) Screaming noises.

She flipped a page.

The doctor is yelling—she can't make it. I'm shouting "The hills!"

Another.

. . . beside some endless translucent film, and a hand begins to push through . . .

Outside the room, Rich was speaking to a nurse. Inside, in the tube, he questioned a soldier. He was in stereo.

164

I'm attached by an umbilical IV line to the project machine, swinging the cord like a jump rope. Commander Stone sits in a corner, just staring at me. "Quit it," I say. "Knock it off." His eyes are recessed deep under his brow, like Rich's. The technician sits at the interfaced control—player piano, ragtime. Then he stands and flakes away as sand. The cord begins pulling me into the machine. Commander Stone reaches out and he's a dust monster, crudely sculpted sand in a Time Seeker's costume. He reaches out, stops, pulls back his hand, and I'm going into the machine, all gaping darkness . . .

The new clock radio read 5:33 in luminescent figures. It was set to go off at seven. She hadn't needed an alarm clock for over a decade. Her skin felt like burning sand. She stretched to find a good position to return to sleep and felt something warm against her back. A body. She was not alone. A dust monster!

She crawled out slowly, anxious not to awaken the quiet life-vampire, then went into the kitchen and put up water for instant coffee. She was afraid to return to bed.

"It's not a dust monster," she said, mouth dry with fever. "It's Sean, it's got to be Sean. Right?" She was unable to go and check the hypothesis.

The teapot screamed and it was every black-and-white thirty-frames-per-second terrified woman screaming for rescue. It was Dr. Insomnia.

They met in the corridor, doctor and patient both wearing robes and slippers. The walls were the same industrial green as Time Seekers' headquarters. He held up his IV bottle. "I'm searching for an honest man."

She hoisted her bottle. "I'll see your isotonic saline and raise you five percent glucose."

Voice suddenly full of concern, he asked, "Do they know what it is?"

"Not yet. More tests," she replied.

He said, "I'm being discharged soon. Mind if I come visit?"

"I'll be here." *I'll never leave.* The walk from her room to the nurses' station and back exhausted her. She lay down and was asleep.

Running across sand dunes toward the electric towers. The dune forms into a hand that grabs my ankle. I fall. Rolling down the dune into more sand that becomes arms grabbing, holding, smothering . . .

165

Jason, there is no answer . . . All time and space depend on you . . . Time. Time is the dust vampire.

As to an afterword—well, I don't know what to say. In high school my friends and I were vampire buffs; we watched *Dark Shadows,* read Bram Stoker, slept under Bela Lugosi posters. Since then I've changed, realizing that vampires aren't tall, dark strangers who will rescue you from mundane adolescent angst and introduce you to the hidden worlds of love, power, and cosmic wonder. Now, I guess I think of vampires as the things that keep you from love, power, and wonder—jobs, responsibility, mortality, and all the other baggage we accumulate by growing up. Maybe I was happier before . . .

On a different note, I wrote the story six years ago, in early medical school. While the jargon is no less accurate than the scientific details in most science fiction, it is a bit embarrassing from my current level of knowledge. But that's just more accumulations too.

Sharon N. Farber

Good Kids

EDWARD BRYANT

I've found that giving Ed an assignment is the best way to get him to finish a new story. It's worked at OMNI, *and it's worked here.*

It's tough for kids growing up in New York City—the world is a dangerous place and so they become tough themselves.

"That blood?" said Donnie, appalled. "That's grossss."

Angelique was peeking over her shoulder at the lurid paperback vampire novel. "Don't draw out your consonants. You sound like a geek."

"I'm not a geek," said Donnie. "I'm only eleven years old, you jerk. I get to draw out my esses if I want to."

"We're all too goddamned bright," said Camelia gloomily. "The last place I went to school, everybody just played with dolls or talked all day about crack."

"Public schools," Angelique snorted.

Donnie flipped the page and squinted. "Yep, he's lapping up her menstrual blood, all right. This vampire's a real gink."

"Wonderful. So her arching, lily-white swan throat wasn't enough," said Cammie. "Oh boy. I can hardly wait til *I* start having my period."

The lights flashed and the four of us involuntarily glanced up. Ms. Yukoshi, one of the Center's three night supervisors, stood framed in the doorway. "Okay, girls, lights out in three. Put away the book. Hit those bunks. Good night, now." She started to exit, but then apparently changed her mind. "I suppose I ought to mention that this is my last night taking care of you."

167

Were we supposed to clap? I wondered. Maybe give her a four-part harmony chorus of "Thank you, Ms. Yukoshi"? What was appropriate behavior?

"No thanks are necessary," said Ms. Yukoshi. "I just know I need a long, long vacation. Lots of R and R." We could all see her sharp, white teeth gleaming in the light from the overhead. "You'll have a new person to bedevil tomorrow night. His name is Mr. Vladisov."

"So why don't we ever get a good WASP?" Cammie whispered.

The other two giggled. I guess I did too. It's easy to forget that Camelia is black.

Ms. Yukoshi looked at us sharply. Donnie giggled again and dog-eared a page before setting the vampire book down. "Good night, girls." Ms. Yukoshi retreated into the hall. We listened to the click and echo of her stylish heels moving on to the next room, the next island of kids. Boys in that one.

"I wonder what Mr. Vladisov will be like," Donnie said.

Angelique smiled. "At least he's a guy."

"Good night, girls." Donnie mimicked Ms. Yukoshi.

I snapped off the lamp. And that was it for another fun evening at the renovated brownstone that was the Work-at-Night Child Care Center and Parenting Service. Wick Pus, we called it, all of us who had night-shift parents with no other place to put their kids.

"Good night," I said to everybody in general. I lay back in the bunk and pulled the covers up to my chin. The wool blanket scratched my neck.

"I'm hungry," said Angelique plaintively. "Cookies and milk aren't enough."

"Perhaps you want some blooood?" said Donnie, snickering.

"Good night," I said again. But I was hungry too.

The next day was Wednesday. Hump day. Didn't matter. No big plans for the week—or for the weekend. It wasn't one of the court-set times for my dad to visit, so I figured probably I'd be spending the time reading. That was okay too. I like to read. Maybe I'd finish the last thousand pages of Stephen King's new novel and get on to some of the stuff I needed to read for school.

We were studying urban legends and old wives' tales—a side issue was the class figuring out a nonsexist term for the latter.

168

We'd gone through a lot of the stuff that most of us had heard—and even believed at one time—like the hook killer and the Kentucky Fried Rat and the expensive car that was on sale unbelievably cheap because nobody could get the smell out of the upholstery after the former owner killed himself and the body wasn't discovered for three hot days. Then there was the rattlesnake in the K-Mart jeans and the killer spiders in the bouffant. Most of that didn't interest me. What I liked were the older myths, things like keeping cats out of the nursery and forbidding adults to sleep in the presence of children.

Now I've always liked cats, so I know where my sympathy lies with that one. Kitties love to snuggle up to warm little faces on chilly nights. No surprise, right? But the bit about sucking the breath from babies' lungs is a load of crap. Well, most of the time. As for the idea that adults syphon energy from children, that's probably just a cleaner way of talking about the incest taboo.

It's a way of speaking metaphorically. That's what the teacher said.

I can see why adults would want to steal kids' energy. Then they could rule the world, live forever, win all the Olympics. See what I mean? So maybe some adults do. You ever feel just how much energy is generated by a roomful of hyper kids? *I* know. But then, I'm a kid. I expect I'll lose it all when I grow up. I'm not looking forward to that. It'll be like death. Or maybe undeath.

It all sounds sort of dull gray and drab, just like living in the book *1984*.

The thing about energy is that what goes out has to come in first. Another lesson. First Law of Thermodynamics. Or maybe the Second. I didn't pay much attention that day. I guess I was too busy daydreaming about horses, or maybe sneaking a few pages of the paperback hidden in my vinyl binder.

Don't even ask what I'm going to do when I grow up. I've got lots of time to figure it out.

Mr. Vladisov had done his homework. He addressed us all by name. Evidently he'd sucked Ms. Yukoshi dry of all the necessary information.

"And you would be Shauna-Laurel Andersen," he said to me, smiling faintly.

I felt like I ought to curtsy at least. Mr. Vladisov was tall and courtly, just like characters in any number of books I'd read. His hair was jet-black and fixed in one of those widow's peaks. Just like a novel. His eyes were sharp and black too, though the whites were all bloodshot. They didn't look comfortable. He spoke with some kind of Slavic accent. Good English, but the kind of accent I've heard actors working in restaurants goofing around with.

Shauna-Laurel, I thought. "My friends call me SL," I said.

"Then I hope we shall be friends," said Mr. Vladisov.

"Do we have to call you 'sir'?" said Angelique. I knew she was just being funny. I wondered if Mr. Vladisov knew that.

"No." His gaze flickered from one of us to the next. "I know we shall *all* be very close. Ms. Yukoshi told me you were all . . ." He seemed to be searching for the correct phrase. ". . . good kids."

"Sure," said Donnie, giggling just a little.

"I believe," said Mr. Vladisov, "that it is customary to devour milk and cookies before your bedtime."

"Oh, that's not for a while yet," said Angelique.

"Hours," chimed in Donnie.

Our new guardian consulted his watch. "Perhaps twenty-three minutes?"

We slowly nodded.

"SL," he said to me, "will you help me distribute the snacks?"

I followed Mr. Vladisov out the door.

"Be careful," said Angelique so softly that only I could hear. I wondered if I really knew what she meant.

Mr. Vladisov preceded me down the corridor leading to the playroom and then to the adjacent kitchenette. Other inmates looked at us through the doorways as we passed. I didn't know most of their names. There were about three dozen of them. Our crowd—the four of us—was pretty tight.

He slowed so I could catch up to his side. "Your friends seem very nice," he said. "Well behaved."

"Uh, yes," I answered. "They're great. Smart too."

"And healthy."

"As horses."

"My carriage," mused Mr. Vladisov, "used to be pulled by a fine black team."

"Beg pardon?"

170

"Nothing," he said sharply. His tone moderated. "I sometimes slip into the past, SL. It's nothing."

"Me," I said. "I love horses. My dad says he'll get me a colt for my graduation from middle school. We'll have to stable it out in Long Island."

Mr. Vladisov didn't comment. We had reached the closetlike kitchenette. He didn't bother to turn on the light. When he opened the refrigerator and took out a carton of milk, I could see well enough to open the cabinet where I knew the cookies were stored.

"Chocolate chip?" I said. "Double Stuf Oreos?"

Mr. Vladisov said, "I never eat . . . cookies. Choose what you like."

I took both packages. Mr. Vladisov hovered over the milk, assembling quartets of napkins and glasses. "Don't bother with a straw for Donnie," I said. "'She's not supposed to drink through a straw. Doctor's orders."

Mr. Vladisov nodded. "Do these things help you sleep more soundly?"

I shrugged. "I 'spose so. The nurse told me once that a high-carb snack before bed would drug us out. It's okay. Cookies taste better than Ritalin anyway."

"Ritalin?"

"An upper that works like a downer for the hypers."

"I beg your pardon?"

I decided to drop it. "The cookies help us all sleep."

"Good," said Mr. Vladisov. "I want everyone to have a good night's rest. I take my responsibility here quite seriously. It would be unfortunate were anyone to be so disturbed she woke up in the early morning with nightmares."

"We all sleep very soundly," I said.

Mr. Vladisov smiled down at me. In the dim light from the hall, it seemed to me that his eyes gleamed a dusky red.

I passed around the Double Stuf Oreos and the chocolate-chip cookies. Mr. Vladisov poured and distributed the glasses of milk as solemnly as if he were setting out communion wine.

Cammie held up her milk in a toast. "We enjoyed Ms. Yukoshi, but we know we'll like you much better."

Mr. Vladisov smiled without parting his teeth and raised an empty

171

hand as though holding a wine glass. "A toast to you as well. To life everlasting, and to the dreams which make it bearable."

Angelique and I exchanged glances. I looked at Donnie. Her face was saying nothing at all. We all raised our glasses and then drank. The milk was cold and good, but it wasn't the taste I wished. I wanted chocolate.

Mr. Vladisov wished us a more conventional good night, then smoothly excused himself from the room to see to his other charges. We listened hard but couldn't hear his heels click on the hallway tile.

"Slick," said Angelique, nibbling delicately around the edge of her chocolate-chip cookie.

"Who's he remind me of?" mused Cammie. "That old guy—I saw him in a play once. Frank Langella."

"I don't know about this," said Donnie.

"What don't you know?" I said.

"I don't know whether maybe one of us ought to stay up all night on watch." Her words came out slowly. Then more eagerly, "Maybe we could take turns."

"We all need our rest," I said, "It's a school night."

"I sure need all the energy I can get," said Cammie. "I''ve got a geography test tomorrow. We're supposed to know all the capitals of those weird little states west of New Jersey."

I said, "I don't think we have anything to worry about for a while. Mr. Vladisov's new. It'll take him a little while to settle in and get used to us."

Cammie cocked her head. "So you think we got ourselves a live one?"

"So to speak." I nodded. "Metaphorically speaking . . ."

So I was wrong. Not about what Mr. Vladisov was. Rather that he would wait to get accustomed to how things ran at Wick Pus. He must have been very hungry.

In the morning, it took Donnie forever to get up. She groaned when Cammie shook her, but didn't seem to want to move. "I feel shitty," she said, when her eyes finally opened and started to focus. "I think I've got the flu."

"Only if bats got viruses in their spit," said Cammie grimly. She gestured at Donnie's neck, gingerly zeroing in with her index finger.

Angelique and I leaned forward, inspecting the throat.

Donnie's brown eyes widened in alarm. "What's wrong?" she said weakly.

"What's wrong ain't pimples," said Cammie. "And there's two of them."

"Damn," said Angelique.

"Shit," said Donnie.

I disagreed with nobody.

The four of us agreed to try not to get too upset about all of this until we'd had time to confer tonight after our parents dropped us off at the Center. Donnie was the hardest to convince. But then, it was her throat that showed the pair of matched red marks.

Mrs. Maloney was the morning-shift lady who saw us off to our various buses and subways to school. Mr. Vladisov had gone off duty sometime before dawn. Naturally. He would return after dark. Double naturally.

"I'm gonna tell my mom I don't want to come back to the Center tonight," Donnie had said.

"Don't be such a little kid," said Cammie. "We'll take care of things."

"It'll be all right," Angelique chimed in.

Donnie looked at me as though begging silently for permission to chicken out. "SL?"

"It'll be okay," I said as reassuringly as I could. I wasn't so sure it would be that okay. Why was everyone staring at me as though I were the leader?

"I trust you," Donnie said softly.

I knew I was blushing. "It'll be all right." I wished I knew whether I was telling the truth.

At school, I couldn't concentrate. I didn't even sneak reads from my Stephen King paperback. I guess I sort of just sat there like a wooden dummy while lessons were talked about and assignments handed out.

I started waking up in the afternoon during my folklore class.

"The thing you should all remember," said Mrs. Dancey, my teacher, "is that myths never really change. Sometimes they're garbled and they certainly appear in different guises to different generations who recount them. But the basic lessons don't alter. We're talking about truths."

The truth was, I thought, I didn't know what we were all going to do about Mr. Vladisov. That was the long and short of it, and no urban myth Mrs. Dancey tempted me with was going to take my mind off that.

Time. Things like Mr. Vladisov, they figured they had all the time in the world, so they usually seemed to take things easy. Given time, we'd figure something out. Cammie, Donnie, Angelique, and me. We could handle anything. Always had.

"Shauna-Laurel?" It was Mrs. Dancey. Talking to me.

I didn't know what she had asked. "Ma'am?" I said. "Sorry."

But it was too late. I'd lost my chance. Too much daydreaming. I hoped it wouldn't be too late tonight.

Donnie's twin red marks had started to fade when the four of us huddled in our room at the Center to talk.

"So maybe they *are* zits," said Cammie hopefully.

Donnie irritably scratched at them. "They itch."

I sat on the edge of the bunk and swung my legs back and forth. "Don't scratch. They'll get infected."

"You sound like my mother."

"Good evening, my good kids." Mr. Vladisov filled the doorway. He was all dark clothing and angular shadows. "I hope you are all feeling well tonight?"

"Aren't you a little early?" said Angelique.

Mr. Vladisov made a show of consulting his watch. It was the old-fashioned kind, round and gold, on a chain. It had hands. I glanced out the window toward the street. The light had gone while we were talking. I wondered where Mr. Vladisov spent his days.

"Early? No. Perhaps just a bit," he corrected himself. "I find my position here at the Center so pleasant, I don't wish to be late." He smiled at us. We stared back at him. "What? You're not all glad to see me?"

"I have the flu," said Donnie dully.

"The rest of us will probably get it too," Angelique said.

Cammie and I nodded agreement.

"Oh, I'm sorry," said Mr. Vladisov. "I see why this should trouble you. Perhaps I can obtain for you an elixir?"

"Huh?" That was Cammie.

"For your blood," he said. "Something to strengthen your resistance. Tomato juice, perhaps? or V-8? Some other healthful beverage?"

Vladisov apart with her bare fingers with their crimson painted nails.

"Follow running blood downhill," I said.

"Jeez," Cammie said disgustedly.

"I mean it. Try the basement. I bet he's got his coffin down there."

"Traditionalist, huh?"

"Maybe. I hope so." I pulled on one Adidas, wound the laces around my ankle, reached for the other. "What time is it, anyway?"

"Not quite midnight. Sucker didn't even wait for the witching hour."

I stood up. "Come on."

"What about the others?" Angelique paused by the door to the hall.

I quickly thought about that. We'd always been pretty self-sufficient. But this wasn't your ordinary situation. "Wake 'em up," I said. "We can use the help." Cammie started for the door "But be quiet. Don't wake up the supervisors."

On the way to the door, I grabbed two Oreos I'd saved from my bedtime snack. I figured I'd need the energy.

I realized there were thirty or thirty-five kids trailing just behind as my roommates and I found one of Donnie's Felix slippers on the landing in the fire stairs. It was just before the final flight down to the dark rooms where the furnace and all the pipes were. The white eyes stared up at me. The whiskers didn't twitch.

"Okay," I said unnecessarily, "come on. Hurry!"

Both of them were in a storage room, just up the corridor from the place where the furnace roared like some giant dinosaur. Mr. Vladisov sat on a case of toilet paper. It was like he was waiting for us. He expected us. He sat there with Donnie cradled in his arms and was already looking up at the doorway when we burst through.

"SL . . ." Donnie's voice was weak. She tried to reach out toward me, but Mr. Vladisov held her tightly. "I don't want to be here."

"Me neither," muttered Cammie from beside me.

"Ah, my good kids," said Mr. Vladisov. "My lambs, my fat little calves. I am sorry that you found me."

It didn't sound like he was sorry. I had the feeling he'd expected it, maybe even wanted it to happen. I began to wonder if this one was totally crazy. A psychotic. "Let Donnie go," I said, trying for a firmness I don't think was really showing in my voice.

"No." That was simple enough.

"Let her go," I repeated.

"I'm not . . . done," he said, baring his fangs in a jolly grin.

I said, "Please?"

"You really don't understand." Mr. Vladisov sighed theatrically. "There are two dozen or more of you and only one of me; but I am a man of some power. When I finish snacking on this one, I will kill most of the rest of you. Perhaps all. I'll kill you and I will drink you."

"Horseshit," said Cammie.

"You will be first," said Mr. Vladisov, "after your friend." He stared directly at me, his eyes shining like rubies.

"Get fucked." I surprised myself by saying that. I don't usually talk that way.

Mr. Vladisov looked shocked. "Shauna-Laurel, my dear, you are not a child of *my* generation."

I definitely wasn't. "Let. Her. Loose," I said distinctly.

"Don't be tiresome, my child. Now be patient. I'll be with you in just a moment." He lowered his mouth toward Donnie's throat.

"You're dead," I told him.

He paused, smiling horribly. "No news to me."

"I mean *really* dead. For keeps."

"I doubt that. Others have tried. Rather more mature specimens than all of you." He returned his attention to Donnie's neck.

Though I didn't turn away from Mr. Vladisov, I sensed the presence of the other kids behind me. We had all crowded into the storage room, and now the thirty-odd of us spread in a sort of semicircle. If Mr. Vladisov wondered why none of us was trying to run away, he didn't show it. I guess maybe like most adults, he figured he controlled us all.

I took Cammie's hand with my right, Angelique's with my left. All our fingers felt very warm. I could sense us starting to relax into that fuzzy-feeling receptive state that we usually only feel when we're asleep. I knew we were teaming up with the other kids in the room.

It's funny sometimes about old folktales (we'd finally come up in class with a nonsexist term). Like the one forbidding adults to sleep in the same room with a child. They had it right. They just had it backwards. It's *us* who suck up the energy like batteries charging . . .

Mr. Vladisov must have felt it start. He hesitated, teeth just a little ways from Donnie's skin. He looked at us from the corners of his eyes without raising his head. "I feel . . ." he started to say, and then trailed off. "You're taking something. You're feeding—"

"Let her go." I shouldn't even have said that. It was too late for making bargains.

"My . . . blood?" Mr. Vladisov whispered.

"Don't be gross," said Cammie.

I thought I could see Donnie smile wanly.

"I'm sorry," said Angelique. "I thought you were going to work out okay. We wouldn't have taken much. Just enough. You wouldn't have suspected a thing. Finally you would have moved on and someone else would have taken your place."

Mr. Vladisov didn't look well. "Perhaps—" he started to say. He looked like he was struggling against quicksand. Weakly.

"No," I said. "Not on your life."

And then we fed.

There's a story I've wanted to write for years. It's about the nasty allegation that cats left alone in a nursery with an infant will suck the breath right from the little tyke's lungs. Twice now I've tried to adapt that aleurophobic slander into a story. Twice I've veered away from the original concept and done something else entirely. Fortunately, both those tangential tales have worked out fine.

The first time was with a story that eventually came to be called "The Baku." That ended up as a script for the CBS series, *The Twilight Zone.* The finished script was at first rejected; then it was heavily rewritten (by me) just in time for the news of the series' cancellation. What's a writer to do? I turned the unproduced script into a novelette for my collection of original fiction in *Night Visions 4.*

Then I decided to use the kitty cat terror angle for a story aimed at the book you hold in your hands, Ellen Datlow's vampirism collection. It didn't take long before the cats in "Good Kids" assumed a rather minimal role.

Maybe the third time'll be a charm.

I hope so. I think cats make terrific characters; and I'm excited about the cutting edge of contemporary dark fantasy that seems to be slicing away the middling paunch of traditional horror.

In the meantime, thanks to the cats who never did appear on stage in "Good Kids," I got acquainted with SL, Donnie, Cammie, and Angelique. I rather like them and suspect they'll return in at least another story. Maybe one of them'll get a cat.

Ed Bryant

The Girl With the Hungry Eyes

FRITZ LEIBER

"The Girl With the Hungry Eyes," published in 1949, is a classic and will probably never become dated. The advertising industry is still searching for "The Look" to sell products to the great American maw. And with new technology continually being developed, the industry becomes more and more adept at insinuating itself into our lives.

All right, I'll tell you why the Girl gives me the creeps. Why I can't stand to go downtown and see the mob slavering up at her on the tower, with that pop bottle or pack of cigarettes or whatever it is beside her. Why I hate to look at magazines any more because I know she'll turn up somewhere in a brassiere or a bubble bath. Why I don't like to think of millions of Americans drinking in that poisonous half-smile. It's quite a story—more story than you're expecting.

No, I haven't suddenly developed any long-haired indignation at the evils of advertising and the national glamour-girl complex. That'd be a laugh for a man in my racket, wouldn't it? Though I think you'll agree there's something a little perverted about trying to capitalize on sex that way. But it's okay with me. And I know we've had the Face and the Body and the Look and what not else, so why shouldn't someone come along who sums it all up so completely, that we have to call her the Girl and blazon her on all the billboards from Times Square to Telegraph Hill?

But the Girl isn't like any of the others. She's unnatural. She's morbid. She's unholy.

Oh it's 1948, is it, and the sort of thing I'm hinting at went out with witchcraft? But you see I'm not altogether sure myself what I'm hinting at, beyond a certain point. There are vampires and vampires, and not all of them suck blood.

And there were the murders, if they were murders.

Besides, let me ask you this. Why, when America is obsessed with the Girl, don't we find out more about her? Why doesn't she rate a *Time* cover with a droll biography inside? Why hasn't there been a feature in *Life* or the *Post*? A Profile in *The New Yorker*? Why hasn't *Charm* or *Mademoiselle* done her career saga? Not ready for it? Nuts!

Why haven't the movies snapped her up? Why hasn't she been on *Information, Please*? Why don't we see her kissing candidates at political rallies? Why isn't she chosen queen of some sort of junk or other at a convention?

Why don't we read about her tastes and hobbies, her views of the Russian situation? Why haven't the columnists interviewed her in a kimono on the top floor of the tallest hotel in Manhattan and told us who her boyfriends are?

Finally—and this is the real killer—why hasn't she ever been drawn or painted?

Oh, no she hasn't. If you knew anything about commercial art you'd know that. Every blessed one of those pictures was worked up from a photograph. Expertly? Of course. They've got the top artists on it. But that's how it's done.

And now I'll tell you the *why* of all that. It's because from the top to the bottom of the whole world of advertising, news, and business, there isn't a solitary soul who knows where the Girl came from, where she lives, what she does, who she is, even what her name is.

You heard me. What's more, not a single solitary soul ever *sees* her— except one poor damned photographer, who's making more money off her than he ever hoped to in his life and who's scared and miserable as hell every minute of the day.

No, I haven't the faintest idea who he is or where he has his studio. But I know there has to be such a man and I'm morally certain he feels just like I *said*.

Yes, I might be able to find her, if I tried. I'm not sure though—by now she probably has other safeguards. Besides, I don't want to.

Oh, I'm off my rocker, am I? That sort of thing can't happen in this

Year of our Atom 1948? People can't keep out of sight that way, not even Garbo?

Well I happen to know they can, because last year I was that poor damned photographer I was telling you about. Yes, last year, in 1947, when the Girl made her first poisonous splash right here in this big little city of ours.

Yes, I knew you weren't here last year and you don't know about it. Even the Girl had to start small. But if you hunted through the files of the local newspapers, you'd find some ads, and I might be able to locate you some of the old displays—I think Lovelybelt is still using one of them. I used to have a mountain of photos myself, until I burned them.

Yes, I made my cut off her. Nothing like what that other photographer must be making, but enough so it still bought this whisky. She was funny about money. I'll tell you about that.

But first picture me in 1947. I had a fourth-floor studio in that rathole the Hauser Building, catty-corner from Ardleigh Park.

I'd been working at the Marsh-Mason studios until I'd got my bellyful of it and decided to start in for myself. The Hauser Building was crummy—I'll never forget how the stairs creaked—but it was cheap and there was a skylight.

Business was lousy. I kept making the rounds of all the advertisers and agencies, and some of them didn't object to me too much personally, but my stuff never clicked. I was pretty near broke. I was behind on my rent. Hell, I didn't even have enough money to have a girl.

It was one of those dark gray afternoons. The building was awfully quiet—even with the shortage they can't half rent the Hauser. I'd just finished developing some pix I was doing on speculation for Lovelybelt Girdles and Buford's Pool and Playground—the last a faked-up beach scene. My model had left. A Miss Leon. She was a civics teacher at one of the high schools and modeled for me on the side, just lately on speculation too. After one look at the prints, I decided that Miss Leon probably wasn't just what Lovelybelt was looking for—or my photography either. I was about to call it a day.

And then the street door slammed four storeys down and there were steps on the stairs and she came in.

She was wearing a cheap, shiny black dress. Black pumps. No stockings. And except that she had a gray cloth coat over one of them, those skinny arms of hers were bare. Her arms are pretty skinny, you know, or can you see things like that any more?

And then the thin neck, the slightly gaunt, almost prim face, the tumbling mass of dark hair, and looking out from under it the hungriest eyes in the world.

That's the real reason she's plastered all over the country today, you know—those eyes. Nothing vulgar, but just the same they're looking at you with a hunger that's all sex and something more than sex. That's what everybody's been looking for since the Year One—something a little more than sex.

Well, boys, there I was, along with the Girl, in an office that was getting shadowy, in a nearly empty building. A situation that a million male Americans have undoubtedly pictured to themselves with various lush details. How was I feeling? Scared.

I know sex can be frightening. That cold, heart-thumping when you're alone with a girl and feel you're going to touch her. But if it was sex this time, it was overlaid with something else.

At least I wasn't thinking about sex.

I remember that I took a backward step and that my hand jerked so that the photos I was looking at sailed to the floor.

There was the faintest dizzy feeling like something was being drawn out of me. Just a little bit.

That was all. Then she opened her mouth and everything was back to normal for a while.

"I see you're a photographer, mister," she said. "Could you use a model?"

Her voice wasn't very cultivated.

"I doubt it," I told her, picking up the pix. You see, I wasn't impressed. The commercial possibilities of her eyes hadn't registered on me yet, by a long shot. "What have you done?"

Well she gave me a vague sort of story and I began to check her knowledge of model agencies and studios and rates and what not and pretty soon I said to her, "Look here, you never modeled for a photographer in your life. You just walked in here cold."

Well, she admitted that was more or less so.

All along through our talk I got the idea she was feeling her way, like someone in a strange place. Not that she was uncertain of herself, or of me, but just of the general situation.

"And you think anyone can model?" I asked her pityingly.

"Sure," she said.

"Look," I said, "a photographer can waste a dozen negatives trying to get one halfway human photo of an average woman. How many do you think he'd have to waste before he got a real catchy, glamorous pix of her?"

"I think I could do it," she said.

Well, I should have kicked her out right then. Maybe I admired the cool way she stuck to her dumb little guns. Maybe I was touched by her underfed look. More likely I was feeling mean on account of the way my pix had been snubbed by everybody and I wanted to take it out on her by showing her up.

"Okay, I'm going to put you on the spot," I told her. "I'm going to try a couple of shots of you. Understand, it's strictly on spec. If somebody should ever want to use a photo of you, which is about one chance in two million, I'll pay you regular rates for your time. Not otherwise."

She gave me a smile. The first. "That's swell by me," she said.

Well, I took three or four shots, close-ups of her face since I didn't fancy her cheap dress, and at least she stood up to my sarcasm. Then I remembered I still had the Lovelybelt stuff and I guess the meanness was still working in me because I handed her a girdle and told her to go behind the screen and get into it and she did, without getting flustered as I'd expected, and since we'd gone that far I figured we might as well shoot the beach scene to round it out, and that was that.

All this time I wasn't feeling anything particular in one way or the other except every once in a while I'd get one of those faint dizzy flashes and wonder if there was something wrong with my stomach or if I could have been a bit careless with my chemicals.

Still, you know, I think the uneasiness was in me all the while.

I tossed her a card and pencil. "Write your name and address and phone," I told her and made for the darkroom.

A little later she walked out. I didn't call any good-byes. I was irked because she hadn't fussed around or seemed anxious about her poses, or even thanked me, except for that one smile.

I finished developing the negatives, made some prints, glanced at them, decided they weren't a great deal worse than Miss Leon. On an impulse I slipped them in with the pix I was going to take on the rounds next morning.

By now I'd worked long enough so I was a bit fagged and nervous, but I didn't dare waste enough money on liquor to help that. I wasn't very hungry. I think I went to a cheap movie.

I didn't think of the Girl at all, except maybe to wonder faintly why in my present womanless state I hadn't made a pass at her. She had seemed to belong to a, well, distinctly more approachable social stratum than Miss Leon. But then of course there were all sorts of arguable reasons for my not doing that.

Next morning I made the rounds. My first step was Munsch's Brewery. They were looking for a "Munsch Girl." Papa Munsch had a sort of affection for me, though he razzed my photography. He had a good natural judgment about that, too. Fifty years ago he might have been one of the shoestring boys who made Hollywood.

Right now he was out in the plant pursuing his favorite occupation. He put down the beaded can, smacked his lips, gabbled something technical to someone about hops, wiped his fat hands on the big apron he was wearing, and grabbed my thin stack of pix.

He was about halfway through, making noises with his tongue and teeth, when he came to her. I kicked myself for even having stuck her in.

"That's her," he said. "The photography's not so hot, but that's the girl."

It was all decided. I wondered now why Papa Munsch sensed what the girl had right away, while I didn't. I think it was because I saw her first in the flesh, if that's the right word.

At the time I just felt faint.

"Who is she?" he asked.

"One of my new models." I tried to make it casual.

"Bring her out tomorrow morning," he told me. "And your stuff. We'll photograph her here. I want to show you.

"Here, don't look so sick," he added. "Have some beer."

Well I went away telling myself it was just a fluke, so that she'd probably blow it tomorrow with her inexperience, and so on.

Just the same, when I reverently laid my next stack of pix on Mr. Fitch, of Lovelybelt's rose-colored blotter, I had hers on top.

Mr. Fitch went through the motions of being an art critic. He leaned over backward, squinted his eyes, waved his long fingers, and said, "Hmmm. What do you think, Miss Willow? Here, in this light. Of course the photograph doesn't show the bias cut. And perhaps we should use the Lovelybelt Imp instead of the Angel. Still, the girl. . . . Come over here, Binns." More finger-waving. "I want a married man's reaction."

He couldn't hide the fact that he was hooked.

Exactly the same thing happened at Buford's Pool and Playground, except that Da Costa didn't need a married man's say-so.

"Hot stuff," he said, sucking his lips. "Oh, boy, you photographers!"

I hot-footed it back to the office and grabbed up the card I'd given to her to put down her name and address.

It was blank.

I don't mind telling you that the next five days were about the worst I ever went through, in an ordinary way. When next morning rolled around and I still hadn't got hold of her, I had to start stalling.

"She's sick," I told Papa Munsch over the phone.

"She at a hospital?" he asked me.

"Nothing that serious." I told him.

"Get her out here then. What's a little headache?"

"Sorry, I can't."

Papa Munsch got suspicious. "You really got this girl?"

"Of course I have."

"Well, I don't know. I'd think it was some New York model, except I recognized your lousy photography."

I laughed.

"Well look, you get her here tomorrow morning, you hear?"

"I'll try."

"Try nothing. You get her out here."

He didn't know half of what I tried. I went around to all the model and employment agencies. I did some slick detective work at the photographic and art studios. I used up some of my last dimes putting advertisements in all three papers. I looked at high school yearbooks and at employee photos in local house organs. I went to restaurants and drugstores, looking for waitresses, and to dime stores and department stores, looking at clerks. I watched the crowds coming out of movie theatres. I roamed the streets.

Evenings I spent quite a bit of time along Pick-up Row. Somehow that seemed the right place.

The fifth afternoon I knew I was licked. Papa Munsch's deadline—he'd given me several, but this was it—was due to run out at six o'clock. Mr. Fitch had already canceled.

I was at the studio window, looking out at Ardleigh Park.

She walked in.

I'd gone over this moment so often in my mind that I had no trouble putting on my act. Even the faint dizzy feeling didn't throw me off.

"Hello," I said, hardly looking at her.

"Hello," she said.

"Not discouraged yet?"

"No." It didn't sound uneasy or defiant. It was just a statement.

I snapped a look at my watch, got up and said curtly, "Look here, I'm going to give you a chance. There's a client of mine looking for a girl your general type. If you do a real good job you may break into the modeling business.

"We can see him this afternoon if we hurry." I said. I picked up my stuff. "Come on. And next time, if you expect favors, don't forget to leave your phone number."

"Uh, uh," she said, not moving.

"What do you mean?" I said.

"I'm not going to see any client of yours."

"The hell you aren't," I said. "You little nut, I'm giving you a break."

She shook her head slowly. "You're not fooling me, baby, you're not fooling me at all. They *want* me." And she gave me the second smile.

At the time I thought she must have seen my newspaper ad. Now I'm not so sure.

"And now I'll tell you how we're going to work," she went on. "You aren't going to have my name or address or phone number. Nobody is. And we're going to do all the pictures right here. Just you and me."

You can imagine the roar I raised at that. I was everything—angry, sarcastic, patiently explanatory, off my nut, threatening, pleading.

I would have slapped her face off, except it was photographic capital.

In the end all I could do was phone Papa Munsch and tell him her conditions. I know I didn't have a chance, but I had to take it.

He gave me a really angry bawling out, said "no" several times and hung up.

It didn't faze her. "We'll start shooting at ten o'clock tomorrow," she said.

It was just like her, using that corny line from the movie magazines. About midnight Papa Munsch called me up.

"I don't know what insane asylum you're renting this girl from," he said, "but I'll take her. Come around tomorrow morning and I'll try to get it through your head just how I want the pictures. And I'm glad I got you out of bed!"

After that it was a breeze. Even Mr. Fitch reconsidered and after taking two days to tell me it was quite impossible, he accepted the conditions too.

Of course you're all under the spell of the Girl, so you can't understand how much self-sacrifice it represented on Mr. Fitch's part when he agreed to forego supervising the photography of my model in the Lovelybelt Imp or Vixen or whatever it was we finally used.

Next morning she turned up on time according to her schedule, and we went to work. I'll say one thing for her, she never got tired and she never kicked at the way I fussed over shots. I got along okay except I still had the feeling of something being shoved away gently. Maybe you've felt it just a little, looking at her picture.

When we finished I found out there were still more rules. It was about the middle of the afternoon. I started down with her to get a sandwich and coffee.

"Uh uh," she said, "I'm going down alone. And look, baby, if you ever try to follow me, if you ever so much as stick your head out that window when I go, you can hire yourself another model."

You can imagine how all this crazy stuff strained my temper—and my imagination. I remember opening the window after she was gone—I waited a few minutes first—and standing there getting some fresh air and trying to figure out what could be back of it, whether she was hiding from the police, or was somebody's ruined daughter, or maybe had got the idea it was smart to be temperamental, or more likely Papa Munsch was right and she was partly nuts.

But I had my pix to finish up.

Looking back it's amazing to think how fast her magic began to take hold of the city after that. Remembering what came after, I'm frightened of what's happening to the whole country—and maybe the world. Yesterday I read something in *Time* about the Girl's picture turning up on billboards in Egypt.

The rest of my story will help show you why I'm frightened in that big general way. But I have a theory, too, that helps explain, though it's one of those things that's beyond that "certain point." It's about the Girl. I'll give it to you in a few words.

You know how modern advertising gets everybody's mind set in the same direction, wanting the same things, imagining the same things. And you know the psychologists aren't so sceptical of telepathy as they used to be.

Add up the two ideas. Suppose the identical desires of millions of people focused on one telepathic person. Say a girl. Shaped her in their image.

Imagine her knowing the hiddenmost hungers of millions of men. Imagine her seeing deeper into those hungers than the people that had them, seeing the hatred and the wish for death behind the lust. Imagine her shaping herself in that complete image, keeping herself as aloof as marble. Yet imagine the hunger she might feel in answer to their hunger.

But that's getting a long way from the facts of my story. And some of those facts are darn solid. Like money. We made money.

That was the funny thing I was going to tell you. I was afraid the Girl was going to hold me up. She really had me over a barrel, you know.

But she didn't ask for anything but the regular rates. Later on I insisted on pushing more money at her, a whole lot. But she always took it with that same contemptuous look, as if she were going to toss it down the first drain when she got outside.

Maybe she did.

At any rate, I had money. For the first time in months I had money enough to get drunk, buy new clothes, take taxicabs. I could make a play for any girl I wanted to. I only had to pick.

And so of course I had to go and pick—

But first let me tell you about Papa Munsch.

Papa Munsch wasn't the first of the boys to try to meet my model but I think he was the first to really go soft on her. I could watch the change in his eyes as he looked at her pictures. They began to get sentimental, reverent. Mama Munsch had been dead for two years.

He was smart about the way he planned it. He got me to drop some information which told him when she came to work, and then one morning he came pounding up the stairs a few minutes before.

"I've got to see her, Dave," he told me.

I argued with him, I kidded him. I explained he didn't know just how serious she was about her crazy ideas. I pointed out he was cutting both our throats. I even amazed myself by bawling him out.

He didn't take any of it in his usual way. He just kept repeating, "But, Dave, I've got to see her."

The street door slammed.

"That's her," I said, lowering my voice. "You've got to get out."

He wouldn't, so I shoved him in the darkroom. "And keep quiet," I whispered. "I'll tell her I can't work today."

I knew he'd try to look at her and probably come busting in, but there wasn't anything else I could do.

The footsteps came to the fourth floor. But she never showed at the door. I got uneasy.

"Get that bum out of there!" she yelled suddenly from beyond the door. Not very loud, but in her commonest voice.

"I'm going up to the next landing," she said, "And if that fat-bellied bum doesn't march straight down to the street, he'll never get another pix of me except spitting in his lousy beer."

Papa Munsch came out of the darkroom. He was white. He didn't look at me as he went out. He never looked at her pictures in front of me again.

That was Papa Munsch. Now it's me I'm telling about. I talked about the subject with her, I hinted, eventually I made my pass.

She lifted my hand off her as if it were a damp rag.

"Nix, baby," she said. "This is working time."

"But afterward . . ." I pressed.

"The rules still hold." And I got what I think was the fifth smile.

It's hard to believe, but she never budged an inch from that crazy line. I mustn't make a pass at her in the office, because our work was very important and she loved it and there mustn't be any distractions. And I couldn't see her anywhere else, because if I tried to, I'd never snap another picture of her—and all this with more money coming in all the time and me never so stupid as to think my photography had anything to do with it.

Of course I wouldn't have been human if I hadn't made more passes. But they always got the wet-rag treatment and there weren't any more smiles.

I changed. I went sort of crazy and light-headed—only sometimes I felt my head was going to burst. And I started to talk to her all the time. About myself.

It was like being in a constant delirium that never interfered with business. I didn't pay attention to the dizzy feeling. It seemed natural.

I'd walk around and for a moment the reflector would look like a sheet of white-hot steel, or the shadows would seem like armies of moths, or the camera would be a big black coal car. But the next instant they'd come all right again.

I think sometimes I was scared to death of her. She'd seem the strangest, horriblest person in the world. But other times . . .

And I talked. It didn't matter what I was doing—lighting her, posing her, fussing with props, snapping my pix—or where she was—on the platform, behind the screen, relaxing with a magazine—I kept up a steady gab.

I told her everything I knew about myself. I told her about my first girl. I told her about my brother Bob's bicycle. I told her about running away on a freight and the licking Pa gave me when I came home. I told her about shipping to South America and the blue sky at night. I told her about Betty. I told her about my mother dying of cancer. I told her about being beaten up in a fight in an alley behind a bar. I told her about Mildred. I told her about the first picture I ever sold. I told her how Chicago looked from a sailboat. I told her about the longest drunk I was ever on. I told her about Marsh-Mason. I told her about Gwen. I told her about how I met Papa Munsch. I told her about hunting her. I told her about how I felt now.

She never paid the slightest attention to what I said. I couldn't even tell if she heard me.

It was when we were getting our first nibble from national advertisers that I decided to follow her when she went home.

Wait, I can place it better than that. Something you'll remember from the out-of-town papers—those maybe-murders I mentioned. I think there were six.

I say "maybe" because the police could never be sure they weren't heart attacks. But there's bound to be suspicion when heart attacks happen to people whose hearts have been okay, and always at night when they're alone and away from home and there's a question of what they were doing.

The six deaths created one of those "mystery poisoner" scares. And afterward there was a feeling that they hadn't really stopped, but were being continued in a less suspicious way.

That's one of the things that scares me now.

But at that time my only feeling was relief that I'd decided to follow her.

I made her work until dark one afternoon. I didn't need any excuses, we were snowed under with orders. I waited until the street door slammed, then I ran down. I was wearing rubber-soled shoes. I'd slipped on a dark coat she'd never seen me in, and a dark hat.

I stood in the doorway until I spotted her. She was walking by Ardleigh Park toward the heart of town. It was one of those warm fall nights. I followed her on the other side of the street. My idea for tonight was just to find out where she lived. That would give me a hold on her.

She stopped in front of a display window of Everly's department store, standing back from the glow. She stood there looking in.

I remembered we'd done a big photograph of her for Everly's, to make a flat model for a lingerie display. That was what she was looking at.

At the time it seemed all right to me that she should adore herself, if that was what she was doing.

When people passed she'd turn away a little or drift back farther into the shadows.

Then a man came by alone. I couldn't see his face very well, but he looked middle-aged. He stopped and stood looking in the window.

She came out of the shadows and stepped up beside him.

How would you boys feel if you were looking at a poster of the Girl and suddenly she was there beside you, her arm linked with yours?

This fellow's reaction showed plain as day. A crazy dream had come to life for him.

They talked for a moment. Then he waved a taxi to the curb. They got in and drove off.

I got drunk that night. It was almost as if she'd known I was following her and had picked that way to hurt me. Maybe she had. Maybe this was the finish.

But the next morning she turned up at the usual time and I was back in the delirium, only now with some new angles added.

That night when I followed her she picked a spot under a street lamp, opposite one of the Munsch Girl billboards.

Now it frightens me to think of her lurking that way.

After about twenty minutes a convertible slowed down going past her, backed up, swung in to the curb.

I was closer this time. I got a good look at the fellow's face. He was a little younger, about my age.

Next morning the same face looked up at me from the front page of the paper. The convertible had been found parked on a side street. He had been in it. As in the other maybe-murders, the cause of death was uncertain.

All kinds of thoughts were spinning in my head that day, but there were only two things I knew for sure. That I'd got the first real offer from a national advertiser, and that I was going to take the Girl's arm and walk down the stairs with her when we quit work.

She didn't seem surprised. "You know what you're doing?" she said. "I know."

She smiled. "I was wondering when you'd get around to it."

I began to feel good. I was kissing everything good-bye, but I had my arm around hers.

It was another of those warm fall evenings. We cut across into Ardleigh Park. It was dark there, but all around the sky was a sallow pink from the advertising signs.

We walked for a long time in the park. She didn't say anything and she didn't look at me, but I could see her lips twitching and after a while her hand tightened on my arm.

We stopped. We'd been walking across the grass. She dropped down and pulled me after her. She put her hands on my shoulders. I was looking down at her face. It was the faintest sallow pink from the glow in the sky. The hungry eyes were dark smudges.

I was fumbling with her blouse. She took my hand away, not like she had in the studio. "I don't want that," she said.

First I'll tell you what I did afterward. Then I'll tell you why I did it. Then I'll tell you what she said.

What I did was run away. I don't remember all of that because I was dizzy, and the pink sky was swinging against the dark trees. But after a while I staggered into the lights of the street. The next day I closed up the studio. The telephone was ringing when I locked the door and there were unopened letters on the floor. I never saw the Girl again in the flesh, if that's the right word.

I did it because I didn't want to die. I didn't want the life drawn out of me. There are vampires and vampires, and the ones that suck blood aren't the worst. If it hadn't been for the warning of those dizzy flashes, and Papa Munsch and the face in the morning paper, I'd have gone the way the others did. But I realized what I was up against while there was still time to tear myself away. I realized that wherever she came from, whatever shaped her, she's the quintessence of the horror behind the bright billboard. She's the smile that tricks you into throwing away your money and your life. She's the eyes that lead you on and on, and then show you death. She's the creature you give everything for and never really get. She's the being that takes everything you've got and gives nothing in return. When you yearn toward her face on the billboards, remember that. She's the lure. She's the bait. She's the Girl.

And this is what she said, "I want you. I want your high spots. I want everything that's made you happy and everything that's hurt you bad. I want your first girl. I want that shiny bicycle. I want that licking. I want that pinhole camera. I want Betty's legs. I want the blue sky filled with stars. I want your mother's death. I want your blood on the cobblestones. I want Mildred's mouth. I want the first picture you sold. I want the lights of Chicago. I want the gin. I want Gwen's hands. I want your wanting me. I want your life. Feed me, baby, feed me."

I originally wrote "The Girl With the Hungry Eyes" for the first issue of a magazine Donald Wollheim was trying to publish. That project didn't work out but instead, the story was published in Avon's original anthology, called The Girl With the Hungry Eyes (1949), edited by Wollheim. Marshall McLuhan quoted from the story in his early (and negatively reviewed) book on advertising, The Mechanical Bride. I later wrote a story called "The Mechanical Bride" as a kind of joke, in response.

Fritz Leiber

The Janfia Tree

TANITH LEE

Vampirism is a recurring theme in Lee's work. In this graceful, ambiguous tale, a woman with no hope invokes a dark god who may or may not exist, just to conquer her own indifference to life.
Vampires often mesmerize their victims with their gaze. In a neat little twist the Janfia tree gives off a seductive, overpowering fragrance as a lure.

After eight years of what is termed "bad luck," it becomes a way of life. One is no longer anything so dramatic as unhappy. One achieves a sort of state of what can only be described as de-happiness. One expects nothing, not even, actually, the worst. A certain relaxation follows, a certain equilibrium. Not flawless, of course. There are still moments of rage and misery. It is very hard to give up hope, that last evil let loose from Pandora's box of horrors. And it is always, in fact, after a bout of hope, springing without cause, perishing not necessarily at any fresh blow but merely from the absence of anything to sustain it, that there comes a revulsion of the senses. A wish, not exactly for death, but for the torturer at least to step out of the shadows, to reveal himself, and his plans. And to this end one issues invitations, generally very trivial ones, a door forgetfully unlocked, a stoplight driven through. Tempting fate, they call it.

"Well, you do look tired," said Isabella, who had met me in her car, in the town, in the white dust that veiled and covered everything.

I agreed that perhaps I did look tired.

"I'm so sorry about—" said Isabella. She checked herself, thankfully,

196

on my thanks. "I expect you've had enough of all that. And this other thing. That's not for a while, is it?"

"Not until next month."

"That gives you time to take a break at least."

"Yes."

It was a very minor medical matter to which she referred. Any one of millions would have been glad, I was sure, to exchange their intolerable suffering for something twice as bad. For me, it filled the quota quite adequately. I had not been sleeping very well. Isabella's offer of the villa had seemed, not like an escape, since that was impossible, yet like an island. But I wished she would talk about something else. Mind-reading, "Look at the olives, aren't they splendid?" she said, as we hurtled up the road. I looked at the olives through the blinding sun and dust. "And there it is, you see? Straight up there in the sky."

The villa rose, as she said, in the hard sky above; on a crest of gilded rock curtained with cypress and pine. The building was alabaster in the sun, and, like alabaster, had a pinkish inner glow where the light exchanged itself with the shade. Below, the waves of the olives washed down to the road, shaking to silver as the breeze ruffled them. It was all very beautiful, but one comes in time to regard mortal glamours rather as the Cathars regarded them, snares of the devil to hide the blemishes beneath, to make us love a world which will defile and betray us.

The car sped up the road and arrived on a driveway in a flaming jungle of bougainvillaea and rhododendrons.

Isabella led me between the stalks of the veranda, into the villa, with all the pride of money and goodwill. She pointed out to me, on a long immediate tour, every excellence, and showed me the views, which were exceptional, from every window and balcony.

"Marta's away down the hill at the moment, but she'll be back quite soon. She says she goes to visit her aunt, but I suspect it's a lover. But she's a dulcet girl. You can see how nicely she keeps everything here. With the woman who cooks, that's just about all, except for the gardeners, but they won't be coming again for a week. So no one will bother you."

"That does sound good."

"Save myself of course," she added. "I shall keep an eye on you. And tomorrow, remember, we want you across for dinner. Down there, beyond those pines, we're just over that spectacular ridge. Less than half a mile. Indeed, if you want to you can send us morse signals after dark from the second bathroom window. Isn't that fun. So near, so far."

"Isabella, you're really too kind to me."

"Nonsense," she said. "Who else would be, you pessimistic old sausage." And she took me into her arms, and to my horror I shed tears, but not many. Isabella, wiping her own eyes, said it had done me good. But she was quite wrong.

Marta arrived as we were having drinks at the east end of the veranda. She was a pretty, sunlit creature, who looked about fourteen and was probably eighteen or so. She greeted me politely, rising from the bath of her liaison. I felt nothing very special about her, or that. Though I am often envious of the stamina, youth, and health of others, I have never wanted to be any of them.

"Definitely, a lover," said Isabella, when the girl was gone. "My God, do you remember what it was like at her age. All those clandestine fumblings in gray city places."

If that had been true for her, it had not been true of me, but I smiled.

"But here," she said, "in all this honey heat, these scents and flowers. Heaven on earth—arcadia. Well, at least I'm here with good old Alec. And he hands me quite a few surprises, he's quite the boy now and then."

"I've been meaning to ask you," I said, "that flowering tree along there, what is it?"

I had not been meaning to ask, had only just noticed the particular tree. But I was afraid of flirtatious sexual revelations. I had been denied in love-desire too long, and celibate too long, to find such a thing comfortable. But Isabella, full of intrigued interest in her own possessions, got up at once and went with me to inspect the tree.

It stood high in a white and terracotta urn, its stem and head in silhouette against a golden noon. There was a soft pervasive scent which, as I drew closer, I realized had lightly filled all the veranda like a bowl with water.

"Oh yes, the fragrance," she said. "It gets headier later in the day, and at night it's almost overpowering. Now what is it?" She fingered dark glossy leaves and found a tiny slender bloom, of a somber white. "This will open after sunset," she said. "Oh lord, what *is* the name?" She stared at me and her face cleared, glad to give me another gift. "Janfia," she said.

"Now I can tell you all about it. Janfia—it's supposed to be from the French, *janvier*." It was a shame to discourage her.

"January. Why? Does it start to bloom then?"

"Well perhaps it's supposed to, although it doesn't. No. It's something to do with January, though."

"Janus, maybe," I said, "two-faced god of doorways. You always plant it by a doorway or an opening into a house? A guardian tree." I had almost said, a tree for good luck.

"That might be it. But I don't think it's protective. No, now isn't there some story. . . . I do hope I can recall it. It's like the legend of the myrtle—or is it the basil? You know the one, with a spirit living in the tree."

"That's the myrtle. Venus, or a nymph, coming out for dalliance at night, hiding in the branches by day. The basil is a severed head. The basil grows from the mouth of the head and tells the young girl her brothers have murdered her lover, whose decapitum is in the pot."

"Yum, yum," said Isabella. "Well Alec will know about the Janfia. I'll get him to tell you when you come to dinner tomorrow."

I smiled again. Alec and I made great efforts to get along with each other, for Isabella's sake. We both found it difficult. He did not like me, and I, reciprocating, had come to dislike him in turn. Now our only bond, aside from Isabella, was natural sympathy at the irritation endured in the presence of the other.

As I said good-bye to Isabella, I was already wondering how I could get out of the dinner.

I spent the rest of the afternoon unpacking and organizing myself for my stay, swimming all the while in amber light, pausing frequently to gaze out across the pines, the sea of olive groves. A little orange church rose in the distance, and a sprawling farm with Roman roofs. The town was already well-lost in purple shadow. I began, from the sheer charm of it, to have moments of pleasure. I had dreaded their advent, but received them mutely. It was all right, it was all right to feel this mindless animal sweetness. It did not interfere with the other things, the darkness, the sword hanging by a thread. I had accepted that, that it was above me, then why trouble with it.

But I began to feel well, I began to feel all the chances were not gone. I risked red wine and ate my supper greedily, enjoying being waited on.

During the night, not thinking to sleep in the strange bed, I slept a long while. When I woke once, there was an extraordinary floating presence in the bedroom. It was the perfume of the Janfia tree, entering the open shutters from the veranda below. It must stand directly beneath my window. Mine was the open way it had been placed to favor. How deep and strangely clear was the scent.

When I woke in the morning, the scent had gone, and my stomach was full of knots of pain and ghastly nausea. The long journey, the heat, the rich food, the wine. Nevertheless, it gave me my excuse to avoid the unwanted dinner with Isabella and Alec.

I called her about eleven o'clock. She commiserated. What could she say? I must rest and take care, and we would all meet further along the week.

In the afternoon, when I was beginning to feel better, she woke me from a long hot doze with two plastic containers of local yogurt, which would apparently do wonders for me.

"I'll only stay a moment. God, you do look pale. Haven't you got something to take for it?"

"Yes. I've taken it."

"Well. Try the yogurt, too."

"As soon as I can manage anything, I'll try the yogurt."

"By the way," she said, "I can tell you the story of the Janfia now." She stood in the bedroom window, looking out and down at it. "It's extremely sinister. Are you up to it, I wonder?"

"Tell me, and see."

Although I had not wanted the interruption, now it had arrived, I was oddly loath to let her go. I wished she would have stayed and had dinner with me herself, alone. Isabella had always tried to be kind to me. Then again, I was useless with people now. I could relate to no one, could not give them any quarter. I would be better off on my own.

"Well it seems there was a poet, young and handsome, for whose verses princes would pay in gold."

"Those were the days," I said idly.

"Come, it was the fifteenth century. No sewers, no antibiotics, only superstition and gold could get you by."

"You sound nostalgic, Isabella."

"Shush now. He used to roam the countryside, the young poet, looking for inspiration, doubtless finding it with shepherdesses, or whatever they had here then. One dusk he smelled an exquisite fragrance, and searching for its source, came on a bush of pale opening flowers. So enamoured was he of the perfume, that he dug up the bush, took it home with him, and planted it in a pot on the balcony outside his room. Here it grew into a tree, and here the poet, dreaming, would sit all afternoon, and when night fell and the moon rose, he would carry his mattress on to the balcony, and go to sleep under the moon-shade of the tree's foliage."

Isabella broke off. Already falling into the idiom, she said, "Am I going to write this, or are you?"

"I'm too tired to write nowadays. And anyway, I can't sell anything. You do it."

"We'll see. After all the trouble I had with that cow of an editor over my last—"

"And meantime, finish the story, Isabella."

Isabella beamed.

She told me, it began to be noticed that the poet was very wan, very thin, very listless. That he no longer wrote a line, and soon all he did was to sit all day and lie all night long by the tree. His companions looked in vain for him in the taverns and his patrons looked in vain for his verse. Finally a very great prince, the lord of the town, went himself to the poet's room. Here, to his dismay, he found the poet stretched out under the tree. It was close to evening, the evening star stood in the sky and the young moon was shining in through the leaves of the Janfia tree upon the poet's white face which was now little better than a beautiful skull. He seemed near to death, which the prince's physicians, being called in, confirmed. "How," cried the prince, in grief, "have you come to this condition?" Then, though it was not likely to restore him, he begged the poet to allow them to take him to some more comfortable spot. The poet refused. "Life is nothing to me now," he said. And he asked the prince to leave him, for the night was approaching and he wished to be alone.

The prince was at once suspicious. He sent the whole company away, and only he returned with stealth, and hid himself in the poet's room, to see what went on.

Sure enough, at midnight, when the sky was black and the moon rode high, there came a gentle rustling in the leaves of the Janfia. Presently there stepped forth into the moonlight a young man, dark-haired and pale of skin, clothed in garments that seemed woven of the foliage of the tree itself. And he, bending over the poet, kissed him, and the poet stretched up his arms. And what the prince then witnessed filled him with abysmal terror, for not only was it a demon he watched, but one which performed acts utterly proscribed by mother church. Eventually overcome, the prince lost consciousness. When he roused, the dawn was breaking, the tree stood scentless and empty, and the poet, lying alone, was dead.

"So naturally," said Isabella, with relish, "there was a cry of witchcraft, and the priests came and the tree was burned to cinders. All but for one tiny piece that the prince found, to his astonishment, he had broken off. Long after the poet had been buried, in unhallowed ground, the prince kept this little piece of the Janfia tree, and eventually thinking it dead, he threw it from his window out into the garden of his palace."

She looked at me.

"Where it grew," I said, "watered only by the rain, and nurtured only by the glow of the moon by night."

"Until an evening came," said Isabella, "when the prince, overcome by a strange longing, sat brooding in his chair. And all at once an amazing perfume filled the air, so mysterious, so irresistible, he dared not even turn his head to see what it portended. And as he sat thus, a shadow fell across his shoulder on to the floor in front of him, and then a quiet, leaf-cool hand was laid upon his neck."

She and I burst out laughing.

"Gorgeous," I said. "Erotic, gothic, perverse, Wildean, Freudian. Yes."

"Now tell me you won't write it."

I shook my head. "No. Maybe later, sometime. If you don't. But your story still doesn't explain the name, does it?"

"Alec said it might be something to do with Janus being the male form of the name Diana—the moon and the night. But it's tenuous. Oh," she said, "you do look so much better."

Thereby reminding me that I was ill, and that the sword still hung by its hair, and that all we had shared was a derivative little horror story from the back hills.

"Are you sure you can't manage dinner?" she said.

"Probably could. Then I'd regret it. No, thank you. Just for now, I'll stick to that yogurt, or it to me, whatever it does."

"All right. Well, I must dash. I'll call you tomorrow."

I had come to the villa for solitude in a different climate, but learned, of course, that climate is climate, and that solitude too is always precisely and only that. In my case, the desire to be alone was simply the horror of not being so. Besides, I never was alone, dogged by the sick, discontented, and unshakable companions of my body, my own restless mind.

The sun was wonderful, and the place was beautiful, but I quickly realized I did not know what to do with the sun and the beauty. I needed to translate them, perhaps, into words, certainly into feelings, but neither would respond as I wished. I kept a desultory journal, then gave it up. I read and soon found I could not control my eyes enough to get them to focus on the pages. On the third evening, I went to dinner with Isabella and Alec, did my best, watched Alec do his best, came back a little drunk, more ill in soul than in body. Disgraced myself in private by weeping.

Finally, the scent of the Janfia tree, coming in such tides into the room, drew me to the window.

I stood there, looking down at the veranda, the far-away hills beyond described only by starlight, the black tree much nearer, with here and there its moonburst of smoky white, an open flower.

And I thought about the poet, and the incubus that was the spirit of the tree. It was the hour to think of that. A demon which vampirized and killed by irresistible pleasures of the flesh. What an entirely enchanting thought. After all, life itself vampirized, and ultimately killed, did it not, by a constant equally irresistible, administration of the exact reverse of pleasure.

But since I had no longer any belief in God, I had lost all hopes of anything supernatural abroad in the universe. There was evil, naturally, in its abstract or human incarnations, but nothing artistic, no demons stepping from trees by night.

Just then, the leaves of the Janfia rustled. Some night breeze was passing through them, though not, it seemed, through any other thing which grew on the veranda.

A couple of handsome, shy wild cats came and went at the villa. The woman who cooked left out scraps for them, and I had seen Marta, one morning, leaving a large bowl of water in the shade of the cypress they were wont to climb. A cat then, prowling along the veranda rail, was disturbing the tree. I tried to make out the flash of eyes. Presently, endeavoring to do this, I began to see another thing.

It was a shadow, cast from the tree, but not in the tree's shape. Nor was there light, beyond that of the stars above the hills, to fashion it. A man then, young and slender, stood below me, by the Janfia, and from a barely suggested paleness, like that of a thin half moon, it seemed he might be looking up toward my room.

A kind of instinct made me move quickly back, away from the window. It was a profound and primitive reaction, which startled me, and refreshed me. It had no place on the modern earth, and scarcely any name. A kind of panic—the pagan fear of something elemental, godlike, and terrible. Caught up in it, for a second, I was no longer myself, no longer the one I dreaded most in all the world. I was no one, only a reaction to an unknown matter, more vital than sickness or pessimism, something from the days when all ills and joys were in the charge of the gods, when men need not think, but simply *were*.

And then, I did think. I thought of some intruder, something rational, and I moved into the open window again, and looked down, and there was nothing there. Just the tree against the starlight.

"Isabella," I said to her over the telephone, "would you mind if I had that tree carried up to my bedroom?"

"Tree?"

I laughed brightly. "I don't mean one of the pines. The little Janfia. It's funny, but you know I hadn't been sleeping very well—the scent seems to help. I thought, actually in the room, it would be about foolproof. Nonstop inhalations of white double brandies."

"Well, I don't see why not. Only, mightn't it give you a headache, or something? All that carbon monoxide—or is it dioxide—plants exude at night. Didn't someone famous suffocate themselves with flowers? One of Mirabeau's mistresses, wasn't it? No, that was with a charcoal brazier—"

"The thing is," I said, "your two gardeners have arrived this morning after all. And between them, they shouldn't have any trouble getting the urn upstairs. I'll have it by the window. No problems with asphyxia that way."

"Oh well, if you want, why not?" Having consented, she babbled for a moment over how I was doing, and assured me she would "pop in" tomorrow. Alec had succumbed to some virus, and she had almost forgotten me. I doubted that I would see her for the rest of the week.

Marta scintillantly organized the gardeners. Each gave me a narrow look. But they raised the terracotta and the tree, bore them grunting up to the second floor, plonked them by the window as requested. Marta even followed this up with a can of water to sprinkle the earth. That done, she pulled two desiccated leaves off the tree with a coarse functional disregard. It was part of the indoor furnishings now, and must be cared for.

I had been possessed by a curious idea, which I called, to myself, an experiment. It was impossible that I had seen anything, any "being," on the veranda. That was an alcoholic fantasy. But then again, I had an urge to call the bluff of the Janfia tree. Because it seemed to me responsible, in its own way, for my mirage. Perhaps the blooms were mildly hallucinogenic. If so, I meant to test them. In lieu of any other social event or creative project, an investigation of the Janfia would have to serve.

By day it gave, of course, very little scent; in the morning it had seemed to have none at all. I sat and watched it a while, then stretched out for a siesta. Falling asleep, almost immediately I dreamed that I lay bleeding in a blood-soaked bed, in the middle of a busy city pavement. People stepped around me, sometimes cursing the obstacle. No one would help me. Somebody—formless, genderless—when I caught at a sleeve, detached me with a good-natured, Oh, you'll be all right.

I woke up in a sweat of horror. Not a wise measure any more, then, to sleep by day. Too hot, conducive to the nightmare. . . . The dream's psychological impetus was all too obvious, the paranoia and self-pity. One was expected to be calm and well-mannered in adversity. People soon got tired of you otherwise. How not, who was exempt from distress?

I stared across the room at the Janfia tree, glossy with its health and beauty. Quite unassailable it looked. Was it a vampire? Did it suck away the life of other things to feed its own? It was welcome to mine. What a way to die. Not messily and uncouthly. But ecstatically, romantically, poignantly. They would say, they simply could not understand it, I had been a little under the weather, but *dying*—so very odd of me. And Isabella, remembering the story, would glance at the Janfia fearfully, and shakily giggle the notion aside.

I got up, and walked across.

205

"Why don't you?" I said. "I'm here. I'm willing. I'd be—I'd be only too glad to die like that, in the arms of something that needed me, held, in pleasure—not from some bloody slip of a careless uncaring knife, some surgeon with a hangover, whoops, lost another patient today, oh dear what a shame. Or else to go on with this bloody awful misery, one slap in the teeth after another, nothing going right, nothing, nothing. Get out, to oblivion hopefully, or get out and start over, or if there's some bearded old damnable God, he couldn't blame me, could he? 'Your honor,' I'd say, 'I was all for keeping going, suffering for another forty years, whatever your gracious will for me was. But a demon set on me. You know I didn't stand a chance.' So," I said again to the Janfia tree, "why not?"

Did it hear? Did it attend? I reached out and touched its stems, its leaves, the fruited, tight-coiled blossoms. All of it seemed to sing, to vibrate with some colossal hidden force, like an instrument still faintly thrumming after the hand of the musician has left it, perhaps five centuries ago.

"Christ, I'm going crazy," I said, and turned from the tree with an insulting laugh. See, the laugh said, I know all that is a lie. So, I *dare* you.

There was a writing desk in the room. Normally, when writing, I did not employ a desk, but now I sat at it and began to jot some notes on the legend of the tree. I was not particularly interested in doing this, it was only a sort of sympathetic magic. But the time went swiftly, and soon the world had reached the drinks hour, and I was able with a clear conscience to go down with thoughts of opening a bottle of white wine. The sun burned low in the cypress tree, and Marta stood beneath it, perplexed, a dish of scraps in her hand.

"Cats not hungry today?" I asked her.

She cast me a flashing look.

"No cats. Cats runs off. I am say, Where you go give you better food? Mrs. Isabella like the cats. Perhaps they there. Thing scares them. They see a monster, go big eyes and then they runs."

Surprising me with my surprise, I shivered.

"What was it? That they saw?"

Marta shrugged.

"Who's know? I am see them runs. Fat tail and big eyes."

"Where was it?"

206

"This minute."

"But where? Down here?"

She shrugged a second time.

"Nothing there. They see. I am go along now. My aunt, she is waits for me."

"Oh yes. Your aunt. Do go."

I smiled. Marta ignored my smile, for she would only smile at me when I was serious or preoccupied, or ill. In the same way, her English deteriorated in my presence, improved in Isabella's. In some fashion, it seemed to me, she had begun to guard herself against me, sensing bad luck might rub off.

I had explained earlier to everyone that I wanted nothing very much for dinner, some cheese and fruit would suffice, such items easily accessible. And they had all then accordingly escaped, the cook, the cats, and Marta. Now I was alone. Was I?

At the third glass I began to make my plans. It would be a full moon tonight. It would shine in at my bedroom window about two in the morning, casting a white clear light across the room, the desk, so that anything, coming between, would cast equally a deep shadow.

Well, I would give it every chance. The Janfia could not say I had omitted anything. The lunar orb, I at the desk, my back to night and moon and tree. Waiting.

Why was I even contemplating such a foolish adolescent act? Naturally so that tomorrow, properly stood up on my date with delicious death, I could cry out loudly: The gods are dead! There is nothing left to me but *this,* the dunghill of the world.

But I ought to be fairly drunk. Yes, I owed the situation that. Drink, the opening medicine of the mind and heart, sometimes of the psyche.

The clean cheeses and green and pink fruits did not interrupt the spell of the wine. They stabilized my stomach and made it only accommodating.

Tomorrow I would regret drinking so much, but tomorrow I was going to regret everything in any case.

And so I opened a second bottle, and carried it to the bath with me, to the ritual cleansing before the assignation or the witchcraft.

I fell asleep, sitting at the desk. There was a brief sealike afterglow, and my notes and a book and a lamp and the bottle spread before me. The

207

perfume of the Janfia at my back seemed faint, luminous as the dying of the light. Beginning to read, quite easily, for the wine, interfering itself with vision, made it somehow less difficult to see or guess correctly the printed words, I weighed the time once or twice on my watch. Four hours, three hours, to moonrise.

When I woke, it was to an electric stillness. The oil lamp which I had been using in preference, was burning low, and I reached instantly and turned down the wick. As the flame went out, all the lit darkness came in about me. The moon was in the window, climbing up behind the jet-black outline of the Janfia tree.

The scent was extraordinary. Was it my imagination?—it seemed never to have smelled this way before, with this sort of aching, chiming note. Perhaps the full moon brought it out. I would not turn to look. Instead, I drew the paper to me and the pen. I wrote nothing, simply doodled on the pad, long spirals and convolutions; doubtless a psychiatrist would have found them most revealing.

My mind was a blank. A drunken, receptive, amiable blank. I was amused, but exhilarated. All things were supposed to be possible. If a black specter could stalk me through eight years, surely then phantoms of all kinds, curses, blessings, did exist.

The shadow of the Janfia was being thrown down now all around me, on the floor, on the desk and the paper: the lacy foliage and the wide-stretched blooms.

And then, something else, a long finger of shadow, began to spill forward, across everything. What was it? No, I must not turn to see. Probably some freak arrangement of the leaves, or even some simple element of the room's furniture, suddenly caught against the lifting moon.

My skin tingled. I sat as if turned to stone, watching the slow forward movement of the shadow which, after all, might also be that of a tall and slender man. Not a sound. The cicadas were silent. On the hills not a dog barked. And the villa was utterly dumb, empty of everything but me, and perhaps of this other thing, which itself was noiseless.

And all at once the Janfia tree gave a little whispering rustle. As if it laughed to itself. Only a breeze, of course only that, or some night insect, or a late flower unfolding . . .

A compound of fear and excitement held me rigid. My eyes were wide and I breathed in shallow gasps. I had ceased altogether to reason. I did not even feel. I waited. I waited in a type of delirium, for the touch of a cruel serene hand upon my neck—for truth to step at last from the shadow, with a naked blade.

And I shut my eyes, the better to experience whatever might come to me.

There was then what is known as a lacuna, a gap, something missing, and amiss. In this gap, gradually, as I sank from the heights back inside myself, I began after all to hear a sound.

It was a peculiar one. I could not make it out.

Since ordinary sense was, unwelcome, returning, I started vaguely to think, Oh, some animal, hunting. It had a kind of coughing, retching, whining quality, inimical and awesome, something which would have nothing to do with what basically it entailed—like the agonized female scream of the mating fox.

The noises went on for some time, driving me ever further and further back to proper awareness, until I opened my eyes, and stood up abruptly. I was cold, and felt rather sick. The scent of the Janfia tree was overpowering, nauseating, and nothing at all had happened. The shadows were all quite usual, and rounding on the window, I saw the last of the moon's edge was in it, and the tree like a cutout of black-and-white papers. Nothing more.

I swore, childishly, in rage, at all things, and myself. It served me right; fool, fool, ever to expect anything. And that long shadow, what had that been? Well. It might have been anything. Why else had I shut my eyes but to aid the delusion, afraid if I continued to look I must be undeceived.

Something horrible had occurred. The night was full of the knowledge of that. Of my idiotic invitation to demons, and my failure, their refusal.

But I really had to get out of the room, the scent of the tree was making me ill at last. How could I ever have thought it pleasant?

I took the wine bottle, meaning to replace it in the refrigerator downstairs, and going out into the corridor, brought on the lights. Below, I hit the other switches rapidly, one after the other, flooding the villa with hard modern glare. So much for the moon. But the smell of the Janfia was more persistent, it seemed to cling to everything—I went out on to the western veranda, to get away from it, but even here on the other side of the house the fragrance hovered.

I was trying, very firmly, to be practical. I was trying to close the door, banish the element I had summoned, for though it had not come to me, yet somehow the night clamored with it, reeked of it. What was it? Only me, of course. My nerves were shot, and what did I do but essay stupid flirtations with the powers of the dark. Though they did not exist in their own right, they do exist inside every one of us. I had called my own demons. Let loose, they peopled the night.

All I could hope for now was to go in and make a gallon of coffee, and leaf through and through the silly magazines that lay about, and stave off sleep until the dawn came. But there was something wrong with the cypress tree. The moon, slipping over the roof now in pursuit of me, caught the cypress and showed what I thought was a broken bough.

That puzzled me. I was glad of the opportunity to go out between the bushes and take a prosaic look.

It was not any distance, and the moon came bright. All the night, all its essence, had concentrated in that spot, yet when I first looked, and first saw, my reaction was only startled astonishment. I rejected the evidence as superficial, which it was not, and looked about and found the tumbled kitchen stool, and then looked up again to be sure, quite certain, that it was Marta who hung there pendant and motionless, her engorged and terrible face twisted away from me. She had used a strong cord. And those unidentifiable sounds I had heard, I realized now, had been the noises Marta made, as she swung and kicked there, strangling to death.

The shock of what had happened was too much for Isabella, and made her unwell. She had been fond of the girl, and could not understand why Marta had not confided her troubles. Presumably her lover had thrown her over, and perhaps she was pregnant—Isabella could have helped, the girl could have had her baby under the shelter of a foreign umbrella of bank notes. But then it transpired Marta had not been pregnant, so there was no proper explanation. The woman who cooked said both she and the girl had been oppressed for days, in some way she could not or did not reveal. It was the season. And then, the girl was young and impressionable. She had gone mad. God would forgive her suicide.

I sat on the veranda of the other villa, my bags around me and a car due to arrive and take me to the town, and Alec and Isabella, both pale with convalescence, facing me over the white iron table.

210

"It wasn't your fault," said Alec to Isabella. "It's no use brooding over it. The way they are here, it's always been a mystery to me." Then, he went in, saying he felt the heat, but he would return to wave me off.

"And poor poor you," said Isabella, close to tears. "I tell you to come here and rest, and this has to happen."

I could not answer that I felt it was my fault. I could not confess that it seemed to me that I, invoking darkness, had conjured Marta's death. I did not understand the process, only the result. Nor had I told Isabella that the Janfia tree seemed to have contracted its own terminal disease. The leaves and flowers had begun to rot away, and the scent had grown acid. My vibrations had done that. Or it was because the tree had been my focus, my burning-glass. That would reveal me then as my own enemy. That powerful thing which slowly destroyed me, that stalker with a knife, it was myself. And knowing it, naming it, rather than free me of it, could only give it greater power.

"Poor little Marta," said Isabella. She surrendered and began to sob, which would be no use to Marta at all, or to herself, maybe.

Then the car, cheerful in red and white, came up the dusty road, tooting merrily to us. And the driver, heaving my luggage into the boot, cried out to us in joy, "What a beautiful day, ah, what a beautiful day!"

Invited to say something about the genesis or content of this story, I'm afraid that all I *can* say is that it was based in part on a dream. Perhaps, in the light of the material itself, this is more than enough.

Tanith Lee

A Child of Darkness

SUSAN CASPER

Sue has written several vampire stories, including one about a fat vampire. "A Child of Darkness" is a more serious study of a young girl so entranced by the myth of the vampire that she longs to be one, despite all evidence that there is no such creature.

The air is damp and tainted with the odors of tobacco, sweat, and urine. What light there is comes from a small bulb in the ceiling, its plastic cover green with ancient grime. Voices echo, re-echo along the concrete walls of the corridor until they sound like an old recording. It is Daria's only contact with the world outside of her little cell and she is torn between a nervous desire to shut it all out, and a need to listen greedily.

Far away a woman begins to sing an old gospel song. Her voice is thin and slightly off key; it gives Daria a shiver. *It makes my blood run cold,* she thinks, then laughs bitterly at the idea. Hers is not the only laughter. From somewhere in the depths comes the cackle of a mad woman—and then another voice joins in, slurred, unsteady, taunting. "That singin' won't help you none, bitch. God knows what you are. Whore of Babylon, that's what *you* are."

The singing stops. "What the hell do you know?" a Spanish accent replies.

"Ain't what I know that counts, bitch. It's what God knows. God knows you're a sinner. He's gonna get you, girl."

The accent protests. She prays, sobs, moans, repents, accuses, but her anguished voice is softer, and weaker, and somehow more frightening than the others.

Suddenly, a shrill, soprano, scream cuts across all the other noises. "Oh, the pain. Oh my God, the pain. I'm dying. Somebody please . . . help me."

"Hey, you, knock it off down there," a cold male voice replies.

Daria can see nothing from her cell but the stained gray wall across the corridor which seems to go on forever, but she finds that if she presses herself into the corner, she can just make out the place where the hallway ends on one side. A guard is sitting there. He is eating a sandwich that he peels from a wax-paper bag as if it were a banana. A Styrofoam cup is perched on the floor by his side. Another cop comes by. She can see him briefly as he passes through her narrow channel of vision, but he must have stopped to talk, because the first man's face splits into a grin and then she can see his lips move. His thumb points down her corridor and he begins to laugh.

Lousy bastard, she thinks.

The Kool-Aid looked a lot like wine in her mother's good stemware. Especially when the light shone through it, making the liquid glow like rubies, or maybe the glorious seeds of an autumn pomegranate. She lifted the glass, pinky raised in a grotesque child's parody, and delicately sipped the liquid. *Wine must taste a lot like this,* she thought, swirling the sugary drink in her mouth. This was what it would be like when she was a lady. She would pile her hair high atop her head in curls and wear deliciously tight dresses, her shoulders draped in mink. Just like Marilyn Monroe.

"Ha, ha, Dary's drinking wi-ine. Dary's drinking wi-ine," Kevin sang as he raced back and forth across the kitchen floor.

"It's not either wine," she said, more embarrassed than frightened at being caught by her little brother.

"If it's not wine then prove it," he said, snatching the glass from her hand. He held it tightly in his fist, one pinky shooting straight out into the air, mocking her already exaggerated grip. He sipped it, then made a face, eyes bugged and whirling. "Ugh, it is wine," he said, looking at her impishly. "I must be drunk." He began to stagger about, flinging himself around the room. Daria saw it coming. She wanted to cry out and stop him, or at least to cover her eyes so that she couldn't see the disaster, but it happened before she could do any of those things. Kevin tripped over the leg of a chair and went down in a crash of shattered crystal.

Her first thought was for the glass. That was one of the things that she hated herself for later. All she could think about was how it was Kevin's fault that the glass was broken, but she would be the one who got the spanking for it. Especially the way he was howling. Then she saw the blood all over her brother's arm. Already there was a small puddle on the floor. She knew that she should get a bandage, or call the emergency number that her mother always kept near the phone, or at the very least, run and get a neighbor, but she couldn't move. She couldn't take her eyes off of the bright-red stain. It was not as if she had never seen blood before, but suddenly she was drawn to it as she had never been drawn to anything before. Without knowing what she was doing, she found herself walking toward her brother, taking his arm in her hands and pulling it slowly toward her face. And then she could taste the salt and copper taste as she sucked at her brother's wound, filling a need that she hadn't even known existed. It was a hunger so all-consuming that she could not be distracted even by Kevin's fists flailing away at her back, or the sound of her mother's scream when she entered the room.

Daria realizes that she has wedged her face too tightly between the bars and the cold metal is bruising her cheeks. She withdraws into the dimness. There is a metal shelf bolted to the wall. It has a raised edge running around its sides and was obviously designed to hold a mattress that is long since gone. There are cookie-sized holes in the metal, placed with no discernible pattern along its length. Words have been scratched into this cot frame with nail files, hair pins, paper clips—mostly names like Barbara and Mike, and Gloria S. There are many expletives and an occasional statement about the "pigs," but no poems or limericks to occupy her attention for even a brief time. The metal itself is studded with rock-hard lumps of used chewing gum, wadded bits of paper and who knows what else. It is uncomfortable to sit on even without these things—too wide. Her skirt is too tight for her to sit cross-legged, and so if she sits back far enough to lean against the wall, the metal lip cuts sharply into the back of her calves. Already, there are bright-red welts on her legs, and so she lies on her side with her knees drawn up and her head pedestaled on her arm, the holes in the metal leaving rings along the length of her body. She pulls a crumpled package of cigarettes out of her pocket and stares at them longingly. Only three left. With a sigh, she puts them back. It is going to be a long night.

*   *   *

The doctor's name was printed in thick black letters on the frosted glass. Who knew what horrors waited for her on the other side. She knew that she had promised her mother that she would behave, but it was all too much for her. With tears streaming down her cheeks, she tried to pull free from her mother's grasp.

"No! Please. No, Mommy! I'll be a good girl, I promise."

Her mother grabbed her by both shoulders and stooped down until she could look into her daughter's eyes. With trembling fingers she brushed the child's hair. "Dary, honey, the doctor won't hurt you. All he wants to do is have a little talk with you. That's all. You can talk with the nice doctor, can't you?"

Daria sniffed and wiped her eyes with the backs of her hands. She knew what kind of people went to see psychiatrists. Crazy people. And crazy people got "put away" in the nuthouse. She allowed her mother to lead her into the doctor's office, a queen walking bravely to the gallows.

The waiting room was supposed to look inviting. One whole side was set up as a playroom, with a child-sized table and two little chairs, an open toybox with dolls and blocks spilling out of the top. A lady in starched white greeted them at the door and pointed Daria toward the corner, but she was not the least interested in playing. Instead, she hoisted herself onto a large wooden chair and sat there in perfect stillness, her hands folded across her lap. There she could hear some of the words that passed between her mother and the nurse. Their voices were hushed and they were quite far away, but she could hear enough to tell that her mother was ashamed to tell the white lady what Daria had done. She could hear the word "crazy" pass back and forth between them just as she had heard it pass between her father and her mother all the last week. And she could tell, even though she could only see the back of her head, that her mother was crying.

Suddenly, the door opened up behind the nurse's desk and Daria's mother disappeared through it. The nurse tried to talk to the sullen little girl, but Daria remained motionless, knowing that she would wait there forever, if necessary, but she would not move from that spot until her mother returned.

Then, like a miracle, her mother was back. Daria forgot all about her resolve to stay in the seat. She rushed to her mother's side. She would go anywhere, even inside the doctor's room if only her mother wouldn't leave her again. When her mother opened the door to the doctor's office and waved Daria through, the child went without hesitation, but then, her mother shut the door without following, and Daria was more frightened than ever.

"You must be Daria," Doctor Wells said without moving from his desk. He reminded Daria of the stuffed walrus in the museum, and he smelled of tobacco and Sen-Sen and mustache wax. He smiled, and it was a pleasant smile. "Your mother tells me that you're very smart and that you like to do puzzles. I have a puzzle here that's very hard. Would you like to try and do my puzzle?"

Daria nodded, but she did not move from her place near the door. Dr. Wells got up and walked over to a shelf and removed a large wooden puzzle. It was a cow. A three-dimensional puzzle. Daria had never seen anything like it before. He placed the puzzle on a little table that was a twin to the one in the waiting room and went back behind his desk.

"Well, you don't have to do it if you don't want to," he said after a minute, and then began to look through some papers on his desk, ignoring her. Soon, Daria's curiosity got the better of her and she found herself standing at the table looking at the puzzle, taking it apart.

Daria had expected the doctor would talk to her, but he didn't really seem interested in talking. He seemed content to watch her play with the puzzles and toys and he asked her very few questions. By the time she left his office, Daria had decided that she liked Dr. Wells very much.

She wakes slowly, unsure whether minutes or hours have passed. Her eyes are weeping from the cold of the metal where her head has been resting, and her muscles ache with stiffness. Her neck and chest, still covered with crusted blood that the arresting officers had refused to let her wash away, have begun to itch unmercifully. She sits up and realizes that her bladder is full. There is a toilet in the cell. It is a filthy affair with no seat, no paper, no sink, and no privacy from the eyes of the policemen who occasionally stroll up and down the corridor. She will live with the pain a while longer.

Suddenly, she realizes what it is that has woken her up. Silence. It is a silence as profound as the noise had been earlier. No singing, no taunting voices, nobody howling in pain. It is so quiet that she can hear the rustling newspaper of the guard at the end of the hall. She feels that she ought to be grateful not to have to listen to the racket, but instead, she finds the silence frightening.

Once again, she pulls the crumpled pack of cigarettes from her pocket. This time she cannot resist. She pulls one from the pack and straightens its bent form, then holds it between her lips for a long time before she begins the finalizing act of lighting it. She lets out the smoke in a long plume, pleased by the hominess of its smell. A familiar scent in this alien world.

"Can you spare one . . . please?" a soft voice calls from the next cell. "Please?" it asks again. The noise acts like a trigger as the tiny gospel singer starts in once more. A hand pokes through the bars in the corner of the cell. It is black and scarred and shaking with the strain of the reach. It is easily the largest hand she has ever seen. Large even for a man. Daria stares at the two cigarettes remaining in her pack. What the hell, she figures, they'll be gone soon anyway. She removes one and places it in the hand. It squeezes her own gently and withdraws.

"So, it has happened again, Daria?" Dr. Wells asked. The child nodded, looking down at her feet. "After three years we had great hope that it wouldn't happen again. But now that you are a little older, perhaps you can tell me what went on in your mind. What were you thinking when it happened? Do you have any idea why you did it?"

"I don't remember thinking anything. I don't even remember doing it. It was like a dream. They had us all lined up outside for gym. We were going to play field hockey. Tanya and Melinda were playing and Tanya hit her with her stick. I only wanted to help, but there was blood all over everything. I remember being afraid. I remember doing it, but it was almost more like watching television, when the camera's supposed to be you. The next thing I knew, Mrs. Rollie was holding me down and there were people everywhere." There was a long pause. "None of the other girls will talk to me now. They called me . . ." The child burst into tears. "They called me a vampire," she said.

"And how do you feel about that?" Dr. Wells goaded her.

"I don't know. Maybe it's true. It must be true, else why would I do what I do?" Tears streamed down her cheeks and she blotted them with a tissue.

217

"What do you know about vampires, Daria?"

"That they sleep in coffins and hate the sun . . . I know, but maybe it's only partly true. I do hate the sunlight. It hurts my eyes. And garlic, too. It makes me sick. Even the smell of it. Maybe the legends aren't quite right. Maybe I'm just a different kind of vampire. Why else would I do what I do?"

"Do you want to be a vampire, Daria?" Dr. Wells asked softly.

"No!" she shouted, the tears streaming down her face unimpeded, then again more softly, "no. Do you think I'm a vampire?" she asked.

"No, Daria. I don't believe in vampires. I think you're a young lady with a problem. And . . . I think if we work together, we can find out why you have this problem and what we can do about it."

There is the jingle of keys and the crisp sound of heavy feet. The dying woman has begun her plea for help again and Daria wonders if they are finally coming to see what is wrong, but the footsteps stop in front of her own cell. She looks up and sees the policeman consulting a piece of paper. "Daria Stanton?" he asks. She nods. He makes her back up, away from the door of the cell before he opens it. He tells her to turn around and put her hands behind her back. He handcuffs her and makes her follow him.

She is surprised to see there is only one cell between hers and the main corridor, something that she hadn't noticed on the way in. The cop she saw earlier is still sitting there, still eating, or perhaps eating again. She wants to ask him why he doesn't at least check on the woman who is screaming, but he doesn't look up at her as she passes. She is taken down an endless maze of corridors, all covered with the same green tile, except where they branch out into hallways full of cells. Eventually, she is taken to a room where her cuffs are removed and she is told to wait. He is careless shutting the door behind him and she can see that it isn't locked, but she makes no move to go through it. What difference can it make. Her fate was decided long ago.

"Daria Stanton? Please sit down, I have some questions to ask you."

Even after six months it still felt strange, coming to this new building, walking down a new corridor. She still missed Dr. Wells and hated him for dying that way, without any warning, as though it had been an act against her, personally. This new doctor didn't feel like a doctor at all; letting her call him Mark. And there should be a law against anyone's shrink being so cute, with all those new-fangled ideas. She paused outside the door, pulled off her mirrored sunglasses, and adjusted her hair and makeup in the lenses.

"Morning, Mark," she said as she seated herself in his green padded chair by the window. She couldn't bring herself to lie down on the couch, because all she could think of was how much she wanted him lying there with her. Seated where she was, she could watch the street outside while they talked. Two boys were standing around the old slide-bolt gum machine that had stood outside Wexler's Drug Store for as long as she could remember. It was easy to tell by their attitude that they were up to something. The dark-haired boy looked around furtively several times, then started sliding the bolt back and forth.

"I have some news for you this morning," Dr. Bremner told her. "Good news, I hope." The blond child kicked the machine and tried the bolt again. "The reports of your blood workup are back and I've gone over them with Dr. Walinski. Your blood showed a marked anemia of a type known as iron-deficiency porphyria. Now, ordinarily, I wouldn't be telling a patient that it was good news that she was sick, but in your case, it could mean that your symptoms are purely physical." A woman walked down the street. The two boys stopped tampering with the machine, turned and stared into the drugstore window until she had passed. ". . . a very rare disease. It is even more unusual for it to evince the symptoms that you have, but . . . it has been known to happen. Your body craves the iron porphyrins that it can't produce, and somehow, it knows what *you* don't . . . that whole blood is a source." The boys went back to the machine. One of them pulled a wire from his pocket and inserted it into the coin slot. "I've also talked with Dr. Ruth Tracey at the Eilman Clinic for Blood Disorders. She says your sensitivity to light and to garlic are all tied up in this too. For one thing, garlic breaks down old red blood cells. Just what a person with your condition can't afford to have happen." Once again the boys were interrupted and once again they removed themselves to the drugstore window. "Do you understand what all this means?"

Daria nodded morosely.

"How does it feel to know that there is a physiological cause for your problem?"

"I don't see what difference it makes," she said, brushing a wisp of straight black hair back from her forehead in irritation. "Insanity, vampirism, porphyria? What difference does it make what name you put on it? Even my family barely speaks to me any more. Besides, it's getting worse. I can't even stand to go out during the day anymore, and look at this." She pulled the sunglasses from her face to show him the dark circles under her eyes.

"Yes, I know, but Dr. Tracey can help you. With the right medications your symptoms should disappear. Imagine a time when you can see someone cut themself without being afraid of what you'll do. You'll be able to go to the beach and get a suntan for Chrissake."

Daria looked back out the window, but the boys were gone. She wasn't sure whether the half-empty globe had been full of gumballs a moment ago.

Hours—weeks—years later they bring her back to her cell. Though she has only been there since early evening, already it is like coming home. The chorus has changed. Two drunken, giggling voices have been added and someone is drumming on the bars with ringed fingers. The taunter still goads the gospel singer even though she has stopped singing and the dying woman is still dying, with a tough new voice telling her to do it already and shut up. Daria slumps back on her slab of metal, her back against the wall with her straight skirt hiked up so that her legs can be folded in front of her. She no longer cares what anybody sees. She has been questioned, photographed, and given one phone call. Mark will be there for the arraignment. He will see about getting her a lawyer. She has been told not to worry, that everything will be all right—but she is not worried . . . she knows that nothing will ever be all right for her again.

She stares at the dim and dirty green light that is always on and wonders if prison will be worse. From what she has read about penal institutions, she will not last very long once they send her away. A vampire in prison. She laughs at the thought and wonders what Dracula would do.

The fire was warmth seeping into her body, making her feel alive for the first time in years. She inched herself a little closer to the hearth. Mark came into the room holding a pair of cocktail glasses. He placed one by her elbow and joined her on the rug.

"Daria, there are things I wanted to tell you. So many things that I just couldn't say while you were my patient. You do understand why I couldn't go on treating you? Not the way I felt."

220

She reached out and squeezed his hand, reluctant to turn her face away from the fire for even the time it would have taken to look at him. He stroked her hair. Why did it make her feel like purring? She wanted him to take her in his arms, but she was afraid. Unlike most twenty-year-old women, she had no idea what to do; how to react. The boys that she met had often told her that she was beautiful, flirted, made passes or asked her out, but the moment they found out anything about her, they always became frightened and backed off. Mark was different. He already knew everything, even though he didn't choose to believe it all.

He took her face in his hands and kissed her. At first she wanted to pull away, but soon a burning started inside of her that made the fireplace unnecessary.

Daria can no longer stand the boredom. She climbs on the bars of her cell just for something to do. It is morning. She can tell by the shuffling of feet and slamming of doors that comes from the main corridor. She can tell by the food trays being brought down the hall, though none comes to her, and by the fact that the man in the chair has been replaced by a sloppy matron. She wonders if Mark is in the building yet. Probably. He has been in love with her since the first day she walked into his office, though she is convinced it is her condition and not herself that he loves. She would like to love him back, but though she needs him and wants him, truly enjoys his intimacy, she is sure that love is just another emotion that she cannot feel.

A different policeman stops outside her cell. He is carrying handcuffs, but he does not take them from his belt as he opens her cell door. "Time for your arraignment," he says cheerfully. Docile, she follows him down the same, and then a different, set of corridors. They take a long ride in a rickety elevator and when the doors open they are standing in a paneled hall. Spears of morning light stab through the windows making Daria cover her eyes. In the distance she can see a courtroom packed with people. Mark is there. He is standing by the double doors that lead inside. Someone is with him. Even on such short notice, he has found a lawyer— a friend of a friend. Mark takes her hand and they go through the double doors together. There are several cases to wait through before her name is called and he whispers reassurances to her while they sit there.

Finally, it is her turn, but the lawyer and Mark have taken that burden from her and she has no need to speak. Instead, she watches the judge. His face is puffy from sleep as he reads down the list of charges, aggravated assault, assault and battery . . . the list is long and Daria is surprised that they haven't thrown in witchcraft. The judge has probably slept through many such arraignments, but Daria knows that he will not sleep through this one. Indeed, she sees his eyes grow wide as the details of her crime are discussed. Interfering at the scene of an accident, obstructing the paramedics . . . there is no mercy in that face for her.

Then Mark begins to talk. Lovingly, he tells of her condition, of the work that Dr. Tracey is doing, of the hope for an imminent cure. He is so eloquent that for the very first time *she* is almost willing to believe that she is merely "sick." The judge's face softens. Illness is another matter. Daria has been so resigned to her fate that she is surprised to find that she has been freed. Released on her own recognizance until her trial. No bail. Mark throws his arms around her, but she is too stunned to hug him back.

"I love you," Mark tells her as he leads her out of the courtroom. He has brought glasses to shield her eyes from the sun.

A vein in his neck is throbbing.

"I love you too," she answers automatically. She tries not to stare at the throbbing vein. *This is a compulsion caused by illness,* she tells herself, *a chemical imbalance in the blood. It can be cured.*

"Daria, we're going to fight this. First we'll get you off on those ridiculous charges, and then Dr. Tracey is going to make you well. You'll see. Everything's going to be all right." He puts his arm around her shoulders, but something inside makes her stiffen and pull away.

Once again she looks at the throbbing vein and wonders what it will be like not to feel this hunger. All it will take is just the right compound stabbed into her arm with a little glass needle. A second of pain.

No, she thinks to herself in the crowded aloneness of the jailhouse steps. She finds inside herself a well of resolve, of acceptance, that she has never tapped before. She will no longer be put off by bottles of drugs, by diets that don't work, by hours of laborious talk. She will be what she is, the thing that makes her different, the thing that makes her herself. She is not just a young woman with a rare blood disease; she is a vampire, a child of darkness, and she had been fighting it for way too long.

Allowing her expression to soften to a smile, she turns to Mark and places her hand gently on his neck, feeling the pulse of the vein under her thumb. "Yes, Mark, you're right," she says softly. "You *will* have to get me off on these charges." So many little blue veins in so many necks. She will have to stay free if she is to feed.

This story stems, in part, from personal experience. (It was a bum rap, honest!) I remember reading an article in one of the science magazines which discussed porphyria as a medical rationale for vampirism. The article stated that this disease could very well explain an aversion to sunlight and garlic as well as a desire to drink blood. For a long time I had been thinking about doing a story about a girl who thought she was a vampire when it was actually more reasonable to believe that she was not. I thought of the seductive pull of vampires as they are expressed in pop culture and the appeal that they might have on a sensitive person who was ostracized because she was different. The prison experience seemed like a good hook to hang it all on.

Susan Casper

Nocturne

STEVE RASNIC TEM

I wanted to use Sylvia Plath's poem "Daddy" but was stymied by the unrealistic demands of the Plath estate. So, on Ed Bryant's recommendation, I asked his fellow Coloradan Steve Rasnic Tem for a poem on the psychology of some arrested male-female relationships. "Nocturne" is his response.

Under neon patina,
her eyes shift toward yellow.
The city enfolds them,
electric hum depleting
the rations of love.
"Do you even care?"
she asks, and still he's speechless,
seething because she cannot believe his rage,
because he cannot love
however much he makes love,
because one woman is never enough,
because he needs the dead visions
of women in pornographic prayerbooks,
raging because he needs.

She closes her eyes,
so he can stand inside her skin.
She feels him inside her,
his fingertips greeting
each inner wall.

kissing her unseen flesh.
He fills her outline completely,
like a balloon,
forcing out her own breath,
pressing out any sense.
She's emptied trying to fill him,
and still he won't be filled.

If she were dead she could not resist.
If she were dead she might fill.

A child, he'd played with dead mice.
He's sick for her smell.
He's sick for her life,
all his potency gone
into rusted etchings of consumed cars,
the slow-motion collapse of abandoned homes,
the sure specters of his childhood play,
the glossy feel of dead women.
Raging at the absence of love,
he burns over the wife he's made his mother,
whom he cannot repay with love,
whom he can only consume.

Her eyes shift toward red,
the taste of her like roasted seed.
He's drained her of sleep;
he's sapped her dreams.
Teeth and tongue to nape,
"You're so sweet," he says,
in hungry infant's voice,
"I could just eat you up,"
imitating mama.
He gives her lines to say.

She's slow to sleep
as pale and lazy as the sheets.

Tasting her like a baby,
using tongue for eyes,
his life becomes so still,
his life becomes so dark.

His breath rank with desire.
His aquiline face, lean nose,
his heavy eyebrows.
Ruddy lips and anemic ears.
He could become a wolf,
if he wanted to;
he could pass beneath a door.
He might speak with waxen beasts
and other neighbors of the night.

If she'd just let him feed.

One of the things poetry does best is to explore the gray areas: the ill-defined regions between genre expectations, those thematic realms which disturb while leaving us inarticulate about exactly what it is that disturbs us. Poetry is a form permitting us to grapple head-on with that inarticulateness, encouraging work about that very grasping after meaning. An ideal form for darker sorts of fantasy, I think.

And an appropriate form for capturing my own feelings about vampirism. On the one hand, admit it, it's a pretty silly idea—a Rudolph Valentino clone in an outdated suit, posturing melodramatically, mascara applied generously to heighten the color. The horror in that figure escapes me much of the time, it seems so far removed from my own apprehensions. But go beyond that—most of us have been in relationships which left us unaccountably drained, have known people whose very presence somehow left us weakened, edgy. People feed off each other. That's not necessarily bad; maybe it's just a natural consequence of having a brain that can aspire, and yearn. But like anything else, some people will take it too far.

Steve Rasnic Tem

Down Among the Dead Men

GARDNER DOZOIS AND JACK DANN

This story was first published in Oui *magazine because initially none of the fantasy or science fiction magazines (including* OMNI) *would take it. It was too "tough" and possibly "tasteless" a subject. There is an actual vampire in this story, and in a world where humans are monstrous to each other is he any worse a monster?*

Bruckman first discovered that Wernecke was a vampire when they went to the quarry that morning.

He was bending down to pick up a large rock when he thought he heard something in the gully nearby. He looked around and saw Wernecke huddled over a *Musselmänn*, one of the walking dead, a new man who had not been able to wake up to the terrible reality of the camp.

"Do you need any help?" Bruckman asked Wernecke in a low voice.

Wernecke looked up, startled, and covered his mouth with his hand, as if he were signing to Bruckman to be quiet.

But Bruckman was certain that he had glimpsed blood smeared on Wernecke's mouth. "The Musselmänn, is he alive?" Wernecke had often risked his own life to save one or another of the men in his barracks. But to risk one's life for a Musselmänn? "What's wrong?"

"Get away."

All right, Bruckman thought. Best to leave him alone. He looked pale, perhaps it was typhus. The guards were working him hard enough, and Wernecke was older than the rest of the men in the work gang. Let him sit for a moment and rest. But what about that blood? . . .

"Hey, you, what are you doing?" one of the young SS guards shouted to Bruckman.

Bruckman picked up the rock and, as if he had not heard the guard, began to walk away from the gully, toward the rusty brown cart on the tracks that led back to the barbed-wire fence of the camp. He would try to draw the guard's attention away from Wernecke.

But the guard shouted at him to halt. "Were you taking a little rest, is that it?" he asked, and Bruckman tensed, ready for a beating. This guard was new, neatly and cleanly dressed—and an unknown quantity. He walked over to the gully and, seeing Wernecke and the Musselmänn, said, "Aha, so your friend is taking care of the sick." He motioned Bruckman to follow him into the gully.

Bruckman had done the unpardonable—he had brought it on Wernecke. He swore at himself. He had been in this camp long enough to know to keep his mouth shut.

The guard kicked Wernecke sharply in the ribs. "I want you to put the Musselmänn in the cart. Now!" He kicked Wernecke again, as if as an afterthought. Wernecke groaned, but got to his feet. "Help him put the Musselmänn in the cart," the guard said to Bruckman; then he smiled and drew a circle in the air—the sign of smoke, the smoke which rose from the tall gray chimneys behind them. This Musselmänn would be in the oven within an hour, his ashes soon to be floating in the hot, stale air, as if they were the very particles of his soul.

Wernecke kicked the Musselmänn, and the guard chuckled, waved to another guard who had been watching, and stepped back a few feet. He stood with his hands on his hips. "Come on, dead man, get up or you're going to die in the oven," Wernecke whispered as he tried to pull the man to his feet. Bruckman supported the unsteady Musselmänn, who began to wail softly. Wernecke slapped him hard. "Do you want to live, Musselmänn? Do you want to see your family again, feel the touch of a woman, smell grass after it's been mowed? Then *move.*" The Musselmänn shambled forward between Wernecke and Bruckman. "You're dead, aren't you Musselmänn," goaded Wernecke. "As dead as your father and mother, as dead as your sweet wife, if you ever had one, aren't you? Dead!"

The Musselmänn groaned, shook his head, and whispered, "Not dead, my wife . . . "

229

"Ah, it talks," Wernecke said, loud enough so the guard walking a step behind them could hear. "Do you have a name, corpse?"

"Josef, and I'm not a Musselmänn."

"The corpse says he's alive," Wernecke said, again loud enough for the SS guard to hear. Then in a whisper, he said, "Josef, if you're not a Musselmänn, then you must work now, do you understand?" Josef tripped, and Bruckman caught him. "Let him be," said Wernecke. "Let him walk to the cart himself."

"Not the cart," Josef mumbled. "Not to die, not—"

"Then get down and pick up stones, show the fart-eating guard you can work."

"Can't. I'm sick, I'm . . ."

"Musselmänn!"

Josef bent down, fell to his knees, but took hold of a stone and stood up.

"You see," Wernecke said to the guard, "it's not dead yet. It can still work."

"I told you to carry him to the cart, didn't I," the guard said petulantly.

"Show him you can work," Wernecke said to Josef, "or you'll surely be smoke."

And Josef stumbled away from Wernecke and Bruckman, leaning forward, as if following the rock he was carrying.

"Bring him *back!*" shouted the guard, but his attention was distracted from Josef by some other prisoners, who, sensing the trouble, began to mill about. One of the other guards began to shout and kick at the men on the periphery, and the new guard joined him. For the moment, he had forgotten about Josef.

"Let's get to work, lest they notice us again," Wernecke said.

"I'm sorry that I—"

Wernecke laughed and made a fluttering gesture with his hand— smoke rising. "It's all hazard, my friend. All luck." Again the laugh. "It was a venial sin," and his face seemed to darken. "Never do it again, though, lest I think of you as bad luck."

"Carl, are you all right?" Bruckman asked. "I noticed some blood when—"

"Do the sores on your feet bleed in the morning?" Wernecke countered angrily. Bruckman nodded, feeling foolish and embarrassed. "And so it is with my gums. Now go away, unlucky one, and let me live."

At dusk, the guards broke the hypnosis of lifting and grunting and sweating and formed the prisoners into ranks. They marched back to the camp through the fields, beside the railroad tracks, the electrified wire, conical towers, and into the main gate of the camp.

Josef walked beside them, but he kept stumbling, as he was once again slipping back into death, becoming a Musselmänn. Wernecke helped him walk, pushed him along. "We should let this man become dead," Wernecke said to Bruckman.

Bruckman only nodded, but he felt a chill sweep over his sweating back. He was seeing Wernecke's face again as it was for that instant in the morning. Smeared with blood.

Yes, Bruckman thought, we should let the Musselmänn become dead. We should all be dead. . . .

Wernecke served up the lukewarm water with bits of spoiled turnip floating on the top, what passed as soup for the prisoners. Everyone sat or kneeled on the rough-planked floor, as there were no chairs.

Bruckman ate his portion, counting the sips and bites, forcing himself to take his time. Later, he would take a very small bite of the bread he had in his pocket. He always saved a small morsel of food for later—in the endless world of the camp, he had learned to give himself things to look forward to. Better to dream of bread than to get lost in the present. That was the fate of the Musselmänner.

But he always dreamed of food. Hunger was with him every moment of the day and night. Those times when he actually ate were in a way the most difficult, for there was never enough to satisfy him. There was the taste of softness in his mouth, and then in an instant it was gone. The emptiness took the form of pain—it *hurt* to eat. For bread, he thought, he would have killed his father, or his wife. God forgive me, and he watched Wernecke—Wernecke, who had shared his bread with him, who had died a little so he could live. He's a better man than I, Bruckman thought.

It was dim inside the barracks. A bare light bulb hung from the ceiling and cast sharp shadows across the cavernous room. Two tiers of five-foot-deep shelves ran around the room on three sides, bare wooden shelves where the men slept without blankets or mattresses. Set high in the northern wall was a slatted window, which let in the stark white light of the kliegs. Outside, the lights turned the grounds into a deathly imitation of day; only inside the barracks was it night.

"Do you know what tonight is, my friends?" Wernecke asked. He sat in the far corner of the room with Josef, who, hour by hour, was reverting back into a Musselmänn. Wernecke's face looked hollow and drawn in the light from the window and the light bulb; his eyes were deep-set and his face was long with deep creases running from his nose to the corners of his thin mouth. His hair was black, and even since Bruckman had known him, quite a bit of it had fallen out. He was a very tall man, almost six feet four, and that made him stand out in a crowd, which was dangerous in a death camp. But Wernecke had his own secret ways of blending with the crowd, of making himself invisible.

"No, tell us what tonight is," crazy old Bohme said. That men such as Bohme could survive was a miracle—or, as Bruckman thought—a testament to men such as Wernecke who somehow found the strength to help the others live.

"It's Passover," Wernecke said.

"How does he know that?" someone mumbled, but it didn't matter how Wernecke knew because he *knew*—even if it really wasn't Passover by the calendar. In this dimly lit barrack, it *was* Passover, the feast of freedom, the time of thanksgiving.

"But how can we have Passover without a *seder*?" asked Bohme. "We don't even have any *matzoh*," he whined.

"Nor do we have candles, or a silver cup for Elijah, or the shankbone, or *haroset*—nor would I make a *seder* over the *traif* the Nazis are so generous in giving us," replied Wernecke with a smile. "But we can pray, can't we? And when we all get out of here, when we're in our own homes in the coming year with God's help, then we'll have twice as much food—two *afikomens*, a bottle of wine for Elijah, and the *haggadahs* that our fathers and our fathers' fathers used."

It *was* Passover.

"Isadore, do you remember the four questions?" Wernecke asked Bruckman.

And Bruckman heard himself speaking. He was twelve years old again

232

at the long table beside his father, who sat in the seat of honor. To sit next to him was itself an honor. "How does this night differ from all other nights? On all other nights we eat bread and *matzoh;* why on this night do we eat only *matzoh?*

"*M'a nisht' ana halylah hazeah. . . .* "

Sleep would not come to Bruckman that night, although he was so tired that he felt as if the marrow of his bones had been sucked away and replaced with lead.

He lay there in the semidarkness, feeling his muscles ache, feeling the acid biting of his hunger. Usually he was numb enough with exhaustion that he could empty his mind, close himself down, and fall rapidly into oblivion, but not tonight. Tonight he was noticing things again, his surroundings were getting through to him again, in a way that they had not since he had been new in camp. It was smotheringly hot, and the air was filled with the stinks of death and sweat and fever, of stale urine and drying blood. The sleepers thrashed and turned, as though they fought with sleep, and as they slept, many of them talked or muttered or screamed aloud; they lived other lives in their dreams, intensely compressed lives dreamed quickly, for soon it would be dawn, and once more they would be thrust into hell. Cramped in the midst of them, sleepers squeezed in all around him, it suddenly seemed to Bruckman that these pallid white bodies were already dead, that he was sleeping in a graveyard. Suddenly it was the boxcar again. And his wife Miriam was dead again, dead and rotting unburied. . . .

Resolutely, Bruckman emptied his mind. He felt feverish and shaky, and wondered if the typhus were coming back, but he couldn't afford to worry about it. Those who couldn't sleep couldn't survive. Regulate your breathing, force your muscles to relax, don't think. Don't think.

For some reason, after he had managed to banish even the memory of his dead wife, he couldn't shake the image of the blood on Wernecke's mouth.

There were other images mixed in with it: Wernecke's uplifted arms and upturned face as he led them in prayer; the pale strained face of the stumbling Musselmänn; Wernecke looking up, startled, as he crouched over Josef . . . but it was the blood to which Bruckman's feverish thoughts returned, and he pictured it again and again as he lay in the

233

rustling, fart-smelling darkness, the watery sheen of blood over Wernecke's lips, the tarry trickle of blood in the corner of his mouth, like a tiny scarlet worm. . . .

Just then a shadow crossed in front of the window, silhouetted blackly for an instant against the harsh white glare, and Bruckman knew from the shadow's height and its curious forward stoop that it was Wernecke.

Where could he be going? Sometimes a prisoner would be unable to wait until morning, when the Germans would let them out to visit the slit-trench latrine again, and would slink shamefacedly into a far corner to piss against a wall, but surely Wernecke was too much of an old hand for that. . . . Most of the prisoners slept on the sleeping platforms, especially during the cold nights when they would huddle together for warmth, but sometimes during the hot weather, people would drift away and sleep on the floor instead; Bruckman had been thinking of doing that, as the jostling bodies of the sleepers around him helped to keep him from sleep. Perhaps Wernecke, who always had trouble fitting into the cramped sleeping niches, was merely looking for a place where he could lie down and stretch his legs . . .

Then Bruckman remembered that Josef had fallen asleep in the corner of the room where Wernecke had sat and prayed, and that they had left him there alone.

Without knowing why, Bruckman found himself on his feet. As silently as the ghost he sometimes felt he was becoming, he walked across the room in the direction Wernecke had gone, not understanding what he was doing nor why he was doing it. The face of the Musselmänn, Josef, seemed to float behind his eyes. Bruckman's feet hurt, and he knew, without looking, that they were bleeding, leaving faint tracks behind him. It was dimmer here in the far corner, away from the window, but Bruckman knew that he must be near the wall by now, and he stopped to let his eyes readjust.

When his eyes had adapted to the dimmer light, he saw Josef sitting on the floor, propped up against the wall. Wernecke was hunched over the Musselmänn. Kissing him. One of Josef's hands was tangled in Wernecke's thinning hair.

Before Bruckman could react—such things had been known to happen once or twice before, although it shocked him deeply that *Wernecke* would be involved in such filth—Josef released his grip on Wernecke's hair. Josef's upraised arm fell limply to the side, his hand hitting the floor with a muffled but solid impact that should have been painful—but Josef made no sound.

Wernecke straightened up and turned around. Stronger light from the high window caught him as he straightened to his full height, momentarily illuminating his face.

Wernecke's mouth was smeared with blood.

"My God," Bruckman cried.

Startled, Wernecke flinched, then took two quick steps forward and seized Bruckman by the arm. "Quiet!" Wernecke hissed. His fingers were cold and hard.

At that moment, as though Wernecke's sudden movement were a cue, Josef began to slip down sideways along the wall. As Wernecke and Bruckman watched, both momentarily riveted by the sight, Josef toppled over to the floor, his head striking against the floorboards with a sound such as a dropped melon might make. He had made no attempt to break his fall or cushion his head, and lay now unmoving.

"My *God,*" Bruckman said again.

"Quiet, I'll explain," Wernecke said, his lips still glazed with the Musselmänn blood. "Do you want to ruin us all? For the love of God, be *quiet.*"

But Bruckman had shaken free of Wernecke's grip and crossed to kneel by Josef, leaning over him as Wernecke had done, placing a hand flat on Josef's chest for a moment, then touching the side of Josef's neck. Bruckman looked slowly up at Wernecke. "He's dead," Bruckman said, more quietly.

Wernecke squatted on the other side of Josef's body, and the rest of their conversation was carried out in whispers over Josef's chest, like friends conversing at the sickbed of another friend who has finally fallen into a fitful doze.

"Yes, he's dead," Wernecke said. "He was dead yesterday, wasn't he? Today he had just stopped walking." His eyes were hidden here, in the deeper shadow nearer to the floor, but there was still enough light for Bruckman to see that Wernecke had wiped his lips clean. Or licked them clean, Bruckman thought, and felt a spasm of nausea go through him.

"But *you,*" Bruckman said, haltingly. "You were. . . ."

"Drinking his blood?" Wernecke said. "Yes, I was drinking his blood."

Bruckman's mind was numb. He couldn't deal with this, he couldn't understand it at all. "But *why,* Eduard? Why?"

"To live, of course. Why do any of us do anything here? If I am to live, I must have blood. Without it, I'd face a death even more certain than that doled out by the Nazis."

Bruckman opened and closed his mouth, but no sound came out, as if the words he wished to speak were too jagged to fit through his throat. At last he managed to croak, "A vampire? You're a vampire? Like in the old stories?"

Wernecke said calmly, "Men would call me that." He paused, then nodded. "Yes, that's what men would call me. . . . As though they can understand something simply by giving it a name."

"But Eduard," Bruckman said weakly, almost petulantly. "The Musselmänn . . ."

"Remember that he *was* a Musselmänn," Wernecke said, leaning forward and speaking more fiercely. "His strength was going, he was sinking. He would have been dead by morning anyway. I took from him something that he no longer needed, but that I needed in order to live. Does it matter? Starving men in lifeboats have eaten the bodies of their dead companions in order to live. Is what I've done any worse than that?"

"But he didn't just die. You *killed* him. . . ."

Wernecke was silent for a moment, and then said, quietly, "What better thing could I have done for him? I won't apologize for what I do, Isadore; I do what I have to do to live. Usually I take only a little blood from a number of men, just enough to survive. And that's fair, isn't it? Haven't I given food to others, to help them survive? To you, Isadore? Only very rarely do I take more than a minimum from any one man, although I'm weak and hungry all the time, believe me. And never have I drained the life from someone who wished to live. Instead I've helped them fight for survival in every way I can, you know that."

He reached out as though to touch Bruckman, then thought better of it and put his hand back on his own knee. He shook his head. "But these Musselmänner, the ones who have given up on life, the walking dead— it is a favor to them to take them, to give them the solace of death. Can you honestly say it is not, *here?* That it is better for them to walk around while they are dead, being beaten and abused by the Nazis until their bodies cannot go on, and then to be thrown into the ovens and burned like trash? Can you say that? Would *they* say that, if they knew what was going on? Or would they thank me?"

Wernecke suddenly stood up, and Bruckman stood up with him. As Wernecke's face came again into the stronger light, Bruckman could see that his eyes had filled with tears. "You have lived under the Nazis," Wernecke said. "Can you really call me a monster? Aren't I still a Jew, whatever else I might be? Aren't I *here*, in a death camp? Aren't I being persecuted, too, as much as any other? Aren't I in as much danger as anyone else? If I'm not a Jew, then tell the Nazis—they seem to think so." He paused for a moment, and then smiled wryly. "And forget your superstitious boogey tales. I'm no night spirit. If I could turn myself into a bat and fly away from here, I would have done it long before now, believe me."

Bruckman smiled reflectively, then grimaced. The two men avoided each other's eyes, Bruckman looking at the floor, and there was an uneasy silence, punctured only by the sighing and moaning of the sleepers on the other side of the cabin. Then, without looking up, in tacit surrender, Bruckman said, "What about *him?* The Nazis will find the body and cause trouble. . . ."

"Don't worry," Wernecke said. "There are no obvious marks. And nobody performs autopsies in a death camp. To the Nazis, he'll be just another Jew who had died of the heat, or from starvation or sickness, or from a broken heart."

Bruckman raised his head then and they stared eye to eye for a moment. Even knowing what he knew, Bruckman found it hard to see Wernecke as anything other than what he appeared to be: an aging, balding Jew, stooping and thin, with sad eyes and a tired, compassionate face.

"Well, then, Isadore," Wernecke said at last, matter-of-factly. "My life is in your hands. I will not be indelicate enough to remind you of how many times your life has been in mine."

Then he was gone, walking back toward the sleeping platforms, a shadow soon lost among other shadows.

Bruckman stood by himself in the gloom for a long time, and then followed him. It took all of his will not to look back over his shoulder at the corner where Josef lay, and even so Bruckman imagined that he could feel Josef's dead eyes watching him, watching reproachfully as he walked away abandoning Josef to the cold and isolated company of the dead.

* * *

Bruckman got no more sleep that night, and in the morning, when the Nazis shattered the gray predawn stillness by bursting into the shack with shouts and shrill whistles and barking police dogs, he felt as if he were a thousand years old.

They were formed into two lines, shivering in the raw morning air, and marched off to the quarry. The clammy dawn mist had yet to burn off, and marching through it, through a white shadowless void, with only the back of the man in front of him dimly visible, Bruckman felt more than ever like a ghost, suspended bodiless in some limbo between Heaven and Earth. Only the bite of pebbles and cinders into his raw, bleeding feet kept him anchored to the world, and he clung to the pain as a lifeline, fighting to shake off a feeling of numbness and unreality. However strange, however outré, the events of the previous night had *happened*. To doubt it, to wonder now if it had all been a feverish dream brought on by starvation and exhaustion, was to take the first step on the road to becoming a Musselmänn.

Wernecke is a vampire, he told himself. That was the harsh, unyielding reality that, like the reality of the camp itself, must be faced. Was it any more surreal, any more impossible than the nightmare around them? He must forget the tales that his grandmother had told him as a boy, "boogey tales" as Wernecke himself had called them, half-remembered tales that turned his knees to water whenever he thought of the blood smeared on Wernecke's mouth, whenever he thought of Wernecke's eyes watching him in the dark. . . .

"Wake up, Jew!" the guard alongside him snarled, whacking him lightly on the arm with his rifle butt. Bruckman stumbled, managed to stay upright and keep going. Yes, he thought, wake up. Wake up to the reality of this, just as you once had to wake up to the reality of the camp. It was just one more unpleasant fact he would have to adapt to, learn to deal with. . . .

Deal with how? he thought, and shivered.

By the time they reached the quarry, the mist had burned off, swirling past them in rags and tatters, and it was already beginning to get hot. There was Wernecke, his balding head gleaming dully in the harsh morning light. He didn't dissolve in the sunlight—there was one boogey tale disproved. . . .

They set to work, like golems, like ragtag clockwork automatons.

Lack of sleep had drained what small reserves of strength Bruckman had, and the work was very hard for him that day. He had learned long ago all the tricks of timing and misdirection, the safe way to snatch short moments of rest, the ways to do a minimum of work with the maximum display of effort, the ways to keep the guards from noticing you, to fade into the faceless crowd of prisoners and not be singled out, but today his head was muzzy and slow, and none of the tricks seemed to work.

His body felt like a sheet of glass, fragile, ready to shatter into dust, and the painful, arthritic slowness of his movements got him first shouted at, and then knocked down. The guard kicked him twice for good measure before he could get up.

When Bruckman had climbed back to his feet again, he saw that Wernecke was watching him, face blank, eyes expressionless, a look that could have meant anything at all.

Bruckman felt the blood trickling from the corner of his mouth and thought, *the blood . . . he's watching the blood . . .* and once again he shivered.

Somehow, Bruckman forced himself to work faster, and although his muscles blazed with pain, he wasn't hit again, and the day passed.

When they formed up to go back to camp, Bruckman, almost unconsciously, made sure that he was in a different line than Wernecke.

That night in the cabin, Bruckman watched as Wernecke talked with the other men, here trying to help a new man named Melnick—no more than a boy—adjust to the dreadful reality of the camp, there exhorting someone who was slipping into despair to live and spite his tormentors, joking with old hands in the flat, black, bitter way that passed for humor among them, eliciting a wan smile or occasionally even a laugh from them, finally leading them all in prayer again, his strong, calm voice raised in the ancient words, giving meaning to those words again. . . .

He keeps up together, Bruckman thought, he keeps us going. Without him, we wouldn't last a week. Surely that's worth a little blood, a bit from each man, not even enough to hurt. . . . Surely they wouldn't even begrudge him it, if they knew and really understood. . . . No, he is a good man, better than the rest of us, in spite of his terrible affliction.

Bruckman had been avoiding Wernecke's eyes, hadn't spoken to him at all that day, and suddenly felt a wave of shame go through him at the

239

thought of how shabbily he had been treating his friend. Yes, his friend, regardless, the man who had saved his life. . . . Deliberately, he caught Wernecke's eyes, and nodded, and then somewhat sheepishly, smiled. After a moment, Wernecke smiled back, and Bruckman felt a spreading warmth and relief uncoil his guts. Everything was going to be all right, as all right as it could be, here. . . .

Nevertheless, as soon as the inside lights clicked off that night, and Bruckman found himself lying alone in the darkness, his flesh began to crawl.

He had been unable to keep his eyes open a moment before, but now, in the sudden darkness, he found himself tensely and tickingly awake. Where was Wernecke? What was he doing, whom was he visiting tonight? Was he out there in the darkness even now, creeping closer, creeping nearer? . . . Stop it, Bruckman told himself uneasily, forget the boogey tales. This is your friend, a good man, not a monster. . . . But he couldn't control the fear that made the small hairs on his arms stand bristlingly erect, couldn't stop the grisly images from coming. . . .

Wernecke's eyes, gleaming in the darkness . . . was the blood already glistening on Wernecke's lips, as he drank? . . . The thought of the blood staining Wernecke's yellowing teeth made Bruckman cold and nauseous, but the image that he couldn't get out of his mind tonight was an image of Josef toppling over in that sinister boneless way, striking his head against the floor. . . . Bruckman had seen people die in many more gruesome ways during this time at the camp, seen people shot, beaten to death, seen them die in convulsions from high fevers or cough their lungs up in bloody tatters from pneumonia, seen them hanging like charred-black scarecrows from the electrified fences, seen them torn apart by dogs . . . but somehow it was Josef's soft, passive, almost restful slumping into death that bothered him. That, and the obscene limpness of Josef's limbs as he sprawled there like a discarded rag doll, his pale and haggard face gleaming reproachfully in the dark. . . .

When Bruckman could stand it no longer, he got shakily to his feet and moved off through the shadows, once again not knowing where he was going or what he was going to do, but drawn forward by some obscure instinct he himself did not understand. This time he went cautiously, feeling his way and trying to be silent, expecting every second to see Wernecke's coal-black shadow rise up before him.

He paused, a faint noise scratching at his ears, then went on again, even more cautiously, crouching low, almost crawling across the grimy floor.

Whatever instinct had guided him—sounds heard and interpreted subliminally, perhaps?—it had timed his arrival well. Wernecke had someone down on the floor there, perhaps someone he seized and dragged away from the huddled mass of sleepers on one of the sleeping platforms, someone from the outer edge of bodies whose presence would not be missed, or perhaps someone who had gone to sleep on the floor, seeking solitude or greater comfort.

Whoever he was, he struggled in Wernecke's grip, but Wernecke handled him easily, almost negligently, in a manner that spoke of great physical power. Bruckman could hear the man trying to scream, but Wernecke had one hand on his throat, half-throttling him, and all that would come out was a sort of whistling gasp. The man thrashed in Wernecke's hands like a kite in a child's hands flapping in the wind, and, moving deliberately, Wernecke smoothed him out like a kite, pressing him slowly flat on the floor.

Then Wernecke bent over him, and lowered his mouth to his throat.

Bruckman watched in horror, knowing that he should shout, scream, try to rouse the other prisoners, but somehow unable to move, unable to make his mouth open, his lungs pump. He was paralyzed by fear, like a rabbit in the presence of a predator, a terror sharper and more intense than any he'd ever known.

The man's struggles were growing weaker, and Wernecke must have eased up some on the throttling pressure of his hand, because the man moaned "Don't . . . please don't . . . " in a weaker, slurred voice. The man had been drumming his fists against Wernecke's back and sides, but now the tempo of the drumming slowed, slowed, and then stopped, the man's arms falling laxly to the floor. "Don't . . . " the man whispered; he groaned and muttered incomprehensively for a moment or two longer, then became silent. The silence stretched out for a minute, two, three, and Wernecke still crouched over his victim, who was now not moving at all. . . .

Wernecke stirred, a kind of shudder going through him, like a cat stretching. He stood up. His face became visible as he straightened up into the full light from the window, and there was blood on it, glistening black under the harsh glare of the kliegs. As Bruckman watched, Wernecke began to lick his lips clean, his tongue, also black in this light, sliding like some sort of sinuous ebony snake around the rim of his mouth, darting and probing for the last lingering drops. . . .

How smug he looks, Bruckman thought, like a cat who has found the cream, and the anger that flashed through him at the thought enabled him to move and speak again. "Wernecke," he said harshly.

Wernecke glanced casually in his direction. "You again, Isadore?" Wernecke said. "Don't you ever sleep?" Wernecke spoke lazily, quizzically, without surprise, and Bruckman wondered if Wernecke had known all along that he was there. "Or do you just enjoy watching me?"

"Lies," Bruckman said. "You told me nothing but lies. Why did you bother?"

"You were excited," Wernecke said. "You had surprised me. It seemed best to tell you what you wanted to hear. If it satisfied you, then that was an easy solution to the problem."

"Never have I drained the life from someone who wanted to live," Bruckman said bitterly, mimicking Wernecke. "Only a little from each man! My God—and I believed you! I even felt sorry for you!"

Wernecke shrugged. "Most of it was true. Usually I only take a little from each man, softly and carefully, so that they never know, so that in the morning they are only a little weaker than they would have been anyway. . . ."

"Like Josef?" Bruckman said angrily. "Like the poor devil you killed tonight?"

Wernecke shrugged again. "I have been careless the last few nights, I admit. But I need to build up my strength again." His eyes gleamed in the darkness. "Events are coming to a head here. Can't you feel it, Isadore, can't you sense it? Soon the war will be over, everyone knows that. Before then, this camp will be shut down, and the Nazis will move us back into the interior—either that, or kill us. I have grown weak here, and I will soon need all my strength to survive, to take whatever opportunity presents itself to escape. I *must* be ready. And so I have let myself drink deeply again, drink my fill for the first time in months. . . ." Wernecke licked his lips again, perhaps unconsciously, then smiled bleakly at Bruckman. "You don't appreciate my restraint, Isadore. You don't understand how hard it has been for me to hold back, to take only a little each night. You don't understand how much that restraint has cost me. . . ."

"You are gracious," Bruckman sneered.

Wernecke laughed. "No, but I am a rational man; I pride myself on that. You other prisoners were my only source of food, and I have had to be very careful to make sure that you would last. I have no access to the Nazis, after all. I am trapped here, a prisoner just like you, whatever else you may believe—and I have not only had to find ways to survive here in the camp, I have had to procure my own food as well! No shepherd has ever watched over his flock more tenderly than I."

"Is that all we are to you—sheep? Animals to be slaughtered?"

Wernecke smiled. "Precisely."

When he could control his voice enough to speak, Bruckman said, "You're worse than the Nazis."

"I hardly think so," Wernecke said quietly, and for a moment he looked tired, as though something unimaginably old and unutterably weary had looked out through his eyes. "This camp was built by the Nazis—it wasn't my doing. The Nazis sent you here—not I. The Nazis have tried to kill you every day since, in one way or another—and I have tried to keep you alive, even at some risk to myself. No one has more of a vested interest in the survival of his livestock than the farmer, after all, even if he does occasionally slaughter an inferior animal. I have given you food—"

"Food you had no use for yourself! You sacrificed nothing!"

"That's true, of course. But *you* needed it, remember that. Whatever my motives, I have helped you to survive here—you and many others. By doing so I also acted in my own self-interest, of course, but can you have experienced this camp and still believe in things like altruism? What difference does it make what my reason for helping was—I still helped you, didn't I?"

"Sophistries!" Bruckman said. "Rationalizations! You twist words to justify yourself, but you can't disguise what you really are—a monster!"

Wernecke smiled gently, as though Bruckman's words amused him, and made as if to pass by, but Bruckman raised an arm to bar his way. They did not touch each other, but Wernecke stopped short, and a new quivering kind of tension sprung into existene in the air between them.

"I'll stop you," Bruckman said. "Somehow I'll stop you, I'll keep you from doing this terrible thing—"

"You'll do nothing," Wernecke said. His voice was hard and cold and flat, like a rock speaking. "What can you do? Tell the other prisoners? Who would believe you? They'd think you'd gone insane. Tell the *Nazis*,

243

then?" Wernecke laughed harshly. "They'd think you'd gone crazy, too, and they'd take you to the hospital—and I don't have to tell you what your chances of getting out of there alive are, do I? No, you'll do *nothing*."

Wernecke took a step forward; his eyes were shiny and black and hard, like ice, like the pitiless eyes of a predatory bird, and Bruckman felt a sick rush of fear cut through his anger. Bruckman gave way, stepping backward involuntarily, and Wernecke pushed past him, seeming to brush him aside without touching him.

Once past, Wernecke turned to stare at Bruckman, and Bruckman had to summon up all the defiance that remained in him not to look uneasily away from Wernecke's agate-hard eyes. "You are the strongest and cleverest of all the other animals, Isadore," Wernecke said in a calm, conversational voice. "You have been useful to me. Every shepherd needs a good sheepdog. I still need you, to help me manage the others, and to help me keep them going long enough to serve my needs. This is the reason why I have taken so much time with you, instead of just killing you outright." He shrugged. "So let us both be rational about this—you leave me alone, Isadore, and I will leave you alone also. We will stay away from each other and look after our own affairs. Yes?"

"The others. . . ." Bruckman said weakly.

"They must look after themselves," Wernecke said. He smiled, a thin and almost invisible motion of his lips. "What did I teach you, Isadore? Here everyone must look after themselves. What difference does it make what happens to the others? In a few weeks almost all of them will be dead anyway."

"You *are* a monster," Bruckman said.

"I'm not much different from you, Isadore. The strong survive, whatever the cost."

"I am *nothing* like you," Bruckman said, with loathing.

"No?" Wernecke asked, ironically, and moved away; within a few paces he was hobbling and stooping, vanishing into the shadows, once more the harmless old Jew.

Bruckman stood motionless for a moment, and then, moving slowly and reluctantly, he steppped across to where Wernecke's victim lay.

It was one of new men Wernecke had been talking to earlier in the evening, and, of course, he was quite dead.

Shame and guilt took Bruckman then, emotions he thought he had forgotten—black and strong and bitter, they shook him by the throat the way Wernecke had shaken the new man.

Bruckman couldn't remember returning across the room to his sleeping platform, but suddenly he was there, lying on his back and staring into the stifling darkness, surrounded by the moaning, thrashing, stinking mass of sleepers. His hands were clasped protectively over his throat, although he couldn't remember putting them there, and he was shivering convulsively. How many mornings had he awoken with a dull ache in his neck, thinking it was no more than the habitual bodyaches and strained muscles they had all learned to take for granted? How many nights had Wernecke fed on *him?*

Every time Bruckman closed his eyes he would see Wernecke's face floating there in the luminous darkness behind his eyelids . . . Wernecke with his eyes half-closed, his face vulpine and cruel and satiated . . . Wernecke's face moving closer and closer to him, his eyes opening like black pits, his lips smiling back from his teeth . . . Wernecke's lips, sticky and red with blood . . . and then Bruckman would seem to feel the wet touch of Wernecke's lips on *his* throat, feel Wernecke's teeth biting into *his* flesh, and Bruckman's eyes would fly open again. Staring into the darkness. Nothing there. Nothing there *yet.* . . .

Dawn was a dirty gray imminence against the cabin window before Bruckman could force himself to lower his shielding arms from his throat, and once again he had not slept at all.

That day's work was a nightmare of pain and exhaustion for Bruckman, harder than anything he had known since his first few days at the camp. Somehow he forced himself to get up, somehow he stumbled outside and up the path to the quarry, seeming to float along high off the ground, his head a bloated balloon, his feet a thousand miles away at the end of boneless beanstalk legs he could barely control at all. Twice he fell, and was kicked several times before he could drag himself back to his feet and lurch forward again. The sun was coming up in front of them, a hard red disk in a sickly yellow sky, and to Bruckman it seemed to be a glazed and lidless eye staring dispassionately into the world to watch them flail and struggle and die, like the eye of a scientist peering into a laboratory maze.

He watched the disk of the sun as he stumbled towards it; it seemed to bob and shimmer with every painful step, expanding, swelling, and bloating until it swallowed the sky. . . .

Then he was picking up a rock, moaning with the effort, feeling the rough stone tear his hands. . . .

Reality began to slide away from Bruckman. There were long periods when the world was blank, and he would come slowly back to himself as if from a great distance, and hear his own voice speaking words that he could not understand, or keening mindlessly, or grunting in a hoarse, animalistic way, and he would find that his body was working mechanically, stooping and lifting and carrying, all without volition. . . .

A Musselmänn, Bruckman thought, I'm becoming a Musselmänn . . . and felt a chill of fear sweep through him. He fought to hold onto the world, afraid that the next time he slipped away from himself he would not come back, deliberately banging his hands into the rocks, cutting himself, clearing his head with pain.

The world steadied around him. A guard shouted a hoarse admonishment at him and slapped his rifle butt, and Bruckman forced himself to work faster, although he could not keep himself from weeping silently with the pain his movements cost him.

He discovered that Wernecke was watching him, and stared back defiantly, the bitter tears still runneling his dirty cheeks, thinking, *I won't become a Musselmänn for you, I won't make it easy for you, I won't provide another helpless victim for you* . . . Wernecke met Bruckman's gaze for a moment, and then shrugged and turned away.

Bruckman bent for another stone, feeling the muscles in his back crack and the pain drive in like knives. What had Wernecke been thinking behind the blankness of his expressionless face? Had Wernecke, sensing weakness, marked Bruckman for his next victim? Had Wernecke been disappointed or dismayed by the strength of Bruckman's will to survive? Would Wernecke now settle upon someone else?

The morning passed, and Bruckman grew feverish again. He could feel the fever in his face, making his eyes feel sandy and hot, pulling the skin taut over his cheekbones, and he wondered how long he could manage to stay on his feet. To falter, to grow weak and insensible, was certain death; if the Nazis didn't kill him, Wernecke would. . . . Wernecke was out of sight now, on the other side of the quarry, but it seemed to Bruckman that Wernecke's hard and flinty eyes were everywhere, floating in the air around him, looking out momentarily from the back of a Nazi soldier's head, watching him from the dulled iron side of a quarry cart, peering at him from a dozen different angles. He bent ponderously for another rock, and when he had pried it up from the earth he found Wernecke's eyes beneath it, staring unblinkingly up at him from the damp and pallid soil. . . .

That afternoon there were great flashes of light on the eastern horizon, out across the endless flat expanse of the steppe, flares in rapid sequence that lit up the sullen gray sky, all without sound. The Nazi guards had gathered in a group, looking to the east and talking in subdued voices, ignoring the prisoners for the moment. For the first time Bruckman noticed how disheveled and unshaven the guards had become in the last few days, as though they had given up, as though they no longer cared. Their faces were strained and tight, and more than one of them seemed to be fascinated by the leaping fires on the distant edge of the world.

Melnick said that it was only a thunderstorm, but old Bohme said that it was an artillery battle being fought, and that that meant that the Russians were coming, that soon they would all be liberated.

Bohme grew so excited at the thought that he began shouting, "The Russians! It's the Russians! The Russians are coming to free us!" Dichstein, another one of the new prisoners, and Melnick tried to hush him, but Bohme continued to caper and shout—doing a grotesque kind of jig while he yelled and flapped his arms—until he had attracted the attention of the guards. Infuriated, two of the guards fell upon Bohme and beat him severely, striking him with their rifle butts with more than usual force, knocking him to the ground, continuing to flail at him and kick him while he was down, Bohme writhing like an injured worm under their stamping boots. They probably would have beaten Bohme to death on the spot, but Wernecke organized a distraction among some of the other prisoners, and when the guards moved away to deal with it, Wernecke helped Bohme to stand up and hobble away to the other side of the quarry, where the rest of the prisoners shielded him from sight with their bodies as best they could for the rest of the afternoon.

Something about the way Wernecke urged Bohme to his feet and helped him to limp and lurch away, something about the protective, possessive curve of Wernecke's arm around Bohme's shoulders, told Bruckman that Wernecke had selected his next victim.

That night Bruckman vomited up the meager and rancid meal that they were allowed, his stomach convulsing uncontrollably after the first few bites. Trembling with hunger and exhaustion and fever, he leaned against the wall and watched as Wernecke fussed over Bohme, nursing him as a man might nurse a sick child, talking gently to him, wiping away some of the blood that still oozed from the corner of Bohme's mouth, coaxing Bohme to drink a few sips of soup, finally arranging that Bohme should stretch out on the floor away from the sleeping platforms, where he would not be jostled by the others. . . .

As soon as the interior lights went out that night, Bruckman got up, crossed the floor quickly and unhesitantly, and lay down in the shadows near the spot where Bohme muttered and twitched and groaned.

Shivering, Bruckman lay in the darkness, the strong smell of the earth in his nostrils, waiting for Wernecke to come. . . .

In Bruckman's hand, held close to his chest, was a spoon that had been sharpened to a jagged needle point, a spoon he had stolen and begun to sharpen while he was still in a civilian prison in Cologne, so long ago that he almost couldn't remember, scraping it back and forth against the stone wall of his cell every night for hours, managing to keep it hidden on his person during the nightmarish ride in the sweltering boxcar, the first few terrible days at the camp, telling no one about it, not even Wernecke during the months when he'd thought of Wernecke as a kind of saint, keeping it hidden long after the possibility of escape had become too remote even to fantasize about, retaining it then more as a tangible link with the daydream country of his past than as a tool he ever actually hoped to employ, cherishing it almost as a holy relic, as a remnant of a vanished world that he otherwise might almost believe had never existed at all. . . .

And now that it was time to use it at last, he was almost reluctant to do so, to soil it with another man's blood. . . .

He fingered the spoon compulsively, turning it over and over; it was hard and smooth and cold, and he clenched it as tightly as he could, trying to ignore the fine tremoring of his hands.

He had to kill Wernecke. . . .

Nausea and an odd feeling of panic flashed through Bruckman at the thought, but there was no other choice, there was no other way. . . . He couldn't go on like this, his strength was failing; Wernecke was killing him, as surely as he had killed the others, just by keeping him from sleeping. . . . And as long as Wernecke lived, he would never be safe: always there would be the chance that Wernecke would come for him, that Wernecke would strike as soon as his guard was down. . . . Would Wernecke scruple for a second to kill *him,* after all, if he thought that he could do it safely? . . . No, of course not. . . . Given the chance, Wernecke would kill him without a moment's further thought. . . . No, he must strike *first.* . . .

Bruckman licked his lips uneasily. Tonight. He had to kill Wernecke *tonight.* . . .

There was a stirring, a rustling: Someone was getting up, working his way free from the mass of sleepers on one of the platforms. A shadowy figure crossed the room toward Bruckman, and Bruckman tensed, reflexively running his thumb along the jagged end of the spoon, readying himself to rise, to strike—but at the last second, the figure veered aside and stumbled toward another corner. There was a sound like rain drumming on cloth; the man swayed there for a moment, mumbling, and then slowly returned to his pallet, dragging his feet, as if he had pissed his very life away against the wall. It was not Wernecke.

Bruckman eased himself back down to the floor, his heart seeming to shake his wasted body back and forth with the force of its beating. His hand was damp with sweat. He wiped it against his tattered pants, and then clutched the spoon again. . . .

Time seemed to stop. Bruckman waited, stretched out along the hard floorboards, the raw wood rasping his skin, dust clogging his mouth and nose, feeling as though he were already dead, a corpse laid out in the rough pine coffin, feeling eternity pile up on his chest like heavy clots of wet black earth. . . . Outside the hut, the kliegs blazed, banishing night, abolishing it, but here inside the hut it was night, here night survived, perhaps the only pocket of night remaining on a klieg-lit planet, the shafts of light that came in through the slatted windows only serving to accentuate the surrounding darkness, to make it greater and more puissant by comparison. . . . Here in the darkness, nothing ever changed . . . there was only the smothering heat, and the weight of eternal darkness, and the changeless moments that could not pass because there was nothing to differentiate them one from the other. . . .

Many times as he waited Bruckman's eyes would grow heavy and slowly

249

close, but each time his eyes would spring open again at once, and he would find himself staring into the shadows for Wernecke. Sleep would no longer have him, it was a kingdom closed to him now; it spat him out each time he tried to enter it, just as his stomach now spat out the food he placed in it. . . .

The thought of food brought Bruckman to a sharper awareness, and there in the darkness he huddled around his hunger, momentarily forgetting everything else. Never had he been so hungry. . . . He thought of the food he had wasted earlier in the evening, and only the last few shreds of his self-control kept him from moaning aloud.

Bohme did moan aloud then, as though unease were contagious. As Bruckman glanced at him, Bohme said, "Anya," in a clear calm voice; he mumbled a little, and then, a bit more loudly, said, "Tseitel, have you set the table yet?" and Bruckman realized that Bohme was no longer in the camp, that Bohme was back in Dusseldorf in the tiny apartment with his fat wife and his four healthy children, and Bruckman felt a pang of envy go through him, for Bohme, who had escaped.

It was at that moment that Bruckman realized that Wernecke was standing there, just beyond Bohme.

There had been no movement that Bruckman had seen. Wernecke had seemed to slowly materialize from the darkness, atom by atom, bit by incremental bit, until at some point he had been solid enough for his presence to register on Bruckman's consciousness, so that what had been only a shadow a moment before was now unmistakably Wernecke as well, however much a shadow it remained.

Bruckman's mouth went dry with terror, and it almost seemed that he could hear the voice of his dead grandmother whispering in his ears. Boogey tales . . . Wernecke had said *I'm no night spirit.* Remember that he had said that. . . .

Wernecke was almost close enough to touch. He was staring down at Bohme; his face, lit by a dusty shaft of light from the window, was cold and remote, only the total lack of expression hinting at the passion that strained and quivered behind the mask. Slowly, lingeringly, Wernecke stooped over Bohme. "Anya," Bohme said again, caressingly, and then Wernecke's mouth was on his throat.

Let him feed, said a cold remorseless voice in Bruckman's mind. It will be easier to take him when he's nearly sated, when he's fully preoccupied and growing lethargic and logy . . . growing *full*. . . .

Slowly, with infinite caution, Bruckman gathered himself to spring, watching in horror and fascination as Wernecke fed. He could hear Wernecke sucking the juice out of Bohme, as if there were not enough blood in the foolish old man to satiate him, as if there were not enough blood in the whole camp . . . or perhaps, the whole world. . . . And now Bohme was ceasing his feeble struggling, was becoming still. . . .

Bruckman flung himself upon Wernecke, stabbing him twice in the back before his weight bowled them both over. There was a moment of confusion as they rolled and struggled together, all without sound, and then Bruckman found himself sitting atop Wernecke, Wernecke's white face turned up to him. Bruckman drove his weapon into Wernecke again, the shock of the blow jarring Bruckman's arm to the shoulder. Wernecke made no outcry; his eyes were already glazing, but they looked at Bruckman with recognition, with cold anger, with bitter irony and, oddly, with what might have been resignation or relief, with what might almost have been pity. . . .

Bruckman stabbed again and again, driving the blows home with hysterical strength, panting, rocking atop his victim, feeling Wernecke's blood spatter against his face, wrapped in the heat and steam that rose from Wernecke's torn-open body like a smothering black cloud, coughing and choking on it for a moment, feeling the steam seep in through his pores and sink deep into the marrow of his bones, feeling the world seem to pulse and shimmer and change around him, as though he were suddenly seeing through new eyes, as though something had been born anew inside him, and then abruptly he was *smelling* Wernecke's blood, the hot organic reek of it, leaning closer to drink in that sudden overpowering smell, better than the smell of freshly baked bread, better than anything he could remember, rich and heady and strong beyond imagining.

There was a moment of revulsion and horror, and he tried to wonder how long the ancient contamination had been passing from man to man to man, how far into the past the chain of lives stretched, how Wernecke himself had been trapped, and then his parched lips touched wetness, and he was drinking, drinking deeply and greedily, and his mouth was filled with the strong clean taste of copper.

*   *   *

The following night, after Bruckman led the memorial prayers for Wernecke and Bohme, Melnick came to him. Melnick's eyes were bright with tears. "How can we go on without Eduard? He was everything to us. What will we do now? . . . "

"It will be all right, Moishe," Bruckman said. "I promise you, everything will be all right." He put his arm around Melnick for a moment to comfort him, and at the touch sensed the hot blood that pumped through the intricate network of the boy's veins, just under the skin, rich and warm and nourishing, waiting there inviolate for him to set it free.

This story started out as a sentence I jotted down in my story-idea notebook: "vampire in death camp, during Second World War."

It stayed in that form for a couple of years, until one night when Jack Dann was down in Philadelphia for a visit—my calendar shows that it was March 6, 1981—and we were sitting in my living room in my rundown old apartment on Quince Street, kicking around potential ideas for collaborative stories. I got my notebook out and started throwing ideas from it out at Jack; one of them was the vampire sentence. Jack took fire with that idea at once. We talked about the overall plot for a half hour or so, brainstorming, kicking it back and forth, and then Jack got up, sat down behind my ancient, massive Remington office-model standup standard typewriter, which lived on one side of my somewhat-unsteady kitchen table, and started writing the story. He wrote like a madman for a few hours, and by the time he stood up again, he had finished a rough draft of about the first nine manuscript pages, carrying the story through the brilliant Passover scene, which was entirely of his own devising. Then he left, headed back to Binghamton, and the ball was in my court. I worked pretty extensively on the story for a solid week (obviously, I work much more slowly than Jack!), and then worked on it off and on for the next couple of months, with one hurried story conference with Jack at that year's Nebula Banquet to hammer out a plot problem, and the passing back and forth by mail of several different drafts of one particularly difficult scene toward the story's end. The story was finished on May 9, 1981. It bounced around for a while, and finally sold to *Oui*. It was reprinted in *The Magazine of Fantasy and Science Fiction,* where its appearance prompted a major horror writer to remark that it was the most morally offensive story he'd ever read. We were quietly proud.

At the core of the story, it seems to me, is the question of identity. In spite of being a supernatural monster, Wernecke is *perceived* by the Nazis as a Jew, and so that's the way they treat him, no better or worse than the other prisoners. To some extent, we are what other people think we are, whether we want to be or not. For me, the real meat of the story is in the two conversations between Wernecke and Bruckman, and in some ways those were the most difficult scenes to write.

I'd always wanted to call a story "Down Among the Dead Men," a line from an old English folksong, and the title certainly seemed to fit the story well enough, so that's what we called it.

Gardner Dozois

Anoted writer of genre horror once complained that this story was in bad taste, as it depicted a concentration camp internee as a vampire. It is our opinion, however, that in order to rise above genre cookie patterns, fiction must take chances and try to reflect that which really *is* the dark side of human nature.

It has been said that the events of the holocaust were so terrible in themselves that they are beyond any kind of fictive telling. Note some of the statistics: In five years the Nazis

253

exterminated nine million people. Six million were Jews. The efficiency of the concentration camps was such that twenty thousand people could be gassed in a day. The Nazis at Treblinka boasted that they could "process" the Jews who arrived in the cattle cars in forty-five minutes.

In 1943 six hundred desperate Jews revolted and burned Treblinka to the ground. These men were willing to martyr themselves so that a few might live to "testify" and tell a disbelieving world of the atrocities committed in the camps, lest those who had died be forgotten . . . lest *we* forget those events which are too terrible to contemplate.

Out of the six hundred, forty survived to tell their story.

"Down Among the Dead Men," like the companion story "Camps," is our attempt to testify, to bring the terror and horror and discomfort to another generation of readers in the only way we know how. Perhaps through the metaphoric and symbolic medium of horror—of the fantastic—we might catch a dark reflection of that terrible event. Even if it is impossible to grasp the terrible reality of what happened in the camps, still, we must try.

In order to survive, the prisoners had to take part in the "process" of killing other prisoners; that was one of the greatest attrocities of the concentration camps. It became a maxim of the survivors—those who did not let themselves be reduced to *Musselmänner,* the walking, living dead—that "first you save yourself, then you save yourself, and then, and only then, can you try to save others." Prisoners could survive only against almost impossible odds, and the guilt was impossible to escape. It was built into the Nazi extermination system . . . into the new technology of genocide.

To live, you had to help kill.

The vampire is . . . *us!*

Indeed, the vampire is a horrifying metaphor. It would have been much more palatable if we had made him one of the Nazis. But perhaps by testifying, by taking chances, by leaning over the edge of what might be construed as "bad taste," we can keep the memory of what happened alive.

254

It is too easy to forget our history.

But as the philosopher George Santayana said, "Those who cannot remember the past are condemned to repeat it."

God forbid. . . .

Jack Dann

...To Feel Another's Woe

CHET WILLIAMSON

*The sharklike intensity necessary to succeed in the highly competitive
New York theater scene is a given. Williamson has obviously brushed
against the life or he wouldn't have written the following piece about
those who will do* anything *to make it.*

I had to admit she looked like a vampire when Kevin described her as
such. Her face, at least, with those high model's cheekbones and
absolutely huge, wet-looking eyes. The jet of her hair set off her pale
skin strikingly, and that skin was perfect, nearly luminous. To the best
of my knowledge, however, vampires didn't wear Danskin tops and Annie
Hall flop-slacks, nor did they audition for Broadway shows.

There must have been two hundred of us jammed into the less than
immaculate halls of the Ansonia Hotel that morning, with photo/résumés
clutched in one hand, scripts of *A Streetcar Named Desire* in the other. John
Weidner was directing a revival at Circle in the Square, and every New
York actor with an Equity card and a halfway intelligible Brooklyn dialect
under his collar was there to try out. Stanley Kowalski had already been
spoken for by a new Italian-American film star with more *chutzpah* than
talent, but the rest of the roles were open. I was hoping for Steve or
Mitch, or maybe even a standby, just something to pay the rent.

I found myself in line next to Kevin McQuinn, a gay song-and-dance
man I'd done Jones Beach with two years before. A nice guy, not at all
flouncy. "Didn't know this was a musical," I smiled at him.

"Sure. You never heard of the Stella aria? And he sang softly, "I'll never
stop saying Steh-el-*la* . . .""

"Seriously. You going dramatic?"

He shrugged. "No choice. Musicals these days are all rock or opera or rock opera. No soft shoes in *Sweeney Todd*."

"*Sweeney Todd* closed ages ago."

"That's 'cause they didn't have no soft shoes."

Then she walked in holding her P/R and script, and sat on the floor with her back to the wall as gracefully as if she owned the place. I was, to Kevin's amusement, instantly smitten.

"Forget it," he said. "She'd eat you alive."

"I wish. Who is she?"

"Name's Sheila Remarque."

"Shitty stage name."

"She was born with it, so she says. Me, I believe her. Nobody'd *pick* that."

"She any good?"

Kevin smiled, a bit less broadly than his usually mobile face allowed. "Let's just say that I've got twenty bucks that says she'll get whatever part she's after."

"Serious?"

"The girl's phenomenal. You catch *Lear* in the park last summer?" I nodded. "She played Goneril."

"Oh *yeah*." I was amazed that I hadn't recalled the name. "She *was* good."

"You said good, I said phenomenal. Along with the critics."

As I thought back, I remembered the performance vividly. Generally Cordelia stole the show from Lear's two nasty daughters, but all eyes had been on Goneril at the matinee I'd seen. It wasn't that the actress had been upstaging, or doing anything to excess. It was simply (or complexly, if you're an actor) that she was so damned *believable*. There'd been no trace of *acting,* no indication shared between actress and audience, as even the finest performers will do, no self-consciousness whatsoever, only utterly true emotion. As I remembered, the one word I had associated with it was *awesome*. How stupid, I thought, to have forgotten her name. "What else do you know about her?" I asked Kevin.

"Not much. A mild reputation with the boys. Love 'em and leave 'em. A Theda Bara vampire type."

"Ever work with her?"

"Three years ago. *Oklahoma* at Allenberry. I did Will Parker, and she was in the chorus. Fair voice, danced a little, but lousy presence. A real poser, you know? I don't know what the hell happened."

I started to ask Kevin if he knew where she studied, when he suddenly tensed. I followed his gaze, and saw a man coming down the hall carrying a dance bag. He was tall and thin, with light-brown hair and a nondescript face. It's hard to describe features on which not the slightest bit of emotion is displayed. Instead of sitting on the floor like the rest of us, he remained standing, a few yards away from Sheila Remarque, whom he looked at steadily, yet apparently without interest. She looked up, saw him, gave a brief smile, and returned to her script.

Kevin leaned closer and whispered. "You want to know about *Ms.* Remarque, *there's* the man you should ask, not me."

"Why? Who is he?" The man hadn't taken his eyes from the girl, but I couldn't tell whether he watched her in lust or anger. At any rate, I admired her self-control. Save for that first glance, she didn't acknowledge him at all.

"Name's Guy Taylor."

"The one who was in *Annie?*"

Kevin nodded. "Three years here. One on the road. Same company I went out with. Used to drink together. He was hilarious, even when he was sober. But put the drinks in him and he'd make Eddie Murphy look like David Merrick. Bars would fall apart laughing."

"He went with this girl?"

"Lived with her for three, maybe four months, just this past year."

"They split up, I take it."

"Mmm-hmm. Don't know much about it, though." He shook his head. "I ran into Guy a week or so ago at the *Circle of Three* auditions. I was really happy to see him, but he acted like he barely knew me. Asked him how his lady was—I'd never met her, but the word had spread—and he told me he was living alone now, so I didn't press it. Asked a couple people and found out she'd walked out on him. Damn near crushed him. He must've had it hard."

"That's love for you."

"Yeah. Ain't I glad I don't mess with women."

Kevin and I started talking about other things then, but I couldn't keep my eyes off Sheila Remarque's haunting face, nor off the vacuous features of Guy Taylor, who watched the girl with the look of a stolid, stupid guard dog. I wondered if he'd bite anybody who dared to talk to her.

At ten o'clock, as scheduled, the line started to move. When I got to the table, the assistant casting director, or whatever flunky was using that name, looked at my P/R and at me, evidently approved of what he saw, and told me to come back at two o'clock for a reading. Kevin, right beside me, received only a shake of the head and a "thank you for coming."

"Dammit," Kevin said as we walked out. "I shouldn't have stood behind you in line, then I wouldn't've looked so un-macho. I mean, didn't they *know* about Tennessee Williams, for crissake?"

When I went back to the Ansonia at two, there were over thirty people already waiting, twice as many men as women. Among the dozen or so femmes was Sheila Remarque, her nose still stuck in her script, oblivious to those around her. Guy Taylor was also there, standing against a wall as before. He had a script open in front of him, and from time to time would look down at it, but most of the time he stared at Sheila Remarque, who, I honestly believe, was totally indifferent to, and perhaps even ignorant of, his perusal.

As I sat watching the two of them, I thought that the girl would make a stunning Blanche, visually at least. She seemed to have that elusive, fragile quality that Vivien Leigh exemplified so well in the film. I'd only seen Jessica Tandy, who'd originated the role, in still photos, but she always seemed too horsey-looking for my tastes. By no stretch of the imagination could Sheila Remarque be called horsey. She was exquisite porcelain, and I guess I must have become transfixed by her for a moment, for the next time I looked away from her toward Guy Taylor, he was staring at me with that same damned expressionless stare. I was irritated by the proprietary emotion I placed on his face, but found it so disquieting that I couldn't glare back. So I looked at my script again.

After a few minutes, a fiftyish man I didn't recognize came out and spoke to us. "Okay, Mr. Weidner will eliminate some of you without hearing you read. Those of you who make the final cut, be prepared to do one of two scenes. We'll have the ladies who are reading for Blanche and you men reading for Mitch first. As you were told this morning, ladies, scene ten, guys six. Use your scripts if you want to. Not's okay too. Let's go."

Seven women and fifteen men, me and Guy Taylor among them,

259

followed the man into what used to be a ballroom. At one end of the high-ceilinged room was a series of raised platforms with a few wooden chairs on them. Ten yards back from this makeshift stage were four folding director's chairs. Another five yards in back of these were four rows of ten each of the same rickety wooden chairs there were on the stage. We sat on these while Weidner, the director, watched us file in. "I'm sorry we can't be in the theater," he said, "but the set there now can't be struck for auditions. We'll have to make do here. Let's start with the gentlemen for a change."

He looked at the stage manager, who read from his clipboard, "Adams."

That was me. I stood up, script in hand. Given a choice, I always held book in auditions. It gives you self-confidence, and if you try to go without and go up on the lines, you look like summer stock. Besides, that's why they call them readings.

"Would someone be kind enough to read Blanche in scene six with Mr. Adams?" Weidner asked. A few girls were rash enough to raise their hands and volunteer for a scene they hadn't prepared, but Weidner's eyes fell instantly on Sheila Remarque. "Miss Remarque, isn't it?" She nodded. "My congratulations on your Goneril. Would you be kind enough to read six? I promise I won't let it color my impressions of your scene ten."

Bullshit, I thought, but she nodded graciously, and together we ascended the squeaking platform.

Have you ever played a scene opposite an animal or a really cute little kid? If you have, you know how utterly impossible it is to get the audience to pay any attention to you whatsoever. That was exactly how I felt doing a scene with Sheila Remarque. Not that my reading wasn't good, because it was, better by far than I would have done reading with a prompter or an ASM, because she gave me something I could react to. She made Blanche so real that I had to be real too, and I was good.

But not as good as her. No way.

She used no book, had all the moves and lines down pat. But like I said of her Goneril, there was no *indication* of acting at all. She spoke and moved on that cheapjack stage as if she were and had always been Blanche DuBois, formerly of Belle Rêve, presently of Elysian Fields, New Orleans in the year 1947. Weidner didn't interrupt after a few lines, a few pages, the way directors usually do, but let the scene glide on effortlessly to its end, when, still holding my script, I kissed Blanche DuBois on "her forehead and her eyes and finally her lips," and she sobbed out her line, " 'Sometimes—there's God—so quickly!' " and it was over and Blanche DuBois vanished, leaving Sheila Remarque and me on that platform with them all looking up at us soundlessly. Weidner's smile was suffused with wonder. But not for me. I'd been good, but she'd been great.

"Thank you, Mr. Adams. Thank you very much. Nice reading. We have your résumé, yes. Thank you," and he nodded in a gesture of dismissal that took me off the platform. "Thank you too, Miss Remarque. Well done. While you're already up there, would you care to do scene ten for us?"

She nodded, and I stopped at the exit. Ten was a hell of a scene, the one where Stanley and the drunken Blanche are alone in the flat, and I had to see her do it. I whispered a request to stay to the fiftyish man who'd brought us in, and he nodded an okay, as if speaking would break whatever spell was on the room. I remained there beside him.

"Our Stanley Kowalski was to be here today to read with the Blanches and Stellas, but a TV commitment prevented him," Weidner said somewhat bitchily. "So if one of you gentlemen would be willing to read with Miss Remarque . . ."

There were no idiots among the men. Not one volunteered. "Ah, Mr. Taylor," I heard Weidner say. My stomach tightened. I didn't know whether he'd chosen Taylor to read with her out of sheer malevolence, or whether he was ignorant of their relationship, and it was coincidence— merely his spotting Taylor's familiar face. Either way, I thought, the results could be unpleasant. And from the way several of the gypsies' shoulders stiffened, I could tell they were thinking the same thing. "Would you please?"

Taylor got up slowly, and joined the girl on the platform. As far as I could see, there was no irritation in his face, nor was there any sign of dismay in Sheila Remarque's deep, wet eyes. She smiled at him as though he were a stranger, and took a seat facing the "audience."

"Anytime," said Weidner. He sounded anxious. Not impatient, just anxious.

Sheila Remarque became drunk. Just like that, in the space of a heartbeat. Her whole body fell into the posture of a long-developed alcoholism. Her eyes blurred, her mouth opened, a careless slash across the ruin of her face, lined and bagged with booze. She spoke the lines as if no one had ever said them before, so any onlooker would swear that it was Blanche DuBois's liquor-dulled brain that was creating them, and in no way were they merely words that had existed on a printed page for forty years, words filtered through the voice of a performer.

She finished speaking into the unseen mirror, and Guy Taylor walked toward her as Stanley Kowalski. Blanche saw him, spoke to him. But though she spoke to Stanley Kowalski, it was Guy Taylor who answered, only Guy Taylor reading lines, without a trace of emotion. Oh, the *expression* was there, the nuances, the rhythm of the lines and their meaning was clear. But it was like watching La Duse play a scene with an electronic synthesizer. She destroyed him, and I thought back, hoping she hadn't done the same to me.

This time Weidner didn't let the scene play out to the end. I had to give him credit. As awful as Taylor was, *I* couldn't have brought myself to deny the reality of Sheila Remarque's performance by interrupting, but Weidner did, during one of Stanley's longer speeches about his cousin who opened beer bottles with his teeth. "Okay, fine," Weidner called out. "Good enough. Thank you, Mr. Taylor. I think that's all we need see of you today." Weidner looked away from him. "Miss Remarque, if you wouldn't mind, I'd like to hear that one more time. Let's see . . . Mr. Carver, would you read Stanley, please." Carver, a chorus gypsy who had no business doing heavy work, staggered to the platform, his face pale, but I didn't wait to see if he'd survive. I'd seen enough wings pulled off flies for one day, and was out the door, heading to the elevator even before Taylor had come off the platform.

I had just pushed the button when I saw Taylor, his dance bag over his shoulder, come out of the ballroom. He walked slowly down the hall toward me, and I prayed the car would arrive quickly enough that I wouldn't have to ride with him. But the Ansonia's lifts have seen better days, and by the time I stepped into the car he was a scant ten yards away. I held the door for him. He stepped in, the doors closed, and we were alone.

Taylor looked at me for a moment. "You'll get Mitch," he said flatly.

I shrugged self-consciously and smiled. "There's a lot of people to read."

"But they won't read Mitch with *her*. And your reading *was* good."
I nodded agreement. "She helped."

"May I," he said after a pause, "give you some advice?" I nodded. "If they give you Mitch," he said, "turn them down."

"Why?" I asked, laughing.

"She's sure to be Blanche. Don't you think?"

"So?"

"You heard me read today."

"So?"

"Have you seen me work?"

"I saw you in *Annie*. And in *Bus Stop* at ELT."

"And?"

"You were good. Real good."

"And what about today?"

I looked at the floor.

"Tell me." I looked at him, my lips pinched. "Shitty," he said. "Nothing there, right?"

"Not much," I said.

"She did that. Took it from me." He shook his head. "Stay away from her. She can do it to you too."

The first thing you learn in professional theater is that actors are children. I say that, knowing full well that I'm one myself. Our egos are huge, yet our feelings are as delicate as orchids. In a way, it stems from the fact that in other trades, rejections are impersonal. Writers aren't rejected—it's one particular story or novel that is. For factory workers, or white-collars, it's lack of knowledge or experience that loses jobs. But for an actor, it's the way he looks, the way he talks, the way he moves that make the heads nod yes or no, and that's rejection on the most deeply personal scale, like kids calling each other Nickel-nose or Fatso. And often that childish hurt extends to other relationships as well. Superstitious? Imaginative? Ballplayers have nothing on us. So when Taylor started blaming Sheila Remarque for his thespian rockslide, I knew it was only because he couldn't bear to admit that it was *he* who had let his craft slip away, not the girl who had taken it from him.

The elevator doors opened, and I stepped off. "Wait," he said, coming after me. "You don't believe me."

"Look, man," I said, turning in exasperation, "I don't know what went on between you and her and I don't care, okay? If she messed you over, I'm sorry, but I'm an actor and I need a job and if I get it I'll *take* it!"

His face remained placid. "Let me buy you a drink," he said.

"Oh Jesus . . ."

"You don't have to be afraid. I won't get violent." He forced a smile. "Do you think I've *been* violent? Have I even raised my voice?"

"No."

"Then please. I just want to talk to you."

I had to admit to myself that I *was* curious. Most actors would have shown more fire over things that meant so much to them, but Taylor was strangely zombielike, as if life were just a walk-through. "All right," I said, "all right."

We walked silently down Broadway. By the time we got to Charlie's it was three thirty, a slow time for the bar. I perched on a stool, but Taylor shook his head. "Table," he said, and we took one and ordered. It turned out we were both bourbon drinkers.

"Jesus," he said after a long sip. "It's cold."

It was. Manhattan winters are never balmy, and the winds that belly through the streets cut through anything short of steel.

"All right," I said. "We're here. You're buying me a drink. Now. You have a story for me?"

"I do. And after I tell it you can go out and do what you like."

"I intend to."

"I won't try to stop you," he went on, not hearing me. "I don't think I could even if I wanted to. It's your life, your career."

"Get to the point."

"I met her last summer. June. I know Joe Papp, and he invited me to the party after the Lear opening, so I went. Sheila was there with a guy, and I walked up and introduced myself to them, and told her how much I enjoyed her performance. She thanked me, very gracious, very friendly, and told me she'd seen me several times and liked my work as well. I thought it odd at the time, the way she came on to me. Very strong, with those big, wet, bedroom eyes of hers eating me up. But her date didn't seem to care. He didn't seem to care about much of anything. Just stood there and drank while she talked, then sat down and drank some more. She told me later, when we were together, that he was a poet. Unpublished, of course, she said. She told me that his work wasn't very good technically, but that it was very emotional. 'Rich with feeling,' were the words she used.

"I went to see her in Lear again, several times really, and was more impressed with each performance. The poet was waiting for her the second time I went, but the third, she left alone. I finessed her into a drink, we talked, got along beautifully. She told me it was all over between her and the poet, and that night she ended up in my bed. It was good, and she seemed friendly, passionate, yet undemanding. After a few more dates, a few more nights and mornings, I suggested living together, no commitments. She agreed, and the next weekend she moved in with me.

"I want you to understand one thing, though. I never loved her. I never told her I loved her or even suggested it. For me, it was companionship and sex, and that was all. Though she was good to be with, nice to kiss, to hold, to share things with, I never loved her. And I know she never loved me." He signaled the waiter and another drink came. Mine was still half full. "So I'm not a . . . a victim of unrequited love, all right? I just want you to be sure of that." I nodded and he went on.

"It started a few weeks after we were living together. She'd want to play games with me, she said. Theater games. You know, pretend she was doing something or say something to get a certain emotion out of me. Most of the time she didn't let me know right away what she was doing. She'd see if she could get me jealous, or mad, or sullen. Happy too. And then she'd laugh and say she was just kidding, that she'd just wanted to see my reactions. Well, I thought that was bullshit. I put it down as a technique exercise rather than any method crap, and in a way I could understand it—wanting to be face-to-face with emotions to examine them—but I still thought it was an imposition on me, an invasion of my privacy. She didn't do it often, maybe once or twice a week. I tried it on her occasionally, but she never bit, just looked at me as if I were a kid trying to play a man's game.

"Somewhere along the line it started getting kinky. While we were having sex, she'd call me by another name, or tell me about something sad she'd remembered, anything to get different reactions, different rises out of me. Sometimes . . ." He looked down, drained his drink. "Sometimes I'd . . . come and I'd cry at the same time."

The waiter was nearby, and I signaled for another round. "Why did you stay with her?"

265

"It wasn't . . . she didn't do this all the time, like I said. And I *liked* her. It got so I didn't even mind it when she'd pull this stuff on me, and she knew it. Once she even got me when I was stoned, and a couple of times after I'd had too much to drink. I didn't care. Until winter came.

"I hadn't been doing much after the summer. A few industrials here in town, some voice-over stuff. Good money, but just straight song and dance, flat narration, and no reviews. So the beginning of December Harv Piersall calls me to try out for *Ahab.* The musical that closed in previews? He wanted me to read for Starbuck, a scene where Starbuck is planning to shoot Ahab to save the Pequod. It was a good scene, a strong scene, and I got up there and I couldn't do a thing with it. Not a goddamned thing. I was utterly flat, just like in my narration and my singing around a Pontiac. But there it hadn't mattered—I hadn't had to put out any emotion—just sell the product, that was all. But *now,* when I had to feel something, had to express something, I couldn't. Harv asked me if anything was wrong, and I babbled some excuse about not feeling well, and when he invited me to come back and read again I did, a day later, and it was the same.

"That weekend I went down to St. Mark's to see Sheila in an OOB production—it was a new translation of *Medea* by some grad student at NYU—and she'd gotten the title role. They'd been rehearsing off and on for a month, no pay to speak of, but she was enthusiastic about it. It was the largest and most important part she'd done. Papp was there that night, someone got Prince to come too. The translation was garbage. No set, tunics for costumes, nothing lighting. But Sheila . . ."

He finished his latest drink, spat the ice back into the glass. "She was . . . superb. Every emotion was real. They should have been. She'd taken them from me.

"Don't look at me like that. I thought what you're thinking too, at first. That I was paranoid, jealous of her talents. But once I started to think things through, I knew it was the only answer.

"She was so loving to me afterward, smiled at me and held my arm and introduced me to her friends, and I felt as dull and lifeless as that poet I'd seen her with. Even then I suspected what she'd done, but I didn't say anything to her about it. That next week when I tried to get in touch with the poet, I found out he'd left the city, gone home to wherever it was he'd come from. I went over to Lincoln Center, to their videotape collection, and watched *King Lear*. I wanted to see if I could find anything that didn't jell, that wasn't quite *right*. Hell, I didn't know what I was looking for, just that I'd know when I saw it."

He shook his head. "It was . . . incredible. On the tape there was no sign of the performance I'd seen her give. Instead I saw a flat, lifeless, amateurish performance, dreadfully bad in contrast to the others. I couldn't believe it, watched it again. The same thing. Then I knew why she never auditioned for commercials, or for film. It didn't . . . *show up* on camera. She could fool people, but not a camera.

"I went back to the apartment then, and told her what I'd found out. It wasn't guessing on my part, not a theory, because I *knew* by then. You see, I *knew*."

Taylor stopped talking and looked down into his empty glass. I thought perhaps I'd made a huge mistake in going to the bar with him, for he was most certainly paranoid, and could conceivably become violent as well, in spite of his assurances to the contrary. "So what . . ." My "so" came out too much like "sho," but I pushed on with my question while he flagged the waiter, who raised an eyebrow, but brought more drinks. "So what did she say? When you told her?"

"She . . . verified it. Told me that I was right. 'In a way,' she said. In a way."

"Well . . ." I shook my head to clear it. ". . . didn't she probably mean that she was just studying you? That's hardly, hardly *stealing* your emotions, is it?"

"No. She stole them."

"That's silly. That's still silly. You've still got them."

"No. I wanted . . . when I knew for sure, I wanted to kill her. The way she smiled at me, as though I were powerless to take anything back, as though she had planned it all from the moment we met—that made me want to kill her." He turned his empty eyes on me. "But I didn't. Couldn't. I couldn't get angry enough."

He sighed. "She moved out. That didn't bother me. I was glad. As glad as I could feel after what she'd done. I don't know *how* she did it. I think it was something she learned, or learned she had. I don't know whether I'll ever get them back or not, either. Oh, not from *her*. Never from her. But on my own. Build them up inside me somehow. The emotions. The feelings. Maybe someday."

He reached across the table and touched my hand, his fingers surprisingly warm. "So much I don't know. But one thing I do. She'll do it again, find someone else, *you* if you let her. I saw how you were looking at her today." I pulled my hand away from his, bumping my drink. He grabbed it before it spilled, set it upright. "Don't," he cautioned. "Don't have anything to do with her."

"It's absurd," I said, half stuttering. "Ridiculous. You still . . . show emotions."

"Maybe. Maybe a few. But they're only outward signs. Inside it's hollow." His head went to one side. "You don't believe me."

"N—no . . ." And I didn't, not then.

"You should have known me before."

Suddenly I remembered Kevin at the audition, and his telling me how funny and wild Guy Taylor had gotten on a few drinks. My own churning stomach reminded me of how many we had had sitting here for less than an hour, and my churning mind showed me Sheila Remarque's drunk, drunk, perfectly drunk Blanche DuBois earlier that afternoon. "You've had . . ." I babbled, ". . . how many drinks have you had?"

He shrugged.

"But . . . you're not . . . showing any *signs* . . ."

"Yes. That's right," he said in a clear, steady, sober voice. "That's right."

He crossed his forearms on the table, lowered his head onto them, and wept. The sobs were loud, prolonged, shaking his whole body.

He wept.

"There!" I cried, staggering to my feet. "There, see? See? You're *crying,* you're *crying!* See?"

He raised his head and looked at me, still weeping, still weeping, with not one tear to be seen.

When the call came offering me Mitch, I took the part. I didn't even consider turning it down. Sheila Remarque had, as Kevin, Guy Taylor, and I had anticipated, been cast as Blanche DuBois, and she smiled warmly at me when I entered the studio for the first reading, as though she remembered our audition with fondness. I was pleasant, but somewhat aloof at first, not wanting the others to see, to suspect what I was going to do.

I thought it might be difficult to get her alone, but it wasn't. She had already chosen me, I could tell, watching me through the readings, coming up to me and chatting at the breaks. By the end of the day she'd learned where I lived, that I was single, unattached, and straight, and that I'd been bucking for eight years to get a part this good. She told me that she lived only a block away from my building (a lie, I later found out), and, after the rehearsal, suggested we take a cab together and split the expense. I agreed, and the cab left us out on West 72nd next to the park.

It was dark and cold, and I saw her shiver under her down-filled jacket. I shivered too, for we were alone at last, somewhat hidden by the trees, and there were no passersby to be seen, only the taxis and buses and cars hurtling past.

I turned to her, the smile gone from my face. "I know what you've done," I said. "I talked to Guy Taylor. He told me all about it. And warned me."

Her face didn't change. She just hung on to that soft half smile of hers, and watched me with those liquid eyes.

"He said . . . you'd be after me. He told me not to take the part. But I had to. I had to know if it's true, all he said."

Her smile faded, she looked down at the dirty, ice-covered sidewalk, and nodded, creases of sadness at the corners of her eyes. I reached out and did what I had planned, said what I had wanted to say to her ever since leaving Guy Taylor crying without tears at the table in Charlie's.

"Teach me," I said, taking her hand as gently as I knew how. "I'd be no threat to you, no competition for roles. In fact, you may need me, need a man who can equal you on stage. Because there aren't any now. You can take what you want from me as long as you can teach me how to get it back again.

"Please. Teach me."

When she looked up at me, her face was wet with tears. I kissed them away, neither knowing nor caring whose they were.

A decade ago I was a member of Actors' Equity, active in stock and regional theater. But when I endured the audition process in New York for a few months, I decided that I preferred those individual writer's rejections that my character Adams speaks of to the blanket rejections that are the lot of actors. I have sat in the halls of the Ansonia, as well as on the other side of the audition table (as a writer and producer of industrial shows), and watched the people bare their souls while contradictorily sheltering their fragile egos. I've seen a few grow old, lose their talents, and eerily vanish from an occupation so unstable that, when people ask me why I became a freelance writer, I can honestly answer, "for the security."

The realities of the acting life can be a far more chilling horror story than the one that arises from Sheila Remarque's odd gift.

Chet Williamson

Time Lapse

JOE HALDEMAN

A father's loss triggers an obsession that ends up violating the trust needed within families. A powerful poem by Joe Haldeman, who is primarily a science fiction writer, "Time Lapse" perfectly captures the need that becomes vampirism in a tortured relationship.

At first a pink whirl
there on the white square:
the girl too small to stay still.

    After a few years, though
    (less than a minute),
    her feet stay in the same place.

Her pink body vibrates with undiscipline;
her hair a blond fog. She grows now
perceptibly. Watch . . . she's seven,
eight, nine: one year each twelve seconds.

    Always, now, in the audience,
    a man clears his throat.
    Always, a man.

Almost every morning
for almost eighteen years,
she came to the small white room,
put her bare feet on the cold floor,
on the pencilled H's,

and stood with her hands palms out
while her father took four pictures:
both profiles, front, rear.

It was their secret. Something
they did for Mommy in heaven,
a record of the daughter
she never lived to see.

By the time she left (rage and something
else driving her to the arms of a woman)
he had over twenty thousand
eight-by-ten glossy prints of her
growing up, locked in white boxes.

He sought out a man with a laser
who some called an artist
(some called a poseur),
with a few quartets of pictures,
various ages: baby, child, woman.
He saw the possibilities.
He paid the price.

It took a dozen Kelly Girls
thirty working hours apiece
to turn those files of pretty pictures
into digits. The artist,
or showman,
fed the digits into his machines,
and out came a square
of white where
in more than three dimensions
a baby girl
grows into a woman
in less than four minutes.

Always a man clears his throat.
The small breasts bud

and swell in seconds. Secret
places grow blond stubble, silk;
each second a spot of blood.

Her stance changes
as hips push out
and suddenly
she puts her hands on her hips.
For the last four seconds,
four months;
a gesture of defiance.

The second time you see her
(no one watches only once),
concentrate on her expression.
The child's ambiguous flicker
becomes uneasy smile,
trembling thirty times a second.
The eyes, a blur at first,
stare fixedly
in obedience
and then
(as the smile hardens)
the last four seconds,
four months:

> a glare of rage

All unwilling,
she became the most famous
face and figure of her age.
Everywhere stares.
As if Mona Lisa, shawled,
had walked into the Seven/Eleven . . .

No wonder she killed her father.

The judge was sympathetic.
The jury wept for her.

273

They studied the evidence
from every conceivable angle:

Not guilty,
by reason of insanity.

So now she spends her days
listening quietly, staring
while earnest people talk,
trying to help her grow.

But every night she starts to scream
and has to be restrained, sedated,
before she'll let them take her back

to rest

in her small white room.

I carried this idea around for almost seventeen years. I remember mentioning the notion of this creepily exploitative father to my brother when his daughter was born. I wrote it a few months after taking her downtown to get her first driver's license.

Why so long a gestation period? Maybe it's because I was thinking of it in too conventional a way. As a plain short story, it couldn't jell, because plot and character were subordinate to the single visual image that's at the center of the story. Written as a narrative poem, though, the story can "radiate" from the image. That's my theory, anyhow. It was fun to write.

Joe Haldeman

Dirty Work

PAT CADIGAN

Deadpan Allie, the pathosfinder, is a character familiar to Pat Cadigan fans, who've followed Allie's career through several science fiction stories (a few of which appeared in OMNI) and the sf novel Mindplayers (Bantam). Because of my fondness for the character and because so many of her "cases" seemed to verge on the subject of vampirism, I asked Pat to write a Deadpan Allie story for this book.

Com1879625-JJJDeadpanAllie
TZT-Tijuaoutlie
XQWithheld

NelsonNelson
NelsonNelsonMindplayAgency
TZT-Easct.Njyman
XQ.2717.06X0661818JL

GO

So, NN, how's the family? Ah, sorry, I mean the agency. Of course. Yes, of course. I'm sending you this instead of coming back myself. Sorry to cut into your Bolshoi Ballet viewing time like this. I won't be transmitting a vocal. I haven't spoken for, I'm not sure, days. Lots of days. Something's happened to my speech center. I'd have to put a socket in my head to vocalize and there doesn't seem to be a surgeon handy. Anyway, I know how much you hate sockets. Then, too, I don't speak any

Romance language. But just about all the merchants sign, so I make my needs known that way. I used to sign a lot back at J. Walter Tech when I was getting my almost worthless education and learning to read Emotional Indexes—Indices?—and I'd forgotten how much I enjoyed it. You know, NN, I like it so much, I'm thinking about just letting my speech center go. I haven't sustained complete damage to language. I can write, and I can read what I've written for as long as my short-term memory cares to hold it. It's a capricious thing, short-term memory. Where was I? Oh. Ever hear of that kind of damage before? I don't know if I can understand anything said to me because I haven't heard any English or Mandarin since I got here. But then, maybe I wouldn't know if I had. I hear them talking here in their own language and it doesn't sound right, it doesn't sound like language. It sounds like noise. Clang-clang, clang-clang. Being a mute may be unnecessary in this day, but it's hardly a handicap in my profession. People talk too goddam much.

You wouldn't see it that way. *You* talked me into this job. Big bonus, you said. Buy the apartment I've been scouting, you said. Just a job, where's my professionalism, you said, and you said, and you said. Nothing wrong with *your* speech center.

But you know it—you would love me if you could see me now. Because one of the other effects of this half-assed aphasia I've got is my facial muscles are paralyzed. You'd never ask me again if they called me Deadpan Allie for nothing.

That's what you asked me when you talked me into this. I can remember. I've got one eye out and I'm plugged into the memory boost (all the equipment's here, I wouldn't want it to fall into the wrong hands. Like yours.) Left eye. I tried the other eye but I don't think my left hemisphere wants to talk to you because I can't type and remember at the same time plugged in on that side. Typing lefthanded, too. I guess I've got enough language on that side of the brain.

I'm meandering. You'll have to bear with me.

I told you when you talked me into this I don't do dirty work. People like me because I'm clean. I was clean with the fetishist, I was clean with the mindsuck composer, I was clean with your son-in-law and he pushed me. But you wanted me to do this one. Do you remember what I said or do you need a boost for it? I told you anyone who insisted on working with an empath didn't need me.

Fine. It's a silly prejudice. Maybe I wouldn't want anyone to get that close to me without the decency of a machine between us. It's my right to feel that way. Why did you send me when you knew I felt that way? Professionalism. I know that. Don't try getting in touch with me to tell me something I already know. Fine. They asked for me. They asked for me. Fine. They asked for me. They asked for me. Fine. They asked for—

Excuse. I got a bounce on that, a real ricochet. I'm not myself today. Or maybe I am, for the first time in a long time.

I'd always thought of the entourage as a thing of the past. Not just entourage, but Entourage, as in the people who tend to accumulate around someone who happens to be Somebody. Now, I've seen performance artists who keep an audience on retainer so they can hone work as they go but an Entourage is a lot more than that, and a lot less, too. Caverty had a whole houseful of Entourage—highly unusual for a holo artist, I thought—and there was a hell of a lot of house. I'd already been told how it was with him—hell, I knew about the empath, didn't I?—but that didn't mean I could anticipate the experience of opening the front door and finding them all there.

Yes, I did open the front door myself. Noisy crowd, they didn't hear me ring so I tried the controls and the door swung open to the entry hall. All those done-over mansions in the Midwest retained the original entry halls, complete with chandelier. Yesterday's gentility, today's bright idea. This one was tiled in a black-and-white compass pattern. When you came in, you could see you were standing just slightly east of true north, if that sort of thing mattered to you. The Compass hasn't permeated everything the way the Zodiac has, but then it's a pretty new idea. Personally, I think *What's your direction?* will always be as dumb a question as *What's your sign?* None of the half-dozen people standing around in the entry hall asked me either question, or anything else, including *Need some help?* as I unloaded my baggage from the flyer. The pilot watched from the front seat; she was union and definitely not a baggage handler, as she'd told me several times on the trip out.

It wasn't until I had all my system components piled up on the center of the compass—excuse, Compass, I mean (they'd want it that way)—that someone broke loose from the group and came over. To examine the boxes, as it turned out. She refused to notice me until she heard the whiny hum of the flyer as it lifted off outside.

"Are these for Caverty?" she asked, putting one hand on top of the pile proprietarily.

I put my own hand atop the pile, even with hers. "Not exactly. I'm the pathosfinder."

The silver-and-gold-weave eyebrows went up. In the middle of the day, they gave her the look of someone who hasn't yet gone home from last night's party. So did the rest of her outfit, which seemed to be a collection of swatches from this season's best fabrics or something, predominantly silver and gold with the textures varying. Some people I know would have tried to buy it right off her back.

"Pathosfinder," she said, tasting the word uncertainly. "I don't think—" she shrugged. "I'm sorry, I don't remember us ordering a pathosfinder." She turned to the other people still clustered over near the foot of a curving marble-and-ebony staircase. "Anyone put in an order for a pathosfinder?"

"Caverty did," I said before any of them could answer. "You should ask him."

The gray eyes widened; not biogems, I noticed, but eyes that looked like eyes. It seemed kind of out of character for her. "Oh, no," she said. "Caverty works with an empath, everybody knows that."

"He still works with an empath," I said, "only he's also going to be working with me temporarily."

The woman shrugged again. "I'm sorry, I don't think you understand how things are. If Caverty ordered some equipment from you, I'm sure he means to use it himself somehow, but I know that he didn't order you to come with it. You can leave the equipment here and I'll see that he gets it and sends your company a receipt but—" She was starting to show me the egress when the chandelier said, in a cheery, female voice, "You're a lousy doorman, Priscilla, you should stick to partying. I'm coming right down."

For several moments, all Priscilla did was gape up at the chandelier with her mouth open. I stole a look at the little group by the stairs; the Emotional Indices ranged from apprehension to mild indignation to somewhat malicious satisfaction. I felt myself going over a mental speed bump. The milieu here was going to be a bitch to get around, and it would no doubt be reproduced in some way in Caverty's mind. Terrific, I thought. As if the job weren't already hard enough, I had a complicated social structure to clamber around on. *NN, you old bastard.*

Then another woman came trotting down the staircase. "Ah, here we are. The pathosfinder. Alexandra Haas, right? Deadpan Allie?" Somehow her hitting the foot of the stairs shooed everyone, including Priscilla, away; they flowed off into a room to the left, or west, according to the Compass.

"Sorry about that," said the woman. She was all business, tailored, no frills, brown all over, including her eyes, which were some kind of artificial gem the color of oak. "Sometimes the Entourage gets a little out of hand around here. I'm Harmony. At least, Caverty hopes I am." She laughed. "I'm kind of the general factotum, grand scheduler, traffic director, hall monitor. I try to keep things harmonious. I'm the one who contacted your agency about you. I've done quite a lot of research on pathosfinders; I'm really happy you were able to take the job."

I nodded. "Thanks. I need a place to stash my equipment and then I'd like to meet Caverty."

"I've had a room prepared for you upstairs, away from the general foofooraw and infighting—"

"Somewhere close to Caverty, I hope?" I said, as she tried to herd me toward the stairs. "I like to be as available and accessible to a client as possible."

Harmony's face clouded slightly. "Oh. Well. I, uh, I'd really have to check that out with Caverty. He has his own section of the house where no one else stays, out of respect to his need for a private working environment. You're experienced with creative people, so I guess you know how that is."

"I understand completely. However, clients sometimes feel that they have to see me right away, in the middle of the night or whatever. I need to be easily available."

Harmony smiled with indulgence. "There's nowhere you can go in this house where you would not be available to Caverty on a moment's notice or less. Everyone here understands that. It *is* his house, after all."

I opened my mouth, thought quickly, and shut it again. Trying to explain to her that I was not just another body added to the general Entourage population wasn't going to penetrate; I could tell. She was sure she knew the kind of people who stayed in Caverty's house, she was one of them. "My system—" I said, gesturing at the stack of components still sitting in the center of the Compass.

"I've already taken care of that. It'll be moved up to your room for you."

"I'll just wait here, then, until I see everything moved."

The professional mask almost slipped. She caught herself before she could sigh and spoke into her brown bracelet instead. "Entry hall right *now*." Four people with straps and handtrucks emerged from a door half hidden by the start of the curve of the staircase. They weren't exactly in uniform but there was a sameness to them and I knew immediately from their posture that they weren't Entourage. They were employees.

"We don't do that much heavy lifting and moving large objects around here," Harmony said as the hired help labored along behind us with my system. "The people who come and go here tend to travel light, although we haven't actually had anyone leave for a long time. Leave permanently, I mean. Which is good. For all of Caverty's—oh, I don't know what you'd call it, wildness of heart or freedom of spirit, I guess—for all that, he really needs a stable living situation. And things have really stabilized here. It's good. I think you'll see that while you're here."

Even though I was getting short of breath on those damned stairs I had to do breathing exercises to maintain the deadpan. She was making my skin crawl.

Whoa. Have to stop sometimes. That boost. Too vivid sometimes. I don't know why I'm reliving this for you anyway, NN. I mean, can you appreciate it? What do I think I'm doing, making art or something? I'm no artist, not in that sense. But I'm the best pathosfinder in the hemisphere. Right? You made me the best pathosfinder in the hemisphere, remember? You did it. And you know, that was nothing compared to what some people can do to you.

I know what you're saying right now. I went into it with a bad attitude. Isn't that what you're saying? I know it is, even though— chuckle, chuckle—I doubt I could actually understand you if I were there right now and you were saying it to me. Clang-clang, clang-clang.

280

Um, bad attitude. Yes, you'd say I'd gone into it with a bad attitude. Now what kind of a thing is that for someone trading on the name Deadpan Allie, and my reputation and all. Well, I'll tell you. It's knowing when you're in a bad situation. I wanted to pack up and go right then. Leaving aside the skin crawling and that stuff (interesting mental image, there, pack up and go and leave aside the skin crawling; there I go meandering again, bear with me, it happens, did I mention that? I guess I did but it's too late to go back and see if I really did because I can't read that part any more). So. Even if my skin hadn't been crawling like a lizard, like a million little tiny lizards, I should have seen it was already too hard. Pathosfinding you need privacy for. Go down and root around in somebody's soul like that; the client gets embarrassed in front of *me* sometimes. Facing someone else can be impossible. Caverty should have known that, he was a professional, he'd worked with a pathosfinder years before, before he'd discovered his empath.

So that was mainly why I stayed, you know. I wanted to check that out, see this empath and Caverty, get a feel for how they worked and why Caverty wanted to work that way. But I think I must have had it in the back of my mind that I was going to leave after that, unless Caverty could disentangle himself from his empath and his Harmony and the rest of the Entourage. So I could work him properly.

Disentangle? Did I really say that?

I don't know. I can't read it any more.

Harmony gave me the house tour. Done-over mansion, the usual things overdone as well as done over. Ten thousand rooms, not counting bedrooms. Ballrooms, dining rooms, sitting rooms, room rooms, an art gallery, a theatre where Caverty showed his holos if he felt like it. That last wasn't the way Harmony put it but that was the general idea, or so I gathered from her Emotional Index.

Reading the Emotional Index of someone who is trying like hell to give you the best impression can be amusing or annoying, depending on your mood. Occasionally I found myself feeling one way or the other about it but mostly I felt uneasy. She'd fallen into some kind of PR ramadoola that she was running on me. Silliness; you don't give a pathosfinder PR because she finds out what the truth is right away. But Harmony was straining to make me happy or get some kind of approval

281

from me. Maybe because she thought then I'd do a better job with her boss?

No, that wasn't it. She was trying to *sell* me something.

Or convert me.

Oh, yes. Once I saw it, there was no way not to see it. But never mind. Sooner or later, I'd get to Caverty and I wouldn't have to bother with Harmony or Priscilla the Party Baby or anyone else in the Entourage.

"I need to see Caverty as soon as possible," I told Harmony as she led me down yet another upstairs hall toward yet another room she thought she had to show me. "He *is* my client, I have to let him know I've arrived."

Harmony turned to look at me with mild surprise. "But—were you thinking of starting work today?"

"If Caverty wanted to start in five minutes, I'd do my best to be ready."

"He won't want to start today, I'm positive. And I'm sure someone must have told him you're here." The smile turned a little hard. "Perhaps Priscilla. Anyway, wouldn't you like to get comfortable, settle in a little, get to know the place? Not to mention all of us. Caverty's group. I know he'd like you to feel like you're a part of things. I mean, if you're going to be here awhile—"

"I don't actually know how long I'll be here. I won't have any idea until Caverty and I begin working together, and even then it'll be hard to say. Pathosfinding isn't a simple business. And that doesn't even come into it. Some extremely complicated jobs have taken less than a day to complete while others that were more straightforward took weeks." I resisted the temptation to look apologetic; not hard, really, because they *don't* call me Deadpan Allie for nothing, but her proselytizing was working at me, trying to find a way in, at least to my politeness sympathies. "I really must speak to Caverty, whether we begin working today or two weeks from now. He's my client."

Harmony spread her hands and then clasped them together with a little sigh. Her nails were also painted brown, I noticed. That shouldn't have seemed bizarre. "Well. If you must, you must. Could I at least phone him and tell him we're coming? Is that all right?"

"Of course."

She stepped into a room which seemed to be a souvenir gallery of some kind—still holos alongside flat pictures promoting one or other of

Caverty's works, things that might have been awards, props, or just items he (or someone) had wanted to keep for sentimental reasons. Not a junk room; it was all neat and very organized. I glanced around while Harmony used a talk-only phone on a seven-tiered ceramic table. She didn't say much and she didn't say it to Caverty, I was pretty sure. The Entourage has a completely different way of talking to the Man (or Woman) than they do to each other, and for each other, they had their own pecking order that was never quite congruent with the Man's idea of who was over whom. Harmony was talking to an equal, without a doubt and, without a doubt, that wasn't the empath.

"He says come right up," Harmony said, replacing the phone. "Caverty lives at the top of the house; starting on this floor, there are elevators so we don't have to climb a million stairs." The smile was forced now, though I wouldn't have been able to tell if I hadn't known how to read an Emotional Index. She really hadn't wanted to take me to Caverty today at all and I couldn't figure that out. She'd chosen me (according to her, anyway); her own comfort was contingent on my helping the Man but she was reluctant to let me near him. Not completely reluctant—just for today. Tomorrow. Mañana, no problem. Entourages could be funny things. I had a passing thought that Caverty had better turn out to be worth it after the obstacle course I was having to run to get to him.

Well, of course, he had the whole top floor of the house, though the main room where he did most of his living and working was a big studio at the rear of the building, where he could look out a fan-shaped, floor-to-ceiling window at cultivated rolling country. He was sitting at the window when Harmony led me in—I was never going to walk with Harmony, I saw, she was always going to lead—off to the left side, looking away from the sunset, which was visible through another much smaller window behind him. A woman was sitting at his feet, one hand resting casually on his ankle. I could just barely hear their voices in quiet conversation. Harmony looked around, saw no one else and nearly panicked.

"I talked to Langtree, *he* told me to come up," she said, ostensibly to me but actually so Caverty would hear and know that she hadn't just taken it upon herself to barge in. Whatever happened to *Caverty says come right up,* I wondered.

"It's all right, Harmony," Caverty called out. There was a slight echo off the mostly empty walls. "I sent Langtree out."

"Oh," she breathed, pretending to fan herself relievedly with one brown-tipped hand, "that's good, I'm glad I wasn't interrupting anything important—"

"You weren't," Caverty said good-naturedly. He had one of those voices that would sound good-natured all the time, even when it was chewing someone out. "You're okay, Harmony, thanks for everything. You can go now, too, take a break, get some rest. Have a drink, have kinky sex, whatever you want."

Harmony gave one of those full-bodied *ha-ha-ha* laughs and sort of backed out of the room, looking from me to Caverty and the woman on the floor and back again.

"The pathosfinder," Caverty said to me.

"The pathosfinder. Yes." I looked around. The holo equipment was in an untidy pile in the righthand corner nearest the door. Except for one of the cameras and a couple of colored lights, it all looked as though it hadn't been touched for a long time, not even to be cleaned. For me, that will always be what a creative block really looks like, in the mind or in the world: a pile of mostly unused equipment, gathering dust.

Caverty didn't get up. "Come closer," he said. "Please."

I walked across the room slowly enough to have time to look at both of them. Caverty was a solidly built man, more good-looking than he really needed to be. Sculpture, of course; these days everyone's from Mt. Olympus, with bone structure to die for (which, of course, you have to pay for and only the filthoid rich can pay for custom designs like the one Caverty had). But on Caverty, there was a sense of overkill about his attractiveness, too many nice things crammed into one place.

The same could not be said about the woman sitting on the floor. There was a naturalness about her that was also very expensive, except she hadn't bought her looks. She stopped short of being delicate—*fine* was the way that old bastard NN would have put it. Aquamarine eyes; the facets in the pupils glittered like tears. Thick, dark straight hair cut ragamuffin-style. Thin as a ballet dancer but without any sense of a dancer's litheness. I realized belatedly that she had stolen my attention away from Caverty completely.

Caverty looked up at me with the start of a smile. "My empath,

Madeleine." He pronounced it *Mad-a-LAYNE*. "We were just enjoying some quiet moments at the end of the day. No matter what I'm doing I try to take time to enjoy those few moments before the daylight fades." He shifted position slightly, adjusting his caftan. It was gray, very thick and heavily textured, mimicking a handweave. "Although we never watch the sunset. I don't believe in such things of course but Harmony says that west is definitely not my direction. I'm northeast. Which is why this house is perfect for me. According to the Compass, I mean, if you believe such things. I don't imagine pathosfinders put any more stock in them than holo artists." He looked at Madeleine. "Or empaths?"

She gave a short, breathy laugh. "We've known each other far too long for you to have to ask that."

"How long is that?" I asked conversationally.

They had to look at each other before they could answer me. "Fifteen years," Caverty said, while Madeleine nodded. "That is, we've known each other for fifteen years; we've been working together for eight. Of course, just knowing Madeleine affected me deeply, even before we began working together. Affected my work. So perhaps we have been working together the whole time we've known each other. She's been working *on* me, anyway." He chuckled, looking at his empath fondly while she sat under his praise smiling demurely at her knees.

"Before that, how often did you work with a pathosfinder?" I asked.

They both looked up at me with mild surprise. "Maybe once, twice a year," Caverty said. "It isn't the sort of thing you can do all the time. Why?"

"I was just wondering. For the sake of the job. It can help before we start if I know a little about your last mindplay experience."

"Bless me, Allie, for I have sinned. It has been eight years since my last mindplay experience. With a pathosfinder. I can barely remember it now, it seems."

Madeleine gave him a soft pat on the leg.

"Could I ask why you feel the need to work with one now after all these years?"

Caverty took a deep breath. "I need something different. My work needs something different. Have you seen any of my holos?"

"I've seen all of them, including your last release, *Dinners Between Dinners*."

285

"Retitled *Food Fight* by the critics," he said with a hint of hurt feelings. "Not that there wasn't something to what some of them said. There is no easy way to look at yourself and see that you're getting stale. Especially when you were considered an innovator early in your career. You have no idea how excruciating it is to have to give up the position of Promising Young Turk because all your Promising Young Turk stuff has become an old story. People begin to recognize the devices you fall back on as, well, the devices you fall back on. I thought it was time to explore some different things."

"And what about you?" I said to the empath.

She sat up slightly, blinking. "What do you mean?"

"What will you be doing?"

"When?"

"While Caverty's exploring these different things?"

"Why, what I always do. I'll be empathizing." Her tiny smile grew even tinier. "Won't I?" She looked to Caverty.

He leaned over to say something to her, paused, and frowned up at me. "Won't she?"

Time for the tightrope walk fifty yards above the glass net. "There are, I'm sure, pathosfinders who will work with a tandem of any kind. And there are pathosfinders who work with empaths—"

"Is there something wrong with empaths?" she asked. Not a bit defensive, either; her Emotional Index was devoid of any hostility. She just wanted to know. I felt myself relax a little.

"Well, when you're mindplaying, the system facilitating the contact between minds imposes a certain amount of order on the encounter— there's a medium for the minds to interact within, strict boundary conditions that keep separate entities truly separate so that there isn't any confusion as to whose thoughts are whose, and a certain amount of protocol that reinforces the personal sense of security."

She nodded. "Yes."

"Yes." I waited and she waited with me. "I mean, that's it. That's what it is."

She looked at me doubtfully. "That's what's wrong with empaths?"

Caverty's posture changed very subtly to a protective position.

"I'm sorry, I didn't actually mean there was anything wrong with empaths. What I mean is—well, that's why I don't work with empaths. I thought the agency made that clear."

Caverty rubbed his chin with two fingers. "They didn't."

"I'm surprised. My agency has always been careful to spell out exactly what the mindplayers do. And don't do."

"Well, that's all right anyway," Caverty said, warmth flowing into his voice from somewhere deep inside. "You don't have to work with an empath. *I* work with an empath. That will do."

"Will it do for you not to work with an empath while you're working with me?"

Caverty's smile shrank somewhat. "You mean while we're hooked in together or the whole time you're here?"

I didn't look at Madeleine. "The whole time I'm here."

"Oh . . ." He slumped back in his chair and stared intently at the toes of his slippers. Doeskin slippers, possibly synthetic but then again, perhaps not. This was the home of the filthoid rich, after all. "I—I'm not sure."

Madeleine reached out to put a hand on his knee and then changed her mind, showing me that she was letting him make his own decision this time.

"I'm not sure I'm capable of doing that," he said. "Madeleine and I—we've been together for so long—not working with Madeleine is—it would be like not working with air."

"Oh, Caverty," Madeleine said. "You have to do what is best for your work."

I wasn't sure I could take the sudden emotional charge pressurizing the room. All at once, there seemed to be a heaviness on my solar plexus, the way you feel when you barge in on some kind of intimate scene, or perhaps when it barges in on you. But they don't call me Deadpan Allie for nothing. (For fun, maybe, hey, NN? Depends on your idea of fun.) I waited it out; Caverty and the empath rode it out. Without moving, either.

Presently, she said, "You should try it, Caverty. You have to try it, you owe it to yourself, you owe it to your work. We both know you've gotten stale—"

"Don't say that too loud, the critics might have the place bugged." They smiled sadly at each other in lieu of laughing.

287

"Try it," she said. "It'll be . . . different. You need something different. Something besides me."

Did she think I was completely stupid? Or just stupid enough not to know how to read an Emotional Index? Hers said she believed he needed nothing of the sort, that she would continue to be the one and only thing he needed, work or no work.

But then, she was an empath. Maybe it wasn't her Emotional Index I was reading but his.

I resisted the urge to blink several times and maintained as much neutrality as I could, which, under the circumstances, wasn't really very much. Just by being there I was pitting myself against her, forcing a choice between us.

She got up suddenly. "Try it now. Just here, just the two of you."

He reached out for her, about to protest.

"No. I insist. This is your *career*, Caverty. It's all right, I'm not going anywhere except out of the room. You know I'll always be here for you."

She gave me a quick, level, professional-to-professional smile as she passed me on her way out. Caverty looked after her with dismay, fear, and guilt fighting it out for dominance on his handsome face. He stared at the door for a long time after she shut it. Then finally his attention came over to me.

"And now what?" he asked, spreading his hands. They were shaking a little.

"Now not so much. I thought we might talk. Get acquainted. I don't like to go cold into contact with someone's mind and I'm sure you wouldn't want to, either."

"Oh, no, certainly not." He shifted position in the chair, trying to get comfortable. It was a very comfortable chair, not one of those living contour things that adjusts itself to your every little move, just a very receptive inanimate, but it was impossible for him now that Madeleine was out of the room. "What, ah, do you need to know? Oh, dinner's coming up. We don't want to miss dinner. The meals around here are *prima*."

The sun had gone down and, as it had grown progressively darker outside, the lights had come up in perfect equilibrium with the fading sunlight so that you almost didn't notice the change.

"We won't miss any meals. Pathosfinding doesn't require that anyone starve for their art." I wanted to go over to him but I had no intention of sitting at his feet. I looked around for another chair, spotted one near the pile of equipment and dragged it over so I could sit across from him.

"That's good," he said, stealing a glance at the door again. "I doubt that I could, any more. I've grown too used to eating regularly and well." Pause, and then a rueful smile. "That being why I called you in."

"At this point, you wouldn't starve if you never worked up another holo. It's a different kind of need now."

He squinted at me with thoughtful surprise. "You *know*."

"Yes, I know. I've worked with many, many artists of many different kinds." *And empaths aren't the only ones who know how other people feel,* I added to myself. "You can do lots of things to keep from starving, but only one thing to produce your art."

"Absolute. Just absolute." He nodded, feeling comfortable for all of three seconds. "That's the truth." He put his hand on his stomach. "Was that me? Did you hear that? My stomach just roared like a wild animal. I think I can smell dinner from here."

Let him go, said some small part of my mind. Probably the last shred of my common sense. Let him go, let him cling to his empath and later you can hook in with him and fail and go home none the worse for wear.

"I need to be able to look at any holos you have available for viewing around here."

"Oh. Certainly."

"And it would be best if we could look at them together."

"Oh. . . . Yes, I guess it would."

"But we don't have to do that before dinner."

"After dinner?" He looked a little pale.

"Tomorrow will be soon enough. I did just get here, after all."

Now he really came to life. "Oh, of course, this is really thoughtless of me, keeping you here when you'd probably like to get some rest and you must be hungry, too—"

He babbled both of us out of the room. I broke away and made a stop at my quarters before heading down to the dining room, which in any other place would have been known as a banquet hall.

*   *   *

289

Now, NN, I *know,* I just *know* you're picking up on my hostility toward the empath. The poor innocent empath. What on earth have I got against empaths? And how can I be so unprofessional as to show it?

Hang me, shoot me—emotional criminal!

I told you, I didn't work with empaths. It feels indecent, doing something like that without a machine.

Hang me, shoot me—emotional prude! You just can't win in this business. I always knew that.

But I'll tell you what else I don't like about empaths. I know all about empathy; you know that, you taught me everything I know, right? You do still claim that, don't you? Sure you do, I know you. Yah, I know all about empathy; empaths are something else.

There's something about empaths touching you—not even touching you, being around you. You just know they're soaking it all up, whatever it is. They're always just—soaking it all up. Drinking you in. You're supposed to feel such kinship with them. You're not alone any more, someone knows exactly how you feel, someone's walked a mile in your moccasins. But what's that for, anyway? Yah, I know, so you feel you're not alone any more, right, we said that, didn't we. Didn't I, excuse me, I'm doing all of the semitalking. But what's it really for? What possible survival value can that have? For you, I mean—you the regular person. What's the survival value of feeling such kinship with someone, of not feeling alone any more emotionally. Pretend you're a regular person instead of a dried-up old bastard just for the sake of example, okay, NN? The survival value of, yes, empaths in terms of you, the regular person. Well, there is none. Not for you

It's all for the empath. When you know exactly how anyone— *everyone*—feels, that's a pretty powerful survival tool. In fact, you'd probably end up doing a lot more than just surviving with it. Survive and thrive, yah; and soaking it all up all the time, you'd get terribly— *accustomed* to it, more than accustomed, *addicted.* Except that's not quite the word. I mean, are you *addicted* to air?

Yah, so what's in it for you, the regular person? (You pretend like you're a regular person, okay, NN, or have I already asked you to do that?) What's in it for you? I mean, shouldn't you get something out of this? Well, sure you should, and you do.

You get to *like* having someone crawling around in your emotions, feeling them with you, and letting you feel other emotions from other people.

Except maybe *like* is the wrong word.

Do you *like* air?

Caverty had thirty pairs of moccasins, by the way, and Mad-a-LAYNE had had her sensitive little soles in every one of them.

It was a banquet hall, but the type of place where you sat down in one spot only if you really wanted to, if you were tired or something. Most of the Entourage were gypsy diners, the type of people who seem to be reluctant to light anywhere even semipermanently, in case they should see a better place to sit. So they were all cruising around, plates or cups or whatever in hand, cocktail-party style, working at enjoying themselves.

I'd stopped off at my room for a change of clothes and a dose of solitude so I could refortify myself. There wasn't time for even the quickest mental exercise with the system, unless I wanted to miss a good portion of the dinnertime dynamics and something told me I didn't want to miss very much in this house.

I managed to arrive in the dining room before both Caverty and Madeleine, which meant dinner was not quite underway. You could tell that by the general demeanor of the room. The entire Entourage was in a waiting mode.

Quite a mixed bag, this Entourage. There had to be at least thirty of them, acting out their inner lives. A few were dressed after certain animals; bears or lions seemed to be the fashion, though I spotted a couple of chicken people. At least, they looked like chicken people to me. A peacock might have been appropriate in some cases but no one cared to be quite that obvious. There was an umbrella woman who took up a lot of space; at various times, her umbrella skirt would open or shut for some private reason of her own, following no pattern I could see. I saw Priscilla with her little group; she'd changed some of the swatches on her outfit and polished her metallics so that she twinkled under the chandeliers. The members of her group were now each wearing an outfit made from one of her swatches. You might have briefly mistaken them for the focal point of the Entourage. On second glance, they'd have reminded you of nothing so much as some kind of in-house organization. Like security guards. It would figure, I thought, helping myself to a bowl of something fragrant.

If definite job assignments weren't made, individuals within the Entourage would automatically fall into certain roles, depending on their personalities. Priscilla was a natural for the cops.

I was looking around for a place to sit when someone finally chose to notice me. I'd noticed him wading along behind me as I'd made my way to the buffet. It would have been hard not to notice him. He was at least six-three and bulky and where he wasn't bulky, he was hairy; the kind of person who makes you feel crowded just by being nearby. I'd figured I'd mix in among everyone as though there were nothing unusual about my being there but he planted himself in front of me, cutting off most of my view of the room and said, "You're new here."

His tone was politely matter-of-fact, not accusatory at all; wherever he fit in here, he wasn't the cops. "Yes, I am," I said, shifting position so a woman in a harlequinesque outfit could pass behind me.

"Did you come to join?" he asked, reaching around me for a bowl of the same stuff I had. His arms were so long he barely had to move.

"No, I'm—"

"Didn't think so." He smiled cheerily. "I always know when someone's coming in to join. Hasn't happened in an awfully long time. Came alone, didn't you?"

I nodded "I was just upstairs talking to Caverty and Mad-a-Layne."

His eyebrows went up very slightly. "It's a good group here. Good balance of all different kinds." Priscilla cruised by closely enough to hear what we were saying. My bulky friend looked at her for a few moments with mild hostility on his dark furry face. "Mostly a good balance. When you've got all kinds, you've got *all* kinds. But as long as they serve their purpose and don't just take up space and eat up all the food, you can tolerate just about anyone." He looked down at me again. "Of course, we're all on the same side here," he added quickly. "There may be a slob here and there, but they're *our* slobs. If you get what I mean."

"Couldn't be clearer."

"I'm Arlen. Some people call me The Bear, but not to my face." He chuckled into his beard. "Of course, they don't know *I* started them calling me The Bear. Planted the name myself. I figured if they were going to be calling me something, I might as well have some say over what it was."

"Is that name insulting to you?" I asked.

"Hell, no. But *they* think it is." He laughed again. "Some people, if they think they're insulting you, it's all they need to know. And that's how you survive in an Entourage." He herded me a few feet away from the buffet table. "What's your name and what are you planning to do here besides survive?"

"Allie. Deadpan Allie, actually, and I'm a pathosfinder."

I'd finally managed to rumple his smooth. "Pathosfinder?' He actually stepped back from me. "For *who*? Not Caverty?"

A white-blond woman in a shimmering blue Japanese-style kimono turned around. "Pathosfinder?" The word echoed, flowing out into the people immediately around us and I found myself in the middle of a minor group within the group instead of just being among them.

"Who called you?" the Nordic-looking woman asked, worry large on her luminous face. "Is it *my* fault?"

Arlen The Bear patted her shoulder gently with a huge pawlike hand. "That's not quite the right question, Lina. Poor Lina thinks any time something goes wrong around here, she's somehow to blame for not spotting the problem early enough."

"For some people, sensitivity has to be cultivated, worked on every moment, waking *and* sleeping," the woman explained to me anxiously. "Otherwise, they get hardened to everything without ever realizing it because being *in*sensitive is their natural state of mind. And it can be contagious, too, insensitivity can. It can spread from just one person to infect a whole group and pretty soon you can have a whole population incapable of feeling for their fellow human being."

"Yes," I said, "but—"

"So that's why I asked if our needing a pathosfinder was my fault." She looked up at Arlen with begging eyes. Icy-blue eyes, I noticed. "*Is* it me, Arlen? You'd tell me, wouldn't you?"

Arlen's laugh was kindly as he gave her a gentle hug. "Sure I would, but by the time I did, you'd already have been told several times by everyone else. Stop worrying. She isn't here because of anything you've done wrong. But she hasn't yet said why she *is* here." His expression was a little less kindly now; I'd upset one of their own. God knew how they were going to receive the fact that I was going to be messing with the entourage's *raison d'être*. But we can't lie to anyone directly involved with a client, whether it's a friend, enemy, parent, Entourage or something

293

even more baroque. Not unless it's to save someone's life. *Suppose it's your own life?* I'd once asked NN. *Don't be silly,* he'd said. *Who'd want to kill you?*

I thought about that as I said, "I'm here for Caverty."

Nobody said anything. A third of my audience backed off.

"Caverty called you?" Arlen asked finally. "He must have. I can't believe it. All these years with Madeleine and now—" He shook his head a little. "What are you going to—I mean, are you—"

"I'm not replacing Mad-a-LAYNE permanently." I could hear the sighs of relief above the general chatter in the room. "I really hadn't meant to create a disturbance," I said, glancing to my right, where the umbrella woman was getting the news that there was a pathosfinder at large from a waifish type in black secondskins. "I'm going to do some work with Caverty and when it's done, I'll be leaving and life will go on."

"Maybe you won't want to leave," said a chubby man in a pouch suit, ordinary except for the fact that it seemed to be padded to make him even chubbier.

"Yah. You might really get to like it here," said the Nordic woman. "That happens."

"I have some things to go back to that are very important to me," I said politely.

"What?" asked The Bear with what seemed to be genuine curiosity.

"Ah . . ." Something told me they weren't going to perceive my career as suitably important. I seized the first thing that came into my head. "There's Nelson Nelson."

"An important *someone?*" asked the Nordic woman.

"Ask him to come here. He might like it," the Bear suggested.

"I, uh, no, I couldn't."

"It's up to you," said the man in the pouch suit. "But don't count it out completely, staying here. You just might. You never know."

The general babble in the room changed its tone and I knew without even looking that Caverty had come in.

Immediately, their attention went directly to him, allowing me to slide out of the spotlight and into the general crowd. Slipping between derelicts and duchess types, I made my way over to a small raised area containing a few small tables where I could sit and regroup. A few chiffon fanciers lingered by the steps up to the area; I managed to pass them unnoticed, in spite of the fact that I'd dipped the corner of somebody's scarf in my dish. If he didn't care, I didn't.

Relieved to be out of the general crowd, I didn't see that there was someone else sitting at the table I'd chosen until I was about to sample the night's entree.

"You're new here," he said.

I paused with my spoon nearly at my lips.

"Only the new people choose to sit up here. The very new and the very old." He smiled with the left half of his mouth; his diamond eyes twinkled. Diamond biogems are seldom a good choice but his olive skin kept him from looking too much like a willing victim of blindness. He was older than someone you'd expect to find in an Entourage, and not as done over as the average citizen. The nose had been broken at least once, but the effect wasn't homely. He'd have reminded you of your father, if that was your orientation. It wasn't mine. To me, he looked only like a graying, older man in comfortably baggy shirt and pants, too sensible to be here but staying anyway for some reason of his own.

"It's Madeleine they're all so worried about," he continued, watching as the room rearranged itself around Caverty's presence.

"Not Caverty?"

"Oh, of course, Caverty. Both of them, really. We don't have one without the other here, as you must know. But they're worried about Caverty in terms of Madeleine and what you mean for her. I know. I've been here with the Entourage since before it was formally an Entourage. I may have founded the Entourage. Or helped found it. I came to him, others came. Then we were a caravan." He paused to watch a woman wearing a jewel-encrusted cage over her face and neck make her way through the room. One of the chicken people stopped her and they embraced warmly.

"I know all their dynamics, small and large. I direct the domestic drama here. At one time or another, I've gotten all of them to play at least some small part. Caverty finds it amusing, I think, to watch other people besides himself have problems, even if they're just staged. And once he based a holo on one of my scenarios—*Dinners Between Dinners,* after my scenario, *Food Fight.*"

"You don't say."

"That was the only instance, though. Usually I cribbed from him now and then. As a kind of tribute to his work. And as a kind of tribute to being fresh out of ideas at the time, too." He fell silent, watching Caverty moving among his Entourage.

The Entourage both moved aside for him and crowded around him all at once. It was as though a new element had been dropped into simmering waters. Caverty slipped among them much more easily than I'd been able to, maneuvering effortlessly, balancing socializing and finger food. He ate a little, held court, ate a little more, held a little more court—a reception, I realized. Every night, the Entourage gave him a reception of the type he'd probably gotten on the debut of a new holo. Not so unusual, really. Performers become addicted to applause quite easily. But Caverty had found a way to get a fix of applause every day—more often than that, if he wanted—without having to go through the tiresome business of working for it.

"Get it direct, from producer to consumer," I muttered.

"Pardon?"

I shrugged. "Just a stray thought."

The man got up with a smile and tossed a cloth napkin onto the table. "Well, I should go say 'good evening' to the great man."

"Do you always do this?"

"Every night, dinner's an occasion here. Didn't they tell you?"

"I mean, you personally going over to pay your respects."

Mildly troubled frown. "I stay here by his good graces. I eat his food, take up space, ply my trade, all by virtue of his hospitality. Once a day, I can let the man know how I feel." He paused, studying me for a moment. "You have to mean something here, you know. Whether you stay or not." Then he looked toward Caverty, prepared a friendly smile, and moved away, straightening his clothes.

It took him over a minute to make his way through the cluster around Caverty, not because it was so crowded, really, but because some of the *couture* was voluminous, like the umbrella lady, and because they were all deferring to each other as well as socializing among themselves, while Caverty favored each person who reached him with more than just token conversation. Didn't the novelty ever wear off, for any of them?

Off to one side, I saw that Harmony had appeared amid the near-fringe of the ragged circle around "the great man" and was subtly directing traffic, moving people along so they could greet Caverty in turn and moving those who'd already spoken to him away without seeming to. Caverty was facing in her general direction, reinforcing the idea of them getting in line for him. It might have been engineered, but it had the look and feel of incidental choreography—they'd fallen into doing things this way and as long as it worked they'd keep doing it.

I tried to catch the expression on each face as the Entourage members paid their respects and turned away but I wasn't close enough to see them all. The ones I could see looked content, or satisfied, or, I don't know—appeased, somehow, the way children look when they all go home from the party with a gift. Which was probably the case.

Caverty looked the same way; a little drawn and besieged, perhaps, but generally content. Appeased. Happy, even.

He shouldn't have been. He should have felt tired and put upon and too in demand. *But then,* I thought, *if he's not giving any of himself to his work, he has plenty left to give to his Entourage. Right, Allie?*

No, wrong— he supposedly wasn't doing any work because he didn't have any inside him, so he shouldn't have had anything to offer this live-in applause machine. So what exactly was he giving them and where was it coming from?

I scanned the room again and found her at last. She was at the opposite end of an invisible straight line that ran from Harmony through Caverty. That look. She could have been in religious trance; she could have been gazing at her firstborn child; she could have been dreaming of a lover or fantasizing a murder behind that look. Her Emotional Index shifted, melted, segued through a thousand different states in less time than it took to think about it.

The food, I noticed, had been completely forgotten. Or maybe not so much forgotten as dropped, like any other pretense.

All right, NN, three quick choruses of *What's It All About?* and if you haven't figured it out by then, you're a candidate for brain salad.

Yah, well, what do you think I did after that? I got the hell out of there and went off to my room, my luxuriously appointed room with the singing, vibrating bed and custom-built lavabo and tried to compose a message which would convey beautifully and inarguably why the Entourage had to leave as soon as they could pack themselves up. Halfway through the start of the sixth draft, I plugged into a memory boost and relived the scene for myself, for reinforcement, so I could make it more—I don't know, urgent? Real? Immediate? So he could see it as I saw it. And then I realized he couldn't see it as I saw it and not be too alienated to work with me. I was already separating him and Mad-a-LAYNE. Madeleine. But I kept thinking of her in that exaggerated way. Mad-a-LAYNE. Mad-a-LAYNE. Mad-a-LAYNE in PAIN falls MAINly in your BRAIN.

I'd started yawning midway through the second holo. By the start of the third, I had to ask Caverty for coffee. He roused himself from the stupor I'd nearly fallen into and dialed some up from the bar near the projection booth.

"Am I supposed to ask you what you think?" he said as we perched on antique stools together.

"I really don't know what you're *supposed* to do."

Caverty laughed a little. "Neither do I, most of the time. As you can probably guess. Actually, I don't have to ask. I was comatose from boredom myself."

"Your own boredom with your work isn't much of a barometer. However you feel about your work is tied up in the difficulties you're having right now, so you're not a terribly reliable judge."

He glanced over his shoulder briefly and I squelched the urge to tell him Madeleine wasn't there. Today he was a bit less uncomfortable in her absence but he was still looking around for her. "Maybe not, but I used to know when the work was good. At least, I thought I did. Now I'm beginning to think I spent close to two decades fooling myself." He stared gloomily into his coffee cup.

We'd watched one holo from his beginning phase and one from his experimental. Both had been narrative pieces, the stories simple while the embellishment was complex, especially in the experimental work. He'd been very young when he'd done that one, though it had come after the previous piece. He'd just been discovering how much fun it was to break the rules and from time to time, ghost images of himself with his holocam had drifted through the piece, recording other ghost images as well as the central scene in progress. It was the sort of thing most artists do sooner or later and usually it's a bad choice but somehow, Caverty had made it work, either through luck or sheer talent, or perhaps a combination of the two. It left an aftertaste in the brain; your memory kept returning to it, going over the core story—boy meets self, boy gets self, boy loses self, boy buys new self—while the trimmings drifted around as vividly in memory as they'd been in the holo itself.

The interesting part was that Caverty had used minimal sound—no dialog, no musical scoring, few sound effects except as a kind of punctuation here and there, and yet you tended to remember more sound than he'd used. While I wasn't sure that I really liked it, it did seem to summarize all of Caverty's strong points as an artist. I didn't want to ask him how autobiographical it was; artists never really know exactly how autobiographical any of their work is. I could find out later if I really wanted to know.

"You're very quiet," Caverty said. "That, uh, well . . . *scares* me."

"I'm not a critic. You have to stop thinking of me as some kind of master evaluator."

"But you are, aren't you? Evaluating my talent, how you can help me. *If* you can help me." Pause while he drained his coffee. "*Can* you help me? How bad off *is* this patient, doctor?"

"How bad off do you feel?"

"If you're going to tell me it's all up to me—"

"Not exactly. It's a matter of how much help you're willing to accept; then it's a matter of how much help you'll be able to accept. Plus a lot of other things." I pushed my coffee aside. "This isn't something I discuss in detail with my clients, as it tends to make them far too self-conscious. I don't want you getting in your own way."

He nodded absently, glancing over his shoulder again. "Well. How many more holos did you want to see?"

"One representative piece from each stage of your career would be fine. And if there are any others you want me to look at, that's fine, too."

He nodded again but his gaze was on some point off to my right, as though he were daydreaming or suddenly remembering something very pleasant, or perhaps getting a new idea for a holo. For a moment, I was uncertain as to whether it was any of those things but then I realized, and just as I did, it touched me.

It was a very light touch, a brush that might have been accidental. A pathosfinder's mind isn't at all receptive to casual telepathy or an empath just cruising; it's all that self-definition and controlled concentration we engage in during the course of mindplay. After a while, it becomes second nature. It's going on all the time somewhere in your mind, an engine on idle. Madeleine brushed up against me and passed on, like someone who'd accidentally knocked on the wrong door and didn't wait for an answer. She was gone before I could sense how close she was.

Caverty sighed cheerfully and then looked down at his hands resting on his thighs. "It's just good to know she's there."

"I can't have that."

"Pardon?" He didn't look up.

"I can't have her coming in like that. Especially when we're hooked in together."

"Oh, she knows that, I asked her to look in on me, as it were. Just so I'd know she was there."

"You'll have to ask her not to do it."

"She knows that, too." His hands came together, gripping each other tightly and I realized she hadn't quite left yet. I let him be until he raised his head and I could see that the faraway look on his face was gone. "She understands, she really does. I know she does."

"Good. I'm glad. We can look at the next holo."

We looked at six more—a couple of display pieces normally presented on loop for continuous exhibition, a juvenile piece that had been badly received, and a thematic trilogy having to do with growing older. The juvenile piece was negligible in terms of his work as a whole—he no longer had any idea what it was like to be a child. The trilogy was interesting as a precursor of his present state; after viewing it, you might have thought he was having difficulty accepting the fact that he himself was growing older. But while he'd alluded to that earlier, I didn't think that was the bulk of his problem.

It was close to suppertime when we finished, so I let him go, pleaded fatigue for myself and headed for my room so I could review/relive everything on boost.

The last thing I had expected her to do was to come to me. How could Caverty possibly cope with his Entourage without her somewhere in the room doing whatever it was she did—I still hadn't figured out exactly what her function was, but whatever it was, she was good at it.

She didn't even knock. Knocking wasn't customary in this house, apparently. I was taking a semimeditative breather from boosted review-ing and she slipped into the room like a bit of cloth blown in by an errant draft.

"Hi," she said shyly, standing with her back against the door.

I gestured at one of the pudgy spot chairs. Not the closest one. She sank into it gingerly, keeping her hands on the sides of the cushions as though she might have to launch herself out of it on short notice.

"I know you must be wondering why I'm not at dinner," she said. "I don't always go. Sometimes I take a night off, eat in my room. But Caverty loves his public."

"Do you think a private Entourage qualifies as a 'public'?"

"In Caverty's case, yes, I think so. Public as opposed to the privacy of his mind."

I didn't feel like arguing it with her so I let it go.

"We live a very balanced life here. You may not think so but it is. Every element is carefully balanced against every other element. The Entourage population stabilized a little while ago and it provides Caverty with the security he needs to be able to work."

"But he isn't able to work."

"Well, no, not now but before he hit this rough patch in his creativity, he was able to work very well."

"You're the second person, I think, who's told me that the Entourage has 'stabilized.' "

She nodded. "And?"

"I wouldn't call it stabilization."

"What, then?"

"I'd call it entropy."

She drew back slightly, as though I'd taken a swipe at her.

"Or stagnation. I'm sorry if that hurts your feelings."

Mad-a-LAYNE laughed. "My feelings?"

"Or whomever's you've got."

Still smiling, she leaned forward. "I could have anybody's. Every-body's. You know us empaths. Especially those of us with a stronger telepathic bent than most."

I felt that brush against my mind again; she didn't persist.

"You're resistant, though. I guess most mindplayers are. All that holding yourself together that you do when you're in contact with someone else's mind. Holding your identity together. Holding tight to what you are. Isn't that the way they put it in mindplayer school, or wherever it is you go to learn how to handle those *machines*? Hold tight to what you are, am I right?"

I had the sensation of the room rearranging itself around us so that we were squared off against each other. Beside me, my system was assembled, the optic nerve connections capped but primed and ready for use.

"*Am* I right? Hold tight to what you are?"

"Generally the client isn't trying to get *at* what you are. So it isn't really necessary to go around clenched like a fist."

"Then why do you?"

"I'm sure it must seem that way to you, having such free access to all the people around here. But I'm really quite normal."

"Normal in whose terms? Them, out there in the world, where you use that *can opener* to break into people's minds?"

I shook my head. "I think I'd better go."

"What?" A look of panic, now. "Wait—why?"

Half out of my own chair, I paused. "*Why?* You must know."

"No, I don't. I *would* know if you didn't shut me out."

I saved my laugh for later, on the trip home. "It's not the sort of thing you need empathic powers to know."

"For me, it is."

I started to disassemble the system. "He's going to know. Caverty, I mean. He'll know what's happened between us just now and he won't be able to work with me."

She got up and came over to me, intending to put her hand on my arm; I stepped away from the system quickly. "Sorry," she said, putting the hand behind her back. "I wasn't thinking. I just wanted you to stop that. You mustn't leave."

"I don't think there's much choice any more."

"I really didn't mean to do this, to try to force you out of here. I was just—" She blew out a frustrated breath. "I'm sorry. I don't even know how to begin to try to explain it to you, I'm so used to just letting people know how I feel. Especially when the feeling is so complex. Do you know how that is, to feel so many different things at one moment?" She paused. "Or is that not being properly *deadpan?*"

302

She wiped both hands over her face and through her hair, turning away from me. "So many misunderstandings because *words* get in the way. People unable to imagine how other people feel because you can't explain to someone with just *words* a feeling of jealousy and gladness mixed up with the desire to see a loved one succeed."

I refrained from pointing out that she just had. "Just because you don't have emotional access to me doesn't mean that I have no understanding. I don't *have* to feel exactly what you feel to know what it is." I shrugged. "In any case, I still have to leave."

"No. Please don't. Caverty would never forgive me."

"Sure he would."

She allowed herself a tremulous, momentary smile. "Yes, he would. But I don't want to put him through the effort. *I* would never forgive *myself,* and the effect of that on Caverty would be horrible. I agreed to your conditions voluntarily, I urged Caverty to go along with them. If I sabotage everything, Caverty won't have a chance."

"Of course he will," I said quietly, though I tended to doubt it.

She looked over at me sharply. "I meant he won't have a chance to find out whether this could have worked for him or not."

"Oh. Yes, that *is* different."

"You see? Another misunderstanding because of *words.* If you'd been open to me, you would have understood what I meant instantly."

I did not tell her I didn't see why that was necessarily a better arrangement than the usual conversational mode of imparting information, emotional or otherwise. Not to mention the fact that there wouldn't have been a misunderstanding had there been *enough* words. NN, I thought, was going to give me a medal for self-control when he reviewed my report.

"Anyway," she said, softening, "you mustn't leave. Please. I promise I won't interfere any more."

"It's not that," I said. "It's that Caverty's going to know what happened between us."

"You'd tell him?"

"No. But you would. You couldn't help yourself."

She drew herself up. "Yes, I can. I can hold as tight to my own as you can to yours. I can keep feelings from him or allow them out as I choose. And I promised not to touch him while you're working with him, so I won't even have to make the effort. I *will* keep from touching him. And you. I *will*." She paused. "Stay?"

I nodded, without words.

I could tell he'd slept well and it surprised me. I'd have thought the prospect of meeting me in his studio/sanctorum shortly after dawn without Mad-a-LAYNE would have kept him on the thin edge of wakefulness for most of the night. It must have been a terrific dinner for him, the whole Entourage love-bombing him with lots of acclaim and reassurance. Either that or Mad-a-LAYNE had been with him after all, in spite of her protests to me. As I worked at reassembling the system, I found myself hoping she had. I would hook in with Caverty, discover she'd lied, disconnect, and go home. End of story.

The way I was wanting forever to get out of there, you'd have thought I'd have done just that, said to hell with it all and risked whatever NN's professional wrath would have brought. If anything. I'd turned down jobs before and NN hadn't sued me. I'd even cut some short and NN had seen the correctness of my action. But I'd never backed out of one and I just wasn't sure how the old bastard would take that. Of course, I hadn't wanted it in the first place but I'd allowed myself to be talked into it—my own fault, really. Which I guess was why I kept reassembling the system in Caverty's studio, and primed the optic nerve connections and got him all settled and comfortable on a chaise and removed his beautiful biogem eyes and hooked him into a building-colors relaxation exercise. It had been my own idea to skip the real-time outside exercises. Somehow a round of *What Would You Do?* or *What Do You Hear In These Pictures?* just didn't seem right for him. There were a couple of others I might have tried with him, including *Finish the Following,* which NN himself had invented for visual artists, involving real-time completion of a partial image but no doubt that would have made him feel as though I were forcing his hand. As it were. Besides, I felt the more time he could spend getting accustomed to being inward without Mad-a-LAYNE, the easier it would be to work with him.

I had the system run continuous checks on his vitals while I prepared myself to meet him mind-to-mind. He showed no signs of panicking or disintegrating so I took my time. I had to; there were a lot of feelings to put away.

He'd been in the relaxation exercise for nearly half an hour before I felt prepared enough to remove my own eyes and slip them into solution and a little longer after I hooked myself up to the system before I allowed it to bring my consciousness and his together.

The contact was gradual. I chose a new color as a vehicle and slipped in among the others he had been forming. He sensed me immediately and accepted the contact just as quickly. The colors cleared out, leaving us in a visualization not of his studio but of the banquet hall where dinner were celebrated every night.

Well, he said, *here we are.*

Is this where you keep your holos?

No. It's where I keep myself. My self, I mean.

What do you do here?

He looked around and I looked with him. The room seemed pretty much as it was in realife, down to the buffet tables, except he had not visualized food on them. I saw the area where I had sat with the domestic actor the first night I'd been there; it too was empty. I was about to repeat my question when the room began to darken, first in the corners and then spreading out in waves of shadows.

This is what I do here, he said. *I don't be alone here.*

I don't be alone is an awkward verbalization of what it was and not quite what he said but that was the way I received it. Before I could get meaning around it, the shadows had formed themselves into images of the Entourage, ghostly and nowhere near as substantial as our own representations but somehow no less present. Immediately they were cluttering up everything, hanging all over us as though we were underwater with a lot of rags and scarves.

Come on now, I coaxed, holding my patience. *You can clear them all out.*

A ghost of the umbrella woman flowed over his face. *Yes, I can,* he said.

I waited and he waited to see what I was waiting for. I felt the warm brush of someone's presence and for a moment I was nose to nose with the woman who'd had a cage on her head. Admiration, envy, a sense of accomplishment . . . the emotions belonged to several different people. I brushed her away.

Caverty?

If I want to. That's what it is, you see. I can clear them all out if I want to. But I don't want to. I don't want to! I! DON'T! WANT! TO!

305

It was a mental blast that blew me into the center of the room. I flew through the ghosts, tasting a thousand different emotions in a second, the admiration, the desire to be close, the envy, the sorrow, the loneliness, the gladness, the fatigue of routine followed by the sense of security, the euphoria, the craving that is addiction and most of all the appeasement that came both from having received something and having had something taken, the sweet need of being increased, the even sweeter need of being diminished.

They meant to pin me but ghosts can't really do anything, not even mental ones. I spread them out easily, clearing an area around myself big enough to accommodate myself and Caverty's ego.

I know you don't want to, Caverty, I said, calling to him through the wraiths wrapping themselves around his face, *but if you're willing to join me here, you can and it won't be me forcing you to do anything. Understand?*

Understand, they all said, Caverty and all of them together. *Don't want to, though!*

Then that's it, I said. *We don't have anything more to do.*

Arlen The Bear floated over me with his big arms held out. *Are you sure about that?* he asked with Caverty's mental voice.

I pulled all the way into myself so they—*he, Caverty,* I reminded myself—so he wouldn't feel my anger for the time and effort wasted when he'd never intended to try working with me. For several mental moments, I was aware only of composing myself. When I came out of it to face Caverty again, he was much closer than before, almost intrusive. My alarm nearly showed; after eight years without any mindplaying, he shouldn't have had that much skill at creeping up on me. Time to go, I thought, threw myself out of the visualization into the relaxation exercise. Caverty followed me and the colors caught him like quicksand and held him.

Even so, the taste of his consciousness seemed slow to fade out of my own mind, as though he were still chasing me anyway. My problem, I thought; sometimes the most unlikely people can get a hook into you and it's hell to get out. When I got home, I'd have myself dry-cleaned. And at NN's expense.

I disconnected from the system the moment it told me I could do so without trauma, groped for my eyes and couldn't contain the sigh of relief at finding them still in the container. I popped them back in and just sat for several minutes in Caverty's comfortable chair, rocking back and forth and breathing my way down to a calm state.

We were alone in the room. I hadn't expected us to be. I'd expected to come out and find them all there, waiting, wanting to—I forced the thought away before my heartrate could increase again.

Caverty lay on his chaise, completely relaxed. I had a strong urge to just leave him like that, limp and blind and harmless, and sneak out of the house and run all the way back to the agency. We hadn't even touched on ideas or holos or creativity or anything vaguely related. I hadn't even found any *memories*—just that damned Entourage, as present in his brain as it was outside of it.

Except for Mad-a-LAYNE, I realized. I hadn't felt her in there anywhere. As though she didn't exist.

I shook away my questions. Ask later; get out now. *Now.* But it was another minute before I could bring myself to touch Caverty even just to disconnect him from the system and put his eyes back in.

"Jesus," he said, sitting up slowly. He rubbed his forehead in a dazed way. "I didn't realize that—I didn't realize." He looked up at me pleadingly. "I don't know what to say to you."

I capped his connections and slipped them into a drawer in the system. "You don't have to say anything. I'll be going now."

"We aren't going to try again?"

"I don't think we can. Not until you do something about the general population in there."

He touched his forehead again. "They are all in there, aren't they?"

"Oh, yes."

"And I think if you hooked in with each of them, you'd find me in every single one."

"That's right."

"Madeleine?"

I nodded. "Prolonged empathy."

A slow smile spread across his face. "Sometimes I was afraid it hadn't worked. But Madeleine was right." His eyes narrowed. "And that's why you don't want to try again. Because I like it."

"Not the only reason, but that's part of it."

"And you *don't* like it."

307

I shrugged. "If you like it, it doesn't make much difference about me."

Without saying anything, he got up, stretched, and walked over to the pile of unused holo equipment. I paused for a moment, watching him, and then capped the set of connections I'd used. "I'd appreciate it if Harmony or someone would call me a flyer." No response. He didn't even look at me. "As for your fee, my agency may give you a partial refund. Minus expenses and time spent in the system." Still no response. I couldn't even get a clear reading of his Emotional Index. Maybe he was thinking about what it meant to give up the art for the audience. I didn't know and I really didn't want to. I moved around to the other side of the system to run a three-second diagnostic before disassembling the components and turned my back to him. It was the dumbest thing I ever did.

Coming to from a state of unconsciousness when you're hooked into the system is like going from death to a dream. For a while, you don't even know you're conscious and when you finally do realize it, the vertigo is furious. You fall in every direction at once, through every idea and thought you have. It seems like you'll fall forever and then you grab onto something, some concept, some belief, some identity thing, and you hold as tight as you can for a long time. And then, a mental century later, you feel steady enough to look around and see where you are and why and who else is there, if anyone.

I was back in the banquet room again, except this one was *my* banquet room, not the one in Caverty's mind, and there was no one there but me. At the moment. I could sense him nearby, though, waiting for me to tell him to come in.

I don't work that way, Caverty, I said and strode to the door. It was a big wooden antique with a shiny carved handle. *I'm coming out to you.*

I yanked at the handle. It wouldn't budge. Smoothing out the panic ripples, I stepped back from the door and gathered my strength into my hands, making them big, even bigger than Arlen The Bear's, and took hold of the handle again, intending to crush it. It swelled to fit my palms and even as I pressed on it, my hands were shrinking.

I jumped back, looking around for another way out.

Forget it, said the chandelier. Harmony. *You don't want to leave. You don't know what it's like to feel that way, to not want to leave. If you did, you'd feel differently.*

I didn't want to deal with that absurdity, nor did I want them to sense how trapped I felt. *All right,* I said, *standoff. I don't get out and you don't get in.*

Wrong.

Softer than a whisper; quieter than a brush against you in passing. She stood in the center of the empty room, very small. Delicate, even; a delicate vessel filled with so many feelings. She came toward me. I tried to back away but the floor shifted under me, keeping me in the same spot but still letting her approach.

They'll know how you feel and you'll know how they feel, she said gently. Cracks appeared in the wall behind her. *Without a word needing to be spoken.* Her arms reached for me.

Somehow, I managed to pull back a little. The cracks in the wall grew larger; faces showed through. Not ghosts this time.

We're all here now. We thought it could work made contact with Caverty after you hooked in together, but we were wrong. Your concentration would allow only limited contact. We were all ghosts and I couldn't even appear. You didn't even recognize us as being present. So I made contact with Caverty and then we hooked you in with him. Much better. It's working now.

She did not quite have me, though; she couldn't quite reach through the layers of deadpan to my core.

Every relationship is something like this, she said, trying to pull me closer. *People feed on each other whether it's lover to lover, friend to friend, audience to artist. We consume, we are consumed. You couldn't live otherwise. We've just refined it, made it more efficient—more satisfying. You'll see. Dinner here is always an Event. Especially when we finally get something new in. A nice change, to have variety in the menu. It's been a long time since the last one.*

I struggled back a little more, gaining ground even though the cracks in the walls were opening wider. *The only problem is I'm not willing.*

And as soon as I said it, I knew *that* was the dumbest thing I'd ever done. Admitting to it, admitting to anything at all gave her the lever she needed to pry off the last of Deadpan, leaving naked Allie.

The walls, as they say, came tumbling down while Mad-a-LAYNE lowered me to the floor. They swelled around her, blocking out the light with their faces.

Unwillingness, she said, face close to mine, *is a feeling. We know how you feel.*

And they did, every single one of them, while she directed traffic. Caverty. Harmony. Arlen The Bear, the chubby man, the domestic drama guy. The Nordic blonde in the kimono. The umbrella woman, the chicken people. Even Priscilla. Even Priscilla. Over and over again. Over and over and over.

Maybe it went on for days. Maybe only hours. When Mad-a-LAYNE disconnected me, I was asleep. In Caverty's studio. They were all gone. Sleeping it off themselves. I staggered around and when my vision cleared, I figured out how to pack my system up.

They should have caught me going down the stairs with it. Priscilla the cop, you know. I got to the bottom of the stairs and that Compass and I thought I *was* caught because someone came out from behind the staircase. I didn't recognize the face but I remembered the style of dress and the manner. Employee. That's when I found out I couldn't talk, right then, because I was going to beg for mercy and nothing came out. Like the record skipped the groove. You remember records. He didn't say anything, either. He just took one look at me and went over to the panel near the front door and pressed a button. I was too fried to run for it so I just waited for them all to come swooping down on me but the house stayed quiet. A little later—I don't know how little, my sense of time was still gone—I heard the flyer land outside. Completely automated, no pilot. I looked through the navigator program and found a picture of a place I liked. Not telling you what it looked like. I just punched for it and off I went and here I am and that's about all.

Yah, so maybe they meant to let me go? Could be. Maybe they figured I'd be too disoriented to turn up anywhere. I guess maybe they didn't want to keep me because they'd *stabilized,* you see. They were all so proud of having *stabilized,* they didn't need a new item on the menu permanently. Just for a change of pace.

Yah, so. I could let you find me and you could get them, right. I mean, this is big-time mindcrime here.

So you go ahead and go get them.

But you're not getting me.

It's peaceful now. I won't ever have to hook in with anyone again or talk, ever. I like that idea. It appeals to my basic deadpan nature, see. I don't want to know how anyone feels anymore. And I don't want anyone knowing how I feel, either. Caverty's Entourage, they're not the only ones who feed off each other's emotions. Everybody does it, even just a little bit. I'm not taking any chances anymore. Nobody else is going to feed off me. They all know how I feel and that's enough.

That's enough.

Clang-clang. Clang-clang.

Ever since the first story about Deadpan Allie, "The Pathosfinder," appeared in 1981, there's been the potential for a story involving vampirism. "Dirty Work" was, in fact, the second story I set out to write, but after two pages, I put it away. It was too soon. Five years later, Ellen Datlow began putting together this nontraditional vampirism anthology and we both agreed Allie was a natural.

Ellen got upset with me for what happened to Allie. "How could you do that to her, you creep?" she said. I thought, *gosh, maybe I should have given Allie more of a break—maybe I've been entirely too merciless.*

And then I thought, *Naaah.*

Pat Cadigan

Contributors' Notes

Leonid Nikolayevich Andreyev

Thanks to Maxim Gorky's introduction to Russian literary society, Andreyev became one of the best-selling authors in Russia during the first few years of the twentieth century. He disliked the Bolshevik regime as much as he had disliked the czarist regime, as reflected in his plays *He Who Gets Slapped* and *Life of Man,* the latter earning him first an attack by the Russian church for blasphemy and later by the communist party for "petit bourgeois negativism." His work was banned for decades after that in the U.S.S.R. In his later years, and after three suicide attempts, he left Russia for Finland, where he died in 1919.

Scott Baker

Scott and his wife Suzi have been living in Paris for several years. In 1982 he won the Prix Apollo for Best SF Novel published that year in France (*Symbiote's Crown,* Berkley, 1978). In 1984 he was nominated for the World Fantasy Award for his infamous novelette *The Lurking Duck,* and in 1985 he won the World Fantasy Award for his short story, "Still Life With Scorpion."

In 1986 and 1987, Tor published his novels *Firedance* and *Drink the Fire From the Flames,* the first and second books in the Ashlu Cycle, a work about Babylonian shamanism.

Edward Bryant

Edward Bryant was born in New York and reared on a cattle ranch in southern Wyoming. He has lived in Denver for about fifteen years. He is best known for his science fiction short stories, two of which have won Nebula Awards—"Stone" and "giANTS." For the last four years he's taken a sabbatical from SF to write horror. He is currently working on *Ed Gein's America,* an *Illustrated Man*-type portrait of a contemporary gothic America.

Pat Cadigan

Pat Cadigan was born in Schenectady, New York, and lives in Overland Park, Kansas. She made her first professional sale in 1980, to *New Dimensions,* and is a frequent contributor to *OMNI, The Magazine of Fantasy & Science Fiction, Isaac Asimov's Science Fiction Magazine,* and *Shadows.* Her first novel, *Mindplayers,* was published by Bantam in 1987.

Susan Casper

Susan Casper is a native Philadelphian who attended Temple University and recently retired from the bureaucracy of the Commonwealth of

Pennsylvania to write full time. Her fiction has appeared in *Playboy, Isaac Asimov's Science Fiction Magazine, The Magazine of Fantasy & Science Fiction,* and *Amazing,* as well as most other science fiction and fantasy magazines and several anthologies, including the prestigious *In the Fields of Fire* (Jack Dann and Jeanne Van Buren Dann, editors).

She has collaborated with Gardner Dozois in editing an anthology entitled *Ripper!*, for Tor Books, and is currently at work on her first novel, tentatively entitled *The Red Carnival.*

Jack Dann

Jack Dann is the author or editor of twenty-one books. Among his novels are *Junction, Starhiker,* and *The Man Who Melted.* His short fiction has appeared in *Playboy, OMNI, Penthouse,* and most of the leading science fiction magazines and anthologies. He has been a finalist for the Nebula Award, the World Fantasy Award, and the British Fantasy Award. Dann lives with his family in Binghamton, New York.

Gardner Dozois

Gardner Dozois is the author or editor of twenty-five books. He was born in Salem, Massachusetts and now lives in Philadelphia. He has won two Nebula Awards for his short fiction, is the editor of *Isaac Asimov's Science Fiction Magazine,* and also edits the annual anthology series *The Year's Best Science Fiction.*

Harlan Ellison

Harlan Ellison has been called "one of the great living American short story writers" by the *Washington Post*. He has won the Hugo Award 8½ times, the Nebula Award three times, the Edgar Allan Poe Award of the Mystery Writers of America twice, the Georges Méliès fantasy film award twice, and was awarded the Silver Pen for Journalism by P.E.N. He recently won the first Bram Stoker Award of the Horror Writers of America for Best Collection, for his thirty-five-year retrospective, *The Essential Ellison*. *Angry Candy*, his most recent collection, was published by Houghton Mifflin in October 1988.

Sharon Farber

A native of San Francisco, Sharon Farber now resides in Tennessee, where she practices medicine. Her stories have appeared in *Amazing, Whispers, Isaac Asimov's Science Fiction Magazine,* and *Universe*. "Return of the Dust Vampires" was nominated for the World Fantasy Award in 1986.

Joe Haldeman

Joe Haldeman was born in Oklahoma in 1943. He currently lives in Florida and Cambridge, Massachusetts. His short stories, novelettes, and novellas have appeared in various science fiction magazines, along with a few appearances in "mainstream" magazines like *Playboy*. He won the Rhysling Award for best SF poem of the year in 1983 for "Saul's Death," which appeared in *OMNI*, and has won the Hugo Award for his novel *The Forever War*, and his short story "Tricentennial."

Harvey Jacobs

Harvey Jacobs is the author of three books: *The Juror, Summer on a Mountain of Spices,* and *The Egg of the Glak*. His stories appear in many magazines and anthologies in the United States and abroad, including *OMNI, The Magazine of Fantasy & Science Fiction,* and *New Worlds*.

Garry Kilworth

Garry Kilworth has traveled and lived extensively in the Far East, Middle East, and America, but now has a cottage on two acres of woodland overlooking a tidal river, with a tenth-century church for a near neighbor. His latest novel is *Witchwater Country*, set in rural England. He loves American literature, especially William Faulkner and Carson McCullers.

Tanith Lee

Tanith Lee was born in 1947, in London. After leaving grammar school at the age of seventeen, she worked for five years in the library service, thereafter migrating to more haphazard employment as clerk, waitress, and shop assistant, and also spending one year at art school at the age of twenty-five. In 1975, publication by DAW Books extracted her from this milieu and allowed her to become a full-time professional writer. By the end of 1988 she will have published more than thirty-five books. Four of her radio plays have been produced in Britain, and she has also done some work for BBC-TV.

Fritz Leiber

Fritz Leiber is the author of such classic novels as *The Big Time* and *Gather, Darkness!* as well as numerous short stories, including the Hugo and Nebula Award winner "Gonna Roll the Bones," which was first published in *Dangerous Visions*. He is credited with coining the descriptive term "sword and sorcery," and created the memorable characters Fafhrd and Gray Mouser to populate his heroic-fantasy adventures. He has just finished a new novel about Fafhrd and Gray Mouser called *The Mouser Goes Below*, to be published with three other Mouser stories to make up the seventh volume of the saga, *The Knight and Knave of Swords*.

Dan Simmons

Dan Simmons was co-winner of the first *Twilight Zone Magazine* short story contest in 1981. Since then his work has appeared in *OMNI* and *Isaac Asimov's Science Fiction Magazine,* and has been put into cryogenic storage in *The Last Dangerous Visions*. Simmons's first novel, *Song of Kali,* was published by Bluejay Books in 1986 and won the World Fantasy Award. Simmons lives in Colorado with his wife and daughter.

Steve Rasnic Tem

Since 1979 Steve Rasnic Tem has sold over one hundred short stories, and an equal number of poems, to such publications as *Isaac Asimov's Science Fiction Magazine*, *Shadows*, *The Twilight Zone Magazine*, *The Saint*, and *The Bennington Review*. He edited *The Umbral Anthology of SF Poetry*, which was a finalist for the first Philip K. Dick Award. His first novel, *Excavation*, was published by Avon Books.

Chet Williamson

Chet Williamson's short fiction has appeared in *Playboy*, *The New Yorker*, *Twilight Zone*, *The Magazine of Fantasy and Science Fiction*, *The New Black Mask*, and others. His story "Season Pass," from *Alfred Hitchcock's Mystery Magazine*, was nominated for the 1985 Edgar Award from the Mystery Writers of America. His first and second novels, *Soulstorm* and *Ash Wednesday*, have been published by Tor Books, and a third, *Lowland Riders*, is just out. A full-time freelancer, Williamson lives with his wife and son in Pennsylvania, writing horror, mystery, humor, and advertising (to give the devil his due).

Gahan Wilson

Confused genetically by being descended from both P. T. Barnum and Williams Jennings Bryan, Gahan Wilson believes he was also seriously affected by being born dead and then brought to life by alternate dunkings in scalding hot and icy cold water.

Gahan wanted to be a cartoonist since childhood, and has become so in *Playboy, The New Yorker,* and other places. While not giving up drawing by any means, he has now wandered on to other activities, such as writing the sort of thing you see here. He is presently trying to meet the deadlines on two novels.